a matter *of* mercy

Lynne Hugo

Blank Slate Press | Saint Louis, MO

www.blankslatepress.com
www.lynnehugo.com

Designed by Kristina Blank Makansi
Interior image: Shutterstock
Set in Adobe Calson Pro

Printed in the United States of America
10 9 8 7 6 5 4 3 2 1

Library of Congress Control Number: 2014943811
ISBN: 9780985808617

For Ciera, Andrew, and Alyssa

"…blessed, beautiful bounty"

a matter
of mercy

Also by Lynne Hugo

The Time Change

A Progress Of Miracles

Swimming Lessons (coauthor Anna Tuttle Villegas)

Baby's Breath (coauthor Anna Tuttle Villegas)

The Unspoken Years

Jessica's Two Families

Graceland

Where The Trail Grows Faint

Last Rights

Author's Note

The 1996 lawsuit depicted in this novel is based on fact, although none of the characters in the book should be construed as being modeled on specific people involved in that event. I do not know anyone involved in the suit personally. My knowledge of it was gleaned strictly from public records, especially reporting in *The Cape Cod Times*.

I have tried to depict the history of the area and aquaculture in Wellfleet, Massachusetts, with accuracy and sensitivity. In this I have been immeasurably helped by Barbara Austin, an aquaculturist whose grant lies off Indian Neck. In a sense, I met Barbara by accident as I was wandering around on those flats literally getting my feet wet as I questioned (i.e., bothered) various aquaculturists. One of them—probably to get rid of me—said, "You really ought to talk to Barbara Austin; *she'll* help you." And help me she did, immeasurably, during a number of visits to a place now as dear to me as the rest of the outer Cape has always been.

Barbara loves to read and was interested in my project, but she probably would have helped anyway, because her heart is as exceptional as her expertise. She was generous with time, with technical explanations and demonstrations, even going so far as to let me put on waders and "work" a bump rake (i.e., get in the way) on her grant. She taught me to cull, took me to the hatchery in Dennis and as she made deliveries in Chatham. On the Shellfish Advisory Board, Barbara loaned me Wellfleet harbor management plans and made suggestions for further reading. She also introduced me widely to her colleagues and answered questions tirelessly in person and by phone. Because of her, it became critical to me to imbue *A Matter of Mercy* with not only the intricate knowledge and skill involved in shellfishing, but its expansive spirit: how the aquaculturists live in respectful harmony with the tides and the ecosystem of the bay.

Other Wellfleet aquaculturists were also kind and detailed in their responses to questions.

Books consulted include *Wellfleet: A Cape Cod Village* by Daniel Lombardo, a useful history of the town, and *The Outer Lands, A Natural History Guide to Cape Cod, Martha's Vineyard, Nantucket, Block Island, and Long Island* by Dorothy Sterling, illustrated by Winifred Lubell. The rangers at the Race Point station of the Province Lands National Seashore were uniformly helpful regarding the ecology of the area.

Chapter 1

The dune fence between their house and the beach still tilted toward the water. It had always seemed an invitation to Caroline, like a gesturing hand, and as a child she'd been secretly glad when her father's work to straighten it didn't last. It had pointed to shiny afternoons at the edge of the shore with her mother. Later it pointed the way for her friends, teenagers gathering on summer nights around a driftwood fire to laugh and drink beer a boy had swiped from his parents. Recently though, since she'd come back, she'd imagined it pointed to an escape route. If she just stuck to the sand and walked west out of Wellfleet, she'd cross the bay beaches of Truro and end up in Provincetown. The passenger ferries to Boston left from the wharf there.

"I don't see why you can't go back to teaching," Caroline's mother said to her back. Strange how her voice could sound so weak, yet relentless, like a hungry kitten. "Can't you apply for reinstatement? It's been a long time."

Caroline sighed and kept looking out through the picture window in the living room. At the shoreline, the water appeared distinct with separate white-lined laps, but toward the horizon it was the color of fog, sea merging into sky, one realm dimming into another in the aging day, just as her mother's life was fading from this world into the next. A silent rise out of the slow breath of sleep—like the blurring of bay and sky—was how her mother's life would likely end. That's how Elsie, the hospice nurse, had described it when she explained the use of a morphine drip. When would be the time to say good-bye in that drifting scenario?

"Rake's not out yet." Caroline's left forefinger examined the nails of her right hand as she spoke. "I'm surprised. The tide's more than half-down." She was trying not to revert to biting her nails by painting them Crystal Mauve. Eleanor used to say polish looked cheap on a woman, but the clay she worked would have made a mess of it, so Caroline attributed the opinion to suppressed envy. She'd thought of offering to paint her mother's nails now, but what would that imply?

"You're changing the subject. Will you look at me please?" her mother complained, and then couldn't curtail herself. "Anyway, it's not Rake there anymore. It's The Junior." Caroline heard the rest as if by telepathy: *I told you, Rake is dead.* "Came back to take over before Rake died. Settled right back home," Eleanor said, the last meaning *it's past time you did the same.* "Sure doesn't look like his father, does he?" She paused and Caroline knew she was supposed to recall the image of the tough, skinny Jake, whose full moniker, Jake the Rake, had been a riff on his resemblance to the bull rake with which he harvested quahogs. "The Junior's built like a brick shithouse." Eleanor had abandoned prim language with no explanation after she was widowed.

"I wouldn't know, Mom. I haven't laid eyes on Rid, or any of those guys, since high school."

"Never heard him called anything but The Junior," Eleanor mused.

"By his parents. I doubt he appreciates it."

"Pffft." Eleanor brushed the notion off with a weak-wristed gesture. She pushed with her heels and wrists, trying to hike herself up in the bed, dislodging a pillow that landed with a *whoof* on the wood plank floor. A wheeled bedside stand, moved aside after she'd relented and taken a little applesauce, held an artful smattering of red, gold and pink dahlias Caroline had salvaged from the garden. They were the brightest color in a room of sparse oak dominated by an old stone fireplace. If there was any daylight at all, the eye was drawn to the view, which Eleanor always insisted *was* the decor.

Caroline left the window to pick up the pillow and resettle her mother who tried to shoo her away with bird-like hands, her bones a network of twigs scarcely covered.

"The Junior is a worker, though," Eleanor pushed on, needing to make some point about a local. The day before she'd gone on about Tomas, the son of another of her retired friends who'd taken over for his parents. "I watched him yesterday. Got a brown dog that runs around the beach."

"See? You *do* love being able to see the water," Caroline said, a bit of

I-knew-it in her voice, glad she'd persisted about moving the furniture around and having the delivery men put the hospital bed in the living room. Eleanor could hear the bay from her bedroom if the window was open, but couldn't see it. Caroline sat next to her mother, but angled the straight-backed chair so she, too, could see the water.

"It's holy to me," Eleanor conceded. "The worst is leaving you and this place behind. I don't know how you ever left."

"You *know* I couldn't stay after the accident."

"People are better than you think," Eleanor said. "There's a time for leaving, I'll give you that, but there's also a time for coming home."

"Mom, no one here is going to celebrate my return by killing the fatted calf. And this isn't about me. I'm here for you. Anyway, what I don't get is why someone would come back to work the *flats*, of all things."

Eleanor's eyes reddened with tears, which she did not try to wipe. After a pause, she said, "Rake worked up a ... life ... to leave The Junior." She attempted an arm swoosh toward the window, though which the bay glinted. "Big call now for Wellfleet oysters. Quahogs, too. They fly 'em to New York and Chicago, all over. Charlotte said she heard there's oysters going to Paris from right here. Best in the world. Right here."

Not for the first time, Caroline wondered if dying was something her mother had arranged just to get her home.

It was dusk when Eleanor nodded off after her mousy nibbling at the edges of food and two-foot journey to the bedside commode with Caroline's help. It might have been two miles, it seemed to exhaust her that much. Elsie had warned Caroline that a catheter would be needed soon, and a diaper. Caroline folded back the sheet across her mother's chest and smoothed it into a neat cuff. She licked the tips of her fingers to subdue a few strands of patchy grayish-white. "A woman's hair is her glory," Eleanor used to say when Caroline was little and she'd wedge her daughter between her knees and brush out her hair before she did her own. "A hundred strokes a day brings out the shine." Caroline shook her head, refusing the tingle of incipient tears, and kissed her mother's forehead with butterfly lips.

The air outside the house was cooler and fresher. She stepped off the porch and started downhill, through a pine and oak scrim to the hundred-step path surrounded by beach plums and rose hips that opened out to clear sand. Many of the houses nearby had been turned into summer rentals, though a few of the old families who hadn't been driven out by ever-increasing taxes still hung on. Up on the bluffs to the east, a spate of new custom homes, with enormous expanses of plate glass, skylights and multi-tiered decks, had been built by washashores, non-natives ostentatious enough to leave them empty in winter while they sojourned in Mexico or the Mediterranean or wherever people like that went to stay warm. To her right, the sunset—peach with magenta streaks—melted over the roofs of houses on the western edge of the horseshoe-shaped inlet. When she reached the sand above the wrack line, she sank down cross-legged to absorb the luminous kaleidoscope over what remained changeless of her mother's holy place.

This was the town's back yard, the bay side, with its natural harbor and gentle variations, domestic and domesticated. This was where people woke, did business, played, ate dinner and lay themselves down at night. Seven miles cross Cape, on the other side of Route 6, was National Seashore, where giant parabolas of brocaded dunes and the raw wild Atlantic offered a natural and spiritual ecosystem far more expansive. Over there, the beach was primeval, the stoneless sand ranged from raw to ultra-fine sugar. Here, one was best advised to walk wearing shoes. All Wellfleet's bay beaches were littered with dusky water-worn stones of pure white, gray, mauve and purple nestled alongside razor-sharp bivalve shells that could ribbon bare feet and leave them bloody. And around Indian Neck, the oyster cultch was murderous. But the contrasts were Wellfleet's ying and yang, just as the summer crowds and the winter isolation balanced each other. Caroline knew natives who hated the summer people, truly hated them for the congestion they brought, packed with their arrogance, even though much of the Cape depended on tourist dollars to keep afloat.

She glanced away from the sunset to take in the whole sweep of beach and bay at twilight and realized that a man approaching from the other side of the inlet was already close enough to speak. Caroline guessed who he was from her mother's brick shithouse summary more than from an image she could call up herself. Jeans, a green T-shirt, tattooed forearms, hair and complexion like sand and dusk, weather-scrubbed as the bluffs behind him.

"Hey, how ya doin'?" he said, looking down at her, not slowing.

"Hey yourself, Rid. How're you?" Caroline composed herself mentally, grateful she'd seen him coming and was spared the startle.

"Uh, hi, uh—I'm sorry." He was off guard, and Caroline realized he had no idea who she was, had only been making a passing greeting to a stranger. She wished she hadn't used his name because now he stopped, a question on his face.

"It's me, Rid, Caroline, from up yonder." She gestured toward her mother's house behind and slightly above them. It still wasn't registering. "CiCi Marcum." She added the nickname of her school years.

"CiCi. My God, I'd never have recognized you." Embarrassed. "Geez. What'd you do? I mean, God. Geez. I'm sorry, I didn't mean it rude like that sounded." He squatted down next to her on the sand. Sticking his thumb and forefinger into his mouth, he produced a shrill whistle. A Labrador retriever appeared within seconds and Caroline paused to watch it lope across the beach. Rid grabbed its collar. "Lizzie, you stick here with me, girl," he said, "Down," and Lizzie slurped his chin with her tongue, sat, and then lay down, reluctant, one brown foreleg then the other.

"That's okay. Yeah, I probably do look pretty different." Caroline knew he was envisioning a heavier girl with a high forehead and long dark brown hair. She'd never put the weight she'd lost in jail back on, and her hair was cropped now, highlighted blonde, a scattering of bangs altering the shape of her face. She'd been two or three classes ahead of him. And fair's fair: her memory of him didn't include this burliness and weathered tan, the smile lines radiating out from the corners of his eyes revealing their secret white centers when his face was at rest. His hairline had started to recede on either side of his forehead, making his round face faintly heart-shaped. She remembered his hair as some undistinguished shade of brown, but now it was sun-burnished, gold.

"I'd say. Um, you here visiting or—?"

"My mother's sick," she said, cutting him off.

"Geez. Is it serious? I mean, I didn't know. I just come in over there, on the access road, you know, and do my work." As he spoke he pointed to the opposite side of the horseshoe, to the dirt road that led out of Indian Neck toward Route 6 where a truck, painted black by the advance of night, was parked. Usually, there were at least eight or ten at low tide; now only his and one other, a sure sign the tide was a good halfway up. "I don't pay much attention to who's—anyway, I'm sorry she's sick. What's the matter?"

Caroline hesitated, inclined by the habit of her history to put him off. For a minute, she let the background sound—incoming mid-tide plashes—emerge, but there was still a gap and he left it unfilled so she answered, more because he was a stranger than because she'd ever casually known him. "Cancer. Ovarian."

"Geez, that's bad. Is it...? I mean, she's gettin' treatment and all, right?"

"It was pretty far gone when she got diagnosed. It's an easy one to miss, I guess. That's the only easy thing about it." Her voice a hybrid of irony and anger.

"God. That's hard, that's bad." He nodded, as if to say *I know.*

It occurred to her, in that same intimate-stranger way, to say, "I'm really sorry about your Dad. Mom told me. Were you there? When he died, I mean. If you don't mind my asking."

"Dad pretty much just keeled over, but I did get to the hospital just before he died," he said lightly, and Caroline wouldn't have pressed for more, but Rid said, "I was already back here then. After. I guess you know I was in prison and all."

Startled. "No, I didn't." She'd wanted to ask about what it was like, seeing his father die, whether he was glad he'd been there or wished he hadn't. The notion of rudeness stopped her. Later she'd think it strange that she hadn't wanted to ask him what his prison was like.

"Yeah, man, I was one messed up dude. Did all kinds of drugs, sold 'em, you name it. It all caught up with me, though. Four and a half years' worth."

"For drugs?"

"Well, throw in a little grand theft auto, but I count that as drugs since I was flying at the time and didn't really need a car." He chuckled and shook his head. "If you get my drift. I was out before Dad died, and that was cool, though. When I came back, see, I started working with Dad because I didn't have a job or a place to go. They always did stick by me. Then he died, and now that's mine." Rid turned and pointed behind him, to an area in the bay across the inlet. "Five acres. Dad got my name on his grant when I turned eighteen, even though I didn't want nothin' to do with workin' it back then. I guess he could see I wasn't headed anywhere else, you know, that I might want to come back to it. I seed 'em, I tend 'em and I harvest 'em. Best oysters in the world. I'm buildin up the quahogs, too, now, getting into them more."

"You really like it?"

"*Look* at it," he said by way of answer, sweeping his arm expansively. Then, embarrassed again. "How's bout you? You went to college, didn't you? And didn't you get married?"

Caroline hesitated, sensing Rid wasn't disingenuous enough to be setting her up. "Yeah," she said. "I went to college, and yeah, but I also got a divorce."

"And now you're a..." he said, inviting her to fill in the blank.

"Oh, God, now I'm nothing. I was a waitress in Chicago. Actually, I just spent three weeks giving notice, subletting my apartment, and all that stuff so I could come back here to be with Mom."

"A waitress? You went to college to be a waitress?"

"Well, I waitressed in the *Plaza*," she said, and heard her defensiveness, so added, "but no, I didn't go to college for that. My degree was in Elementary Education."

"So you're a *teacher*."

"Ah, no, not any more. Long story."

This time he caught the put off. "There's a sure sign of fall comin' on," he said gesturing with his chin. Overhead, a great blue heron's wings beat against the sky. "That's my guy. He and his buddies love the bait fish around the grants this time of year." The sun slid below the horizon degree by degree, a great red neon ball being lowered from an invisible string held by God, fiery and benign. The bay answered with tongues and darts and minnows of color. "Well, nice talkin' to you, CiCi. I'm sorry about your Mom. Listen, I'm around here every low tide just like Dad used to be—I mean, if you need a hand, you know, just watch for me and yell."

"Thanks. I'm fine, though." The auto-answer. "There's a hospice nurse that comes," Caroline got to her feet a second after Rid did, pretending not to see the hand he held out, keeping her head down until he'd tucked it in his pocket to save them both the moment. The last of the sun slipped toward tomorrow, but its remains bled onto the water. Rid bent to caress Lizzie's ears. When he straightened, he stood shorter than Caroline's five-eight by a sideways thumb.

 *Chapter 2*

"I hate the idea of you being alone after I'm gone," Eleanor said. "I wish there'd been a baby or two. Before. You couldn't have done anything about it, then. For heaven's sake, what would you have done, stuffed 'em back inside?" Eleanor chuckled, the first time she'd laughed out loud in a couple of days. Caroline had always liked the throaty laugh that leaked out of her mother like a man's chuckle, and even though what Eleanor said offended her, she didn't shoot back. The oncologist had privately suggested to Caroline that she consider having her ovaries removed prophylactically, and soon, unless she wanted to have a baby first. Eleanor's was an aggressive cancer and likely an inherited gene. He suggested they do a genetic test to make sure, as if Caroline could think about that now. When she couldn't block his words from her mind, she imagined a time bomb with a silent, cold-burning fuse uncoiling and shortening inside her.

"Obviously it wasn't meant to be, Mom. So you'll just have to hang around and live after all."

"Nonsense." As if to prove her point, Eleanor's breathing grew heavy for a moment as a tide of pain washed over her. "Not going to happen, honey. Don't forget to order firewood. Call Pete DeRego for that. And return Noelle's casserole dish. Sorry I let you down."

"Now that's nonsense."

"Not too late. You still could have one."

Caroline was parked next to the hospital bed in an uncomfortable chair not meant for long sitting. She made another note to herself to move the furniture around again and position the blue upholstered chair where this straight-backed one was. She'd brought in more flowers—marigolds and white geranium heads this time, dotted with deep fuchsia dahlias—and rehung some of her mother's favorite seascape paintings where Eleanor could see them. Though she'd had to shove the coffee table way out of place, Caroline had arranged some of Eleanor's salt pottery on the hutch, the big blue and brown bowl and matching pitcher her mother had fashioned like an antique washstand set, trying to keep the room satisfying to an artist's eye.

It was a Sunday, the third in August, and Caroline had been home just long enough to know that Sunday was the hardest day to get through. No Elsie the hospice nurse, no Julia the respite care provider who came twice a week. It was all on her shoulders.

And it meant that if Eleanor got on a subject Caroline wanted to steer on by, say, for example, Caroline's phantom, unborn children or her own ongoing dying, it was even more difficult to divert her. Unless pain accomplished the diversion for her, which was something Caroline could hardly wish for. She learned to sit in silence or let a feathery response drift from her mouth. Sometimes Eleanor accommodated by nodding off, this especially after her pain pills. They hadn't increased the morphine to a drip yet, though Elsie, nursey-crisp in her efficiency but kind in her smile and street clothes, had told them both that it was available anytime. "When you're ready," she said to Eleanor. "If" Caroline had corrected Elsie, and Elsie didn't answer, only stroked the web between Eleanor's thumb and first finger with her own thumb, as if it were the outer petal of a rose.

Other times, though, there was no escape. Some days they might as well have been mother and ten-year-old on the beach again. With July sun scorching her back, CiCi used to bury her mother's feet over and over again. No matter how deep the preparatory hole, no matter how much cement she created with sand and red plastic buckets of water to pile and pound over her mother's wide size eight feet, Eleanor would finally just pull them out with no discernible effort. She'd wiggle her unpolished toes, and Caroline's sculpted mound would crack as Eleanor's rising feet erupted from the fortress.

So when she could speak—especially on Sundays—Eleanor was determined to have her say. Like last Sunday, when it was, "You know, you'll look back and not believe you were so profligate with it. Your life, I mean. That once you were a little girl, and then you had a little girl and even then it was still all ahead of you. You never think about it because just a school year is the length of forever. You want it to pass. You confuse looking ahead with wanting something over. Two different things."

Caroline hadn't twitched. Hadn't done anything, in fact, that could possibly be interpreted as encouragement to continue in this vein. She'd busied herself with an unnecessary check on the water in the pitcher on the bed table. "This is just room temperature," she'd said. "How about I get some fresh ice?" But Eleanor had gone on, her hands too feeble that day to gesture as she normally would have. Caroline couldn't believe the damn morphine wasn't kicking in.

"Remember when you had that terrible sixth grfade teacher? What was her name?"

"I don't know, Mom," though of course, Caroline did.

"Yes, yes you do. What was it? Mrs. Socci? No, that was second…"

Eleanor could have gone on forever naming elementary teachers if she had to. Caroline capitulated in self-defense. "Mrs. Bladen?"

"That's the one." Eleanor plucked at her covers, and Caroline adjusted the sheets for the twentieth time in an hour. But she'd relaxed a bit, thinking Eleanor had finished with her unconceived babies and death talk *du jour*. But no, instead she was refining her technique, Caroline had soon grasped, combining the topics.

"See? I wanted that year to pass for you—and for me, too. Terrible year. Wanted it over. I really didn't do a very good job with it."

"Sure you did, Mom. You tried to get me switched out of that class."

"I mean my life. Why didn't I catch on about things?"

"Oh Mom, don't say that. Please."

"No, I spent my life avoiding what I should have embraced. Why didn't I catch on? I want you to. Learn from me." An offshore breeze rattled the open horizontal blinds that Caroline had partly closed against the late August afternoon sun overheating the room. "I almost think a body can use it as a sign when they avoid something, I mean. Here I am, seeing it now. So much too late."

Caroline had rubbed her forehead then, pinching the bridge of her nose. She was sweaty in her jeans. She wanted to shout, *I get it already. You're not exactly subtle, Mom.* Then, at that moment, she couldn't bear the airlessness of denim another moment. She'd stood abruptly, unzipped and stepped out of her jeans, intending to carry them back to her room and get a pair of shorts. Eleanor didn't miss a beat.

"I've done that, too. Your father had an elegant penis. Not large. Leroy's was much bigger, but your father's was tapered. Elegant."

Caroline had been too stunned to get a sound out for at least fifteen seconds. She'd stood by the bed in her underpants and T-shirt. Who the hell was Leroy? Eleanor's eyes were starting to close. *Oh no you don't. You don't go to sleep on me now, I don't care how much morphine is in you.*

"What, Mom? Who's Leroy? Mom? Mom?"

Eleanor's eyes were at half-mast. Caroline had repeated the question as Eleanor's eyes shut. The response she received was a drugged snore. Later on, she'd tried again, asking in a tone casual as light breeze lifting the edge of a curtain who Leroy was.

"I don't believe I've ever known a Leroy, dear," Eleanor said calmly as she eyed the supper tray Caroline had made of beef barley soup, neat triangles of buttered toast, and applesauce. "And I don't believe I'm hungry at all. The smell is making me a bit sick. Would you mind taking it away? Maybe later."

Caroline brought it up again the next day, but Eleanor didn't know any Leroy, and Caroline couldn't make herself say why she was asking.

That had been the one time she wanted her mother to talk.

What she wanted every other day was just to make it. To do her job and bear what was and what was to come. To be patient, something that didn't come naturally. To be loving. To redeem the ways she'd disappointed her mother, the ways she'd disappointed herself.

What she didn't want were surprises that undid her, the eruptions of history and memory that broke the surface of her composure the way her mother's feet used to destroy the sand mounds she'd constructed over them when she was a child. Tuesday morning, for example. Caroline took Eleanor's power-of-attorney to the Seamen's Bank and retrieved the contents of her mother's safe deposit box. This time there was no warning toe wiggle, just an explosion of memory. Tucked in with Eleanor's and Bill's birth certificates, their marriage certificate, Bill's death certificate, the canceled mortgage, insurance policies, car title and some letters from long-dead parents, was a newspaper clipping. A hot flush of recognition: Eleanor's handwriting was on the bottom margin, slightly blurry, the way the ink from a felt pen fans out on newsprint: *Cape Cod Times*, November 12, 1994. *Friday Auto Accident in Provincetown Proves Fatal* blared the headline. Beneath it, slightly smaller type declared, *Teacher Charged with DWI Following Death of Four Year Old.*

All she had done to bury that night crumbled away like the mucky wet sand over her mother's feet. Eleanor had saved the only edition of the paper that didn't give more details than the child's name and age, details like, for example, that he'd been born without arms. Or that stubby hands emerged from wrists attached to his shoulders, although the hands weren't themselves complete. Other days, the paper had chronicled his numerous birth defects, complete with all the pictures necessary to break everyone's heart, including what remained of her own. Eleanor hadn't saved those, it seemed. It didn't matter; Caroline saw them anyway. Six and a half years after the accident, after a single moment had ruined everything, her grief was fresh as pressed cider. She put her head down on the fake wood veneer table and cried.

 *Chapter 3*

"Don't panic," Elsie said, touching Caroline's arm. "I think it's a pleural effusion. It's a common complication in advanced ovarian cancer." Caroline nodded as if she understood. She found it nearly unbearable to watch or listen to her mother trying to draw in a breath. *What must it be like to endure?* "If we hospitalize her overnight—Dr. Simcoe has already approved it—an x-ray will tell for sure. It'll just show up as a big area of fluid in her lung. Your mother will be much more comfortable if it's drained, and she'll only be in the hospital overnight."

Caroline waited until Eleanor was settled and asleep after the procedure, mid-afternoon. "You don't need to stay," she'd said, and Caroline wondered if her mother knew how much she didn't want to, in that terrible way mothers have of seeing through their children as if they were translucent. Nothing was in her control here, anyway. Not that at home the real outcome was in her control, either. But at home she could go into Executive Mode. She could do what she thought needed to be done. She could switch on the light that pushed back the edges of darkness, and she could keep it on, keeping her thoughts at bay. She could scramble eggs in the kitchen, rearrange furniture in the living room, give pills, and plump pillows wherever there were pillows. She could wait. And wait and wait and wait. She could wait for doctors to return calls, and pills to take effect, for test results, and for late respite care workers. Sometimes it was terrifying and hopeless, ducks she tried to keep in a row all waddling off in opposite directions to die while she wept. But mostly, she coped by staying in charge, by making lists and schedules, by doing. The hospital made Caroline quite crazy.

"You don't need to stay. You know she'll likely sleep pretty much from now on," the charge nurse said, echoing Eleanor. "You could get a break. Caregiving is exhausting. And with this storm coming, you shouldn't wait until you'll be driving in it." So Caroline swallowed her guilt and slipped out of the hospital furtively, as if her purse was full of stolen goods.

An hour later, she was curled up on the couch with a novel and a cup of tea trying not to worry about whether thunder would waken her mother. The afternoon light was fading fast. Eleanor was used to Cape storms, but she might be disoriented, Caroline thought. *Maybe I should have stayed.* She put down her book. It was almost too dark to read, and she needed to turn on a few lights. The radio said the storm was going to be a big one. *What if Eleanor wakes and doesn't know where she is?* Caroline stood to look out the living room window. That's when she saw him: Rid out on the tidal flats. Later, when she tried to retrace the course of events, it seemed her whole life once again had turned on chance.

❦

Forecasters said the eastern edge of the hurricane that had grazed the Atlantic coast from Virginia to Connecticut had bounced off and spun oceanward. They thought it might miss the Cape entirely. They were wrong. An ominous sky and high hot winds had buffeted Rid all afternoon. He could have gotten an earlier start pinning the nets over the quahogs he'd planted in early spring if he'd realized how much storm was going to make its way back to the outer Cape. His Chinese hats—the cement dome-shaped forms the aquaculturists molded to catch wild oyster seed in the bay, much cheaper than buying seed oysters—were in the water and loaded with spat. Not only that, he had nursery bags with beautiful matchhead quahogs, a small fortune's worth in a year when the hatchery in Dennis didn't have a lot of seed to sell and were rationing them in fairness. He'd gotten these beauties by luck, from a hatchery up in Maine. He had to get extra U-hooks down to hold the nets in his raceways, plus pull the nursery bags of seed clams out of the water. He had to pull the hats out, too.

Some of the others left everything in, even in a nor'easter, but Rid knew what Hurricane Bob had done to his father: demolished trays, nets, rerod, everything, leaving parts of the grant literally bare, even old cultch snatched and deposited somewhere else. Other parts of his grant had been a mess of tangled torn nets, U-hooks lifted out by an easy lick of storm tongue and hopelessly chewed up along with broken trays and racks and hats, some his and some of Mario's, Tomas', Barb's, Austin's—even some of Tweed's and Clint's, whose grants were at the Blackfish Creek end of the harbor. Rake had lost more than a year's harvest and even now, Rid was still paying on the loan his father had had to take to resupply with equipment and seed. Rake had picked in the wild to make enough to feed the family all the while he was working his grant back into shape. And money had nothing to do with the time it took to build new hats and trays, cut new nets. The whole winter after that hurricane had gone into the effort. Some of the other farmers had losses almost as crippling, but were temperamentally still more inclined to take their storm chances than he was. A few had been stung to cautiousness as great as Rid's. It depended on where the tide was when the worst of any storm hit, of course. A moon tide rising was the worst time for bad weather, but moon tides are the best for working because the stronger gravitational pull makes the water recede farther. Yet even a storm that clouts during the front of a moon tide can be capricious enough to leave one grant almost untouched while those adjacent might be fouled or wiped out.

Twice Rid moved his truck further inland after the turn, when the water started advancing on him and crept halfway up his rear tires while his back was turned. It was coming in fast and this whole blow would be compounded by it being a moon tide anyway, the biggest of the month and getting toward the biggest of the year, which would come in October. Only Clint's and Barb's trucks were parked on the shoals now. The rest had left already, maybe nobody pulling out or anchoring as much as he was trying to. It bothered Rid, mostly because if their stuff got loose and washed onto his grant it could do a lot of damage. Technically, it would be the other guy's responsibility to replace what he lost, and they'd all say as much themselves, but he'd have to be able to show whose stuff had damaged his. And they couldn't give him back the two years it took to grow quahogs, and three-year oyster aches of nursing his seed toward picking and sale. They couldn't replace his legal-size oysters and clams if their own were as lost as his. No way. They wouldn't have the stock and they wouldn't have the money. Insurance was a joke; so expensive you'd be broke before your first harvest, so none of them had it. No, starting over was a matter of taking thirty thousand dollars, throwing it in the bay, breaking your back and gambling that you can beat predators, weather and disease for three years before the first harvest while you live on more borrowed money. Who among them could do that anymore? Not Rid. Not anyone he knew.

❀

Caroline watched from the front window near Eleanor's empty bed, tension rising on the back of wind while the barometer slid down and then further down. The northeastern sky blackened, the storm chasing its tail and coming back to swipe them on its downsweep. The incoming tide was relentless. Rid slogged through shallow water in his waders. Every few steps he bent over and stuck something in the water.

And then a single boom of thunder that wasn't like distant fireworks or artillery. A jag of lightning at the same instant, sky-splitting, too bright, too close, palpably electric on and around them. Beach, breakwater, bay, truck, road, even Rid flickered in black and white illumination, and Caroline's heart thudded in her ears. The bay was an engine of noise beneath the intermittent cracks and booms. *He knows what he's doing*, she advised herself. *He'll get himself inside if it's dangerous.* In a different life she'd been a person who'd leap in anywhere to help anyone—whether the recipient wanted help or not—and that woman would have been out the front door pulling up the hood of Eleanor's slicker, Eleanor's boots in hand, a good five minutes before the new Caroline was.

Of course, he didn't hear her over the rising wind and turning tide so she had to keep running along the high water mark on the beach until she was parallel with him, but then he didn't see her either because now he was backing up, into the wind. Caroline hopped on each foot in turn as she pulled a rubber boot on the other one and then headed across seventy-five feet of mucky sand and cultch to where he worked. She'd not realized just how many raceways of hard-shelled clams he'd planted, how much netting was down, how large his grant was. From above the tide line, all that was visible on Rid's or anyone else's grant were Chinese hats and oyster trays and racks where the larger shellfish were being nurtured to legal size. Even those could only be seen when the tide was out. Once Caroline slogged out beyond his truck, backed onto the flats an hour before low tide, now resting in about three inches of rapidly incoming water, she found she had to detour several times to avoid stepping on quahog beds.

"Rid! Rid!" She shouted his name four or five more times before he turned even though she was now only a couple of feet behind him. She couldn't get to the side or front where he could see her without stepping on netting. "Rid!"

Now he turned, startled. He took a step toward her and Caroline leaned in to shout in his ear, but she'd miscalculated; he wasn't letting her break his work stride even long enough to hear what she had to say. Rid bent over and stuck a U-hook into the sandy bottom to anchor the net even though he already had rerod bars weighing it down. She saw that's what he'd been doing—every other step, sticking another U-hook into the sand to double secure the netting.

Infuriatingly, he wouldn't stop. She did the only thing she could if she wanted to tell him anything, bobbing up and down to keep her mouth near enough his head, stepping backward in concert with him like a bizarre dancing couple.

"Come in—you can come to my house. There's lightning," she shouted, gesturing skyward, feeling foolish showing him the obvious.

Rid just shook his head. "Gotta anchor these ... not enough rerod.... tide...." The thread of his words unraveled on the wind.

Caroline backed up as he advanced, watching as Rid placed three more anchors. Then, putting her hand on the mesh bag of U-hooks, she blocked his next step as she shouted, "I can do this." She pointed to the end of the raceway. "I'll keep going here so you can get the other side." Maybe he couldn't make out what she was saying; the sky and bay rumbled, arguing constantly. Several more lightning strikes had zigged over the horizon, these still distant but advancing.

Rid started to shake his head no; hesitation was on his face, but Caroline bent and put in a U-hook and must have gotten it right because he released the bag to her and was gone. He didn't go get more U-hooks though. He waded in deeper, bent again, and this time hoisted a nursery tray out of the water, and carried it to the bed of his truck where he shoved aside racks, crates and a bull rake to make space for it. Then another, another, and another, all the while Caroline made slow headway toward shore, stopping to place a U-hook every eighteen inches. When she looked up between steps, she saw Rid scanning the sky while he shouldered another tray. Rain began, not with single drops here and there, but in a pelting downpour.

Caroline quit standing up between securing hooks because water poured in the gap between her neck and chin when she did. Her jeans were soaked from the flapping slicker, but if the wind plastered it momentarily against her body, rainwater slid directly into her boots. She couldn't feel her hands anymore although the water felt warmer than the air now.

She'd not quite finished when she saw the black rubber of his waders sloshing toward her. Her back locked into its bent-over position, she splashed in the hook she was holding and started to unfold herself, but before she could, Rid had her elbow and was pulling.

"Too close!" He shouted, leaning into her ear. "…Now! Gonna sink the truck." The yank on her arm was in the direction of the pickup. The big tires were donuts half dunked into the black bay coffee. Straightening painfully and splashing behind Rid as best she could, Caroline realized that most of the apparatus of the grant was already submerged.

Rid wrestled opened the passenger side of the truck, boosting her into the seat with a hand on her rear before slamming the door and running through a fury of rain to climb into the driver's seat himself. Later, Caroline would remember that she found the gesture oddly chivalrous. The engine coughed twice and caught. Rid dropped the gearshift into reverse, then rocked it into a forward crawl toward the beach. At the highwater mark, he made the left turn and drove along the sandy strip toward the access road. He stopped at the edge of the access road, still on the sand. Caroline's house was faintly silhouetted across the horseshoe beach. She could feel as much as see the trees, dizzy in the torrent.

"God. Whew. Thanks," he said, as their panting slowed and Caroline used her wet sleeve to staunch the trickle running from her hair into her eyes. "Wait, I've got something, I think." Rid twisted to rummage behind the passenger seat and came up with a crumpled, ragged towel. "Oh," he said. "This isn't pretty. Sorry."

"Gimme that." Caroline laughed and grabbed it. "When you're desperate, you're desperate." She blotted her hair. "You probably need to go, I know."

"Nah, let's wait for it to die down. Can't drive you closer to the house than you are here. Can't very well walk in this," he said. "Stuff's okay outta the water. I wanted to get the hats too, but they'll do better than the nursery trays might've. I can't replace that stock, ARC can't get any seed now, it's too late to plant anyway, and … you don't know what I'm talking about, do you? Just thanks. Really, I mean it. *Thanks.*" Then, an afterthought. "But is somebody with your mother?"

"She's in the hospital tonight."

"Oh no, is she worse?"

"I don't know. The doctor says it's terminal, but not right now. This is to drain fluid from her lung so she'll be more comfortable. I was already there most of the day. She'll be home again tomorrow. She's on hospice. I'm hoping to be able to keep her at home—I mean, you know, the whole time."

He shook his head in sympathy. "You want a beer?"

Caroline was confused. "You want to go into town?"

"No. Here. I got it," he said, interrupting. Rooting again, under his seat this time, he pulled out first one, then a second bottled beer and handed one to Caroline after he flicked off the cap with his thumb. "Warm," he said, an apology.

Caroline gave a small shiver. "It's just as well. Warm's good."

Rid made no comment but started the truck up again and put the heat on. Caroline stuck her hands in front of the vent.

Fists of rain pummeled the top and hood and the jumble of equipment and nursery bags in the truck bed. No lights at all now from the rise around the bay inlet. Rid sucked a long draw of beer and sighed. "Power's out. I hope my nets don't get too fouled."

"Weird, isn't it? I mean logically, you wouldn't think more water," she gestured at the rain, "could mess up things that already grow under water."

Rid pulled in his chin and looked at her sidelong.

"What?"

He rolled his eyes. "God, that's so *woman*."

"That sounds dangerously like an insult, Mr. Neal. How so?"

"Using logic to be completely illogical."

Caroline smacked his sleeve with the back of her hand.

They teased that way for several more minutes. Rid drained his beer and when Caroline finished hers, he pulled two more out from under the seat. Again, he popped off the top before handing Caroline hers.

"Sir, you are a gentleman," she said lightly.

"Uh oh. Sounds like a compliment. A minute ago you were as good as calling me a pig."

"Okay. A gentlemanly pig."

In full darkness now, the rain flogged on. The truck felt like a tank to Caroline, impervious, though every now and then the force of the wind swayed it and occasional debris banged the exterior. Rid glanced at the bay, winced, and looked away. There were breakers, as if they were on the ocean side instead of in the quiet natural harbor.

The second beer and most of the third and fourth were spent on comparing kids they'd known in high school, cataloging geeks, preps, dopers, drudges.

"You were just a baby," she complained. "You're naming people who were little brothers and sisters of people in my class."

"Oh, yeah, and you are sooo ancient."

They went on to teachers, praising a few, trashing more. "Nah," he said once. "Didn't take Algebra or Geometry, none of that stuff. General math, and I do believe I failed it, too. Truth is I pretty much fit the stereotype of the dumb local. I was probably the mold for it, in fact. Had a *lot* of fun, though." He laughed and shook his head. After that, Caroline was careful not to talk about teachers who'd had only college prep classes. American History, English and Government; everybody had to take those. Not French, not Chemistry, not Anatomy and Physiology.

When he said no, he hadn't taken Music and not Art either, she said, "Why didn't you? I mean, you're smart, Rid. You could have gone to college. Did you just not want to?"

"Outta my league. God, I spent more time suspended than I did in class. I could talk a good game, but I never could keep it together to pay attention to all that stuff when it came to taking tests or writing reports. Plus no money for it. Plus it did not sound like fun."

Her old teaching mind wondered if he had a learning disability and she asked if he'd ever been tested. Dyslexia? Attention deficit disorder?

"Prob'ly. Don't remember, don't care." He looked at her then and grinned. "Listen to you. *Teacher.* Why'd you really quit anyway?"

There was a strange vulnerability in the question, Caroline thought. Still, she didn't like his pressing her. She'd already put him off the subject once, and he was risking the implicit rejection were she to shut him down again. She hesitated, an honest answer on one side of the balance scale in her mind, a joke on the other. She looked across at him, weighing her response. The darkness erased the squint and sun lines around his eyes and the sanded tan of his skin. He had a light growth of beard on his square jaw, and in this light, he looked young, like a memory of himself years ago.

"You must know about it. It was in the papers. The accident."

He swung his head no. "What accident? Was this while I was in prison?"

Caroline realized he was reminding her of his history. "It was such a big story, I mean, I assumed you'd know."

"What happened?" Again, the forthright question. She'd never seen before how asking a question left you unguarded, sometimes as much as giving an answer.

But still, she couldn't say it headlong, give it out straight. "There was an accident," she said. "A fatal accident. Actually, a lot of lives were lost. Including but not especially mine. And that's why I got divorced, too. Or, more accurately, I should say *was* divorced." Her little laugh was almost a giggle, the scalloped edge of drunkenness.

"How so?"

Pleased that she'd been clever, leading him to a branch off the main path he'd been following, she tipped her head back onto the headrest and exhaled. "I was the divorced, not the divorcee. I mean, the divorcee wasn't actually the divorcer. She was the divorced."

"Huh?"

Giggles, like bubbles through the wand of her mouth. "A divorce was enacted upon me, I was not the enactor."

He wasn't as far gone as she. Maybe he'd had a late lunch. He didn't laugh. "You mean you didn't want the divorce? That's rough. Did he have someone else?"

"Not then, but now. And a baby."

"Why'd he want a divorce?"

Was there no end to these naked questions? They weren't so bothersome now, though. She felt almost nothing when she answered, "He wanted children. I couldn't bear—get it, bear? —to have them. A plus B equals C. Oh, sorry. I forgot about you and math." She was short-changing him with her flippancy, and she suddenly felt cheap, a too-bright portrait of herself. "The *couldn't* was a *wouldn't* turned to stone. There's just too much *bad* that can go down. I couldn't give it a chance to happen again," she said quietly.

It was more than she'd said to anyone about it almost ever. Rid gave an empathetic *yeah*, that he got it, how things could turn out that way. Caroline shook her head, and he started to say something else when his stomach made a feral growl. He slapped a hand against his belly and laughed.

"You want something to eat?" she said, glad to divert him.

Rid peered through the windshield, squinting as if he could discern something, but the darkness was exceptional, elemental and mysterious. To their left, Caroline could make out stutters of white surf lines that broke like arguments, the incoming tide hard and its own answer.

"Drive between lightning strikes, huh? Where do you want to go? Couple places in Eastham got generators, might be open. Road might be closed, though. Prob'ly trees down." Rid leaned forward and grasped the key, dangling from the ignition as it had been when they got in.

"My house," she said, reaching to stop him. She wasn't so far gone that she'd think about letting that truck move, not with someone who'd been drinking at the wheel. She'd put her body in front of it first. And not entirely because of her history, reason enough, but she wanted his company, a small bonfire by which to warm herself. He had a good laugh, chest-deep and unreserved.

"That wind is dangerous. Debris flyin'. And we'll get wet," he said. It was several hundred yards across open beach just to the dirt lane in front of Caroline's path, another hundred feet to her house.

"A big problem, that one, since I'm so incredibly dry right now." She held up a strand of wet hair for him to inspect. "Fortunately, I don't melt. Do you?"

"I work the flats. Let's go." With that, Rid flung open his door. He'd made it almost around the truck as Caroline was still getting out of her side and he grabbed her elbow and tried to slam her door hard, as he had his, but the wind fought him for it until he used two hands and the weight of his body to lever it. He shouldered a half-step ahead of her into open beach and hammering rain. Sometimes the wind pinned them in place or lurched them backward. Rid grabbed her hand as they pressed on, heads down. Once he jerked her sharply to the side to avoid a long chunk of driftwood. Flocks of debris had taken to the air, as beach grass flattened under the torrent. Rid tripped. "Watch it," he yelled as he caught his balance. The umbrella of pines and hardwoods only slightly dulled the density of the rain once they crossed the lane, where Caroline splashed calf deep into a dirt pothole, another spill of water into one of Eleanor's boots, and were on the brief pine straw path. The darkness was primal, the edges of the house utterly obscured. Caroline pitched forward when she miscalculated where the first step should be, her feet slogging in waterlogged shoes inside waterlogged boots. She dumped both on the front porch.

Inside, they were both gasping. "Whooie," Rid said. "Nasty night."

Caroline felt for furniture edges and walls, making her way to the corner cabinet drawer handle, her feet cold in wet socks. Yes. Still there, a supply of candles and matches. There were flashlights in the emergency box in the basement, and a Coleman stove and lantern, but she wanted the candles. She struck a match and used its small circle of amber light to find a wick that in turn made a bigger circle. "Hold this." She handed the first candle to Rid while she used its light to gather up holders. She took back the lit candle and used it to light five more, finally setting up the one she held and distributing them about the room. Self-conscious, she tried to finger-fluff her hair, but it was too wet. She imagined it, drab and flat, and was glad for the darkness. She shivered and clung briefly to her own elbows, feeling gangly and uncomfortable in her skin and clothes.

"I gotta get out of these," Rid said. He unhooked the suspenders of his waders and peeled them down, stepping out of them. "I'm sorry about the mess," he said, pointing with his head toward the wet spots around him.

"Forget it. I did at least as much damage as you. Wet floors are the least of our problems."

"Hmmm. What's the most of them?"

Caroline opened the refrigerator door. "Food. Everything I've got is, um, let's see…applesauce…ice cream…mashed potatoes…you'll love the contents of my refrigerator if you're a hospice patient. Ah ha. Now we're making some progress." She pulled out a block of cheddar cheese. "I can't believe we don't have any oysters. How derelict of you!" She closed the refrigerator and started opening cupboards. "But look! Hospice comes through again—saltines. And the true *bonanza*, which I can't say is hospice fare, but actually caregiver fare." She lifted a bottle of cabernet sauvignon over her head triumphantly. "This stuff may have been here since 1980, but hey, it all improves with age, right?"

"Of course. Like the lady."

"You sweet talker you."

Caroline handed him the bottle and an opener. "You may do the honors, sir. I'll fix us emergency rations."

"You got it, sweetheart." It was a bad imitation of some movie star she couldn't identify, but Caroline smiled. "Not only that, I'll get a fire going. Where's your wood?"

"Ah, well. Didn't get around to that yet."

Rid shrugged. "I guess you haven't been back that long. Sure your Mom doesn't have any?"

"No wood. We can set the couch on fire if you want. Or you can just open the wine." Caroline searched the cupboards, finding a can of marinated mushrooms and a jar of artichoke hearts to drain and add to the tray of cheese and crackers, baby carrots and Granny Smith slices she'd scrounged from the refrigerator. Little party toothpicks and napkins from one of the hutch drawers, leftovers from her wedding to Chuck, completed the spread.

Rid whistled. "Not bad. Wicked good, in fact."

The beer they'd had in the truck first. Candles on the mantelpiece, candles on the coffee table, the tray of food between them, the wine glasses refilled and then refilled again, the afghan knit by Caroline's grandmother around both their backs, the wind and rain beating on the windows. His hand on her thigh in sympathy when she got teary about Eleanor dying. Later when Caroline tried to figure out why this time, this man—Rid, of all unlikely choices—she catalogued these elements and was ashamed that she'd just had too much to drink and succumbed.

No place felt clear of baggage except the floor, which had been Caroline's choice, so they'd started on the braided rug and the good green quilt she'd dragged out, but it hadn't been long before they agreed they were both too old to lie on the floor and pretend they were comfortable. Rid had tried to lead her to the hospital bed, but she'd resisted. Her own room had a narrow twin. They ended up in the big bed in Eleanor's room, no longer in use. *My parents' bed*, she thought afterward.

Later, candlelight flickered against the darkness and his fingertips lightly circled one of her breasts as they sipped the last of the wine. Maybe it was the afterglow of candlelight, sex, and wine, but she found herself talking more than she'd been willing to in years.

"Funny how we're both back where we were born," she said. "Did you feel like you had to? I mean, Mom's cancer is what brought me back, but I won't be staying after.... Did you come back because you didn't have any place else—or because your Dad needed you—or...?"

"Turned out Dad needed me, but I was back before then. It was weird, ya know? Dad put my name on his grant when I was a kid, even though I swore I didn't want to work the flats. It was like he knew I wasn't going to do anything else. 'Course I gave him plenty reason to think that, too. Wonder how many times I got suspended from school?" He laughed. His hand was square, callused. A violent offshore wind was picking up sand and flinging it against the windows; tomorrow they'd be milky with salt, and cleaning them would be Caroline's chore.

"I never understood how that worked, the grants, I mean."

"There's only so much space in the harbor and a certain amount is reserved for picking in the wild—where the public can go. The sea farmers get their leases—same thing as a grant—from the town, see, and there's only so many. When they're gone, they're gone. By Dad putting my name on his grant, that meant that if—or when—he died, it would pass to me. It meant I'd always have a way to make a living. I never knew why Dad wanted to do it. God, you break your back, and...."

"Yeah," Caroline murmured.

"Well sure, there's a million problems. Your oysters get diseased, your nets get fouled, the price of seed goes sky high just when you have the least spat yourself, the flies eat you alive or you're wet and freezing, your bull rake breaks, your dingy leaks, somebody underbids your best account and they never heard of loyalty. Whatever."

"Sounds like a great life." She was sarcastic, softening it with a smile. But what she wanted to ask was why on earth would anyone—no, why would *you*— do this if you had any other choice? "There must be something else you could do," she said instead.

"Well of course. I'm not a complete loser. Or, in spite of the fact that I am a complete loser, yes, I *could* do something else. Don't wanna."

Caroline looked at him, waiting, her brows slightly tented, and he returned her gaze, his expression that of someone waiting for a joke.

"Look," he said finally, "all that stuff about it being backbreaking and unpredictable—all that bad stuff is true. But, CiCi, if you could see what I see—the sky painted colors when it's a sunset tide and how it bleeds into the water as if it's all made of the same stuff. And in the mornings, just being able to see as far as my eyes can see and it's bay and cliffs and sky. You can't believe the different birds, oh my God. Have you ever seen laughing gulls make love?" He shook his head, smiling at the image he conjured. "And then there's my grant and all the trays and nets that are mine." He drew a map in the air. "I'm here, Mario's got the grant next to mine, and Tomas, he's got the one on the other side. Mario does most everything half-assed, and Tomas does everything out of, oh, I don't know, *The New Science of Aquaculture* book, but we'd do anything for each other." Caroline watched Rid's face, saw that he wanted her to understand.

"Barb, Mario, Tomas, geez, Austin, Woody, Clint, Karl, Peg, Richard, Todd, Toby, and shoot, Tweed, and Bogsie—I'm not naming but a fourth now, but all of 'em—we help each other out like family. And this family lives by the tides to support the community. Between us, we can figure most anything out. Barb, she's an encyclopedia with a heart. It's like I'm part of something that's always been here. Even the crabs have a place, you know? They'll finagle their way right into any nursery tray with the smallest opening and eat your seeds like popcorn, so we all hate 'em. But they keep the bottom clean. They have their place, too, when you think about it. See? It's a world, CiCi, that all works together, and I get to be out in it every day. Sure there's crappy days, but you know, mostly the air is so plain good, and the water's clear glass and I pick up one of my own oysters, shuck it right there, slide it into my mouth and I know damn well it's probably the sweetest and the best in the world. It's not a job, it's a life. Every bad day earns me the ones that are—geez, I *told* you I couldn't explain it."

"You love it," Caroline said quietly.

"More 'n anything. I wish to hell I hadn't wasted so many years, but...." A shrug and another head shake, his tone unguarded and sad.

"But you're here now."

"That I am, ma'am." He cooperated with her attempt to be chipper.

"Is there anyone? I mean, I'm surprised you're not married, or living with someone, or involved. Or *are* you?" How could she not have asked first? Rid could have had a wife and two girlfriends and her mother wouldn't have known it unless they'd all been out picking oysters together.

Rid laughed easily. "Not hardly. Been there, done that. *All* done with that, I should say. Lizzie's the only female in my life now."

She tried not to show relief; he might misinterpret, think she wanted something.

"So anyway, you're back here as much as I am. Place in your blood, too, then?" Rid said.

"More like returning to the scene of the crime, I guess." She shrugged, then steered in a more comfortable direction. "Really, I'm here for Mom. As long as she needs me. Until...."

She was grateful he was neither stupid nor disingenuous and merely said, "And then?"

"I have no idea."

 *Chapter 4*

Caroline didn't think she'd be able to sleep, but then she woke needing to pee, amazed that dawn was already mixing into the blackness, lightening the world from black to charcoal gray. She cracked the bathroom window to listen for the weather; it sounded normal enough, though there were no bird sounds. The bay might still be churning whitecaps, but the tide was out so she wouldn't hear it. Still, it was clear the storm had passed.

She flipped the bathroom switch to check for power. Nothing. Her feet were cold on the ceramic floor, and she thought it was just as well she couldn't see herself in the mirror. Smeary makeup, bedhead, a sweatshirt, underpants.

Caroline used the toilet, rinsed her hands and swished water around in her mouth to freshen the sourness. Her toothbrush was upstairs. In the dark she washed her face to take off the eye makeup, then felt for the toothpaste and used her forefinger to swab her teeth with a glob of the minty stuff, more for her breath than her teeth. On her way out, she finger combed her short hair, fluffed the sides and back where she'd slept it flat.

Tiptoeing back to the bed in which they'd slept, she slid back in next to Rid more from chill than confidence. He rolled over as she did.

"Hi."

It was still dark enough that Caroline couldn't tell if he'd opened his eyes, although outside the gray had already lightened several shades since she'd gone to the bathroom. How quickly, how imperceptibly, life moved on.

In a sudden gesture, he flung off the quilt and jumped up. "Holy shit. I've got to go let Lizzie out. Her back teeth will be floating, and she won't speak to me until next Tuesday for not feeding her last night." Then he was standing, hopping on one foot, pulling on boxers. "Did you see where I threw my jeans?"

It wasn't like she'd thought he'd stay. She'd not consciously decided she even wanted him to, for that matter. So was it pride or something else that made her first vaguely insulted then overcome with a terrible loneliness, like the last unpicked rose hip, that he was in such a hurry to leave? She got up, too, following him into the living room, so he couldn't escape and leave her as if nothing had happened.

"Rid, last night, I didn't give you an honest answer to something you asked." Caroline could see his jeans, in fact, over behind the rocking chair, but didn't let his eyes follow hers there.

He had the decency to stop and look at her. "What was that?"

"You asked me why I wasn't teaching. I can't teach. I lost my certification. But no place would hire me anyway. That fatal accident I mentioned?" She paused, and he nodded. Caroline dropped her head and stared at her hands, one rubbing the other in her lap as she moved to sit on the sofa. The gray T-shirt that had been the layer next to Rid's skin, and the final one to come off last night, was wadded beneath her. Rid took the two steps and sat next to Caroline, his bare thighs goosebumped in the chill. She was cold, too, but the fact that he sat there chilled as she started to talk left open the question as to whether he intended to bolt. So she dragged his shirt from under her rump, handing it to him wordlessly and pulled the green quilt up from the floor over their legs.

Rid pulled the T-shirt over his head. Satisfied then, Caroline continued.

"I was the driver in that fatal accident. Chuck—he was my husband—and I had had this argument, and I got in the car and took off … that's not the point. I was charged with DWI, and I pled guilty. Rid, I was in prison."

"God, CiCi, I didn't know. I'm really sorry."

Maybe he'd signaled her then, because he didn't ask any questions, but the accident was something she never talked about, the stone-weight on her chest, and suddenly here she was, rolling it away to test some man, and now inertia kept it rolling. "It was in P-town. I didn't even hit another car on the *road*, it was a parked car."

Rid had to ask then. "Was it icy or something?"

"No. I wish it had been, to tell the truth." She waited for him to take the bait, to ask more, and he did.

"What happened?"

She sighed. "The other car was parked. I guess I misjudged how close I was, you know how narrow those streets are, but also, I didn't expect—see, a woman, the mother actually, had just opened the back door and was lifting a child out. I don't know *why*, I never understood why she was on the street side, but she was, and I hit that open car door and them."

"She was killed?" Rid said, eyes opening, more blue in his incredulity.

"She was pretty badly hurt, but she lived. The four-year old—he's the one who died." Tears were coursing down Caroline's cheeks now. A man who'd been in prison himself would understand, even if it meant she'd changed her whole notion of who she was, with what kind of people she belonged.

"CiCi, I'm real sorry. That's just got to be so hard." He shook his head as if to ward off the image of such sorrow, an empathic gesture, but at the same time, Caroline saw it: a nearly imperceptible clouding-over of his eyes, thigh muscles contracting to rise.

She couldn't let him. "And there's even—"

He stopped her with a hand on her knee as he slid himself forward in the first motion of standing. "I can't believe what you must have been through, Ci. It must have been hell. You're doing good to get over it." He paused, not long. "Right now, I've absolutely got to get going—I need to run and get Lizzie and get out to my grant, you know, check for damage, but also get those trays and hats back in while I've still got the tide. It's already coming." He looked at his watch, which he'd not taken off at all last night, and made an exaggerated face of alarm. "Hey, thanks so much for last night. I mean really, for helping me pull my stuff in." He started toward the hallway. "I'll just quick use the john. Oh, there's my jeans. And look, whaddya know. Shoes too." He picked them up in swoops, a gull diving for prey.

Rid disappeared into the bathroom, and Caroline heard his long hard stream overcome by the flushing toilet before it even ended. A quick rinsing sink sound, and he appeared again, this time with jeans and shoes on. She'd not had time for more than gall and hurt and an inchoate need to keep him from leaving her alone now.

Rid came back into the living room and gathered his waders and slicker, now dry, off the kitchen chair backs where he'd finally arranged them last night.

"Let me get you some breakfast," Caroline said, moving quickly into the kitchen area. "I can fix some—"

"No, really, thanks, but I've *got* to run." He was putting his wallet in his jeans pocket and picking up his truck keys, body angled to the door, talking to her over his shoulder. Behind him the light said dawn, almost morning now. As she'd known they would be, the windows were so occluded Caroline could not tell the weather.

"Just some cof—" Ridiculous, she realized. The power was out.

It didn't matter. "Really, thanks though," he said, opening the door.

"Then let me go with you. I can help."

"Actually, CiCi, what I've got to do today is probably easiest to do myself, you know, rather than take the time to show you. Another time, though. Thanks for the offer. If you need help with your mother—she's coming home today, right?—you just wave me in off the grant, okay? See ya later."

He was on the porch. The screen door had slapped shut behind him already. Caroline, still barefoot, still in only underpants and a sweatshirt, stood in the doorway and called after him. Called toward the beach and the bay and his back, and later, flushed with humiliation, had only this to cling to: the hope that the sound of the waves, the gulls' caws, the onshore breeze was enough to garble it, the pathetic non-sequitur. "Rid, the four-year-old was deformed. It was somebody's deformed child that I killed. *How could I ever get over it?*"

When she replayed it in her mind, she could make it come out either way because she'd only seen his back. Could be he hesitated a nanosecond then kept walking, pretending not to have heard. Or, he strode on to his truck those stupid, sad, desperate words separated and far-flung as bits of dry rockweed skittering along the beach in a high wind, none of it reaching any goal, none of it remaining coherently together. She *could* make it come out either way. But an AA leader in Chicago had lectured, "Tell the real truth, if only to yourself," when speaking about conducting a searching moral inventory. Attendance at four AA meetings had been one condition of her early parole, even though she'd never had a drinking problem. Still, she'd taken the AA message away and it had freed her even when she didn't like it. It was, well, simpler.

And the truth was simple: just enough beer to put her over the legal limit, an argument with Chuck, a figure opening a car door into a narrow street, a mother injured and her son dead.

Rid had hesitated.

Caroline went inside, broke the slam of the screen door, then softly closed and locked the main door. She knew it would be best if she turned on the radio, and busied herself with showering and making coffee—if the damn power ever came back on—or at least changing clothes and straightening the room.

Instead she stood half-dressed in the silence and took in the disarray of a place where something wasteful had occurred and now would all have to be put right again. The room looked as if something feral had been loosed there, snapping, pouncing, killing again while she'd pretended she was still something good, tender, in the bed of a dying old woman.

She tried not to let herself look for him, but she did. Saw him come back to the flats and park below the high-water line, where the others had already moved their trucks back from the incoming tide. His dog jumped out and ran on the beach, like her mother had said, but then Rid put her back in the truck. Another sea farmer waded over to talk to him. She tormented herself by watching him work, leaving the window to strip the bed and start the sheets in the washer, and then returning. Leaving again to fold the green quilt. Erasing the signs. Returning. By the time she was ready to pick up her mother, the tide was in and he was gone.

That night, awake in the bed that had been hers through a childhood in the same whitewashed pine room, the same white curtains at the window overlooking the perennial garden—the annuals were in a Jacob's garden (her grandfather's old dory) on the driveway side and the vegetables had always been planted by the kitchen door, just not this year—she thought how perversely things had turned out. There was Rid, who left high school with nothing and managed to lose even more, ending up in love with his life at what? Must be thirty-eight anyway, since she'd just turned forty. His father a third, maybe fourth, generation Portuguese fisherman turned oyster farmer, his mother a fallen-from-grace local girl who'd had to get married, if Eleanor had her ancient gossip straight. Their house was three or four miles inland, cheaper property even when waterfront prices weren't only for people with money falling out of their pockets. Rid's father had scratched his way up, but hadn't made a go of it until after Rid was gone and oysters went yuppie in the eighties. Back when it mattered, the road into Rid's future had looked unpaved, potholed, and dead-end. Exactly the sort of guy she'd been subtly steered around.

Being native Wellfleet was a mixed bag. It was a fishing village, pure and simple, which meant life on the tidal flats, or maybe picking up work on shrimp and scallop boats, or running your own deep sea operation, going after, say, tuna. The taproots of the year-rounders, the locals, were long and deep. You knew who you were, and so did everyone else. People inherited houses that had been built in the seventeenth and eighteenth centuries—some floated over on barges from Billingsgate Island, once a community across the bay before the sea claimed it entirely back in the nineteen twenties. Now it was no more than a shoal just off Great Island. Little cottages like Susan Atwood's, who was born back in 1804, were still graced—or ghosted—with the voices of the people who lived there first. "The sea is my cemetery," Susan was known to have said; every male in her family, seamen all, had been lost to it. In Wellfleet, history was close as your pillow at night and your mirror in the morning.

In towns like Wellfleet, when there's one thing everyone does, people start thinking it's the only thing anyone *can* do. Respect and disdain rub uneasy elbows and become indistinguishable as they join, and *local* becomes a term of derision and deference at once. Caroline's mother had managed what only a skillful few had done before her. Eleanor was a local who'd kept the deference and lost the derision by becoming part of the wider world while never forsaking home. Caroline's father, Bill, was the Cape Cod rep for a Connecticut marine insurance company who'd married Eleanor right after he graduated from Boston College. Eleanor had been in art school then, on her way to becoming a potter whose work sold briskly in a glutted market. When she inherited her parent's house on the Wellfleet bay shore, Eleanor wanted to go back for good.

"It's the Cape, Bill, my *home.*"

Of course, she wasn't coming back to work the flats or bag groceries at Lema's Market. She was returning as an up-and-coming artist to the Wellfleet village where Main Street was already becoming an arts mecca, especially in high summer when gallery doors are propped open for the tourists with their Gucci sunglasses and platinum credit cards.

Bill transferred to his company's Cape Cod branch, and they built Eleanor a separate studio behind the house, her design, with a skylight, a good wheel, kiln, and plenty of shelves. She taught part-time at the Castle Hill Art School in Truro and tried to keep up with orders for her work. Caroline, an only child, had the gift of their expectations, attention and income.

She'd had every chance. Although CiCi was from an old native family which established her in the community, she hadn't had the pall of it over her head like Cape fog. Her parents weren't involved with fishing, and Eleanor smartly affected expectations for her daughter by quietly working the schools, where the life stories of the locals were often written at the same time the pregnancies were announced: early marriages and menial support jobs for the girls, the flats or the sea for the boys. Although Caroline hadn't been raised a snob, to her mother's mind, perhaps she turned out a bit of one. Or got a dram too much of her father's washashore blood. Either way, by the time she graduated from Provincetown Regional High School, and left for college, CiCi could have been anything, done anything. And she did. She'd had everything until she didn't anymore, until here she was, back home with nothing.

 *Chapter 5*

Rid turned the key in the ignition as he slammed shut the truck door. The engine churned but caught quickly enough and with the same smooth mesh of motion, he had the truck in reverse, his head swiveled and his foot weighing the accelerator. The weather was unsettled after the storm, dank, the morning's onshore wind shifty. As he backed up from the protected place he and CiCi had left the truck, between the access road and the beach, he saw that the others were out on their grants, checking and resetting nets and trays and that the outermost part of his grant was already partly submerged. "Shit," he yelled as he banged the steering wheel with the heel of his right hand. He thought of heading out on his grant now, leaving Lizzie another couple of hours. But since she was with him pretty much all the time, and would have been last night if he hadn't tried to spare her the incoming blow, something she was afraid of, he was already guilt-pocked at having left her at all.

Now he'd done worse, left her to shiver it out alone under his bed, unfed and in the dark with no one there to let her relieve herself. No, he had to make a quick run to go get her first. As he shifted into drive, he saw Barb stand and give him a hands-up puzzled gesture, and he knew she wasn't the only one who'd ask him where he'd been. Missing a tide wasn't something any of them usually did; too much to do, and the work on the grant itself could only be done about two hours at a time once a day (except in the blessed months of extra daylight when there are double tides), the hour before and after dead low. Other than that, everything was under water.

That's what made the whole fuss with the upland owners so dumb. Beyond dumb. They were just spoiled rich people fussing about how the sea farmers' trucks and paraphernalia spoiled their view even though all of it, every single bit was under water except for two hours around low tide. For God's sake, he and his friends made their living on these grants—grants the town had given them, grants they were able to put their children's names on, to pass down the right to work and carry on the traditional way of living on which Wellfleet was built. Not only that, the town's economy was based on what they did. That's how shortsighted and selfish the complaints were.

He shook his head remembering CiCi's tone as she asked him why anyone would want to work a grant. She'd sounded like she was interrogating a garbage collector. What he'd wanted to say about it was, for one, *it's mine.* If she was out there with him at, say, a morning tide, he'd sweep his arm out expansively to show her, *this is my office. There's the view out my window, my ceiling. This is the air I breathe. Can you hear the bay water lapping around my feet, and those crazy herring gulls feeding? That's my elevator music. Other people pay a fortune to get this for a week. It's mine every day.* He was well beyond the point where he could imagine another life. Nor did he want to. It probably *was* a blood thing, he guessed, although shoot, CiCi was native Cape, too. Going to the tides must be a blood-type thing, like A negative or some sort that needs an exact match.

That's, of course, why you couldn't talk to the upland owners. They'd never get it; washashores never did. They were clueless that the bay itself was a living, working being, that the oysters from it were the best in the world because of the particular mix of fresh water from the creeks and rivers emptying into the salt harbor, the sweet clean cool of the place, and that the rhythms of putting in and taking out were fascinating and beautiful. They could glory in them from their fancy decks, if they had a shell's worth of sense. In fact, instead of driving to Aesop's Tables in town and ordering from the raw bar, they could climb down the fancy stairways they built from their manicured yards to their blasted *private* beach, walk over, make friends, and he'd have pulled twice as many oysters and given them freely, with a smile and handshake. Where the hell did they think those oysters had come from anyway? He was the one who had the contract with Aesop's and what he sold the restaurant for sixty-five cents each, the restaurant laughed and sold for double that. Sometimes triple, he'd seen that, too.

At least he'd been able to pull the nursery trays out, thanks to CiCi securing the nets for him. What seed he'd gotten was premium, nearly the size of plantable field clams, which would cost thirty-six dollars a thousand, but he'd only paid the eighteen dollars that matchheads cost. Losing even some of it in a nor'easter would have been—well, he just couldn't, that was all.

As he got a couple of miles inland, closer to Route 6 where his house was just barely on the harbor side of that bisecting road, the protection of the pitch pines and the oaks lessened the force of the wind on his truck and gave him hope that Lizzie might be asleep. No such luck. As his front tires started to crunch the driveway gravel, she was already giving him what-for.

"All right, all right, I'm sorry girl, I'm coming," he called, leaving the truck door open in his fumbling haste for his house key.

The Lab shot out and into a squat in the weedy grass. "Whew," Rid whistled. "I know, I know. Wow, that's a lot. You really had to go bad. I'm really sorry, girl."

As soon as she was upright again, the dog did an ecstatic dance around him, leaping to take tongue swipes at his face. Rid squatted and let her kiss and nuzzle him, his arms around her in a hug that shortly resulted in his being knocked onto his rear. "Okay, okay," he laughed. "I'm happy to see you, too. D'ja think you I was gonna let you starve? Ya wanna *eat*?"

At the word, the dog backed up and barked.

"C'mon, girl, we gotta hurry, we're losing the tide," he said, striding to the kitchen where he scooped dry dog food into a metal bowl, and slamming the house door behind him, carried it to the truck, Lizzie barking and jumping in famished eagerness alongside all the way. Once in the front seat, she snarfed the food as he jammed the truck in reverse and raced back to the tide.

❀

He'd lost way too much time. Some of his nets were already under so much water that if they were fouled, he really couldn't do anything about it now. "Crap," he muttered, throwing the truck into park fairly near the high-water mark, seeing that Barb and Tweed and Woody were already throwing some equipment into the backs of theirs in preparation to move them in some. On a moon tide like this one, so much of the grant was exposed that it was worth it to move the truck two or three times, farther out and then back in some on the flats rather than leave it in the shallows and have to trudge back and forth. It was their most valuable work time of the month, not that tomorrow's tide wouldn't be good, too, but last night had been the full moon, so from now on it wouldn't be quite *as* good, and now he'd missed it when there might be repairs needed, on top of the digging and picking he'd planned to get done to fill the weekend orders down in Chatham.

Lizzie bounded out of the truck and immediately—he could have predicted it, having given her no time in the yard—did her business on the beach. Rid winced, hoping the owner whose precious sand Lizzie was polluting wasn't doing an eagle-eye patrol behind some enormous expanse of window. He'd not thought to bring a plastic bag to pick it up with; maybe someone had one lying around his truck. Rid was always careful—all of them were—about antagonizing the upland owners. Sometimes when he was early and waiting for the tide to drop enough so he could work, he'd play ball with Lizzie in the shallows, always scrupulous to keep her off the beach, and while he worked, he kept her in the truck. He reminded himself: *don't forget to clean that up* as he pulled his waders on and hooked one of the shoulder straps.

"Where the hell you been?" It was Mario, shouting from in front of the big rock that handily marked the border of his grant. He looked at his watch in an exaggerated motion. He'd already thrown his bull rake in the truck, which meant he'd dug the quahogs he needed to fill immediate orders. Behind him, the wind whipped the surface of the bay into frothy whitecaps. The mottled sky kept moving.

Rid wasn't going to take the time to answer. "Got held up," he shouted back, and slung the first two nursery trays he'd pulled from the water last night over his shoulder to carry out and reset. "Much damage last night?" he yelled as he slogged out.

"Some. Not too bad," Mario called, from closer. Mario didn't believe in pulling stock before storms or even burying his oysters in a pit for winter. Most of the time he got away with it, but when he didn't, he lied about it. He was crossing to Rid's grant, zigging to avoid oyster cages and skirting the edges of Rid's netted-over raceways. "Hey, d'ja talk to Tomas since the second tide yesterday?"

"Nope." Rid kept moving, to be clear: *man, I've got to get this done.* It wasn't that they didn't visit out there. For sure they did, but they all had times when they let each other know *not today.* Actually, he was surprised Mario was sparing five minutes himself if he'd had any digging to do along with checking the whole grant for storm damage. "You done?"

"Not yet. Listen, we got trouble. Something about a lawsuit, trying to take away our grants."

"Huh?"

"Yeah. Tomas got an appointment with a lawyer for tomorrow."

"What the hell're you talking about?" This was one of Mario's stupid games, and one Rid did not have time for today.

Mario paused and eyed him. "Didn't ya get your mail yesterday?"

"No, guess I didn't pick it up." He'd been at CiCi's, of course, not that it was Mario's business.

"Buddy, you're being sued."

"Me? For what?"

"We're being sued, us three with grants in front of Pissario's place. Don't you know? We're on *private* property." Typical Mario, acting tough and amused by disaster, water sloshing at his boots now, one hand shielding his eyes although there wasn't a hint of sun and he had on a backward baseball cap anyway. If he actually had to deal with it, Mario would blow like Hurricane Bob.

"What the hell? The town gave us these grants, we're perfectly legal. We stay off their damn beach." Rid felt himself flushing, hated it.

"Except when your date decides to take a shit up there," Mario said, using his chin to gesture at Lizzie where she sat in Rid's driver's seat watching them.

"Goddammit, Mario," Rid said.

Mario laughed, then having received the message, sobered enough to mollify Rid. "They're claiming that the town don't have the *right* to give us the grants because *they* own all the way out to mean low water, not mean high water. Well, it's not a *they*, actually, it's Pissario, suing us for being on '*his*' property." When he said "his," Mario put quotation marks around it with fingers in the air, and underscored it with sarcasm. "And in case that ain't enough, the prince is also suing the town for leasing *his* land out to you and me and Tomas. We just happen to be the lucky bastards whose grants are the ones the prick claims he owns. Anyway, your paperwork, you'll be pleased to hear, is in your mailbox. Ain't that just a kick in the pants?"

Rid struggled to wrap his mind around what Mario was saying. "That would…."

"Yeah. Shut us down."

"But he can't—"

"Hell no. He ain't gonna get away with this."

"What does Wardy say?"

"Hell, Wardy works for the town, he'll do what they tell him to do. It ain't like he's got guts of his own now, is it? I don't guess they told him nuttin yet because I ain't seen hide nor hair of him."

Rid looked down at the tide climbing his ankles. "Christ, man, I've got to check my nets and get these trays back in. I can't think about this now."

"Whatever." Mario gave a half wave, half shrug and turned back toward his own grant. Mario was like that, offended if you didn't join his jocularity or gossip. Rid would have to talk to Tomas and the shellfish warden, although he had to admit that Mario was right about one thing: if they had to rely on Wardy for help, they all might as well stick their heads between their legs and kiss their asses goodbye.

"Your nets fouled bad?" Rid called to the back of Mario's head.

"Yeah."

"Real bad?"

"Yeah."

Rid sighed. All the grants on the flats anywhere near Blackfish Creek got a lot of shifting sand in every big blow that had to be cleared from the raceway nets within a day or the quahogs planted underneath would suffocate. Oysters, too—if they were buried and couldn't filter the water for nutrients, they'd die. Even too much weed on the nets would steal oxygen from the water and slow their growth. Rid was always looking for ways to get to market sooner, not later; they all were. The longer until his animals reached legal size, the more likely he was to lose them to predators, pollution and disease. And in the meantime, well, that was his money lying there, his investment account underwater, and as likely to drown as not.

It wasn't until Rid left the grant, frustrated, the last to go, waiting until the wheels of his truck were sinking in the advancing water and there was no part of his grant he could work, that CiCi crossed his mind again. He'd not have thought about her then—his mind was mired in the mess of his nets and worrying the whole expanse of this lawsuit business—except that he saw her house over across the little horseshoe-shaped beach as his truck bumped up onto the access road. The houses near CiCi's had been there forever and belonged, for the most part, to natives. But as the property up on the bluffs over the bay had all been snatched up, there was increasing *opportunity* (the real estate agents' favorite word) to sell the old places down at sea level, the ones without the spectacular views. Already, a couple had been demolished to make way for the glass castles. One was only a couple of houses from CiCi's traditional Cape, a huge angular structure with jutting decks and skylights, ridiculously out of place to Rid's eye. He'd said as much to Tomas, who'd replied that the owner didn't care how it looked now: he'd just had the foresight to build there while he could still get the land, and get it more cheaply than up on the bluffs. Soon enough all the sea-level houses would be sold and demolished, the natives moved, and the house in question would be ideally placed. Like most natives, Rid looked on the newcomers and their mansions with a mixture of derision, anger and secret envy.

The horseshoe beach, reserved by the town for swimming, didn't have grants in front of it. Rid briefly wondered if that would actually be a selling point. When he saw CiCi's house, that's what he thought first, would she sell it after her mother died, and to whom, for what? How could the tidal flats be private property? That made no sense. There was obviously a mistake in all this, one that would be straightened out in time. His mind wouldn't hold an unbroken thought, only pieces. Still, when he saw her house, he did think of her. And when he thought of her, he was ashamed.

He'd felt it before, with other women. They try to be dignified, let a man leave when he needs to leave. Wants to leave. Whatever. Something like desperation starts to leak in right at the end, though, as if a good watertight seal just springs a tiny leak. And any leak can sink a boat. Just give it time to work, work, work. Anyway, he'd heard her, though he pretended not to. The business about the accident-child being deformed. Like that made some difference. The reason he hadn't turned around was simple and direct. He had to get to his dog and his grant. He couldn't let himself be finagled into staying, not today, not after a blow had done whatever to his nets and his stock. There was another reason, too, though. He didn't have any idea what difference it was supposed to make, what she expected or hoped for in reaction, that she'd have sailed that out like a lasso to snag him. He didn't know what to say or how to help. If he had, maybe he'd have turned around and said, "Why don't you come on with me today after all?"

❀

"Apparently, you're not fishermen. You're farmers. Sea farmers. *Big* difference," the attorney said.

Of course, it would be Tomas—burly-looking in his overalls, untamed gray mane, weather-beaten face and hands—who spoke for them in his refined, educated voice and vocabulary. Among them, he was the scientist, the one who read, who studied environmental conditions and growing techniques. Just now he was working with the new Australian lines, hanging nursery bags from lines suspended in deeper water to increase their exposure to nutrients. The only one of them who began to know as much as Tomas was Barb, only she wasn't being sued.

Tomas cleared his throat. "We're acquaculturists, actually, but it would properly be considered a form of commercial fishing, sir. My research says that fishing is exempted under the Colonial ordinance of 1641. Isn't that correct?"

The three of them had agreed. They would pay for a joint defense. Tomas would speak for them with this Barnstable lawyer who'd agreed to take their case. Now Rid and Mario glanced at each other, tacitly congratulating each other on their wisdom. Tomas had book smarts. What they knew was that they had been raised always to stay below the high water mark when driving to and from their grants as a legal bow to the rights of the private beach owners. Once in the shallows, actually on the tidal flats, they were on their own grants. Neither of them understood—nor particularly wanted to—how something that had functioned so simply and so well for so long was suddenly the focus of litigation. Tomas, on the other hand, would make it his business to understand and fix it.

The attorney sighed. "Yeah. It's correct. And there's a loophole the size of your harbor in it. See, the Colonial ordinance of 1641 was designed to encourage commerce—to get settlers to build wharves and the like. To do this, the lawmakers extended waterfront land ownership all the way out to mean low water—which, as you three well know, is a huge distance—what? five football fields?—rather than just to mean high water like practically every other coastal state in the country. And yes, you're right, they *did* provide that commercial fishing and navigation could go on in the water above the land—hell, even swimming, if you can believe that, as long as the swimmer's feet don't touch bottom, for God's sake."

"So, there's our defense," Tomas said. "And the town's."

"Except...," said the attorney. He leaned back in his swivel chair. It wasn't a fancy office, but decent enough. Framed diplomas. Boston University. A wooden desk, not too scratched up. A second floor office, an abandoned reception desk just now. David Lorenz, Esquire himself: balding, wearing an open-necked Oxford shirt, khakis, steel-rimmed glasses. A habit of twirling the end of his mustache. Bitten fingernails.

"…Except that your pea-brained state Supreme Judicial Court of 1993 affirmed a definition of aquaculture as farming. Not fishing. Therefore the grants are not a protected use. Therefore Pissario's claim that you are on private property may well be valid. The town may not have the right to issue these grants at all."

"What position is the town taking?" Tomas still sounded measured and matter-of-fact, which was the only thing preventing Rid from grabbing the lawyer's throat and demanding to know what the hell he was going to *do* about this. He didn't dare even look at Mario now. The guy had been in the Marines; at least that's what his tattoo claimed, but Rid figured him to have been tossed out of boot camp for sniffing Agent Orange or for putting his drill sergeant in a headlock. Mario was a good-hearted, hotheaded moron. Rid would rather have been sued with anybody else on the flats.

"I couldn't tell you. The town attorney seems rather befuddled. As does the shellfish warden. I realize that there's … er … expense involved for you, but my best advice is not to rely on the town to resolve this for you."

Mario erupted onto his feet, his hand onto the lawyer's desk. *"That's my grant, my father put my name on it, and I'll fucking kill the bas—"*

David Lorenz drew back. In the same motion in which the attorney moved, Tomas was on his feet, his bulk equal to Mario's but easily five or six inches taller. Still, the fluid grace of a fish. He slid himself between Mario and the desk, a hand on Mario's shoulder, Mario then abruptly back in his chair. Rid sensed, rather than saw the force the hand had applied. That was the thing with Tomas. You never actually saw the force he applied to anything. "Hey, man," Tomas said very quietly, speaking eye to eye to Mario. "Mr. Lorenz is our friend. Keep that straight, or we can split up and defend ourselves separately. *Right?"*

Mario's eyes were coal fires, but he mumbled, "Right." He looked out the window where the sky was the pure periwinkle of the Cape in September. It helped. The bay would have helped more.

The attorney's shoulders and eyebrows—which could use a trim—dropped back into place.

"Look," he said, resuming. "There *is* some good news. Remember that Pissario is also suing the sea farmers—"

"That's aquaculturists," Tomas corrected quietly. His hands rested on thighs that looked exposed without waders over them. His voice was strong, even though it was always low and calm.

Lorenz blinked and went on again. "Right, excuse me, aquaculturists, he's suing the other acquaculturists who drive over his beach to get to their grants. Now if I have this right, there are four whose grants are between the access road and Pissario's who don't drive over his beach so they're not included in the suit." He ran a hand from his forehead back, as if there were hair falling down but there wasn't.

Tomas nodded. "That would be Barb, Clint, Tweed, and Karl."

Rid directed the question to Mario and Tomas. "Have they heard anything from the people above them? Any complaints, I mean."

Tomas answered. "Barb just says she's always gotten along with them. You know, she sees them out walking, she gives 'em a couple dozen oysters and chats awhile. Nothing different since Pissario filed, but maybe they don't know about it yet. I doubt it though. People love Barb, and rightly so."

"It's a subdivision up on the bluffs, of course," Lorenz said. "Sometimes neighborhoods like that will band together if a leader like Pissario emerges. Don't be surprised. But that won't affect you."

"Yeah." It was Mario, bitter. "Our asses have already been sued. What else they gonna do? Shoot us at dawn?"

Tomas shot Mario a look. It was enough to shut him up, but he twisted the baseball cap in his hand until Rid wanted to grab it away. He was nervous enough with Mario's fidgeting, restraining himself from speaking to avoid Tomas's reprimand as well as the embarrassment of sounding like Mario. The truth was that his head was about to detonate; he couldn't trust himself not to explode in his own death threats.

"Look, could we stick to the point here? I have other appointments." Lorenz straightened his calendar after leaning over, ostensibly to consult it. "The *point* is that while there are four aquaculturists not included in the suit for whatever reason, there are six or seven others also sued because they drive across Pissario's beach to get to their grant areas, although their actual grants are in front of other upland owners' properties. The *point* is that perhaps you could draw some or all of them in to fight this together—pool your resources, as it were."

"Six or seven others?" Rid couldn't contain himself, although he had enough control, unlike Mario, to stay seated, refrain from shouting and not cuss. His mother would have been proud. "How'd he figure that? There are twelve or thirteen grants down past Pissario's toward Blackfish Creek."

"I have no idea how he decided whom to sue. That's a mystery. Maybe they had too many letters and numbers on their license plates for him to copy down or something. I really have no idea. It seems pretty random."

"I know Bogsie and Smitty are in it, I saw 'em yesterday," Rid inserted. "As far as I know, they haven't done anything like get a lawyer yet."

"We can get that information easily enough. You three are his primary targets though, I'm afraid, since you're engaged in illegally farming his land." The attorney put up two fingers of each hand to bracket *engaged in illegally farming his land* in imaginary quotation marks. "Do you need time to think about this?"

Rid couldn't contain himself. "As opposed to just committing suicide here in your office?" He'd worn his newest jeans, the unfaded dress ones, a clean plain white T-shirt and deck shoes. The outfit was his equivalent of a tuxedo. He felt ridiculous and furious that Pissario—or anyone else—should bring him to his knees this way when nothing else had. Before Tomas could humiliate him, he forced himself to look at the lawyer directly and say, "I apologize. That was uncalled for."

David Lorenz shook his head. "Look, it's all right. You've got every right to be upset. You've just got to realize that I'm on your side here, and what we've got to do is research, strategize and present a hell of a case. You men are going to have to put emotions away for us to do that or we'll waste a lot of time. It's time you're paying for. *Presuming*, I mean, that you decide to fight this. You *can* walk away, you know. Go do something else."

Rid sensed that Mario was about to blow. He put his hand up and out to the side where Mario sat, a warning. "That's not an option," Rid said.

From behind his desk, David Lorenz glanced warily at Mario. "I assume you feel the same way?"

Tomas slid his own voice into the available space. "Yes, sir, he does. We all do."

"Well, then, we'll proceed. I'll need a ten thousand dollar retainer to get started. Our first step is to prevent an injunction that would stop you from working your grants while this thing makes its way through the courts. It could take years. I hope you're prepared for that."

Rid had never gone there in his mind, considered maybe they could be shut down, stopped from working at all. Each of them had thousands of dollars lying in the shallows of the harbor. All their nursery stock, all their maturing and ready-to-harvest shellfish. All their trays, their nets, their cages. His stomach roiled. His peripheral vision picked up Mario twisting his cap.

Tomas wiped one side of his face with his gnarly hand, a narrow gold wedding band part of the flesh. "Yeah. Okay. We'll need to get that together for you."

Rid allowed himself to look at Mario on the way to looking over at Tomas. Mario's eyes glittered unnaturally and for a moment Rid thought a dangerous rage was about to erupt. It was that hard to imagine tears.

Chapter 6

In the weeks that followed, Caroline carried around the hope Rid would call like a sand dollar in a zippered pocket. Not that he'd asked for her number, but it was in the book. It wasn't like he didn't know her mother's name, even if he thought she might be using a married name, which she wasn't. She'd resumed her own Marcum name before the divorce was final. Not that he'd asked about that, either.

She watched him surreptitiously through the big windows near Eleanor's bed as he came and went from his grant at low tides. Surreptitiously not because he could see her from that distance, but because Eleanor watched her as sharply as Caroline wished she could watch Rid, so she could not. And it wasn't actually Rid she watched anyway, but more his truck. She had to actually see the truck arrive to be able to track his movement out to his grant. Otherwise, the figures looked too much alike from a quarter mile, and, lacking any discernible border, one patch of sandy bay bottom littered with oyster cages looked exactly like the next.

He didn't call. The first few days were hardest, but then Eleanor was worse—sicker, weaker, more pain—and Caroline stiffened herself by stuffing hurt and sadness in a bag of anger. So *I'm lonely and scared here* became a muttered *Fuck you, Rid* when she walked down onto the beach at mid- or high tide. If Elsie or a respite care giver were there for Eleanor at low tide, she went into town or over to Newcomb Hollow beach on the ocean side and walked until she was so tired she worried about making it back to the car. Not thinking about him, not rebuking herself, was fairly simple at home because her attention was so much on her mother. But when she was out of the house, however briefly, there was no neutral or restful place for her mind.

🏵

October. Some days the offshore wind unsheathed its blade, but others were butter-soft, shining. The first two weeks offered a late Indian summer with beach grass gilt and silver shining in the Cape's crystal light, waving under a topaz sky. Whitecaps. A symphony of gulls swelling overhead. Bluefish running. One warm Friday afternoon, Caroline opened all the windows in the living room and raised the head of the hospital bed, trying to bring the day to her mother, bring her mother to the day.

Elsie had bathed Eleanor in the morning, a process Caroline intermittently forced herself to watch and couldn't bear. Afterward, the sublingual morphine finally won and Eleanor was asleep, but it had taken much too long. Now Caroline and Elsie were in the yellow kitchen. The light beyond the window was an insult to what was happening indoors, a day Eleanor would have called an ode to joy. Instead she was oblivious to it, only able to focus on an argument with pain, and the recognition broke Caroline's heart. Even visits from Eleanor's friends had become difficult, the effort leaching her, leaving her worn and pale. Caroline had started putting visitors off when she could get away with it, trying not to give offense, sometimes accepting a homemade soup or pudding on the porch and saying that Eleanor was sleeping when she wasn't. Otherwise they lingered, like a nice cake going stale from too much air, and her mother's face looked like a snow sky when they left. Sometimes, though, when it was Eleanor's best friends, like Noelle or Sharon, Karen or Carol, it was Caroline who couldn't bear their presence, how they took what Eleanor had to give when it was Caroline who needed it most.

"Your mother should have the drip now," Elsie said, as she organized a late lunch for the two of them. She was making tea, practiced and efficient in her motions. Her sable hair was cut in a child's straight bob, hardly a bit of gray in it though she looked to be in her late fifties. She definitely wasn't the sort to color it, Caroline was sure; she didn't wear a speck of makeup and her clothes were utilitarian, without a discernible style.

Caroline slumped against the refrigerator, her face in her hands.

"If you can be ready, you'll help her be ready." Caroline felt Elsie touch her shoulder and she lowered her hands from her face, which felt sticky. There was pressure over her eyes.

"I'm not. How can I pretend to be?"

"Don't pretend. Can you start to accept it?"

Caroline felt a flush of anger. "Easy to say."

"I don't mean it to sound that way. Is there something that would help?" Elsie leaned toward Caroline, her brown eyes intent and direct.

"When my father died, I felt cheated—you know? He died at his desk at work. He'd stayed late, the secretary had gone home. Mom finally went to the office to look for him when he didn't answer the phone. A massive heart attack and we didn't even know there was anything wrong with his heart. A little overweight, a little high blood pressure, no big deal. No goodbyes. No nothing. But in comparison to this? In retrospect, it seems a mercy."

Elsie crossed to Caroline, took one of her hands and led her to the kitchen table. She pulled out a chair and sat Caroline down, as if she were a child. The table was set, a turkey sandwich and a cup of tea at Caroline's place. The tea, in one of Eleanor's mother's bone china cups, had a translucent round of lemon studded with cloves split on the rim like a slice of sun. The sandwich, too, was on the good china and had a pink cloth napkin folded next to it. A bowl of mixed fresh fruit was a little to the left. Once Caroline was seated, Elsie sat down with the corner of the table between them, the breath of her own tea rising next to Caroline's.

Tears came to Caroline's eyes. Again. "This is so pretty. So nice of you. Where did you get...?"

"I brought extra. Take a bite."

"Thanks," Caroline whispered. She wanted a shower and a long, dreamless sleep in a cool room and to wake with her mother well and giving unsolicited advice, all of which she would cheerfully take for the rest of her life. She took a small bite and put the sandwich back down. "Last night was bad." The jeans and gray sweatshirt she wore were the same ones she'd had on for the past two or three days. She'd lost track. It wasn't that there wasn't anything else clean; a respite worker had done the laundry. It was just easier to pick up the same thing off the floor and put it on, no need to think. She really had to stop doing that, no matter how tired she was when she got up, as tired as when she'd laid down.

"Can you listen to me for a minute?"

With her free hand, Caroline pressed against the ridge between her eyes.

"I know it doesn't feel this way, but this time can be a gift."

"Oh, definitely." Caroline was faintly ashamed of her sarcasm in the face of Elsie's kindness, yet not enough to retract it. "Have you been through this?"

Elsie didn't appear to notice, or at least not to take offense. Instead she stroked Caroline's shoulder with her left hand, and with her right, she reached across the table and took Caroline's other hand, which lay inert next to the sandwich missing its small half-moon bite.

"Yes. With my mother. And with many patients. I'm not trying to force something on you. Some people can do it, some can't."

"Do what?"

Elsie paused. "Well, not fight it so much. Not run from it. Be with her in it, if you know what I mean. This is a time you can share. You can help her complete her life."

"What's that supposed to mean?"

Again Elsie overlooked the sarcastic edge in her voice. "I mean that if you can give her the chance to say '*I forgive you, forgive me, I love you, thank you and goodbye,*' and you can say those very same things to her—more or less—for most patients and most families, it gives a great deal of peace."

Elsie held Caroline's eyes as she spoke. For a few seconds, some curtain was raised and Caroline glimpsed what Elsie was talking about. But either she was too tired to hold the vision or the window fogged over and the clarity was gone. She stopped meeting Elsie's gaze, dropping her head and pressing her fingers against the bony part of her brow again, where some punk rock band seemed to be warming up.

"Headache?" Elsie said.

"Always."

"Okay. You eat. I'll get you a couple of Tylenol. We'll finish our lunch and—maybe you'd like to get in a shower before I leave?"

"Hmm. Starting to get a bit ripe, am I? No wonder my dating life is slow."

"I didn't mean that. No, not at all. You said earlier that you wanted to shower and I...."

Kindness, not humor, was Elsie's forte. "Elsie, I was just kidding. Yes, I'd really like to shower and wash my hair. And thank you for lunch. It's delicious. Really." Actually, it helped to have to yank herself back abruptly like that. She'd been skirting the abyss. What Else had been talking about was too big, as if while Caroline was lost, chartless in an ocean fog, she was expected to navigate the mystery of her mother's life and death. Too big, too much. Now she was speaking to the nurse's back, as Elsie was over at the kitchen sink where a large bottle of extra-strength Tylenol was on the windowsill. Elsie came back and put two capsules into Caroline's hand.

Caroline took them, drinking from the cup. "Ooh. That tea is so good."

"We have a whole pot of it," Elsie said with a smile. "Can you taste the cinnamon? There's a stick of it in the pot. Not too much, I hope." She sat down again. "Goodness, your neighbors are having a time of it with that lawsuit, aren't they?"

"Lawsuit?" Caroline asked. Good, sweet Elsie, talking about anything but death and dying now.

Elsie pointed vaguely upward, out the side of the kitchen to the east, toward the bluffs. "The people up there suing the oystermen."

"I don't know what you're talking about."

"Oh, well, it's been on the front page of *The Times*, and living right here, I thought you'd know. One of the people up on the bluffs is suing some of the oystermen because he says he owns the flats."

"I haven't looked at the paper. I stopped delivery last month—I was picking it up and dropping it into the trash, and it was just a waste." As she spoke, Caroline's mind skipped ahead: Rid. Was he involved? "I don't see how anybody up there can sue, though. I mean the town gives those grants. It's town property." Wasn't that what Rid had explained to her?

"I don't know the details. Something about how the town doesn't really own it. It's quite a mess, anyway. It'll put those oystermen out of business if they lose. And if it spreads to other upland landowners, it doesn't just wipe out the fishing families, it wipes out a town."

That night, Caroline watched the local news on television but there was no mention of it. She called and had delivery of *The Cape Cod Times* resumed, but there was nothing about a lawsuit. Not for nearly a week. She thought about whether to call Rid, whether to walk down and ask him. She didn't though. Something else took center stage: she awakened nauseated, ate lightly and promptly threw up. That made her pay attention to the missed period she'd attributed to stress and to the tender breasts she'd attributed to the missed period.

The damn lawsuit was consuming him. He had nothing to compare it to except maybe a hurricane warning: something you knew was coming, saw the sky darkening, frantically tried to defend against but realized could take everything you'd worked for. It was all they talked about on the flats, even those who weren't being sued. It was eclipsing this weekend's Oysterfest, something they all had fun with the middle of every October. Barb would probably win the oyster shucking contest again—he could've beaten her last year if he'd concentrated more—but now he wasn't even going to enter. Too far behind on orders, having wasted time standing in the shallows with Tomas, looking up at the Pissario house. There was no sign of activity up there, which was, in itself, infuriating. He had to hold himself back around Mario to avoid inciting the hothead to some retaliation that could boomerang back on them all.

"I'd like to know exactly how we can be such a terrible problem for Mr. High and Mighty," Mario would rant bitterly, squinting up to where the sun glinted off the Pissario house like an ice sculpture. "Ain't nobody there. Four friggin' decks overlooking his friggin' view that we working scumbags mess up but there ain't nobody ever on one of 'em. Too busy out hiring lawyers, I guess. Now, if them plate glass windows of his was to get shot out mysteriously some night, I'm thinking he'd have a problem worth his time. I don't see what choice we got. It's not like we got *help* from our *friends*." The others named in the suit had, one by one, opted out of a joint defense. They were trying to work out a settlement, they said. So far the upland owners above their grants were sleeping giants, and all they needed was to cross Pissario's beach. Obviously, they thought Mario, Rid and Tomas had zero possibility of winning against Pissario and wanted to avoid going down with them.

Rid stopped picking oysters out of a cage then, even though the tide was moving in and he didn't have enough for his restaurant order yet. He stood up between Mario and shore for the third or fourth time that afternoon. "Man, you gotta back off. We've gotta go with Tomas, with the lawyer stuff. That's the way to fight this."

Privately, though, he felt the same rage, the same urge to strike back. Visceral prison memories—the slide and clang of an auto lock steel door, the smothering closeness of the cement walls and ceiling—kept him in check.

When the tide came after dark or was small—meaning it didn't drop below the mean low-tide mark because the moon was waning or new—Rid, Tomas and Mario met early to drink at The Reading Oyster Restaurant, across from the town pier and the shellfish warden's office. "The Oyster" was where they always went, where everyone went, but now they sat apart, not at the bar with the others, but at one of the high tables along the wall. When the others came in, it was later, and earlier when they left. Everyone spoke to them. They were slapped on the back, cheered on, given sympathy, outrage, and thumbs up variously. But then they veered off, as if discreetly trying not to catch a communicable disease.

The main topic for Tomas was raising money. "I don't think you two are adequately aware of how far this may go. The retainer is just the beginning." Tomas had gone into his children's college fund for his share. So far, his wife was with him, but the children came first for her. Tomas didn't think Marie would be willing to follow him into a hole. "If we don't fight it, obviously we lose everything. But we may lose everything anyway, because it may take all we've got and more. That's why we've got to decide now exactly how far we're willing to take this." Tomas spoke in his patient, cultured voice, usually looking at Mario.

For Rid, the issue was trying to keep Tomas from giving up on a joint defense because Mario was such a wildcard. Mario had more money than he did, and he was hoping that Mario would advance some of his share until he could come up with it. There was a question in his mind—probably in Tomas' mind too—about the source of Mario's money. They all had side jobs; they had to. Tomas and Marie ran a bait shop with Marie's brother in Eastham. Some cut and sold firewood, or jumped on a scallop or shrimp boat out of New Bedford for a week or ten days, which would bring in a quick couple of thousand extra in the winter. Rid had done both, depending on the year.

It wasn't impossible that Mario ran some drugs. He reminded Rid of himself ten years ago, which ran up a red flag or two. But there wasn't room to worry about that. For one, he and Tomas needed the money, for all of Tomas' talk about going it alone. And Rid had more than enough to worry about. He *should* have been home repairing cages. He hadn't fixed all the damage from the hurricane tail swipe last month, and winter was coming on. There was no way he should have been sitting on a bar stool.

It was mid-October. The summer tourists were long gone, and it was the local fishers and year-rounder business people in the restaurant. The fishermen were in the bar; the tide had been at five-fifteen and had run them into darkness. Most had come in for a drink right off their grants. On the other side, the restaurant served a couple celebrating an anniversary, a lone man in a suit, a smattering of nondescript others. The bar, as usual on weeknights, was the heartbeat of The Reading Oyster, which was the heartbeat of the town, especially in the off-season.

The restaurant was named for the dark and dusty bookstore at its rear, crammed with ancient paperbacks and magazines and rare books, some suspended over string along the beamed ceiling, many stacked precariously along the narrow aisles. Old, yellowing movie posters were tacked to any wall space not covered with shelves from which old, random books tumbled, here and there an astonishing treasure surrounded by garage-quality junk. The family that owned the restaurant kept the bookstore in operation a few hours a day, not that there were many customers, because it was the collection of their ancient patriarch, who sat guard at the antiquated cash register by the door. Maybe it also kept him out of the restaurant, where he'd be in their way.

Even the bar was slow tonight. Or it was slow now, at seven thirty, because most everyone had come, had their after-tide beer and gone on home to work on their nets or cages or, in the unlikely event that they were caught up with those, to struggle with the paper work. Cash out and cash in was always best. It all used to be under the table, but things were changing, regulations being enacted, inspection procedures becoming more and more rigorous, put in place faster than some of them could keep up. Federal HACCP—Hazard Analysis Critical Control Point—regulation, with its boatload of rules controlled every single clam and oyster if you wanted to deal wholesale, and the damn rules so complicated the government made you pay to take their class.

Rid, Tomas and Mario were still on their stools. They weren't drunk, nor were they entirely sober, except for Tomas who never showed beer anyway, even after five or six. Tonight he'd had only three. All of them ordered sandwiches, Rid and Mario mainly so they could keep drinking, and Tomas to keep them all sober enough to stay on track.

"Look," Tomas said. "It's money now or money later. If we lose our grants we're out our income and everything we've invested. Or even short term— remember, he *could* get a restraining order. We're got to stop pissing and moaning and focus. That's the point. Or we fold now." The last was rhetorical. They all reiterated regularly that they weren't giving up their lives and livelihood, but Tomas still brought it up as an option.

Mario banged his fist on the table. "Why us? Why not the others?" His face was red, a bit bleary in the semi-darkness of the bar, but Rid recognized it as Mario's pent-up anger as much as the beer.

Tomas sighed.

As much to intervene as because he thought it was actually workable, Rid said, "Maybe we could ask all the others to help us out. With the money. You know, make a case that they're all in danger, too. 'Cause if Pissario wins, then the upland owners above them, hell, they're all likely to just say, hey, that's my land you're on, I want you off, or I want sixty percent of everything you pick off my land. Whatever. I mean, isn't Pissario setting precedent? They could all be laying back, letting Pissario absorb the cost of the first suit, and if he wins, then they pounce."

"Yeah," Mario said, "that's what I'm getting at," although, of course, he hadn't been. His cap was on forward tonight, with the bill bent up and back.

Tomas closed his eyes a moment and rubbed his chin. "That's good. That's good. We should be able to make that argument," and Rid was as pleased with himself as he'd been since the one A he'd gotten in high school. Over behind the bar, glassware clinked as Billy hung them in the overhead rack, pretending he wasn't trying to eavesdrop. Usually the bartender wasn't too bad about spreading gossip, but doubtless this topic was too hot to resist. Probably Billy had leaned so far over the bar he'd caught his earring in a barstool. Rid wished he'd paid more attention to making sure they weren't overheard. Mario, especially, barked like a damn seal when he got going. The last thing they needed was for it to get around that they were going to ask for money before they had a chance to do it themselves.

"We've never organized," Tomas sighed again and shrugged one shoulder under the strap of his overalls. It was a strangely delicate movement for his hefty frame, and out of character, too. "Too independent a bunch, and I suppose if any of us had wanted to work with anyone else we wouldn't be working the flats in the first place. But okay. We've got to start somewhere. So we see if we can get everyone to contribute something. Everyone with a grant on Indian Neck. Maybe we should go beyond Indian Neck. Hell, maybe Mayo Beach area? All the aquaculturists in Wellfleet, even. This law affects the economy of the region, after all."

"Okay, how we gonna do this? We just each of us talk to who we know best, and—" Mario shoved his cap back further on his head and plunged in.

Tomas interrupted. "Slow down. Let's be organized about how we approach this. Different arguments will appeal to different people. Let me think about this and let's assign each of us to talk to certain people. This is akin to forming a union." He made eye contact with Mario. "Listen to me. Do *not* say a word to anyone. We don't want a half-baked plan leaking out, and we sure as hell don't want it getting to the upland owners, who might decide to get together and help Pissario. The tide's at six forty-nine tomorrow night—we'll only be able to use the front side of it. How about we meet here about seven-fifteen, maybe a little earlier? All right?" He was already shoving his seat back from the high table, putting his arm in the sleeve of his windbreaker, but as he did he again looked at Mario hard.

"Sure," Rid answered with a head gesture to Mario, pulling him into agreement with Tomas' proposal.

"Yeah, I guess," from Mario.

A half-hour later, Rid had hardly unloaded the truck and gotten into the house when the phone rang. He answered it on the run, switching on lights as he passed them.

"You and I have to handle this ourselves," Tomas' voice came through the receiver. "Mario isn't the person to be talking to people about this. He doesn't inspire confidence."

"I thought that's what you might be thinking." Rid slumped into his recliner, wishing he'd had time to get a beer out of the refrigerator before he'd answered the phone. Lizzie curled into a circle on her bed next to him, their television watching posts. "What do you want me to do?"

"Manage him or distract him. We can't have him making threats or inciting people, and we can't have him—"

"I know."

"I'm not saying I don't care about Mario but I'm not going to let him take us down."

"I'll talk to him."

"Okay. I'll figure out a list tonight dividing who I'll talk to and who you cover."

# Chapter 7

A mackerel sky was just brightening over the steely morning tide when Rid bumped his truck off the access road. Most of his grant was exposed already, but he'd had to wait until it was light enough to work. He was glad only two other trucks, Barb's and Clint's, were out on the flats. He hadn't figured out just how to handle Mario yet, and he needed to get his digging done while he thought things through. His cages, rake and buckets rattled in the truck bed while Lizzie rode shotgun, her head out the passenger side window, sniffing the wind, ears flapping like flags. Rid took a long swallow of the coffee he'd picked up at the Cumberland Farms store on Route Six and made a face. It was old. Usually he made a thermos at home, but this morning he'd been hurried and distracted. Already this damn lawsuit was affecting everything, sucking up what he loved. Like right now, a morning tide was usually when he reveled in his life—the sun coming up soft on the water, the birds coming to work, too— and him there, outside, free, grateful. Grateful *because* he was free, he guessed. Now, here he was instead all worked up and worried, trying to figure out how to deal with frigging crazy Mario, who shouldn't be his problem.

The truth was, he didn't see her huddled on the revetment, the rock wall the upland owners had built to keep the sea water from eroding the sandy cliff during storms when the tides could run exceptionally high. Most of them had their own wooden stairways built up from the beach, too, some even with a platform built halfway up where they could put folding chairs and have drinks as if the fancy tiers and decks and sliding patio doors on their mansions overlooking the bay weren't enough. It was Lizzie, with her typical enthusiasm for any potential playmate, bounding out of the truck to where CiCi sat. Rid actually didn't recognize her at first; she had a sweatshirt hood up, for one, and it had, after all, been weeks since the one time he'd seen her. A flush of guilt washed over him, then defensiveness, then wariness. But he had to intervene. Lizzie was leaping at CiCi, her tail a blur, and Rid knew her tongue was flashing at CiCi's face by the woman's ineffective swipes at her own cheek with one hand as she tried to hold Lizzie down.

"Off, girl," Rid called, slamming the truck door and breaking into a reluctant jog toward them. "Get back to the truck. Hey, hi, I'm sorry. She's not even supposed to be out of the truck," he added as he caught up and grabbed Lizzie's collar. This was the last thing he needed. A woman he'd slept with and never called again who could technically be considered one of the waterfront landowners, and here was his dog loose on a private beach molesting her. Could it get worse? And dammit, he needed to get to work, and he needed to figure out how to lock Mario in a box.

"No problem." At least she was laughing. But she looked terrible, charcoal thumbprints under her eyes. She'd put makeup on, he could see, and her hair was fixed, he could tell that now that she'd flipped the hood back. Still, her face was almost gaunt, as if hollows had been spooned out.

"She's just over-friendly. I thought she'd grow out of it, but she's almost six and I can't hardly call that a puppy anymore. Just acts it. What're you doing here?"

"I brought you some coffee," she said. "I didn't know how you liked it, so I brought creamer and sugar in plastic bags." Sure enough, behind her, standing on one of the boulders was a thermos. She pulled two bags out of her gray sweatshirt pocket as she said it, and took two awkward sidesteps over to lay them next to the thermos.

"Thanks. I usually bring a thermos myself. Didn't have time this morning so I stopped at Cumberland. Got it already." It sounded just on the line of rude, but he was uncomfortable. What did she want? Then he remembered. "Your mother, she didn't...?"

"Not yet. Thank you for asking."

"Um, well, thanks anyway. I should be getting to work. Was there something you needed?"

He could see she was stung. But what did she want? The tide wouldn't wait for him, and Lizzie pulled and squirmed trying to get away. "I'm sorry, please excuse me, but I've got to get her back in the truck. Come on girl." Rid released the collar and strode to where his truck was parked on the wet flats, the Lab prancing back and forth and around him. Cultch snapped and crunched beneath his waders. CiCi couldn't follow him. She was only wearing sneakers.

Impossibly, she did, though. Her feet had to be getting wet, no matter how gingerly she picked her way trying to avoid the eddies and go from one high spot to the next. In another minute she'd be onto a raceway and then she'd tear a net.

"Hold up. I'll be right back." Rid help up a hand in a stop sign gesture behind him.

He opened the driver's side door of the truck. Lizzie hesitated, her pleading expression on her face. Rid pulled a biscuit from his shirt pocket, pointing to the seat with his chin, and the dog immediately leapt inside. "You have a good nap, girl. Keep my spot warm." The Lab took the treat from his hand and he caressed her ears before shutting the truck door and turning back to where CiCi stood as if rooted where he'd stopped her. "Shit," he muttered under his breath. He had too much on his mind this morning to worry about an ex-prom queen jailbird looking for a soul mate.

"Didn't want you to walk over the netting," he explained as he approached her. "I'm sorry, I don't have time to visit just now. I gotta use the tide, y'know?"

"I understand. I know about the lawsuit, too, and I was just wondering if we could get together sometime, to talk."

Rid stiffened. What the hell did she want, this soon-to-be waterfront landowner? Maybe he was spoiling *her* view, too.

"Yeah. Well, I'm pretty busy with this right now."

The sky was lightening and beneath his feet the sand was draining. Almost dead low.

She looked down. "I thought maybe I could help. And I wanted to talk to you."

"No thanks." Tomas' injunction was still ringing in his head. He was treating her like a washashore, which was ridiculous because she was native. He had no reason to assume she'd think of her hometown as a postcard rather than a working place—that she'd try to take that away. But she'd left, and only come back when she had to. That made her suspect.

CiCi's head snapped up, startled, her eyes rounded like targets. "No thanks what?" Her bangs blew the wrong way in the wind and she held them out of her eyes with one hand which made her forehead look high and bald. Behind her, the revetment was solid, unyielding, a wall of carefully fitted boulders rising at a steep slope. Random loose rocks lay embedded in the sand around the high water mark. When the tide was full, there was virtually no beach here.

Rid met her eyes, not backing down. Again, he noticed she looked haggard in spite of the makeup, and felt himself soften. She must be going through hell with her mother. He was being a prick. But there was Tomas's truck just then, jostling over the rough patch from the access road onto the beach and it fortified him to stay the course. Too much was at stake.

"No thanks, I don't need help. And I'm sorry, I just don't have time to talk. I'll try to give you a call sometime. Uh, thanks for the offer." He turned then and walked between two raceways, grabbing his bull rake and several buckets out of the bed of his truck as he passed it. October was a big harvest month. He needed to dig six hundred fifty oysters and four hundred clams for two weddings and a small raw bar today. And deal with Mario, plus whatever Tomas assigned him. Enough was enough.

❀

She'd made a fool of herself. Her feet were wet and here she was carrying the untouched thermos of coffee. He'd blown her off. Whatever had she been thinking? Hadn't she been humiliated adequately the first time, when she'd been pathetic enough to stand out on the porch and call out after him? He'd kept right on going then, hadn't he? So why had she expected anything else? Or hoped.

On the other hand, at least she'd tried. It made the decision to have an abortion easier, really.

Caroline looked up from the cultch-strewn sand just ahead to her mother's house in the middle distance. The horseshoe cove was fully drained now, the tide all the way out. How could she be this exhausted from walking over to Rid's grant and halfway back? It couldn't be a half-mile round trip, and only some of it had been in soft sand. She had to pee desperately, otherwise she'd just go lie down hidden up by the beach plums and scrubby wild vegetation that scalloped the beach between the access road and where the revetment began its steep ascent.

She stopped just to breathe. Then she swung and walked backward for a moment to have the wind at her back. All up and down Indian Neck, trucks were parked like giant beetles on the sand and the detritus of the sea farmers was uncovered, the stacked oyster cages and Chinese hats, a couple of dinghies and random buckets. The farmers themselves were out in force. They must have been arriving steadily while her back was turned. Caroline felt a quick stab of guilt. He'd said he had to work. Possibly she had been keeping him, like when she used to waitress and a friend would drop by and expect her to be to stand and chat. Still, that didn't explain his coldness. That was something else entirely.

She turned back and faced into the wind, forcing one foot in front of the other, infuriated by the sting of the air, how it made her eyes water so.

And she'd had no business leaving the house. Eleanor was awake when Caroline came in, though she'd eased the door open as silently as possible, shrugging out the sweatshirt off, then the layer beneath it before she even went over to the bed. She'd been that certain her mother wouldn't rouse until the hospice aide showed up to bathe her and do catheter care. But when she tiptoed bedside, Eleanor's eyes fluttered open.

"Where were you?"

"Oh Mom, I'm so sorry. I just took a short walk. Are you all right?"

"My baby." Eleanor's eyes closed and for a moment Caroline thought perhaps she'd only awakened momentarily. But then she moved her hand, feeling for Caroline. "My baby. How can I leave you like this, with no one of your own?"

Caroline sank into the chair that was always at the head of her mother's bed. She kissed the hand she held, and set her head down in the hollow between her mother's shoulder and breast wanting nothing more than to climb in and have both her mother's arms close around her. Caroline was, at first, just trying to hide the tears of frustration with Rid, and what lay ahead. Then her mother's hand was on her head without the strength to stroke her hair, but there. How many times had this soft place been her shelter? Then she was crying, really crying, for the first time, over the looming unchosen death.

"Don't leave me, Mom. Please, *please* don't leave me."

 *Chapter 8*

Her name tag said Teresa DiPaulo but no one had ever called her that. "It's just Terry," she'd say. The head librarian at the Truro branch where she worked didn't think nicknames were professional, especially now that they were in their big new building which was airy and beautiful with computers, open stacks, plants and separate children's room. Rhonda didn't seem to notice that this same staff talked quite loudly among themselves and wore jeans to work. As long as they didn't use nicknames, she seemed to think she'd dramatically elevated the standard from the old library, the size of the average walk-in closet, from which they'd recently moved. Rhonda herself, in fact, wasn't all that quiet in the library, though she wore skirts, kept her hair in a neat pageboy and her bright red mouth in a librarian-worthy serious line.

Being called Teresa by her boss was a small price to pay as long as Rhonda didn't make her work in the children's section. When she'd applied for the job, she'd forced herself to ask if she'd have to.

"My assistant and I generally work in all areas of the library. After all, the rest of the staff each works part-time, and, of course, the community volunteers really set their own schedules. You see, the structure of the library is such that…." Rhonda had rambled on before skidding to a halt on, "Why do you ask?"

And Terry had intended to just tell the truth, except that she'd felt the underground river start to rise to the surface and decided that tears in an interview were worse than no answer. "Ah, no reason." She felt Rhonda's eyes light on the gold angel pin on her sweater, and involuntarily, Terry's hand went up to protect it. Well, so she'd blown this interview. All right. She shouldn't have asked. She should have sucked it up and tried to work in that room—with its little tables and chairs, bright colors, high border of sweet, fanciful animals. She plain needed a job now.

But maybe no one else had even applied and Rhonda had been desperate, because the next day, she called and offered Terry the job. There'd been no mention of working in the children's room or not working there, but so far, she hadn't been assigned there. Part-timers had shelved those books, or ordered the new ones, or catalogued the incoming orders. Terry showed her gratitude by trying to look professional for Rhonda. She took pains to curl her long hair which she'd turned blonde when she was fourteen, wore skirts, stockings, dress shoes, and, of course, her pin.

It was possible Rhonda had known. Maybe one of the job references told her and the position had been offered out of pity. Usually people who knew avoided her, though.

It wasn't that John hadn't grieved with her. He'd closed the shop, stopped eating, stopped showering, and choked on his sobs. But she could do nothing to help him. She was drowning herself, and didn't even notice whether her husband had a worn a clean shirt or whether he'd shaved for the visitation. His sister came to attend to him while Terry's brother and her mother, one on either side of her like crutches, had gotten her into St. Mary's of the Harbor for the funeral.

The fourth week, John had gone back to work. He'd had to. There wasn't insurance that would replace the income they were losing. By then, people from out of town had gone home, the casseroles that had been coming in daily slowed to four, then two or three times a week, and Terry and John were slowly left to stagger on by themselves, like robots or zombies. When Terry felt suicidal, John took her to Dr. Telmaun, who prescribed drugs that made no difference.

Around them, the house had a sterile, unlived-in look, yet was increasingly in a state of disrepair. One night during the second year, John pointed around him and said, "Look, we're not even people anymore. We're like shadows. On Saturday, I'm going to fix the garage door."

"Don't you think I want to go on?" Terry said later that month. They'd been in the kitchen, where it had been Chinese take-out again, as opposed to pizza, as opposed to deli sandwiches. It was May and the lilacs outside the baby's window were blooming. They'd never stopped calling him the baby, even though chronologically, he wasn't one. Not one item in his room had been changed. Some of the clothes he'd worn still had his smell, even if John didn't get it. On her worst days, Terry shut herself in his room and buried her face in his red sweater or his denim jacket.

"We have to go on *together*," he said, wrapping his arms around her back and stroking her hair with one hand. She'd forced herself not to pull away although she felt like something carved out of cold stone, like the marble marker over her baby's grave.

"What do you want from me? I'm trying."

"Let's have another baby." It wasn't the first time he'd whispered this. Of course, family on both sides had prescribed it. "I am not trying to replace him," John insisted that night. "I *am* trying to start over."

"I'm not ready."

"Are you ever going to be?"

"I don't know. Goddammit, John, leave me alone."

When he moved the stack of read-aloud books off the coffee table in the living room, Terry raged at him. "Put them back, put them back, put him back," she shouted.

John started sleeping in the spare room, saying it was too frustrating to sleep in the same bed. They had a bitter fight about money; Terry was calling in sick a couple of days a week because of her headaches. She'd used all her sick time and then days and days more. Sometimes she couldn't get out of bed. *Wouldn't* get out of bed was the way John saw it, as in *not trying*. He said as much.

Still, when he actually left, it was like the cruel surprise of a patch of ice in May, one that flew her feet out from underneath her and landed her hard on her back, breathless and alone.

At first it was much worse to have no one there and then, finally, in a bizarre way it was better. No one criticizing her, no one serving up guilt like a daily gruel. If she got up, she got up. If she didn't, well, she didn't. Same with taking a shower.

Predictably, she lost her job in the hardware store. She was fired with great kindness. "We'd love to have you back when you feel better. We just have to have someone here every day."

Suicide was forbidden in her religion but God was on her shit list so she no longer ruled it out.

Then, the strangest thing happened—something that affected her in a way the church she'd repudiated had not. Something that gave her peace unlike the drugs that hadn't helped at all, or helped enough, or the trite and vacant words of well-meaning family and friends. Late one night when she was playing hopscotch through the channels, she landed on the shopping network where a woman was selling guardian angel pins, a psychic by her side. Viewers were invited to call in and the psychic would try to contact a loved one on the other side of the veil. If the psychic was able to receive a message, the viewer would presumably wish to purchase a fourteen karat gold guardian angel with the birthstone of the loved one as tangible evidence of the contact. The angel was available in yellow or white gold and a choice of twelve birthstones.

It took Terry forty-eight minutes to get through. She hadn't expected to believe, in fact she'd expected not to. But when the psychic said, "I have only this message for you from the other side: your baby wants you to know he is all right, and whole now," she couldn't discount it. That word, *whole*. And then the psychic had said, "He loves you and he'll see you again later."

He'll see you later! That's what the baby had said after she or John had read him his last story and tucked him in at night. *I love you, sleep tight, see ya later, alligator,"* was their line, and the baby would answer, *love you, see ya later.*

❦

There really were only two downsides to the library job. Rhonda hadn't asked Terry to work in the children's section, not once in three years, but she did have to check the books out when someone handed them to her. The first time someone handed her a too-familiar-cover, she shut herself in a bathroom stall and stifled sobs, until she worked it out. After that, when any young mother with a toddler boy in her arms handed her a book like *Goodnight Moon*, she was ready. "I'm sorry, this should haven't been shelved. It's been reserved," Terry would say, cool. Lying for her baby was easy. His favorite books should never be touched by children who wouldn't appreciate them. *Goodnight Moon* would disappear, swaddled in a drawer at home with the others marked TRURO PUBLIC LIBRARY. Since Terry was in charge of book orders, there would be no replacement.

There wasn't something comparable she could do when someone from her old life up in Provincetown happened into the library. Furtive studies of the angel on her shirt, then her face, then the quick, guilty aversion of their gaze galled her. Peoples' eyes were palpable as cotton on her skin when they looked at her that way.

Terry felt that prickle when the tall woman with the highlighted hair checked out a strange sandwich of books. The top and bottom volumes were on funeral planning, the middle title was *Living With the Decision: A Woman's Choice*. She saw the woman's eyes read her nametag, then travel to her pin. Even as Terry's hand was traveling to cover the angel, pinned on her blue turtleneck where a college girl would fasten a fraternity pin, her eyes brushed Terry's face. The woman hadn't intended eye contact; immediately, she pretended interest in the clock behind Terry and then studied the flurry her own hands were making of extracting her card and rummaging for her keys. Terry guessed that she must be from Provincetown, someone who'd worked with John or known a family member. She was one of the people who knew who Terry was, as if her ruined life gave off an embarrassing odor or left a scar on her forehead. Sometimes Terry wanted to slink and hide from those people and sometimes she wanted to draw a fist, or spit on their shoes.

 *Chapter 9*

He'd made himself look like a real dickhead, and Rid knew it. It still ate at him as he picked the largest oysters out of the tray, weighing and checking each by feel, tossing empties and partially open shells onto the cultch-strewn bottom where they landed with a soft plash. Those that weren't quite large enough yet clinked back into the tray. Rid was as fast and efficient as his father had been. He hardly had to look anymore to know exactly how good an oyster was.

He was bent from the waist over one of the big four-by-six-foot trays toward the back of the grant, exposed now at dead low tide. It was backbreaking and time consuming, but not absorbing; his mind was free to sail the coast of his worries. Too many of this tray had suffocated when he hadn't gotten the sand off them fast enough after the hurricane in September. These were three year oysters, too, the most frustrating to lose. He hadn't repaired all the trays that were damaged in that blow yet, either. He was behind in his orders, which could cost him even his most patient and loyal customers, because he was stealing work time to talk to people about fighting the lawsuit. And now he'd been an asshole to CiCi and he couldn't say why, except that he couldn't afford one more thing on his mind, even a woman he liked. Especially a woman he liked with a trunk full of her own problems who didn't have the first clue about his.

He glanced over at her house. Or still her mother's house, he guessed. He hadn't seen a death notice in the paper. It had to be rough, and he felt bad for her. When his Dad died, his mother had moved in with his sister and brother-in-law down in Falmouth, and he knew he was lucky that way. By straightening up—which he had to do anyway, his back was complaining—and taking ten steps deeper into the bay, which let him stretch his legs, Rid could see the parking area to the side of CiCi's house. There'd been a detached garage back there once, but it had been rebuilt into a studio for her mother. He could see its skylight glinting from where he stood. There were two cars there now, so he guessed CiCi wasn't alone. Sometime he really ought to knock on the door and ask if she needed anything. Maybe leave off a couple dozen quahogs she could steam for dinner.

He shook his head at his own stupidity. Who takes clams to a dying woman's house? It's supposed to be soup or homemade something, like his mother or sister would do. Something way out of his league.

A couple of the guys had kicked in way more than he and Tomas had thought anyone would for the lawsuit. They'd collected almost five thousand and they weren't through talking to everyone, so there was some good news. On the other hand, there was the ominous unknown. Just yesterday, Tomas had parked his truck below the high water mark but come directly onto Rid's grant where he was already at work, rather than to his own. "Something's up. Lorenz wants a meeting in his office in the next couple of days. Maybe Pissario got wind we're organizing?"

"Or maybe *Lorenz* wants to *break* wind and have us there to discuss it so he can send another bill," Rid had muttered. He and Tomas had fielded a lot of questions about how high the bill might go, and neither of them could even fake an answer.

"Yeah, could be that," Tomas said, squeezing his forehead between thumb and forefinger and then rubbing his eyes. He looked tired.

It was the afternoon tide, still the front side, but Rid had been following it out, early for once, working each section of his grant as the water receded. A cold sting of offshore wind whipped spray against his face, chapping early this year.

"So what do we do?"

"We go. All we can do. I thought day after tomorrow rather than tomorrow because the second tide will be too late to work anyway—too dark. Wanted to check with you first, though. And Mario. Okay if I tell him three o'clock?"

Rid pieced the sentences together as a word here or there was swooped away on the wind. "Sure. Want me to tell Mario?" he said.

"I'll do it."

"I should finish with my list of people?"

"Now more'n ever."

"Right."

So today, he had to get ahead on picking for the weekend restaurant orders in P-town and Chatham. It was a good thing there wasn't a private party or a wedding this weekend, though that was always good money, because he had six or seven more people on his list to talk to, and the meeting with Lorenz tomorrow. He had a heaping plateful to be worrying about now, and he just couldn't add CiCi to the pile.

Rid turned and sloshed back to the oyster tray. He stood and looked down, studying it a moment, then raised his head and slowly took in the measure of his grant. His gaze covered the salt marsh where Blackfish Creek entered the harbor at his far left, up over Lieutenant's Island and the Audubon sanctuary and the sailboat-dotted sweep of the bay all the way around to his right to what he could see of where the harbor jutted out on the far side of the horseshoe beach and on toward Great Island. His father might have liked his beer too much to be what anyone would call a good family man, but he'd sweated for this place, clung to it, babied it into abundance, put Rid's name on it and taught him what he knew before he died. Once Rid had comforted himself that his father had loved him because he'd given him the grant, but as he stood ankle-deep and thought of losing it, he thought *no*, it all had to do with loving *this*. Dad couldn't stand the idea of not having it any more. And, more amazing to Rid, he now understood and felt the exact same way.

Beneath him, Rid's legs felt like broken pencils, wobbly, insubstantial next to this blessed bountiful beauty over which a late weak sun fought the cloud cover to unveil the first hint of sunset. He lifted his face to the west, toward the wispy tendrils of pale fire and thought *come on, you can win this*, and tears came until he wondered if he was melting into the water, his salt mixing into the bay as his father's had.

❧

Strange, all of them cleaned up this way again in the middle of the day. This only happened when they were going to a funeral. As soon as the word came to mind, Rid wondered again if CiCi's mother had died yet, but he was immediately distracted by their attorney, who was tapping the eraser of his pencil against his desk as he spoke. It made him seem nervous, which made Rid nervous.

"Mr. Pissario has, I'm afraid, filed asking for an injunction to stop your work until the court rules on the suit." Lorenz's face did not flicker when he spoke and it was impossible to guess his emotion or if he had any.

"He can't do that!" It was Mario, in an instant boil. Without even looking at him, Rid, in the middle of his two partners, shot a restraining hand onto Mario's arm. The amount of pressure he exerted was a warning.

"He can try," Lorenz said, pushing up his glasses with his index finger. "We have the opportunity to file a response showing why the judge shouldn't issue the injunction. That's why you're here. We have to make that case. So let's get to work."

The attorney's office, in the weak light of a waning gray day, was even less impressive than Rid remembered. It wasn't exactly run down, but sparse and devoid of any particular sign of financial success, even though Barnstable itself was a wealthy area. It reminded him of a public defender's office, and public defenders hadn't exactly saved Rid's ass in the past. Lorenz had had two things to recommend him. First, his initial consultation fee had been just over half of what the two big Hyannis firms had quoted. They were the ones, presumably, with the shoe-swallowing carpet, leather chairs, and precedent-researching paralegals. Second, Lorenz had been slow deciding to take the case, which made all of them think that they might have trouble getting another lawyer. None of it gunned their confidence to a roar, that was for sure.

"Who's the judge?" Tomas asked quietly.

"Judge Atwood, most likely."

Tomas sat back and grinned.

"I like seeing that on your face, but I don't know where it's coming from. If he knows you, or has any personal connection, he'll have to recuse himself."

"What's his first name?"

"Sam."

"Heard of him, don't know him." He swung his head to Rid and Mario in turn. "Either of you two know him?"

"Nope." Mario said, not getting it.

"Not me." Rid echoed.

"Excellent," Tomas said.

"So what's the deal?" Lorenz asked.

"Just that Atwood is an old, old Wellfleet name back from the seventeenth and eighteenth centuries. Lotta people named Atwood lost at sea. I mean, take your pick: Sukie Atwood's house still is over on Chequessett Neck Road. Her first husband, her second husband, her son, then her grandson all went down. She's the one who said, 'the ocean is my cemetery.' Sometime around 1870, that was. Anyway, in 1929 the family moved her house from South Truro to where it is now, overlooking the harbor."

Rid started to grin widely, enjoying Tomas' meandering because he knew where his friend was headed. Not too many people knew Wellfleet history like Tomas. Lorenz looked befuddled.

Tomas registered the attorney's confusion, and disingenuously took the long route to clarification, enjoying himself. "Oh, yes, sure, she's long gone. But see, there's the Simeon Atwood house on East Commercial Street, too. Now that guy was a state legislator in the 1860s; did everything from that to being an inspector for the port of Wellfleet, a justice of the peace, a church choirmaster, and Republican moderator. Lived about six lives in one. Old, old family, like I said. Long roots buried deep. Mr. Lorenz, I'm just not thinking that a Wellfleet native is real likely to issue an injunction to shut us down because some washashore wants him to. You see where I'm coming from? Fishing *is* Wellfleet. It's what we do and who we are. I'm not one to complain about the art stuff around town now. It's fine, but it's not what supports us. *The flats* are home to the natives."

Lorenz tilted his chair back, a slow smile of comprehension starting in his eyes and spreading finally across his mouth. "Well. Well, well. All right then. From your lips to God's ears. And you do understand that this is just the opening round. The suit itself is a different matter. That has to do with *ownership*. A sympathetic judge still can't rewrite the law. Right now I'm looking into every precedent, every interpretation. And, you know, it's occurred to me: I really should check the specific deeds for the Indian Neck subdivision. It's time-consuming. I'm sorry about that."

He was referring, of course, to the mounting bill. He sent it monthly, regular as the moon. They'd made three payments but each month the total was higher than it had been before they'd made the last payment.

Tomas was undaunted. "You know, I just have to believe that there's more to ownership than a piece of paper. If Pissario got an injunction, I don't know how we'd be able to keep going. But I'm betting it's not going to happen."

"He's right," Rid added, slapping his thigh lightly. "Tomas *knows* what he's talking about." He hoped this meant Marie would back off Tomas some. He didn't know what he'd do himself if he had a wife and kids to worry about now.

"Yeah, man. A local's not going to screw us," Mario chimed in. Rid could tell Mario was dying for a smoke, going for the Marlboros in his shirt pocket and then dropping his hand back to his lap as he remembered he couldn't light up in the office. He'd asked in the first meeting, and the attorney had said no.

"All right, then. Once again: from your lips to God's ears. Let's prepare the argument about the impact of an injunction. We've got to give the judge the excuse to rule with his sympathy, presuming you're right."

 *Chapter 10*

Caroline's heart thudded on long after she was in the car. She started the engine and pulled out of the library parking lot but instead of going home, she went a half-mile in the wrong direction on 6A, up to Dutra's Market, where she parked outside the little grocery store, feeling as if she were being followed. That was ridiculous. Teresa DiPaulo hadn't given any gesture of recognition. And why would she? It wasn't as if Caroline's name had been on her library card. Nothing but a bar code there. Anyway, if it had been, it would have been a long jump with just a first name as a starting point. All she'd ever known was the name Caroline Vance, that of a married woman now long gone from the face of the earth. Teresa hadn't been in court when Caroline had pled guilty and been sentenced. Only the child's father, John, and other family members had been present. Caroline had heard the child's mother was under sedation.

Caroline looked at the book titles next to her on the passenger seat and flushed with shame. She tried to calm herself. There was no way she could have known Teresa DiPaulo worked there. She'd gone to the Truro library because it was big and new and right off Route 6 on her way back from the Stop & Shop in Provincetown. Wellfleet didn't have any big chain grocery stores, so every two or three weeks she went either to Eastham or P-town to stock up. The little family-owned local groceries were poorly stocked in the off-season.

There was nothing to do but go on home. Of course, she'd never return the books, not to the Truro branch. There'd be no need, thank goodness. Her card was good at any public library on the Cape. She could just go back to Eastham or P-town. Even the Wellfleet library, though people would know her there for sure.

❦

"Honestly, she's hanging on for a reason," Elsie said. "I don't know what it is she needs. Maybe something from you."

The morphine drip had been in place for several weeks, and most of the time Eleanor alternated between fitful and deep sleep. When she was awake though, she knew Caroline and responded to her. "Her mind is certainly intact," the respite caregiver had commented the day before. "She asked me where you were."

The November chill permeated the low-slung grayness, and Caroline had lit a fire. She and Elsie sat near the fireplace, while Eleanor slept in her bed, pushed up close to the window so she could have an unimpeded view of the bay. Not that Eleanor's eyes were often open anymore.

Elsie's bangs fell in a fine spray across her forehead, which she furrowed as she spoke. A long-fingered plain hand wrapped around a mug of tea in her lap. When she leaned forward, Caroline thought surely it would get on her clothing, but it didn't. "Have you told her it's all right to let go?"

Caroline hesitated. "I don't want her to think—oh, I don't know. That I *want* her to just go ahead and die. That I don't need her." She pushed her hair back off her face. It was dirty, and her lips were chapped. "I had no idea how much I needed her," she whispered.

Elsie leaned forward. "I truly don't mean to pry. I hope you won't mind my asking, but are you pregnant? I saw some reading material you'd left in the kitchen."

Caroline had looked all over for it, in fact, and decided she'd accidentally thrown it out. It was material from the Women's Center in P-town and Planned Parenthood in Hyannis. She didn't have a lot of time left.

Caroline let silence answer for her.

"Maybe you want to tell her?" Elsie said. Caroline wasn't sure if it was a question or a statement, the inflection was that subtle.

"I ... don't think I'm going to keep it."

"But you've not made a final decision?"

"I think I have."

"Maybe this has to do with trouble letting her go?"

Caroline flared. "Something else to feel guilty about."

Elsie didn't take the bait. "Not at all," she said calmly. "Your mother would be the first to say that your needs are as important as hers. Maybe you still need something from her. Or maybe you just want her to know. Either way."

"That seems so terribly wrong, so unfair. To burden her now. Of all times, I mean."

A long pause. "Ordinarily I might agree with you. And I'm not trying to tell you what to do. This is your mother, your call. But maybe something is burdening her *now*."

❧

An early darkness slid into place on Elsie's departure. An aide would be there at eight in the morning to change the sheet, empty the catheter bag and bathe Eleanor, but Caroline felt the weight of the night and already it was cold and heavy. The hospice chaplain was still due to stop in. Jean Keller would read poetry to Eleanor in a voice that was edgeless as cotton batting. But it was getting late, and perhaps she'd been held up elsewhere. If she had, Caroline would be alone with her dying mother until morning. She wasn't worried about the caregiving part—she'd long since been taught exactly what to do and when—rather, it was isolation and fear that got to her.

Eleanor wasn't eating anymore, not to speak of anyway. A couple of spoonsful of applesauce sometimes, and she still liked ice cream for its coolness, always chocolate. Ice chips whenever she wanted them. Caroline didn't understand what was keeping her alive. "I love you, Mom," she said, smoothing back imaginary whispers of hair on Eleanor's forehead for an excuse to stroke her mother's head. Tears slid down her cheeks. She wanted this to end; she wanted it never to end, so she would not have to say goodbye. She couldn't bear to watch the effort of her mother's breaths, even with the oxygen that was supposed to make her more comfortable, and equally she couldn't bear not to be at her side. She watched her mother dreaming, Eleanor's closed eyes following some distant storyline Caroline could not share, a fact that only increased her loneliness.

When it was obvious the chaplain wasn't coming, and Eleanor seemed marginally awake, Caroline made herself say it. She'd put the public radio station on—Eleanor liked classical music—and chamber music was soft in the background. The only light was from the fireplace and the little brass hurricane lamp on the far table. "Mom, I've been thinking that—maybe...." Oh no, that was all wrong. Not the way to tell her. "Mom, I don't know what I'm going to do, but I want you to know...." That was wrong too. Eleanor had closed her eyes anyway. It was just as well. Elsie was probably out of her mind.

Eleanor opened her eyes. "What?" It was the clearest word she'd said all day.

Caroline froze. How could she do this? "It's okay, Mom. It's nothing, really."

"Tell me," her mother said.

And Caroline was too tired to figure all the angles, to remember what she'd rehearsed or to puzzle what would burden her mother or what would relieve her. It was like a Rubik's cube, beyond her capability to solve.

"I'm pregnant, Mom. I thought you'd want to know."

The available light was low and amber but Caroline didn't miss how Eleanor examined her with her eyes before she closed them again, and how her face relaxed then into a smile.

"Good."

"Mom, I'm not sure I...." It didn't feel right to finish the sentence when Eleanor squeezed her hand with what pressure she had the strength for.

"You won't be alone." There was a long pause and Caroline thought her mother had drifted into sleep again. But then Eleanor's lips moved again with one word: "Stay." It was all she said, even through the evening when Caroline swabbed her mouth with the glycerin stick to keep it moist, or rubbed lotion into the fragile skin on her arms and hands and face. Busy work, anything to feel useful. She sat by Eleanor waiting, sometimes watching dark urine snake its way down the catheter tube toward the bag as if it were the most interesting thing on TV.

The next day was a fog indoors and out. Eleanor hardly seemed to wake at all, and her eyes were hardly moving in their dream dance. But there was the morphine, so who could tell? Elsie came although she wasn't scheduled. With her stethoscope to Eleanor's abdomen, she said, "I don't hear bowel sounds now." She stroked Eleanor's hand gently and said, "I've been thinking of you all evening, Mrs. Marcum. You're a beautiful and brave spirit who has blessed us all."

After she'd checked the morphine and, it seemed, everything else she could check and double check, she gestured Caroline away from the bed. "I don't think she'll still be with us tomorrow. Her systems are shutting down. Hearing is the last sense to go, so go right ahead and talk to her as much as you like." She picked up Caroline's hand and held it. "You've done an amazing job, and you're seeing it through." She put her arms around Caroline and pulled her into an embrace that Caroline did not resist. "I'll try to stop in again late this afternoon," she said. "I'm scheduled at the nursing home down in Eastham, but I'll do the best I can."

"Please. If you can," Caroline said. "I'm so scared."

"I know. I'll call the office and see if they can send over an experienced volunteer," Elsie said. And then Caroline was alone again.

Through the day, Caroline occasionally thought she was handling herself well, but then, just as often, that she was failing every test. Exhaustion overtook her and then she'd rally. She'd find courage to sit with her mother, hold her hand and say, "Don't worry about me, Mom. I'm all right. I'll *be* all right. I promise you." But then tears would win and she'd duck into a bedroom. No one came.

In the mid-afternoon, Eleanor's breathing slowed. Caroline's first impulse was to call for help, to try to rouse her mother, and failing that, to run from the scene herself, out to the porch or farther, to the beach. To be anywhere but here. But Elsie's voice came into her head: *you can help her … hearing is the last sense to go.* And there was a competing impulse: not to let her mother down in the end if, this was the end. Caroline sat on Eleanor's bed and gently removed the oxygen tubes so she could get to her unimpeded. She worked her arms beneath her mother's back, leaning her own body forward and lifting her, the weight of twigs now, into a full embrace.

"Mom, if it's time, it's all right to let go. I'm here, and I'll always love you. You've been a wonderful mother, and I'll carry you in my heart forever. Thank you for your good life, thank you for all your love. Thank you for being there for me." Caroline stroked her mother's cheek with her own, speaking softly into her mother's ear.

Her mother exhaled a *whoosh* sound once. Then there was a pause and a ragged intake of breath, and Caroline knew.

"I love you, Mom. Godspeed," she whispered.

A kiss. A last exhalation, and then nothing more. Caroline held her mother and wept.

 *Chapter 11*

She'd been terrified that she'd attend her mother's death alone and of course that's exactly what happened, but now it felt right. Then, fifteen minutes later, it was untenable to be in the house with her mother's body, yet she didn't want to relinquish it to a stranger. Her eyes were runny and wet, but she wouldn't give way.

Instead of calling the funeral home or even one of her mother's friends, she called Elsie's cell phone. "No, it's all right. I'll get there as soon as I can," Elsie said. "Make yourself a cup of tea, take a blanket to stay warm and go out and sit on the porch. Would you like me to call someone else for you?"

No, there was no one else. Only Elsie could be trusted while her mother was lying there, vulnerable as a pale orchid.

She did, however, what Elsie told her. The nurse's instincts were right. Caroline needed to be out of the house yet guard her mother. The morning had been foggy and overcast, but now a weak sun was trying to break through and she angled her face southwest, leaning against a porch support. She sat on a cushion borrowed from a chaise lounge, the blue blanket from her room shawled around her, over her jacket. Ginger peach tea, a gift from her mother's friend Sharon two or three weeks ago, in the thermos Eleanor used to take into the studio with her.

The tide was high, a good thing because it would have been painful to see Rid, or, more accurately, his truck. Caroline thought of his dog and wished the Lab were with her now. Annie—no, he'd called her Lizzie, yes, Lizzie—would curl next to Caroline now with her chin on Caroline's thigh while she fondled the velvet ears and whispered, *you stay right here now girl, good girl, good, good girl.* The dog would wash Caroline's face with that eager kissing tongue and comfort her.

She had to pee twice, which she accomplished in a thicket of beach plums on the far side of the house. This constant pressure like an insistent thumb on her bladder was because she was pregnant. Eleanor had smiled and said, "Good. Now you won't be alone." Eleanor must have been out of her head from the morphine when she said that. The air was getting colder, the light thinner: that was how Caroline marked the passage of time toward dusk. No watch on her wrist today. She'd had the presence to note that her mother died just after two o'clock. They'd want to know that for the death certificate.

Maybe she was breaking some dumb-ass law by not calling anybody but Elsie, come to think of it. She shrugged her shoulders slightly. It wouldn't be the first or the worst law she'd broken, so the hell with it. What could they do to her that wouldn't make her life easier now? If they put her back in jail, at least she wouldn't have to plan her time. Caroline rested her head on her knees, which she'd drawn up against her chest for warmth. She'd go back to Chicago after she finished things up here. Would she sell the house, though? Lord, that would kill Eleanor. Now there was an ironic word choice. But could she afford the taxes if she weren't living and working here? How about renting it out? Why hadn't she figured all this out in advance?

Elsie's car crunched at the top of the gravel drive. Caroline lifted her head to watch it come into sight. She wasn't aware of tears, though she'd blown her nose a couple of times, but her faded jeans had navy circles dark and moist as the receiving earth staining her knees when she stood.

❦

Elsie had parked in the early Cape twilight and the two women hugged.

"You're shivering," Elsie said, drawing the blanket back up and around Caroline's back from where it had slipped down. "Let's get you inside. Would it be all right for me to say goodbye to her?"

"I think so. I've already said goodbye, though."

"You don't need to do it again. What you need is to go upstairs, take a warm bath and maybe lie down. Have you called the funeral home?"

Caroline felt a flush of shame. "No. I know I was supposed to, but…"

"Shh. You've done everything exactly fine. Nobody could have done a better job than you've done here." Elsie touched Caroline's cheek and lifted her face like a child's, by a finger under the chin. "Look at me. I'm telling you the truth. I'll make the call now. You're using Adams Mortuary, right?" she said.

Caroline nodded. In the dusky light, Elsie's face was pale and tired looking. Caroline realized it must be past the time for her to have gone home, but didn't mention it.

"Who else should be called? Your mother's friends. You call one of her closest friends and ask her to call the rest for you. Then you take a bath. I bet it would feel good to put those lavender bath salts I was using for your mother in it, you know? I'll bring up something to eat and some tea." And Elsie led her into the house.

After calling Noelle, Caroline headed upstairs at Elsie's urging. Halfway up, she turned back to the nurse who had positioned herself at the bottom between Caroline and her mother's body. Caroline could see the shape of Eleanor's legs and feet and wanted to hold her again, even knowing that some embrace had to be the last, and the one she'd already given, the one in which their mingled breaths had hung in the air between them, should be the one.

"I told her. I think it helped her let go. I didn't promise her, but I know what she wants. I just don't see how I can do it."

"You don't have to deal with this tonight. Just go get undressed. I'll be up in a few minutes with the salts. Remember, warm—not hot—water."

Minutes later, Caroline studied herself in the bathroom mirror while the bath water ran foamy, lightly scented: puffy, bloodshot eyes, circles smudged beneath them as if by Eleanor's thumb in one of her charcoal renderings. In fact, now that she looked closely, her whole face looked swollen. Her roots were showing; it was way past time for a highlight job, unless the gray could be considered a substitute. And look, she thought: matching new wrinkles around both sides of my mouth. Even if I wanted to, I'm too old and beat up now to have a baby. *How can I look so old and feel like such a child?* An orphan. Who in the world do I have to help me? Elsie will be leaving. Oh God, where did my mother go?

And suddenly, she was crying at the too-largeness, the mystery of things, needing to make them small enough to think about, to get her arms around. But there was another death coming. And there'd be no Elsie to pull the blanket up around her, draw a bath, make her tea, with kind, recognizable words in a familiar world. She was stammering, in the realm of the inexplicable and unanswerable; comprehensible language had become both utterly trite and desperately needed.

☙❧

    It had to be done. It was the right thing to do, and yet Caroline's mind went flimsy as milkweed seed over a memorial service. Bless Eleanor for having told the hospice chaplain what she wanted. One of her own clean-lined vases on the altar with autumn foliage in it. A matching urn in which Caroline had had the mortuary put her ashes. A flutist, a vocal soloist, some of Eleanor's favorite poems and readings, a picture of her at her wheel out in the meetinghouse foyer.

    Caroline didn't have a black dress. Eleanor had one, though, and so Caroline, who didn't care if it was a little tight, found herself sitting in the front row of the Unitarian Meetinghouse in Provincetown in her mother's dress with Elsie beside her, Julie behind her, and her mother's oldest, best friends, completing a protective circle. *In case I faint,* she thought, which didn't seem entirely impossible as she'd thrown up that morning. *And they don't even know.*

    She tried to listen. This is important, she told herself. This is to honor your mother. Pay attention. But she was distracted by nausea and astonishment: the church was standing room only. If she herself died now, who would come? She'd cut off her own roots so thoroughly, twice really, first from here when she'd fled to Chicago and now from Chicago, where she'd never made real friends anyway.

    "Eleanor asked that we close this memorial service with a specific sung version of the twenty-third psalm," Caroline heard Barbara say. "She particularly wanted these words as a gift and comfort to her daughter, Caroline, for whom her love will endure beyond all boundaries of earth and time."

    Caroline jolted at the sound of her own name. Elsie took her hand and held it on her own gray wool thigh. The soloist stood and sang, and when she reached the last verse, Caroline heard her mother's last words to her. "…no more a stranger or a guest, but like a child at home."

    The benediction followed, a final directive from Eleanor. *God be with you till we meet again.* And it was over. She had only to make it through coffee in the big room downstairs, the people wanting to hug and kiss her, people she knew by name from childhood, people she was embarrassed to see, people who knew she'd been to prison and who'd have even more to talk about if they knew she was pregnant.

    Sharon had people sign a guest book. Noelle stood behind the coffee table while Karen and Carol kept replenishing the cookies they'd all baked. Such kindness, even though she'd pushed them beyond arm's distance. How were they finding it in themselves to be so nice?

It was exhausting to respond to people, saying the same thing over and over. They formed a straggling line to speak to her but then lingered, talking to each other, balancing cups and the background noise grew. Finally, she reached the end of hands that wanted to squeeze hers and search her face for something she couldn't give them. "Say the word when you want to go," Elsie said, when the crowd was finally thinning. "You've put in enough face time. These people will all go when you do."

"Do you go to all your patients' funerals?" Caroline asked, thinking how hard that must be, when every patient is terminally ill, how many funerals a year Elsie must have to go to.

"No," Elsie said. "I have different relationships with different patients. And it makes a difference when a family member doesn't have anyone else, you know? I tend to get closer then."

Caroline hugged her, tearing over. It was another surprise, what made her tear and what didn't. "Thank you for being here. It's not enough, but thank you so much."

"Don't feel cut adrift. We'll stay in touch. You remember—we do things differently out here."

As the women gathered coats and purses, both Noelle and Sharon offered to have Caroline come to their homes for the night. When she declined, they offered to spend the night with her. "Really, I'm all right," she said. It had to be faced. There was no point in putting it off.

That night, she opened a bottle of wine and lit a fire. Alone. She shouldn't drink, but it didn't matter. She wasn't going to keep the baby. She put on the public radio station, too tired to pick out discs. Feet on the coffee table, she began reading through the guest book to see which names she could still match with faces. So much of the day was a blur, she could understand how she'd missed most of it but not this—in black block printing, toward the front of the book. Ridley Neal.

The night wasn't as problematic as her mother's friends thought it would be. The next days were much worse. The service behind her, Caroline was left with a collection of sad details like so many dying bouquets, one of which was, literally, so many dying bouquets, even though she'd requested memorial contributions to hospice instead of flowers. The hospital bed hadn't been picked up yet, although she'd called twice. She was donating the bedside commode to hospice, along with Eleanor's cane and walker.

Her mother's clothing would be the worst. Opening the door to her mother's bedroom on the fourth day, she took a few steps in and sank down on the big bed Eleanor hadn't slept in for months, but she and Rid had. That much drained her.

It took another three or four minutes for Caroline to make it to the closet. Even though she'd been in that closet a hundred times since she'd been home, she'd not taken in how it held her mother's scent, lingering as something light and faintly citrus, and it was as overwhelming to Caroline as if her mother had appeared. Eleanor's wardrobe was simple and classic. She'd also had many of her clothes for a decade, some longer. Caroline's plan was to avoid much sorting, rather to just carry clothes on their hangers out to Eleanor's car, hers now—and take them to the women's shelter. But she'd walked the beach with her mother, talked with her while she fired clay; they'd made spaghetti sauce and done dishes together, all while her mother wore these clothes. There, in cleaner's plastic, stuck against the wall was the dress her mother had worn to Caroline's wedding to Chuck.

Caroline started to bunch the first ten hangers together, and then she simply couldn't do it. The whole of their time together could not be emptied out of a closet and driven away. She had to take care of emptying herself and emptying this damn closet, but the order wasn't going to matter.

As it turned out, she was no better at getting the other task accomplished. Two more mornings came during which she opened the phone book to Women's Services but made no call. She refused dinner invitations from three of her mother's friends, rather shopped for frozen entrées and canned soup at the Stop & Shop, picking from the vegetarian section, and buying some organic produce, which she'd never done before, and didn't bother to explain to herself. Elsie left a message while she was out and she left a message for Elsie when she came home, but they didn't connect. She drove over to Newcomb Hollow and up to Race Point, ocean side beaches where she could walk without fear of running into Rid. She told herself she was thinking, but the surf washed thought from consciousness, and she was nothing but movement without direction.

❦

She wasn't lying when she told herself she hadn't planned to go to the library in Truro on the way back to Wellfleet. Her mindset, in fact, had been to avoid it assiduously. She'd gone up to P-town, intending to just go in to the Women's Center and talk to someone, make the appointment to have it done. But then she'd decided to walk to Long Point from the west end, because the tide was all the way out and she hadn't done that for years. It was easy to get marooned out there if you didn't time it right—the tide could come in, although, she guessed, she *could* walk back on the slippery jetty. It was something she'd done in high school with her friends. They'd gone out there with beer for a party and not watched the clock, the one time that Caroline had gotten in serious trouble with her parents, who forbade her to ever go there again. But it was spectacular, the solitary little finger of land's end, with ocean beach on one side, bay beach on the other and a swatch of dune grass striping the middle where terns and gulls nest.

And there was this: within a couple of days of Eleanor's death, Caroline had started talking to her mother. "What should I do, Mom?" she'd ask, in the same way she once might have said, "God, what should I do," not particularly expecting a response, and not slowing for one, yet now when she was trying to focus on something, much of the time it was in the form of a one-way dialogue. So that first afternoon she found herself at the Truro Public Library on the way back from the Provincetown Stop & Stop and Long Point, when she hadn't gone to the Women's Center again but definitely would tomorrow, what she said to herself was, "Mom, what am I doing *here?*" But she went ahead and took the *Cape Cod Times* from the rack and sat in one of the couches with a clear view of the circulation desk, raising the paper to cover her face. She hadn't read it for the past couple of days anyway, she told herself, and then lowered it briefly for a look at Teresa DiPaulo, in an unflattering purple sweater, checking out a stack of books for a blue-haired woman. Caroline could see that yes, that gold angel was pinned over her heart again.

❦

There was, of course, no need to go to the library to read the paper. She had resumed the subscription. But each day, she tossed the rolled up paper into the recycling bin and went to the Truro library to read it, scanning first for any mention of the lawsuit against the sea farmers, and then reading the rest between sneaked glimpses at Teresa. Three or four times, she feared Teresa caught her, too quickly jerking the paper back up, its sudden rustling like a telltale gunshot in the silent room. She was a lousy spy. And spies were supposed to be looking for something, weren't they? She had no idea what her mission was. All she had determined so far was that yes, Teresa did wear the gold angel every day. That piece of information weighed like a stone on Caroline's heart. And still she didn't go to the Women's Center.

Elsie called again.

"I called to see how you're doing. Sometimes it's harder when things are suddenly easier," she said. "It's one of life's ironies. Have you seen a doctor?"

"Ah ... not yet." Caroline was on the kitchen extension, and she twisted the cord around her own waist as she got over to the kitchen window. From there, she could see the access road. She was watching the oystermen arrive for the late tide. Rid hadn't appeared yet, and she didn't want to be distracted from seeing him by talking to Elsie. Up on the bluffs, the afternoon light reflected off vast windows as if the glass were armor, metallic and blinding.

"Caroline," Elsie started, and then hesitated. "I don't mean to sound like a busybody, and—"

"I know, I know." Realizing she sounded curt, Caroline put a wash of cotton over the sharpness of her tone. "I really do know. I have to do it. It's just hard to get ready, I guess. Emotionally."

"Are you sure this is what you want?"

"Geez, I can see what you're getting at. A baby would just be the perfect addition to my life right now. I mean it's ideal, what with my devoted husband, and then there's always the great career I've got going." Immediately she was ashamed of her sarcasm.

"Sometimes when we don't act on a decision," Elsie started, her words tangling with Caroline's, "Oh Elsie, I'm so sorry. I didn't mean to sound like such a shit."

"It's all right. I'd just like to support you—and to help however I can, whatever you do." Elsie's voice was faintly cool this time.

"Elsie, please forgive me. I don't know what's the matter with me. You're helping me—you *have* helped me. I couldn't have gotten through Mom's death without you." She spoke in a rush. There wasn't enough air in the room.

"It's a confusing time. And your hormones are probably berserk."

The afternoon light was melting toward dusk. Out on the shining flats, the oystermen were silhouettes, like so many ants crawling on the water. The tide was dead low now, and it must be a moon tide, Caroline realized, because they were so far out from the beach, some working the backs of their grants. She'd been trying to figure out what visual markers she could use to identify Rid's grant, to watch him at work, but all the trucks looked alike from this distance. She'd even looked for his dog, but remembered that Rid kept her in the truck while he worked. She'd have to see him arrive, identify the truck just as it bumped off the dirt access road onto the beach, and then figure it all out. That was difficult to do without setting up camp in front of a window. Or out on the beach.

"Hormones. Yeah, I'd say so. Definitely." Was Elsie's voice back to normal?

"Is this something you'd like to talk about, or do you want me to mind my own business?"

"Elsie, I just don't know what I'm doing right now. I don't even know what to talk about." At that moment, she just wanted to get off the phone, because unless she was mistaken, she'd figured it out. She'd just watched a figure return to a truck, open a door, and a dog was wild with joy.

 *Chapter 12*

"I'm returning these." Caroline slid the pile of books across the circulation desk.

"Are they overdue?"

"No, I don't think they're due until November 23." When she turned over the top book, a novel she'd carefully put on the top of the stack, she flushed and tried to rotate the pile so Teresa wouldn't see the title on the book underneath, *What To Expect When You're Expecting*. She'd just checked out the book to see what it said about morning sickness remedies. Fumbling, Caroline tried to use the novel she was holding to block Teresa's view, making a show of checking the due date on the sticker. "Yup, November 20, actually, still not overdue."

"Oh, well, unless material is overdue, you can just put it all in the drop slot, or leave it there, where it says 'Returns.' You sure didn't take much time to do all this reading. You can keep this one longer. It's excellent. I mean you might want to if you're..."

As she spoke, Teresa reached under the novel Caroline held, picked up *What To Expect* and made as if to hand it back to Caroline, her face holding a friendly question mark. At the moment she was encouraging Caroline to hang on to *What to Expect*, she glanced down again and saw that the next title in the stack was *Coping With Abortion*.

"Uh, I don't think I need to keep it. I, ah, read it already." Why had she flirted with a situation like this? She'd known damn well she could put the books in the drop box. "I mean it's not for me. I mean I'm not—"

"Goodness, it's none of my business," Teresa interrupted Caroline's stammering to put the books on a cart behind her. "I'm not supposed to comment on the books anyone checks out. Really, I apologize. Now, is there anything else I can help you with?" She was so clearly trying to end the conversation that she was almost saying *shoo*.

It was like an out-of-body experience. Caroline was instructing herself to walk away from the counter even as she took a breath and plunged on, spinning expertly as any spider.

"Actually, there is. I'm staying in the area while I work on a feature story for *Cape Cod Life*. We've—the editors, I mean—become aware of the legal action pending against the local aquaculturists, and we're interested in doing a human interest story. You know, the, uh, the whole slant of the landowners against the aquaculturists, I mean how the local population feels about it, of course, but also, an update on where the lawsuit stands right now. I'm wondering if you can help me with the research."

Teresa got an odd look on her face, not suspicious, but certainly puzzled. "The court proceedings would be a matter of public record. I imagine you know how to access those."

A small heat rose in Caroline's cheeks. She hoped it didn't show, hoped her jeans and sweatshirt hadn't already given her away. What did journalists wear, and would Teresa know? She felt faintly nauseated, sure she was transparent. "Actually, I'm from Quincy myself, so unfortunately I'm not familiar with the ins and outs here. I was just hoping you could save me some time. And, I'm really looking to research deep background on this." She hadn't even a tiny idea of how one went about looking up what was going on in some court or another, hadn't even thought of tracking Rid's fate that way. She'd been relying on the *Cape Cod Times* and the *Provincetown Banner*, combing them daily for any mention. The last she'd read, a judge named Samuel Atwood had denied the plaintiff's motion for an injunction against the shellfishers continuing to work on their grants during the time the suit was pending. Caroline had exhaled a long sigh of gratitude, and then wondered why she cared, except that Rid had come to her mother's service. And why was she putting on *this* charade here, now, with *this* woman of all people? It was reckless, an inexplicable disconnect from sensibility.

"I'm really not a research librarian," Teresa said. "You could come back tomorrow when Rhonda is here. She's out sick today, but she knows a lot more about—"

Caroline cut her off. She spread the most engaging smile she owned over her nerves, a stage actress on opening night. Reaching across the counter, she touched Teresa's hand with the lightest, quickest touch, as if it were a rose petal she didn't want to bruise. "Goodness, I promise, nothing too technical. Mainly questions about local things. Would you mind? I mean, even an orientation to this library would be helpful, save me a lot of time."

Teresa shook her head slightly as her shoulders raised in a small dubious shrug, but she said, "Okay, I guess."

"Thank you so much." She could have gotten out clean then, but no, she had to push on. "Ah, would you be willing for me to interview you? If you like, I can keep it off the record, just use it for deep background." Where on earth was she coming up with this bullshit?

There was a smear of lipstick on one of Teresa's front teeth, red enough to be mistaken for an injury. Her hand had swept across her cheeks once too many times with the blusher, and her teal cardigan, the angel pinned in place, was a half-shade off flattering. Or she was a half-shade too pale. She appeared fragile in the weak, moat-filled afternoon light that made a stage of the circulation desk, and then Caroline felt nauseated again. She needed to leave here and go back to Provincetown, to the Women's Center.

"Me?" Teresa said.

"Do you live in this area?"

"Yes, but—"

Again, the ingratiating smile. "I promise to make it painless. First, though, if you have the time, maybe you could help by telling me how to get into the newspaper archives here. Are they on microfiche, or…?" Yes, this was it. A quick switch to a question Teresa couldn't refuse to answer. She was hanging on, wanting something from the woman whose life she'd ruined. It was insane, she knew. Was Teresa going to say "Hey, by the way, Ms. Reporter, some drunken woman hit my car and killed my child, but write this down: I've forgiven her and I hope she can have a good life because mine is fine again now?"

"I'd suggest you use the Internet first," Teresa said. "The newspapers have their own search engines. But wouldn't you want the court records? You don't get those here." Again, a hesitation in Teresa's voice, a hint of a sidelong glance as if to say, *surely you know this.*

"Of course." Had she already given herself away? Then, though, what to say came to her. "I really haven't been too clear, I realize. I'm really looking to learn about aquaculture—for background. I think anything I can learn about the work will be helpful." Maybe she thought Teresa would say, "And by the way, having a child is like putting all the eggs of your life in one basket. Some crazy, selfish person can get drunk just once, get in a car, and run over the basket. That's what can happen and does happen, so if you're scared to death of that, you're right. But it's still worth it." *Oh Mom, I have lost my mind.*

"We do have a fair amount of literature on aquaculture. Just use the catalog to find the books, and the *Reader's Guide to Periodical Literature* for articles. Here, I'll show you where those are. Although it looks like you've already been using our library pretty well. I mean, since you've checked books out." Teresa came out from behind the desk, lifting a hinged section of the counter and replacing it behind her. She wore a navy pleated skirt, stockings and high-heeled shoes. As Caroline followed her across the carpeting, Teresa kept talking, slowing and directing her voice over her shoulder. "Anyway, then you can check the magazine websites to see if you can get back issues or—any particular material could be available on the Internet, of course."

"Of course." Caroline nodded, and ran her hand through her hair. "Thank you again. Once I get myself going on this, I'd still like to interview you and get ideas about others I should talk to."

"I imagine you'll go to the flats and talk to the oystermen themselves?"

"Definitely." Caroline pictured herself sitting on the rocks that fronted Rid's grant, trying to pull that off. Rid would have narrowed his eyes and seen through her in a jailhouse minute. People who have done time have radar for bullshit, she knew, because everyone inside spends a lot of time either slinging or listening to it.

"Well, good luck," Teresa said, edging back toward the circulation desk.

"Will you be here tomorrow?" Caroline couldn't believe her own nerve.

"Yes, but not until noon because we're open until eight.

"Maybe I can catch you then."

"Maybe. If we're not too busy."

"I'm CiCi, by the way." A name Teresa would never have heard. It had been Caroline Vance who'd hit that parked car and destroyed so many lives. "Cici Marcum. And I can see by your nametag that you're Teresa." Teresa DiPaulo, a name seared on Caroline's mind as permanently as a cattle brand.

"Terry, actually."

This nugget of information was a bit stunning and a small flash of gold for Caroline. Sometimes she couldn't get over how young Teresa—now Terry— looked from across the room, with that long curly blonde hair like a teenager's,

and how it didn't fit with the age around her eyes up close. The name Terry fit
with the hair, not the eyes.

"I'm glad to have met you, Terry. I, well, I appreciate your time." She'd been
going to say *I like your pin*. Really she didn't, though. The pin was a splinter in
her heart.

❀

All these books and articles. Who knew clams and oysters were so
complicated? She'd finally come up with a decent story as to what she was
doing there. Terry was quite right that to really know what was going on in
the lawsuit, she'd have to get court documents. And those, for heaven's sake,
weren't in the library. She'd made herself look like a rube, though fortunately,
Terry didn't seem suspicious. Sometimes the locals really *aren't* too bright, she
thought.

She went back to the pile on the table in front of her. Wellfleet Natural
Resources and Shellfish Management Plan, 1986, happened to be on top.
These people had wrestled with harbor management plans over and over, with
tables and charts and figures enough to make her mind collapse in on itself.

They'd detailed history back to the 17th century. The Wellfleet harbor itself
was a rare natural gift, its sack-shape and shallow, hard sandy bottom created
a large, ten-foot tidal range and rapid tidal currents of fairly warm water. But
it was continuously cooled by the amazing number of creeks and estuaries that
emptied into it: Herring River, Duck Creek, Mayo Creek, Blackfish Creek,
Sewell's Gutter, Power's Landing, and Middle Meadow. Nutrients thrived in
the warm tidal water, extra nutrients came in from the generous creeks, all that
fresh water lowered the salinity in the basin, and *voilà!* Wellfleet oysters were
uniquely sweet and salty at the same time, while the coolness of the bay water
kept the animals extremely fresh and safe. The combination was unmatched in
the world.

It was predictable that people had been greedy and shortsighted. So many
oysters were harvested in the 1700s that they became almost extinct. Cultch
was being scraped up too, then, for lime and mortar, so there was nothing
to catch spat from the remaining oysters. The town forests were overcut for
lumber and grazing, clogging the harbor with silt. They'd actually passed
environmental protection laws as early as 1742 because it looked as if the
harbor might become too blocked for shipping, let alone oysters and quahogs.

Oysters had to be imported from the Chesapeake Bay to redevelop the beds that had once teemed, an abundant birthright for natives.

And the 19th century brought more misguided development: construction of a railroad embankment across Duck Creek, a breakwater, and the enlargement of Shirt Tail Point to make a place for the town marina. Those projects, by slowing and diverting the tidal currents, lessened the inflow of nutrients that fed the harbor's food chain. Caroline read, captivated, about how oysters and clams actually eat the little microscopic stuff that floats in the water by sucking it in, filtering the algae nutrients, and spitting out the rest. Wellfleet harbor is a junk food haven for shellfish—twenty-five thousand varieties of edible microbes come in and the animals go berserk on them. How had she grown up here and not known that? The 20th added pollution from road runoff and defective septic systems that produced a black muck, rank with hydrocarbons—*what the hell are hydrocarbons?* she wondered—and heavy metals and bacterial pollutants. Back in the '80s, already task forces and shellfish constables and shellfishers were studying how this history of abuse had affected each species, trying to restore the harbor's ecosystem. Sometimes Caroline got lost in reading and would forget to observe Terry. Twice she went to the library when Terry wasn't there and because there was nothing else to do until the tide, she just stayed and picked up where she'd left off her bogus study.

Caroline got into a rhythm based on the tides and library hours. If, for example, it was a double tide day, an hour before the first daylight low tide, she'd set herself like an old-time sea wife to watch for Rid's arrival and track his movements. Now she could tell when he was picking oysters as opposed to when he was digging clams. Sometimes his silhouette would be bent over a rack like a question mark for an hour at a time, picking in a two-handed rapid fire, slowing only briefly to inspect an animal. If it was too small, it went back in the rack; if it was damaged or the shell was empty, it was tossed into the shallows, more cultch to catch seed. Every little bit helps. The good, legal oysters went into a plastic milk crate, and when one was filled, he'd straighten and carry it to the bed of the truck and trudge back with another empty crate. He must have a huge order to fill, she'd thought several times. But, then, it was still a month that ended with R—fall, the traditional best shellfish harvest months—and he'd want to pull every legal size animal he could sell because there was no telling what he might lose over the winter. The long-range weather forecast kept talking about a hard winter. She'd read that ice could damage shellfish production, sometimes wipe out whole grants. The better aquaculturists pulled out all their oysters and buried them in specially constructed pits in their yards at home.

When she finished spying on Rid, an hour later, she'd dash to the library to spy on Terry. The only difference was that she spoke to Terry, making up questions if she had to, but usually able to pull something out of her "background research on aquaculture" to ask for help with.

"I love moon snails," Caroline said one day. She'd flagged Terry down as she passed the table at which Caroline was working, ostensibly to show her a lavish full color plate in a book about shells. "I mean they're so beautiful, the way they swirl in on themselves in such a pretty circle. Now I feel guilty. Did you know they're big predators of clams?"

"Actually, I did know that. I've got cousins who are licensed. Nobody with a grant though, they pick in the wild. But they know pretty much everything about oysters and quahogs."

It yanked Caroline back to hear Terry use the lingo so comfortably, as if she and Rid were related. Her separate secret worlds suddenly intersected, and Caroline felt exposed, trapped in the interstice. She covered her discomfort.

"Oh. Gosh. I really *do* need to interview you! You'll be a great source."

"CiCi, if you were from around here, you'd know that everyone knows as much as I do!" Terry laughed. "It's really nothing special. Most of us know *something* about it. It's in our blood." She walked on, pushing a cart of books she was re-shelving, her plaid skirt swinging around her calves.

It was a good thing Terry had gone back to her task. Caroline couldn't have hidden her watery eyes. *It's in our blood.* Were those her mother's words or Rid's—or had they both said it? And yet later, after she calmed herself, it was a very good day for Caroline. She'd discovered that yes, Terry DiPaulo could laugh. Even after everything.

She'd killed two more weeks with this mad routine, promising herself each night that she'd stop, and each morning compelled to repeat it. At the library, she fancied herself Terry's friend, then a moment later would be sure that Terry had identified her and was, even that moment, calling the police.

Thanksgiving came and went, the first that hadn't been observed in her mother's house with the biggest turkey Eleanor could buy, even in the rare years that it was only the three of them for the holiday. She'd freeze whole meals of fragrant leftovers complete with gravy for surprise dinners on frigid January and February nights. Eleanor claimed she saved them for the worst weather nights, "because it's a hearty cheerful meal," but CiCi and her father hadn't been taken in that easily. Eleanor had whipped out those dinners on nights when she'd stayed too long at her wheel, absorbed in the creation her hands raised from it. "It was a good day. Like being God," she'd said once, then blushed and laughed at herself.

This year, Caroline had had invitations from all her mother's friends. "I'm not good company right now," she'd said, at which they'd scoffed. In the end, she'd gone to Noelle's for dinner and Sharon's for dessert so that neither would be slighted. Noelle had asked her what her plans were, but didn't push when she said she didn't know yet. Sharon didn't even ask, only wrapped her in a hug. She needed to think about getting them some little thank you present for Christmas, and something for Elsie, too. It crossed her mind: maybe a little gift for Terry? For helping with the research? *Who do you think you're kidding?* she scolded herself, ashamed.

That day, the sunset bled ferociously into the water, as if the western sky were the last wound of the world, while Caroline scrambled some eggs for supper, and told herself that seeing Terry laugh once had to be enough. *Let it go, now. Please.* She might be losing her marbles, between talking to her dead mother and talking to herself. A taco short of a combination plate, Eleanor used to put it. A sandwich short of a picnic. "Mom, I am the whole basket short of a picnic," she whispered. Tears again.

Her body was changing. She avoided the mirror, even avoided looking down in the shower, as if she were a child who could cover her eyes and make things disappear. But her breasts were bigger, the areolas blooming like big dark flowers, and although she could zip her jeans, she couldn't button them. She hadn't been nauseated lately, but sometimes she was so tired she fell asleep sitting up. She'd put her head down on the table at the library more than once, unable to stay awake.

She brought her plate—the eggs, whole wheat toast, a green salad with orange segments—over to the window where she'd created her Rid-watching station. It was twilight, but she knew he'd be at the tide. They were using lights now, which made the upland owners crazy. Pissario had cited the lights in his lawsuit. But no matter. She simply had to stop these games and either tell Rid or not tell him, get the abortion or—well, she just had to get off this train that had no destination. It was December first already. The last R month. The end of the first trimester when it is safe and easy to harvest.

 *Chapter 13*

Rid stood up and leaned on the handle of his bullrake. December already. When the winter really hit it would be a slam according to the forecast, but the fall had stretched out like a sleeping dog. Hard frosts, of course, but they softened by mid-morning and the cold in the water didn't feel like it was cracking his bones yet. He had on multiple layers under his waders and while his feet were frozen, the early afternoon sun had him sweaty above his waist. He flipped back the hood of his sweatshirt and let the air cool him off a moment while he stretched his back, looked around and decided what to do about filling this order.

There was CiCi's house. He'd gone to her mother's funeral because it seemed the right thing to do. He'd offered to help and then never had. She hadn't asked him, though she'd come to the grant that day wanting *something*, he had to admit that. He felt bad about the whole thing, ashamed and defensive at once. Then she was surrounded by people at the service, and he was embarrassed and it was time to get to the tide anyway, so he'd just slipped out intending to call. He still intended to call her to say he was very sorry about her mother. He thought of it, of her, most every time he noticed her house. Like today. And sometimes he went far enough to remember how she'd helped him the night of the hurricane, the knack she'd shown for anchoring the nets. How gutsy she'd been as the storm lashed its tail across them. She'd put herself in harm's way. For him. Who'd ever done that before? And the way they'd laughed in his truck, how much he'd liked her the whole night of the hurricane.

For now, though, he couldn't think about that. He sloshed across his grant, weaving up, across, down and steadily west until he got within easy voice range of Mario, who was picking oysters.

"Where you been? Haven't seen you in a couple days."

"Yeah, Bonk and me was picking in the wild. Get 'em free, ya know, why sell my own stock when I can sell stuff I didn't have to raise, right? Over off Lieutenant Island. Had to come work my own heap today, I figure, can't let it go *too* long." He laughed and shoved his cap brim up and sideways. His teeth flashed white in his grin, his face still tan although not as deeply so as in high summer. It was probably true about picking in the wild since he said Bonk was with him, although whenever Mario disappeared for a couple of days, Rid suspected he was running drugs. He'd asked him straight out once, and Mario had snorted a denial and added, *ha, you're pissed off 'cause nobody's hired you to!*

"Good picking?"

"Great."

"Listen, can I borrow a couple bushels of clams off you? I got an order to fill tonight and I'm short. I can have 'em back to you tomorrow—day after tomorrow at the latest. It's a good customer." He hated asking Mario, but he'd hate asking anyone and he just wasn't going to beat the tide, that was obvious.

Mario had the good grace not to miss a beat. "No sweat. There's a bushel and a half in the truck. You can dig another half bushel in a flash from that front raceway. I'll give you a hand. Help yourself." He pointed. "I got a bump rake, might be faster if you want. Tide's comin'."

"I got it, thanks." If his voice sounded gruff, he hadn't meant it to. "We got that meeting tomorrow morning, ya know."

"I'll be there. Hope he ain't just runnin' up our bill. Wanna ride down together?"

"Yeah. At the rate I'm going, I'm really hoping that too."

He felt Mario's eyes on his back as he moved to dig from Mario's grant. The difference between Mario's raceways and his own was that every other quahog wouldn't be dead. Even Mario, who didn't pull his stock in the winter but took his chances with ice, even Mario had cleared his nets right away after that hurricane had landed. Or maybe Mario's nets hadn't been as badly buried as Rid's; there were always those vagaries of whose grants happened to take the worst hits in any given weather. Whatever. This time Rid had no one to blame but himself. He should not have let that woman hold him up more, that was for sure.

Rid heard Mario in the water behind him before he felt him catch up. "Hey man. You got problems on your grant? I mean you okay?"

"Yeah. Just short and outta time," Rid answered without looking at him. It wasn't like they were close friends. He'd already said more than he'd meant to. "I'll drive tomorrow. Pick you up at 8:30? We can swing by the Dunkin Donuts in Eastham, grab some coffee." If he drove, it would even the score some, make him feel better even though Mario would talk incessantly. Tomas would appreciate it, though. One of them had to ride herd, make sure Mario didn't flip out over something the lawyer said and go off half-cocked on the way home. Usually Tomas got the honor. Rid had been taking advantage and driving his own truck down to Barnstable while Tomas picked up Mario.

"Yeah. All right. Hey, just fill the rest of that basket, take those. You can just give 'em back whenever." Mario gestured to the bed of his truck, where there were five and a half wire bushel baskets of quahogs and three crates of oysters—a fortune compared to what Rid had harvested today—along with a bump rake and a jumble of other gear. The Ford was parked facing the rock revetment, the tailgate open for ready access as Mario worked. That's how they all did it, keeping their trucks as close as possible so they wouldn't have to carry things so far, sometimes moving them two or three times as a tide receded and came back in. Some of the grants were five and six acres, after all. Rid's was five, and so was Mario's, if he remembered rightly. Mario ought to be more careful, though. Right now his tires were in a good five or six inches of water. It should be moved to safer ground, Rid thought. Like my whole life.

This was a first. The lawyer was smiling. He shook each of their hands in turn, swept a hand unnecessarily toward three chairs and, another first, didn't sit behind his desk but this time in a fourth chair that completed a sort of three-quarter circle in the small office. Another first; a plate of glazed donuts was on a table newly wedged into the middle. "Who needs coffee?" Lorenz asked as they took the seats he indicated. He himself bounced back up and went to the door, poised to give their orders to a woman who was in the outer office.

"She's actually an attorney, my partner," he whispered in a confidential, almost giddy tone. "I can get her to make coffee because mine is so vile that she's embarrassed for clients to drink it. It's my System of Studied Incompetence.

Women fall for it every time. Try it. No extra charge."

"I'll have a cup." Rid, even though he'd had a big cup on the way down.

"Sure." Mario.

"Yes, please." Tomas, the one with the manners.

"All right then, we'll all have some. Four cups. She'll make a pot and I'll just bring it in. Don't want to push my luck by asking her to serve it, you know. Be right back."

Once Lorenz had cleared the room, Mario directed a suspicious mutter to Tomas, whose face was unreadable as a foreign newspaper to Rid. "What the hell is going on?"

"For once, it doesn't look like bad news," Tomas said. "Let's stay calm and wait. Could be nothing."

The three cleaned-up versions of themselves sat uneasily. "Do you think it's okay to take a donut?" Mario said into the silence minutes later. As if on cue, his stomach growled.

"Jesus, Mario. Go ahead," Rid answered, then stifled irritation. "Yeah, man, it's okay. Probably that's what they're there for." He grinned. "Try not to drool on yourself." He was hungry himself, but held back. He'd follow Tomas' lead.

Lorenz returned with a tray. "She gave me a dirty look, but she did it." He set the tray on the table, spread out the Styrofoam cups and said, "I'll let you help yourselves. There's creamer and sugar right there. And napkins. Not too fancy, here. Oh, help yourself to donuts. I picked those up myself on the way in." His glance found Mario, napkin on his lap, half-donut like a crescent moon in hand. "Oh, good, you already did. Great."

Tomas took a breath, waited a moment and then said quietly, "Mr. Lorenz, it seems clear to us that something has happened. We'd like to know what it is." Big hands were quiet in the lap of his overalls, big feet lined up like two shovels on the floor.

David Lorenz got the message. Immediately he leaned forward in his seat and said, "You're right. I do have news and it's potentially very good. Relax. Pour some coffee, sit back and prepare to be pleased. I'm sorry. I've enjoyed discovering this, and anticipated telling you so much that I got carried away. And by the way, don't worry about the clock. Celebration time today is on me." He stood and reached for some files on the top of his desk, then sat back down, all business, opening a file and distributing a copy of one piece of paper to each of them. "Everybody ready?"

"We're ready, sir," Tomas said, even as he scanned the piece of paper, but quickly looked back up. "I'm not sure what this means."

"What it means, Tomas—and by the way, you three should call me Dave—is that Mr. Pissario, while he *thinks* he owns out to the mean low water mark and under Massachusetts law by all rights he *should* own out to the mean low water mark, as best I can tell, he *doesn't*.

"What?" Mario erupted. "Man, we're home free!"

"Wait a minute," Tomas interrupted. "Why doesn't he? And more importantly, who does?"

Lorenz held up a hand. "I'm getting to that. Let me explain. Here's the story." He pushed his glasses up on his nose and sighed. "Careless real estate work, careless legal work. When the Indian Neck property up on the bluffs was originally subdivided forty years ago, the real estate developer—some outfit named Cape Shore Properties, it's defunct now—didn't register the tidal flats with the County Registry of Deeds." He dipped his head toward his chest and shook it back and forth. "Stupid, stupid, stupid. His bad, works to our good." With the attorney's head bent, Rid saw the squished crescent of his receding hairline, how it was working back toward the bald spot in the back. Reflexively, Lorenz ran his hand over the top of his head, his fingers raking his hair like a shag carpet. Still there.

"So it's over?" Mario interrupted eagerly. Sometimes, like now, his real age and boyish demeanor were at odds with the wrinkles that spread out like a delicate fan from the outside corners of his eyes. Theirs was a life that showed on them, at least their faces and hands and backs.

Lorenz sobered. "Not exactly. Well, not at all. I wish I could tell you it was. But, now there's the possibility of a whole new strategy, especially if you can keep absolutely quiet while we work the angle." He uncrossed his legs, reached to the table, and took his first sip of coffee. He looked meaningfully at their untouched cups. "Hey, guys, you'd better drink up or my ass is grass with my partner." He was obviously trying to keep the tone light and celebratory. "C'mon, have a donut. I'll explain."

Tomas reached for his cup, and Rid followed suit after putting in two packets of sugar. He'd have put creamer in, but Lorenz was waiting for them to be settled and drinking coffee before he went on.

"No donut?"

Rid obediently reached for a donut. At this point, he'd have eaten cow dung to get Lorenz to spill his guts. Tomas took one, too.

"Go ahead, Mario, have another one. They're pretty good, those Krispy

Kremes, you know."

Mario didn't need any more encouragement.

Satisfied, Lorenz opened the folder he'd retrieved from his desktop. "Okay, they've been claiming that they own the tidal flats out to 1,650 feet under the Colonial ordinance, as you know. They're backed up by wording in their deed which gives them title to land *'in Wellfleet harbor.'* You can see how this can be interpreted to support their claim. We, on the other hand, have been basing our objection on the fact that another part of the deed specifies that they own 'to the high water mark,' which would include the beach, but not the tidal flats. See what I mean? The deed itself is ambiguous. They are wanting a strict interpretation of the words 'in Wellfleet harbor' and citing the Colonial ordinance to get the court to specify that they own all the way out. Which would put you out of business."

"We always thought they owned the beach anyway," Rid said. "We keep off it, you know, drive below the high tide line and the like. Of course, there's not much beach at full tide. The line's pretty close to the bluffs. But we don't even come until the tide's three quarters out."

"Well, of course," Lorenz said. "If the court were to say they own the beach, it's no skin off your nose. But if the court interprets the deed the way Pissario wants it to...."

"So back to the part where he thinks he owns it but he doesn't. The new strategy." Tomas said. Rid could tell he was getting impatient.

"Exactly. As I said, the tidal flats were never registered by the developer. They should by all rights be part of Pissario's land—and the property of the other upland owners above other grants too—but somebody forgot to register them. Whoever owned that land before Cape Shore Properties bought it for development technically still owns the rights to the tidal flats!" Rid, watching his face, thought *this is a lawyer's version of being a kid in a candy shop.*

Rid and Mario both looked at Tomas to see if he'd already calculated how to use this information. The big man had his eyes closed.

"So, I think I might see where you're going," Tomas said when he opened his eyes. He rubbed his forehead and unruly graying hair, combed and gelled into submission for this official business. "But it's already in the court."

"And the court may still rule in your favor. I see it as a fail-safe backup."

"Huh? What are you talking about?" It was Mario interrupting, but Rid was glad, because he had no idea either.

"Correct me if I'm wrong," Tomas said to Lorenz, then swung toward

Mario. "Conceivably, we could find out who does own the tidal flats that Pissario thinks he owns and buy them."

"Bingo," said Lorenz. "Of course, you've got to keep this absolutely quiet. Pissario has got to keep thinking he and the other upland owners own the beach and—according to him—own the flats, too. He can't find out that the flats weren't registered or they might do the same thing. Either tie it up in court forever, trying to prove it was somehow a mistake and they do own them, or, you know, go buy them."

"Do we tell the court what we're doing, though?" Rid hoped he wouldn't sound dumb. He hated to think how long they'd been in here. The light in the room had changed. You got sensitive to things like that when you worked outside. It had been over an hour. He'd have checked his watch to know exactly but it seemed rude. On the other hand, Lorenz—*Dave*—had said celebration time was on him. Did that mean no bill at all for today?

"No, we just go ahead. They may rule in your favor anyway, and by the time they rule, you may have a purchase worked out. You know how slow the system is. This is a sort of insurance policy."

"So our next step would be…" Tomas, ever practical. Thank God for Tomas.

"If you're willing to incur the additional expense, then we can research exactly who owns the tidal flats. It'll likely be someone who has no idea he or she does, because this whole thing was a mistake to begin with. Sloppy work, as I said. You all consider forming a realty corporation of some sort, a legal partnership to purchase the flats outright, if the owner is willing to sell." Lorenz paused for dramatic effect, sat back and grinned. "Then you can tell Pissario to go piss in the wind. As long as that wind isn't blowing onto *your* beach and flats. What do you think?"

"There's a risk," Tomas pointed out. "The legal owner could decide to shut us down. Are we opening another can of worms?"

"Possible. But the land really isn't good for anything but aquaculture. Shit, guys. It's under water, for God's sake. There's no beach at high tide. If he or she can turn it into some cold cash, I think it's a decent bet they'll want to. But you're right. It's your decision. If it pays off, you're your own masters forever."

"Of course, if we win the suit, we win the suit." Tomas, in his overalls, seemed to be matching the attorney point for point.

"He'll appeal if you win. And appeal and appeal all the way to the State Supreme Court." Lorenz reasoned. "This can, and probably will turn into a war of attrition. An expensive war of attrition."

"I say we go for it," Rid said suddenly. He was not entirely sure what the word attrition meant, but he liked the idea of owning the flats outright.

"I'm in," Mario said.

Tomas sighed and leaned back in his chair. "Give me a minute to think this through." The other men fell silent. The lawyer took a swallow of coffee. Rid squeezed the bridge of his nose between his thumb and third finger and then pressed along the ridge of his eyebrows where a headache was budding.

Tomas opened his eyes. "So what should we name our realty company? Presuming there's a seller who wants to deal with one genius, one very fine ex-con and one juvenile delinquent AWOL Marine?"

❧

Even Tomas might have trouble masking his elation if they went to the bar at The Oyster to celebrate that night, although of the three of them, he was the most inclined to say, "It's looking a lot better," as opposed to shrieking war whoops of victory. That was Mario's style. Instead, they went to the beach over on Jeremy Point on Great Island, the most deserted spot they could come up with. Not technically an island but a peninsula, Great Island was the westernmost part of harbor land. Billingsgate Island—which the sea finally swallowed completely in 1942, now just a shoal marked by a buoy—was off its tip. Back in 1850 there were thirty homes there, a school, a plant to render the oil of the pilot whales that the Wampanoag Indians had taught the first whites how to hunt. Blackfish, they called them. There was a succession of three lighthouses on Billingsgate, each one in turn eaten by the encroaching water, each built on higher ground, until 1910 when the bay ate the sand out from underneath and the beacon was removed from the last one. In 1922, it crumbled and the bricks were floated across to the village of Wellfleet, like a number of the houses had been.

At Jeremy Point, there was no need to mask anything. They were alone with the reveling ghosts of Smith's Tavern, where their ancestors had celebrated. A woman's fan, made of ivory, whale bones, a harpoon shaft, a piece of a man's skull: they'd all been found at the abandoned site, but no place was more desolate now than the forest and beaches of Great Island, utterly uninhabited except by spirits.

Mario's truck was parked on the beach below the tide line. He'd come ahead of the other two to dig on public land while they went to get wood and supplies. When Rid pulled in and parked next to Tomas above the wrack line, he saw Mario had a bushel and a half of quahogs in his truck bed and thought, *I should be the one digging. I'm the one who needs 'em.* They'd all agreed to stay away from their own grants that afternoon; for Tomas and Rid, it had been about keeping Mario quiet, away from the other oystermen until they all calmed down. Now it was just the back side of the tide, and while he could have still done some raking, he let it pass. Tomorrow he'd go at it hard, both tides. He'd do what he could in darkness, wearing a light. December was always hard; so little daylight, no usable double tides because of it.

"Hey, man, get your butt up here—we need more wood," Rid called, thumbing behind himself to the forest. No reason Mario should be making money while he and Tomas were dragging deadfall out of the woods. He wanted to stay in a good mood. For God's sake, he couldn't remember the last time he'd had anything to celebrate.

"Yep, on my way," Mario called back. He slung his rake and a quarter-full basket into his truck bed, and trotted up the beach toward Rid.

"Gonna pull your truck up?"

"I'll get it in a bit," Mario said.

Jeremy Point was a rich source of driftwood, and the forested areas replete with downed and rotting trees. The three gathered a huge brush pile with which to feed the flames, and wood to sustain it. The warm spell had held and the fire they built was high and hot. As dusk rose off the beach skyward, the men unrolled old sleeping bags to sit on and shield their backs from the evening chill.

Tomas and Rid had brought two cases of cold beer, two packages of hotdogs, and buns, and six bags of chips. Mario rummaged in his glove compartment to contribute packets of mustard and ketchup he'd stolen during the summer from a mid-Cape burger stand.

None of them held back. They'd been popping caps before the fire sparked and once it flared up, further flushing their faces, they let loose. It might be premature, but there was more than hope now. There was a plan. They needed to keep quiet, they'd probably need to raise a bunch more money, but their minds were running marathons with possibilities. "Hey, man, maybe we end up giving grants to the town!" Mario shouted and then laughed hysterically. "Burn me a dog, buddy." Tomas had several sticks of them going at once.

"Damn. Why didn't we get some marshmallows? Those are what's good to burn." Rid said.

"I still want to burn Pissario's stinking house." Mario, of course. His face illuminated red in the firelight, full darkness behind him now.

The notion was immediately quashed by the voice of reason, even after however many beers they'd put away. Tomas sounded stone sober, although five minutes earlier he'd seemed as lit as Rid and Mario. "No way. We got the bastard now. This'll do him worse. If we pull it off, we'll be calling the shots. First time you step over the line, do something illegal, you give him ammunition. You gotta stay cool."

"I'm cool," Mario said. "I'm absolutely cool."

Rid suddenly startled, scanned the beach, stared into the darkness and started laughing. He untangled his legs and feet to stand, but doubled over laughing and staggered, holding a hand out to Mario as he did. "Yeah man, you are absolutely the King of Cool. You better get up fast, dude, oh King of Cool, because I do believe you have done sank your truck."

"Shit," Mario shouted, on his feet, Tomas lumbering upright behind him. The men ran down the beach toward the water, the truck taking shape in the darkness as they approached the advancing surf. "Goddammit, goddammit." There was enough moonlight to calculate that waves had reached the floorboards.

"I got a tow rope in the truck,"Tomas yelled in Rid's direction. "Go, go, go."

Rid shouted to Mario, "Get your waders."

"They're in the truck! Tomas is strongest anyway. I'll drive."

"Like hell. It's your goddamn truck. Put mine on." They were running up the beach toward Rid's and Tomas' trucks. Rid grabbed his waders out of the bed and threw them in Mario's direction. Tomas had climbed in his own truck bed, pulled on his waders and was rummaging for the tow rope he kept in the toolbox. At the same time he found it, Rid was in his own driver's seat, starting his engine and throwing it into gear to drive across the beach. Once he was lined up with Mario's truck, he turned and put it in reverse, backing it down toward the shallows into towing position.

Tomas and Mario ran ahead down the beach to attach the rope to Mario's bumper. Rid saw them slosh into the water, dark figures like hyphens breaking the white line of the incoming surf. One of them emerged back onto the sand with the end of the rope to attach to his rear bumper. Mario. He held up a finger in the wait sign. Rid put his truck in forward and advanced just until the rope was nearly straight. His headlights went into the forest where they were aimless.

Looking over his shoulder, Rid saw the driver's side door open and shut as Mario climbed in. Tomas appeared, knee-deep in the water, his raised left palm telling Rid to stop while he gestured a slow forward to Mario with his right hand. Then, he slowly started spiraling his left to Rid indicating a slow advance. "Easy, easy," he shouted, and again, "Go easy."

But Rid's tires only spun in the sand. They tried again with the same effect. Tomas beckoned Rid out of the truck. "Let's try to rock it."

Rid shook his head. "No waders," he yelled.

Tomas ran to the back of Rid's truck, then to the driver's side where he thrust Rid's rubber boots into the door Rid opened. Rid pulled them on, realizing even as he did that it was pointless: the water would overrun the top. And it did, almost right away as he followed Tomas into the icy breaking surf.

He and Tomas slogged to the back of Mario's truck. Tomas pumped a rhythm by keeping his left arm within sight of Mario's side view mirror, his right shoulder on the truck. "Rock it, rock it, rock it, rock it." Mario gunned the motor, on and off the accelerator as Rid and Tomas pushed.

Adrenalin is a wonderful thing, Rid thought on Tomas's right, both hands and a shoulder to the truck. Otherwise, I'd already be paralyzed. His hands ached against the tailgate as he pushed, the cold of the metal as penetrating as fire.

"We need more help. Someone to back my truck up, couple guys to push," Rid finally yelled to Tomas. The truck was rocking but not moving forward. If anything, he thought, it might be digging itself deeper. Tomas signaled Mario to stop.

"By the time they get here, it'll be too late," Tomas said.

"Depends on how far in the truck is from high water line. Do you know?"

"Not really." Tomas banged his fist on the tailgate. It was completely unlike him. "We better take a look."

As the two passed the driver's side, Tomas rapped on Mario's window. "Stay put. We're checking how far gone you are."

"We need more help?" Mario called. "Hey, let's call Pissario! I bet that sumbitch'll come help us out!"

Tomas either didn't hear or ignored him. Rid pretended not to, yielding to Tomas.

On the beach, they found the wrack line. "We can still get him out. Tweed and Clint, maybe Bogsie, too."

"We're not dragging them into this," Tomas said quietly.

"We can't get that truck out by ourselves. He'll lose it."

"Who parked it there? He's got insurance. We get those guys out here, it attracts a whole pile of attention to us. What are we doing here having a party anyway? No. Mario's way too drunk now not to say anything tonight. That's why we came out here in the first place. I've got Marie and my kids to think about."

"Those guys are already involved. They gave us money to fight Pissario"

"If Pissario gets wind that he doesn't own those flats, do you seriously think he can't outbid us for them? No way. This stays between the three of us. We don't get anyone else out here. Mario sank his truck. Any oysterman who doesn't know the tide comes in deserves to sink his truck. We'll help him pull it out tomorrow. He can flush it out and make whatever insurance claim he wants." Tomas' hearty face was clarified to only planes and hollows in the pale light, steely and resolute as his voice.

"But he'll know. I mean, we could get him out with help. We've gotten out worse."

"He doesn't have a cell phone. *You don't have yours with you.*" It was a directive.

Rid's cell phone was in the center compartment of his truck. "Yours?" he asked, as much stalling for time as by way of agreement.

"I'll try it."

"Huh?"

"*I said, I'll try it.* Just drop it now."

What was that supposed to mean? But Tomas didn't give him the chance to push. He turned his back and walked fast into the deepening water, back to where Mario waited in his truck. Rid could see him pounding the steering wheel with his fists.

"Might be enough time," Tomas called into the window Mario opened. "Hurry up. Call Tweed, have him call Bogsie. Better call Clint too. Hurry."

"Man, I don't carry a cell phone. One of you guys gotta call."

Tomas called to Rid, six feet behind him on purpose. "You got your phone in the truck?"

"It's home on the charger," Rid called back.

"Dammit." Tomas turned and ran toward his own truck, well up on the beach. Meanwhile, Rid loosened the tow rope and pulled his own truck up above the tide line. He sure as hell wasn't going to risk sinking *his* while they fooled with trying to pull Mario out.

Mario was out of his truck then chasing Rid down, sand spraying behind each foot as soon as he got on dry terrain. "What the hell!? You gotta get me out! You gotta…." He was sputtering, desperate. *And* slurring his words. Tomas had a point.

"We can't do it without more help. Tomas is calling." Darkness was a fine thing. He couldn't look Mario in the eye, kept his back turned and kept walking. Freezing, teeth chattering, boots waterlogged, jeans soaked, legs chafing, shivering, feet numb and burning at once, he headed for the homing beacon of the fire, his hands outstretched. When he reached it, he yanked the boots off and stood as close to the fire as he dared, a sleeping bag draped around his back. Mario kept talking at him, begging, but Rid tuned him out. "I can't *do* any more right now, man," he said, a couple of times, and "I'm sorry."

Tomas reappeared in the fire-lit circle like a specter. "I forgot Marie took my phone today. She was going to her mother's and wanted to check on the kids after school." This from Tomas, the straight-arrow honest man. His voice sounded breathless, apologetic. Rid looked at the ground.

Mario was frantic. They all knew without discussion that they were too far from town to fetch help in time. "WhatamIgonnado? Ohmigod! WhatamIgonnado?" He looked beseechingly at Tomas, then Rid, his arms outstretched in supplication. "Man, I gotta have my truck!" He was right, of course. They were all dependent on their trucks.

"Let's get your equipment and what you harvested out of the back so it doesn't get lost, for one," Tomas said. "The truck may be salvageable. We'll get it out in the morning. You know, we'll flush it out, see if it runs. You can file an insurance claim. We'll come up with something. Rid, you stay put. We've got waders on."

Still begging, gesticulating, Mario followed Tomas as he strode resolutely back down the beach toward where the truck foundered like a dark whale. Rid turned his head and stared into the fire.

In a bit, when the front of him felt seared, he reversed, draping the sleeping bag across his chest to hold in the warmth and putting his back to the fire. Now he could see the faint figures of Tomas and Mario moving, a black pile amassing high on the beach where the sand was soft and dry.

One of them walked toward Rid, no big hurry now. When he had closed about half the distance, Tomas called, "Rid, can you go get my truck? Keys are in it. Bring it over here so we can load this gear?"

Rid dropped the sleeping bag and headed in the opposite direction, toward the forest and the access road where Tomas' truck was parked near his own. When he got in, he hesitated a moment before starting the engine or pulling on the headlights, he checked the center compartment. Everything neatly organized: gum, pens, pencil, sunglasses, paper, some notes, a space the cell phone might fit. Then he flipped open the glove compartment and felt around. No phone. He was surprised, gratified. Maybe he'd misunderstood the whole thing. He turned the key and the engine answered.

Then another impulse. He leaned forward and felt around under the driver's seat. Nothing right away. But then he reached further back. Rid left it where it was and drove the truck.

 *Chapter 14*

Terry couldn't say exactly what it was about CiCi that made her uneasy. It was like the feeling you'd get entering a familiar room in which no one thing was in the wrong place, but many things might have been moved an inch—or not. It was the way CiCi came to the library every day, for example. A lot of magazine stories are written every year about the outer Cape, for heaven's sake, but what reporter had ever come to the library every day for weeks on end doing background research? And her story was about the Indian Neck landowner's lawsuit against those oyster farmers. How much did she need to know about aquaculture, anyway? The court documents weren't here in the library, and neither were the men being sued.

"You must be about finished with your research by now," she'd baited CiCi just yesterday afternoon. No obvious hook; she'd said it exactly the way she said everything else, but inside she knew.

"Gettin' there," CiCi had answered. "But it's a lot more complex than I realized."

"Your deadline must be coming up?"

Had CiCi blushed? She'd hesitated a nanosecond, then said, "Oh, well, the editor was going to run the story in the spring, but it's been pushed to the summer issue. I guess he's hoping there'll be a resolution—in the court, I mean— to include in the story."

"How convenient."

Had she given away her suspicion by sounding sarcastic? From behind the cart of returned books, Terry manufactured an engaging smile.

And she'd looked over CiCi's shoulder. The pages of notes on aquaculture were real. But one day over lunch Rhonda said, "Your friend sure spends a lot of time here. Do you see her much outside of work?" They were in the staff break room where a small fake Christmas tree was blinking at them. Terry wished she could pack Christmas and bury the whole goddamned thing next to Alexander. She'd wanted to shout this at Rhonda, who'd decorated the library, and wrap the ugly tinsel roping from the checkout desk around Rhonda's neck while she was at it.

"She's not my friend," Terry said sharply. "She's a patron."

"Oh really? I thought—well, I assumed. I mean I see her talking to you so often, I presumed you were personal friends and I thought it was starting to get in the way of your work a bit. I was going to—never mind, she's a patron."

"She's the journalist I've sent to you a couple of times on research questions, the one working on aquaculture."

"Hmm. She's not talked to me. Well, whatever."

"Really? Didn't she ask you about where to find records or laws about aquaculture leases? She was asking about whether they could become part of an estate, or if it was always done by just writing a son or daughter's name on the grant. I guess her point was what if another heir wanted to work it, but hadn't had their name written on it, in the case of a sudden death—she didn't ask you about that?"

"Nope, sure didn't. Now don't fuss about this. Probably you gave her as much help as she needed and didn't realize it." Rhonda gave an encouraging smile as Terry fingered her pin.

"I apologize if I've been talking with her too much. I was answering questions."

"In that case, you're doing your job and doing it well, as usual."

Terry waited until Rhonda's day off, Thursday that week. CiCi came in around eleven. She wore jeans, sneakers, and a baggy gray sweatshirt that made her look like she'd just come off the flats. She looked tired, too, gray smudges around her eyes. Her hair looked bristly, one step away from unkempt, like it needed shaping by a stylist. If she was wearing makeup at all, it needed refreshing.

Terry kept an eye on her, but didn't approach. Finally, about a half hour later, CiCi reached out to stop Terry as she walked by the table where CiCi was ensconced, surrounded by papers and books. "Terry, hi. Look! I found some great stuff on juvenile oyster disease! I'm hoping you can help me find more about other diseases, though. By the way, how are you? It sure is getting colder out, isn't it? Winter is definitely here. Are you a Christmas lover or a Christmas hater?"

"Sure is. Winter's here, I mean. Hey, I've been meaning to catch up with you and ask if Rhonda helped you find what you needed—about inheriting grants, if there's a law or precedent, what they do if it's disputed."

There was the tiniest hesitation, as if CiCi couldn't quite decide which direction to go at a crossroad while people were honking at her. "Oh I'm all set on that," she said.

That wasn't enough. Terry infused her voice with concern. "Was she nice about it? I mean, not to be unprofessional, but sometimes I worry. She's the research librarian, but if you hit her on the wrong day with a question, she can sort of brush you off. How did she respond to you, if you don't mind my asking?"

"She was all right. I'd rather work with you any day. She's a little brusque. But I got what I needed on that question. If you don't mind, though, I'll continue to ask you first."

Terry felt heat inside her body and hoped it didn't show. She'd worn a real wool sweater that John's mother had knit her when the baby was three, the same blue as his eyes, and suddenly she was sweaty and suffocating. "Okay, then, I'm glad to hear she helped you." She moved away toward the desk, hearing her heart echoing too loud and fast in her ears.

After that, she couldn't settle herself down. Her mind whipped and twirled like a weathervane in a hurricane. *You're getting completely paranoid*, she admonished herself, but then imagined the tobacco-rasped voice of her crazy cousin who'd moved to western Massachusetts, the volunteer sheriff's deputy, Citizen Watch Area Commander: *only a fool don't know that sometimes they really are out to get ya.*

Boo was considered insane by the rest of the family. He set himself up for the opinion by dressing in fatigues and a flak jacket and sermonizing that the outer Cape was a hotbed of lawlessness and immorality. Before Terry's little boy was killed, when Boo and his big-haired wife Luann came to family occasions, it had been great fun to leave leaflets advertising the female impersonators' revues and Gay Tea Dances in Provincetown around the living room. Watching the veins in Boo's forehead throb, especially the big one, and seeing if the blood vessels in his eyeballs burst had been family sport. How long he lasted before Luann had to lead him by the hand out to his truck, and whether she let him drive was the subject of the family betting pool. Unlike Boo, all the year-rounders on the outer Cape knew dozens of gays and lesbians and didn't think anything of it. They were just good neighbors living and working, with or without children, with or without partners like everybody else.

For a big extended family, toying with bigoted Boo about it was just good-natured cruelty. There was plenty to ridicule. The funny-looking kid with the face like a flattened ball had started seriously insisting he was an FBI informant at nine. It would have been one thing if he had outgrown it. By twelve, though, he was mocked as Peekaboo Pete by everyone but his parents, and once it was shorthanded to "Boo," even they picked it up. He'd enlisted, wanting to be assigned to Military Intelligence. Mysteriously, he ended up back home in eighteen months, the family speculating behind his back that he'd lacked the Intelligence part. What he did have was a pumped-up patriotic fervor with no place to put it except into his family, and he'd finally settled into appointing himself a one-man army dedicated to defending them against all enemies, domestic, foreign, animal, vegetable or mineral.

Terry hadn't seen her cousin since the baby's funeral, but now she entertained the idea of calling him. He'd go gangbusters at this CiCi woman who almost certainly wasn't what she claimed to be. Terry thought how John would disapprove of turning the family nutcase loose. But John thought she'd become a nutcase herself, and that wasn't John's first or only mistake. *Who's crazy, John? Is it Boo, or you? What does love mean?*

She stayed at the desk, attending to checking books out and other robotic tasks. *Don't fall apart.*

About an hour later, CiCi pushed back her chair, bundled into a goose down jacket that looked too small, as if it wasn't hers, gathered up her papers and moved toward the door, which was just to the left of the circulation desk. Her pattern was to stop and chat on her way out. Terry steeled herself. *Act normal.*

"I'm headin' out."

"Another day's work, another half a day's pay, huh?" Terry offered with a laugh.

"So true."

"What's it like down on the flats now? Must be freezing." She hadn't been able to resist it.

"Pretty much. I don't know how they stand it."

That gave nothing away to Terry because, cold as it was, the aquaculturists probably were out working on their grants. It was still an R month, and probably most of the oyster farmers hadn't buttoned up their grants for the winter quite yet.

Once CiCi had cleared the parking lot, Terry got to work. Most of what she was about to do was against library policy, so she couldn't do it when Rhonda was there, and for sure she wasn't about to wait until the next time Rhonda wasn't around.

CiCi was using a CLAMS library card, good at any public library on the Cape, even though she'd said she was from Quincy. By itself, this was no big deal. They gave them out to visitors and summer people all the time, just for filling out a form, so CiCi could have gotten one easily. She pulled up the record of what CiCi had checked out of all branches of the library, not just Truro. Aquaculture and some novels from this branch. Cancer management, death and dying, a pamphlet on funeral planning, pregnancy and abortion from the Provincetown branch, except for one time she'd taken some of that out from this branch, but never again.

We'd have asked for ID, Terry thought suddenly. The computer showed that CiCi hadn't given a Quincy address when she registered for a card. Sweet Jesus. She was a resident of Wellfleet.

Fingers flying, Terry went into real estate records through the Internet. The house had been owned by Eleanor Marcum until sixteen months ago, at which time it had been sold to Caroline Marcum for one dollar. Could CiCi be a nickname for Caroline? That made sense. Terry checked the tax records. The bills were still going to the same address and were paid up, but that didn't tell her who'd been writing the checks. *What am I missing?*

County records showed that the Marcums had owned that house for over forty years. Caroline, or CiCi, or whatever her name was, must have been raised there. That meant that Terry could almost for sure find *someone* who'd known her back when.

She was fitful that night, changing to pajamas before picking at a frozen dinner, drinking too much wine, her legs tangling the bedclothes. Up and down, up and down after she went to bed, getting water, making a list of ideas, trying to figure out an approach that would not give away her intent and then wondering why she felt as if she were doing something wrong. Once, for a few minutes, she was sad, realizing that she would miss CiCi.

At two-thirty five in the morning it came to her. It really wasn't difficult, once she worked it out. And she didn't even have to be at work until one, so she could do it when she woke up. Not where she worked, where Rhonda could glance over her shoulder, or worse, CiCi could come in and search her out to ask for "help" right as Terry was pulling up information.

❦

At eleven she was at the Provincetown branch of the library, on Commercial Street. She was dressed for work, in stockings and black dress shoes not meant for walking, but she'd known it wouldn't matter. Off-season Provincetown is a hair short of a ghost town, the empty streets nearly a promenade for the year-rounders who come together as one neighborhood as they dodge the wind between the cafes, the post office, the town hall, hardware and liquor stores, and up on Shank Painter Road, the Stop & Shop. Terry parked within twenty steps of the sagging portico of the eighteenth century building.

The clerk at the desk was staring into space. Rhonda would never put up with that. "Do I need to sign up for Internet time?" Terry said.

"I guess. Prob'ly. Lemme ask. I'm new." The girl had a pierced tongue that she clicked on her teeth as she went up on her toes to look for another employee. A greasy ponytail slouched down her oversized sweatshirt. Rhonda would no more hire her than leap naked off Pilgrim Monument. The girl flagged an employee, conferred, and returned to Terry.

"I need to see your card, then you can sign up for a half hour. But if nobody's signed up for the half hour after you, we won't kick you off. The sign-up sheets are over there." She pointed. "Prob'ly in the winter you can have a computer all day. There's hardly nobody around."

Terry showed her card. "Thanks." Through this, her stomach was off-kilter and she felt lightheaded, a faint buzz in her ears like a white noise fan. Why was she so upset about the P-town library looking shabby?

She sat at the computer, and went to the website for the *Provincetown Banner*. She could always go to the larger newspaper later. "Eleanor Marcum" she typed in to the search engine. Two or three seconds later the results popped up. Just by scanning the titles, she knew a good deal. The woman was a potter, she'd had a number of gallery openings that had been reviewed, she'd been a member of multiple civic organizations, and she was dead. Terry clicked on the obituary. Yes. There it was. One surviving daughter, Caroline Marcum of Chicago. Not Quincy. But Caroline Marcum was listed as owning the house.

It must have been put in her name because the mother had cancer and knew she was dying.

All right. But none of that explained what Caroline Marcum could possibly want by stalking her. Unless she really was a journalist. If so, then she'd be easy to find on the Internet, too, Terry reasoned. A Google search yielded nothing.

Terry went back to the *Provincetown Banner* website and typed in "Caroline Marcum."

When the results came up, in reverse chronological order, she thought she'd made an error in her haste. A flush spread over and through her body and with it, a panic. She thought she'd entered her own name by mistake. She hadn't. "Local Teacher Charged With DWI Following Death of Four-Year-Old Alexander DiMarco." *What the hell?* But there were other stories listed: old ones. And there it was, like a hand reaching for her throat. *Caroline Marcum and Charles Vance Wed in Wellfleet Saturday.*

Terry clicked the mouse on the story. Doubtless, there'd be a picture of Caroline Vance, nee Marcum, of Wellfleet.

# Chapter 15

December was killing her softly, as the song said, although now that Christmas was within shouting distance, the bleakness was relieved by the year-rounders' determination to drape Christmas lights on anything that moved or didn't. The days were the color of dirty wash water, though, and crawled in a relentless lonely line. Day after day Caroline made up excuses, postponed and procrastinated. She'd learned a lot about aquaculture, not that she knew why—well, there was Rid—except that she needed an excuse to watch Terry. *I want to know if she's all right.* A lie. She already knew it was impossible. A few times she caught Terry looking at her, and her pulse sounded like surf in her ears as heat rose on her cheeks. But then Terry would give her small smile. The look had been innocent, Caroline could see that, and relief would slow her pulse. *What am I doing?* she said over and over, *what am I doing?* and had no answer, skating on ice she knew she couldn't trust.

Caroline had gone to the Truro library Monday morning, knowing Terry should be there. The staff schedule was posted on a bulletin board to one side of the circulation desk near the Internet sign-up sheet. When no one was covering the desk, it was easy to go look like she was signing up for Internet time. Then she'd pretend to be distracted by something—say, a school class was out in the parking lot and the kids were like thirty springs bouncing noise and color before their teacher shushed them to come in all quiet and respectful, which wouldn't last forty seconds—and instead of looking out the window, she'd study the schedule and memorize Terry's for the next two weeks.

Only Terry wasn't there. Caroline asked a familiar volunteer with a squirrel face who wore a denim jumper like a uniform if she could speak to her. The volunteer's eyes twitched and darted as she said, "Oh my dear, I think she took some vacation time. Did you need something? Rhonda is here. She's in the back." She spoke anxiously, poking back her gray bangs, perhaps worried that Caroline was going to ask for help with one of her esoteric research questions.

"No, that's all right," she'd answered. "I'm all right." The farthest thing from the truth. She'd picked up her things and gone to her mother's car in the parking lot. *Her* car, she corrected herself, sitting behind the wheel, wearing Eleanor's old blue goose down jacket, the idling motor indistinguishable from the buzz in her head. She felt as if she were floating, her mind unanchored and adrift while she waited for Eleanor to reappear. Now she put her head down on the top of the steering wheel and wept.

Five minutes later, when another car parked next to her in the library lot, though, she hastily lifted her head and started the engine. She got herself home, washed her face, combed her hair, microwaved some tomato soup—which immediately gave her heartburn, she should have remembered—and tried to pull herself together. The tide was at two-twelve, so Rid would be arriving sometime close to one. Not all the oystermen came every day now, but even while he was still harvesting legal size, Rid was taking his youngest oysters off the grant for the winter months. She'd seen him the last days piling his truck with racks and cages and driving them off. Obviously he had a pit in his yard in which he stored them. She'd read about it, labor-intensive, but insurance against damage and loss. The quahogs would stay buried under their nets.

Caroline took up her Rid-watching post by the side window in the living room. A little earlier than she'd expected, his truck bumped over the access road and out on to the beach. She could even make out the silhouette of his dog in the passenger seat. Perhaps because Terry hadn't been there, perhaps because she was in a hormone fog, perhaps because she was alone and grieving, on impulse she slid her arms into Eleanor's jacket, pulled boots over her sneakers, wrapped her mother's white scarf around her neck and checked the pockets for gloves. The screen door—she'd not figured out how to change it over to the storm door—banged behind her as she headed toward the shallows. She needed him.

"Rid? Rid?" Caroline felt every inch a pathetic idiot, calling and waving, trying to get his attention. His back was to her. She'd timed the first call all wrong, just as he was trying to lift a rack to his shoulder. He was in the very front of his grant, at the first apparatus to be exposed as the tide receded. When he turned mid-hoist in the ankle-deep water, the rack blocked his vision and teetered precariously. Caroline hurried to help balance one end of it. *Stupid, stupid, stupid,* she berated herself.

"Hey," she said. She pulled one hand back. Bay water from the soaked wood had already penetrated her glove.

"Hey yourself," he answered, pleasantly enough as he got control of the wooden frame. The air was quieter than usual for December, the plashes of the bay soft around their feet. Still, it was dankly cold, sky low-hung and opaque, water the color of pencil lead. Only a few other oystermen were out today, widely scattered.

"I thought I'd see if I could give you a hand. I've got time to burn. Are you picking today, or just pulling stock out to move it to your pit?"

He looked at her strangely. His face looked raw and chapped.

"Mainly, I'm *pittin' oysters*, but I've got a good size order to fill too, so I gotta get moving." Was he correcting the way she'd said it?

"Is it for oysters or quahogs? Well, either way, I could cull them for you...."

"Huh?"

"What didn't you understand? I'm just offering to help."

He started moving toward his truck, gesturing with his chin to lead them off in that direction. "Since when are you such an expert on aquaculture?"

"Sheesh, who said I was?" Awkwardly, holding her end of the rack, she sloshed alongside him toward the open tailgate. "I didn't say I was."

He stared at her.

"Don't we sound like we're back in junior high school...." she said. A small awkward laugh.

"You didn't speak to me when we were in junior high school. High school either."

Tears started in some strange place behind her nose or in her throat, not making it to her eyes, but turning into anger. "Well goddamn. Who peed in your Cheerios? I came down to offer to give you a hand."

"Who asked for your help? Next thing I know you'll be suing me for spoiling your waterfront view."

The anger in his voice stunned her. She stopped moving in concert with him and let go of her end of the rack. Perhaps a third of the oysters spilled out into the sandy cultch-strewn water.

"Shit, now look what you've done." Rid used a knee to brace the middle of the rack, caught Caroline's end with his other hand and staggered the rest of the way to the truck bed. He grabbed a bucket and came back to pick the fallen oysters out of the water.

"I didn't mean to let those drop," she said as he scooped them in. Her voice was neutral, neither conciliatory nor hostile now. "Oh. These aren't legal size yet, are they?"

"What do you mean?" he challenged, standing up with the bucket. "What is it you want?"

"I did come to offer to help. And I need to talk to you."

"I don't need help. Look, I didn't mean to sound so…."

"So mean?"

"Yeah. I didn't mean to sound so mean. I've just got a lot on my plate right now. I'm being sued, I'm trying to do my own work, and I'm trying to do deliveries for a friend who doesn't have his truck. It's just a bad week is all." He paused, relaxed his face, and smiled at her. "I'm actually a very nice guy masquerading as a prick lately."

Caroline shivered, and tucked the hand in the wet glove under the opposite armpit. "I'm really sorry. I—I've been putting this off. I wasn't going to say anything, but…." She used her free hand to raise the scarf over the lower part of her face to so her breath would warm her chin and cheeks.

Her apology both warned and alarmed him. "What? *Are* you getting in on the lawsuit action? Jesus."

"Rid, this has nothing to do with that." A breath, and on the exhale, "I'm pregnant. I haven't completely decided—"

"What?"

"I'm pregnant," she reiterated. "I should have told…."

He took a step backward, shock registering across his features, which stopped her, diverted into watching Rid struggle to process the complete sentence she *had* gotten out. He closed his eyes a moment, shutting his face down. When they opened, he wore a rigid mask of suspicion.

"Rid, listen to me, I'm—"

"And what's to say it's mine?" he interrupted on the offensive, but then flushed and backed up a step.

"I've not been with anyone else, not once, not before, not since, not in years.

You have my word on it." Caroline felt sorry for him then.

"What do you want from me? I'm telling you, I don't have a thing to give you. I mean, I can help pay for an abortion, I guess. I mean, you're having an abortion, aren't you? Why haven't you? That was months ago...." Stammering.

"I planned to get one. I just haven't, I don't know why. I guess I'm thinking about keeping it. Keeping the baby. I don't know what the right thing to do is."

"If you're thinking you can get money from me, you're thinking about blood from stones. Bad, bad time to think about getting money from old Rid. Go right ahead. Slap a goddamn paternity suit on me. Everybody else is suing me. Get in line." His eyes glittered, wet.

"Rid..."

He turned his back and went to his truck, setting the bucket down hard in the bed and closing the tailgate in a hard slam. Another slam of the driver's door, and the truck was moving back onto the beach and the access road, leaving Caroline surrounded by the apparatus of Rid's grant, his undone work, the retreating tide.

Twice. Twice she'd made her way back to the house from Rid's grant rejected. She was on fire with embarrassment, as if the few oystermen at work and the people up on the bluffs and over in the little houses by hers were watching from behind their horizontal blinds and knew exactly what had happened. Caroline walked off the grant, cultch crunching under her boots. She even tried to continue heading on up toward the marshes and Blackfish Creek—the tide was out far enough now that it was possible to get there without climbing up on the rocks—just so her phantom observers would think she had just stopped to chat while out walking, and Rid had hurried off to an appointment. As she did, though, the self-consciousness started to mix with anger, fear, humiliation, sadness and (this was new) protectiveness for the baby. "How dare you!" she said aloud once.

She didn't even make it an eighth of a mile before she turned around. Now she was doused with cold, one hand was wet, her baby's father was a prick, and she was alone in the world and at the decision deadline, if she hadn't passed it already, for a simple procedure. Which was nobody's fault but her own.

Caroline walked well below the tide line, where the sand stayed moist and hard-packed and made for less effort. She was undone so quickly these days, falling asleep sitting up sometimes, blanketed by exhaustion. She'd been keeping her eyes on the sand just ahead of her feet, avoiding clumps of rockweed and some larger stones. Now she raised her gaze to her own house, disheartened by how far away it was, and her utter isolation.

She saw movement. Something or somebody was on the side of her house, under her kitchen window. She couldn't make out a form. Whatever it was looked like the bushes, but she was almost sure she could make out a head in relief against the siding. Immediately her eyes flew to her driveway, checking for a car, but there was none except hers, where it belonged. Maybe she was wrong. But then she saw movement again. *Someone's looking in my window.* She picked up her pace, squeezing her eyes to make out what was there. Frightened, she checked the access road, hoping Rid might still be in the area. Of course he was long gone, and it was a silly thought anyway.

۞

"Elsie? It's me, Caroline. How are you?" Caroline was splayed on the couch after supper that evening. She'd had an organic frozen dinner, spinach lasagna this time, and a green salad with avocado slices and baby tomatoes. She thought she was doing a pretty good job on that score. If she was to keep the baby.

"Caroline, it's good to hear from you! How are you doing?" Elsie's voice sounded a bit tinny and distant, but familiar and warm, like home.

"Oh, loose-ended, I guess. Elsie, I just need somebody to talk to."

"Go right ahead, dear."

The endearment started to undo Caroline. She could almost feel herself regressing. She wanted her mother, she wanted to curl up and cry and be comforted.

"I—I tried to talk to the uh, the father today."

"So you haven't had an abortion."

"No."

"And you've decided not to."

"That's the thing. I haven't decided not to, and I haven't decided to. It's like I've fallen in some hole, and I can't move and I can't even see daylight. Finally today I made myself tell him, you know, just tell him. So I walked out to where he was working."

"Is he one of the oystermen?"

"Not only that, he's one of the one's being sued, Elsie. You remember about that lawsuit?"

"Of course."

"Not that the lawsuit was going on when I got pregnant."

"So how did he take the news?"

"He was terrible. He got mad and stormed off, left me standing out in the water. Just threw stuff in his truck, slammed the door, and peeled out, as much as you can on a beach with sand flying from the back tires. He just *assumed* that what I wanted was money." Indignation was mixing into her tears now.

"What *did* you want?"

"I ... ah ... I don't really know."

"It might have been hard for him to meet your expectations, then."

"Well, I didn't expect him to be a total shit," she defended herself. Now Elsie was letting her down, too. The night looked unrelieved by moon or stars beyond the living room windows, and she was getting cold. She should have closed the blinds before collapsing on the couch. She should have laid a fire, she should have turned on the radio, she should have moved the afghan from the chair back to the couch, she should have made herself a cup of tea. She was so tired of being alone, of having to think of everything.

"I shouldn't have bothered you," she said. "I was just having a bad night. I'll get off the phone now." She wiped her eyes with the bottom of her sweatshirt. When she picked it up it exposed her abdomen. She couldn't button her pants. That had been the case for several weeks, of course. Now, though, even zippers wouldn't reach the top. She was using an oversized pin. She'd have to buy maternity clothes right away. If.

"Hold on, there. I wouldn't be doing my job as your Mom's stand-in if I didn't say some of the hard things, would I? Aren't I sort of your connection to her right now?"

"I hadn't really thought of it that way," Caroline said.

"What would she say?"

"She always wanted me to have a baby," Caroline said. "You remember, right before she died I told her I was pregnant."

"But you don't have to have a baby for your mother. That's not a good reason. What do *you* want? For *you?* She might have had her thoughts about what that would be, but in the end she'd have let you decide."

"Elsie, I'm so scared that something will be wrong with the baby."

"Like what do you mean, wrong?"

"Like maybe that it will be deformed or...." While talking, Caroline shifted from her back, which was starting to ache again, onto her side. As she did, she thought she saw something at the side window. A quick ducking movement, a blur, really, and it vanished. Had it been a face? Like an overturned bug, she struggled for a moment trying to get up. "Hang on a second, Elsie. I'll be right back," she interrupted herself.

In an awkward, rolling stumble, she made her way off the couch and to the window. Nothing. Heart speeding, she went to each window and lowered the blind, letting each drop hard and fast on its sill and hurrying on to the next.

On the way back to the couch she grabbed the afghan and shawled it around her like a cocoon. "I thought someone was looking in my window," she said into the phone.

"Maybe you should call the police." Controlled alarm.

"I thought someone was around my house this afternoon, too. But I've looked outside and I don't see anything."

"Just stay put and stay on the phone. I'll be right back."

Keeping the phone to her ear, Caroline sat upright, scanning the windows and doors. Elsie's alarm heightened her own some, but the crime rate in the area hovered between nothing and practically nothing.

Two minutes later, Elsie's voice came back on the line. "I've called the Wellfleet police on my cell phone, just to come check around your house. You stay on the line with me while they do that. Don't be frightened when they pull into your driveway."

"I feel like an idiot, I'm sure it's all right. I probably just got spooked, you know?"

"Don't feel foolish. It's the safe thing to do. In the meantime, your worry about a deformity? *Every* mother worries about that, but it's very rare. You'll have ultrasound in the fourth or fifth month, too. It's routine now. Are you thinking of adoption or raising it yourself?"

"Raising it myself." The words were scarcely above a whisper, tentative and apologetic. Weren't the sins of parents passed to their children? What would Elsie know about that?

"I think you'd be a wonderful mother," Elsie said warmly. "I'm sure that if you take this on, it means you'll have thought it through and decided you can do it yourself. Do you have the resources?"

Caroline sighed and sank back into the couch. "Thanks to Mom, I do. I mean, ultimately I want to go back to work, but yes, I can do this. That wasn't why I told Rid. I wasn't asking for money."

"What *would* you want from him if you were to keep the baby?"

Caroline sighed. "You know, at one point I really, really liked him or this wouldn't have happened," she said softly. "Maybe I just wanted to know how he felt. If he'd want to be involved. I guess I found out."

"Not necessarily."

"What do you mean?" Tires crunched on the gravel then. "I think the police are here. That was quick! Let me look." Another upturned bug struggle, complicated this time by the afghan. Caroline huddled into herself, chilled as she stood without the blanket. At the kitchen window, she raised the blind she'd lowered moments before. Yes. Red and blue lights flashing on top of a squad car, two flashlights bobbing their way in divergent directions, one toward her porch, one toward Eleanor's studio. "Yes, it's them. Maybe I should call you tomorrow. Thank you so much, Elsie. I'll be all right now."

"Let me know that you're all right."

"Thank you. Thank you so much." This was punctuated by a knock on the porch door, the one facing the beach. Caroline hung up, went to the door, and peered through the glass.

A patrolman was shining a flashlight on his chest, to illuminate his badge and ID. "Police, ma'am. We were called that there might be a prowler here." Caroline opened the door. The outside air was palpable, heavy, and smelled of rain, or maybe snow. A closer look at the officer wasn't reassuring; small statured, fine-boned, complete with acne, he could have passed for fourteen. She wanted to ask if his mommy knew he was out playing with cars and guns.

"I thought I saw someone looking in that window," she said instead. Best to just let him look around and go away. She gestured to the unkempt side of the house to the right of the drive, where beach plums and wild roses were high, thick and unruly. There was ground pine, too, all surrounded by the taller woods. "This afternoon I was out for a walk on the beach, and on my way back, I thought I saw someone in the yard." Now she gestured to the opposite side of the house, left of the driveway, the side that looked toward the grants, where land sloped lower and the beach was visible. "I just don't know. It could be nothing," she added apologetically.

"So that's two different times you thought you saw someone?"

"Yes."

"Male or female."

"I don't really know. I wasn't close enough this afternoon, and tonight I wasn't even sure I saw anything. It was like a flash of motion at the window that could have been a face ducking down."

The other policeman stomped his way up onto the porch then, following the beam of his light. He looked older, like a bulldog, with heavy jowls and a neck that merged into his shoulders way too soon. He took off his hat, which the kiddie-cop hadn't. Nodding to her in an old-school respectful manner that made her feel ancient, he said, "Evening, ma'am. We're investigating the prowler. Have you seen anything since the call was made?"

"No, nothing. I really wasn't sure."

"She saw someone around the house this afternoon, too," the kiddie-cop interrupted.

"Anyone you recognize?" Bulldog asked.

"No. No."

"We'll walk the perimeter again, and check back during the night, ma'am. So if you hear our car outside, don't be afraid. We'll keep an eye out for you," said the fourteen-year-old. "Now don't hesitate to call again if you hear or see anything."

"I appreciate that. Thank you both." Caroline felt as if she were in a low-budget movie, that they were all reading poorly written lines. She'd over-reacted and created this ridiculous scene, the same as going to the doctor and having no symptoms once you got onto the table in the one-ply paper gown.

After the police were gone, Caroline suddenly thought to throw on the yard lights between the house and studio. She'd forgotten they were there. The porch light could stay on overnight, too. Tomorrow night before dark, she'd put on the light over the studio door. Eleanor used to work at night sometimes, so the whole studio could be lit up, which would make it awfully hard for anyone to be in the yard or driveway unseen. The only approaches were from the beach or the road. One side was impenetrable right up to the house with wild beach vegetation, and on the other side, beyond the cut-out yard it was largely the same.

She called Elsie back to tell her that no one had been in the yard, but that the police were watching just the same. The microwave beeped, and juggling the phone to her left hand, she dropped a bag of decaffeinated green tea in a mug. She should have milk, she thought. But she shouldn't have any trouble sleeping, she was so tired. So terribly tired.

"I'm relieved to hear from you," Elsie said. "I was going to wait another half-hour and call you just to check. And will you let me know how I can help, about the baby, I mean? Do you need a doctor?"

"One way or the other, yes. But I think what I mean is yes, I need a doctor. If you know what I mean." She gave a small half-laugh. "God, I hope you do, because I sure don't." Carrying her mug of tea, Caroline made her way back toward the bedroom. She'd been sleeping downstairs lately, in her mother's bed. The goose down pillows and Eleanor's quilt comforted her.

"I believe I do. I'm sure I can get a referral."

"I'm, well, I'm sort of old." She hated saying this. "I'm going to be forty-one when it's born. He or she, I mean."

It was obvious she'd not thought Caroline was that age, or so Caroline interpreted the seconds of silence on the phone line before Elsie answered, "Let me see what I can do. For the time being, take two multivitamins a day, and get lots of extra calcium." Still and ever the nurse, Caroline thought with a smile.

"Thank you so much, Elsie. Good night now."

Elsie said, "Good night, dear," and then something strange happened. Caroline was pulling back the multi-colored quilt on her mother's bed just as she started to say *Hold on a minute* because she wanted to tell Elsie that she'd like a woman doctor in any event, but Elsie had already hung up. The line had a hollow, open sound and Caroline hesitated. Then, distinctly, there was another click.

 *Chapter 16*

For once, Rid didn't care about the shock absorbers. He let the truck slam-bam-bang off the beach and onto the potholed access road, his foot angry on the gas. Anything to get away from Caroline and whatever it was she wanted from him because whatever it was he wouldn't give it to her. Couldn't. Didn't have it.

He hit the steering wheel once with his fist. In the passenger seat, Lizzie anxiously darted in to lick his neck. Absently, he caressed her ears. "It's all right, girl," he muttered. "I'm not mad at you. Not at you." As he drove, tears argued with anger. Or were because of it. He hated how he'd acted. She brought out the worst in him.

In his weedy gravel driveway, another round of door slamming with a side order of foot stomping. That he couldn't afford to lose this tide was a true fact. Just a damn true fact. He had a fat order to fill for Big Al and John who were catering a ninetieth birthday party for their father and wanted everything over-the-top perfect. His plan had been to use the first half of the tide to pick that order, which was for an extravagant twelve dozen oysters, and then to keep pulling out his stock to bury for the winter. He still had a fair number of hats and racks to get out, which was what happened when you stretched the season like tourist taffy, trying to eke out every penny. He could pick legally as long as there wasn't ice, and he had to raise cash. Yet he couldn't risk stock by leaving it in too long, either. This month was going to be tricky.

He was not going to think about what CiCi'd said, and certainly not about whether the baby was a boy or a girl or how she suddenly knew so much about aquaculture. He was going to figure out how to fill that damn order. If the weather held, he could pull more stock tomorrow and the day after. Right now, though, he had to pick and he didn't have a lot of time. Rid glanced at his watch. Shit. Only twenty minutes until the tide would turn. He had plenty of legal size on his own grant, but she could be still be there, like a mine in the harbor.

More than one way to skin a cat. Back in the truck, relieved to have come up with a Plan B that would give him a shot at filling the order without running into CiCi again: Mario was picking in the wild at Lieutenant Island and Rid stomped on the gas and headed that direction. Mario's laissez-faire practice of not buttoning down for the winter gave him more time to turn a profit, that was for sure. There'd been a problem more than once with his apparatus getting loose in a blow and doing damage. As it was, Rid knew there'd been words between Mario and Bogsie, whose grant was on Mario's west side. There'd been words between Mario and a lot of people. Mario liked his beer better than he liked diplomacy, but he sure had a nose for dollars. He cut corners, did things like pick in the wild every chance he got rather than using his own stock to fill orders, then motor across the bay on a skiff and hastily work his own grant on the back side of a tide. No part of his grant was as well tended as any parts of theirs, but somehow every time he seemed to come out ahead. About the only time Rid had seen him come up short was when he lost his truck, and knowing Mario, he was playing the insurance game to the hilt. Meanwhile, Rid and Tomas were playing chauffeur and making his deliveries while Mario nursed his mood.

Now Rid sped down Route 6. Lizzie pulled her head in from the window when he told her to and he raised it. He thought again about CiCi and shook his head in reflexive refusal. "Can't think about that now," he said out loud, and switched the radio on to a hard rock station.

❧

He saw Mario. It would piss him off that Rid would fish the same place, but Rid knew—everybody did—that Mario had a knack for finding wild shellfish, like a built-in divining rod. Normally he was secretive about where he went, but he'd had to tell Rid where he was having Tomas drop him; how else could Rid pick him up? It must be killing Mario for the two of them to know. Hell, it served him right. Tomas had needed his truck that morning, or Mario would have used it. Just another day or two and there'd be at least a rental. The problem was using it commercially, and on the flats. That was proving complicated to work out.

Lieutenant's Island, south of Blackfish Creek, was deserted as usual, especially this time of year. Part of it was an Audubon Society bird sanctuary. Its shallows had had cultch refreshed right about three years ago. Rid had forgotten all about it to his irritation now. Probably most everyone had. Mario was right on, realizing that oysters there would be reaching legal size.

Now from a distance, Mario looked like some overdressed snowman with his waders and waterproof sleeves over a heavy jacket. The wind must have picked up and it must be cold as a witch's tit, too, because he had a hood up over his hat. Mario was bent from the waist, hands flying, hardly stopping at all to inspect for size or whether an oyster was good. He knew by feel. They all did. He already had two crates filled, a very good sign. No one else was around, also good.

Rid put the truck in gear. When he got out, he avoided slamming the door. Mario hadn't looked up yet. He pulled two plastic milk crates from the truck bed, gave a sigh as heavy as Lizzie ever did, and headed in Mario's vicinity.

Mario sensed his approach. His head swung in an exaggerated slow motion, encumbered by clothing. He straightened, his body all annoyance, or maybe Rid was just reading that into his stance. Mario crossed the flat to Rid, his feet crunching cultch lying atop the wet sand as he did.

"What're you doin' here?" Mario demanded, squinting as if there were sunlight.

"Got an order to fill, had to pick you up anyway." Defensive, and for no good reason. He had nothing to be ashamed of. Rid didn't look at him, but put down the crates and made a show of scanning the area.

"I thought you were buttoning your grant." The smallest whiff of sarcasm in Mario's voice.

Rid was suddenly too tired to dissemble. "Look, man. There's a chick, she was waiting for me on the grant, wanting to talk and all, and I can't deal right now. If I stayed—so anyway, I'll pull my stuff out the next couple of tides, whatever. Got an order to fill now and figured I could pick that here. But I gotta move or it'll be too late. Tide's turned."

This was something Mario understood, trouble with a woman. "Shit, man. Pick what you can. If you're short, you can take what you need outta there."

"Thanks. What deliveries you got for me?" Rid was making them, while Mario dickered with the insurance agent.

"Down to Chatham, like I told you yesterday."

"Christ," Rid muttered, though he *had* known it. Also that it would kill the afternoon. "What's Tomas doing?" A sweep of offshore wind carried dry sand from the dunes, and Rid automatically turned his back to the land to protect his face, exposed and vulnerable as jellyfish at the same moment Mario did the identical dance of experience.

"Man, I have no truck. You *said*. Look, never mind, I'll get Bogsie or Tweed to—"

"No," Rid cut him off. "It's cool. We three, we handle this together, remember. I got your back. Chatham it is." He forced a jocular tone and smile. The three men harbored enough anger between them to fill their two working truck beds, Mario's ruined one, and probably the whole goddamn bay. For no good reason. They weren't really mad at each other.

Night sealed the town like a dome, starless, moonless, complete, and Rid slouched at the bar in the Reading Oyster, putting away beer and nursing a burger and fries when it should have been the other way around. Tomas had Marie and the kids to get home to, as he was always reminding Rid. But Rid really couldn't grouse since Tomas had talked his wife into having Mario for dinner. Rid was supposed to go over later for the three to go over lawsuit finances. Really, of course, it was a pretext to babysit Mario or he'd be in here drinking alongside Rid, a dangerous picture.

Across from Rid, Billy wiped the bar up to the spot Rid occupied and picked up on the other side. "Another one?" he asked, an afterthought. The rafters above their heads were low, dark wood and between them were the racks from which glasses hung, gleaming in the low light. Billy wore dangle earrings in both ears tonight, which Rid thought was over the top. He considered starting something about it, but postponed a decision when a stranger he'd not heard come in quietly took the stool next to his. The proximity felt intrusive with the rest of the bar empty.

"Yeah, gimme another one," Rid said, at the same time he openly looked at the man next to him who was definitely not a fisherman. No fisherman would be caught dead or alive in that get-up. Had the country declared war while he'd been down in Chatham?

"Hey," the stranger said, nodding to Rid.

"Yeah," Rid answered, with an obvious scan of his boots and fatigues, on up to his head, which was shaved. "You, uh, stationed around here?"

"You might say that."

The man's face was a moon with a nose that appeared to have been flattened by contact with, say, a steel door. Rid tried to figure out what breed of dog he was reminded of: boxer? No, bulldog, maybe. Or shih tzu. A normal enough face until it got squashed like that.

There weren't any military bases nearby. "Like where?"

"I'm not at liberty to divulge that."

Rid snickered. "Oh, yeah, some kinda secret mission, huh? A Green Beret? Or I guess you must be a SEAL, just swum up off the sub."

"Perhaps. Your name is Ridley Neal and I'm here to speak with you."

Instantly cold water sober. "Who are you?"

"You don't need my name. All you need to know I'm about to tell you." He was wide-shouldered, big-thighed, the body of a high-school football player ten or fifteen years since the last down.

Billy edged toward them and Moonface glared at him. "I'll take a draft and privacy," he said and waited while Billy, sullen, drew the beer and put it in front of him. The bartender checked the near-empty room and lacking an excuse, disappeared through the swinging kitchen doors.

"You got a problem, I'm gonna help you with it."

Rid guessed the man was somehow connected to Pissario, maybe here to try to scare him off his grant. Curiosity fought with irritation and lost. "First off, I don't have a problem, and if I did, I wouldn't ask you for help. Everything's under control, thank you very much. That's my grant and I'm stayin' on it. You can tell your boss to fuck a duck." Almost as he said the words, Rid knew he'd gone too far. Pissario wasn't supposed to get any whiff that they weren't retreating.

But the man just shrugged. "You have no idea what you're talking about, and you're receiving my help purely as a byproduct. Helping you isn't my goal, I assure you. But since you'll get it anyway, I want something in return."

Rid studied the man next to him more closely, making no attempt to hide what he was doing. Now he wished he'd contradicted the stranger and told Billy to stay in the room. Maybe he could manage to call the cops. None of them had figured Pissario for this kind of crap, but there was no other explanation.

"Why don't you be straight? What do you want?" He tried to keep his voice even.

The man's mouth hardly moved with his humorless laugh. "Well, I'd certainly be the only straight thing out here. Look. You got a big problem that's also a problem for someone else. I'm taking care of it for the someone else. You'll benefit. Here's what I want from you: I'm giving you a name and address. She needs help, you make sure she gets it. On the *QT*. You just watch out for her from a distance. Drive past her place every now and then, make sure everything's all right. If it's not, you pay cash, send someone to go fix it. No names. Long-term requirement. Simple as that. Here's the name and address, all wrote out nice and clear." He slid a small piece of pocket notebook paper across the bar to the top of Rid's plate.

Rid thought maybe he'd had too much to drink. He felt his mouth open in surprise. "What?"

"What don't you get?"

"You're doing what?" Anything to slow this down, give himself time to figure it out. The paper remained on the bar. No way he was going to pick it up.

"Me? I'm taking care of your *problem*." The man put quotation marks in the air around the word.

"Huh? How? Who the hell are you?"

"You're on the slow side, know that? You ain't gonna be makin' no monthly payments. Okay? Your part's small potatoes compared to that."

The scene had taken on a surreal quality. Later, that was Rid's only explanation to himself, that he was over the edge of drunkenness and a weird stranger with a pushed-in face dressed like a cartoon—*dressed like a cartoon!* he kept saying to himself—had come into Rid's everyday place and said things so bizarre he couldn't conjure up the right reaction. At the time, Rid had started to say "What're you—what do you mean?" as if he really were slow-witted. For God's sake, was he being threatened? Monthly payments?

The man had downed his beer then and swiveled his barstool toward the door. "*You stay outta the way, y'hear?* There's the name and address. I expect you'll do your part. Y'hear? I'll figure it out if you don't." And the moon face had loomed over Rid as he stood and picked up piece of pocket notebook paper, folded and shoved it in Rid's shirt pocket. He resettled his belt, and walked out the door with Rid staring after him. On the way out, he lifted a jacket from the hooks by the door in an unhurried motion, without breaking stride. There was something bulky in his hip pocket. Did anyone carry a pistol in a pocket? Rid shook his head and blinked, his mind unable to work fast enough.

"Wait a minute," he called, a good ten seconds after the restaurant door had opened and closed. He got up, tripping himself, and stumbled in a lurching run for the door. The air was heavy, wet and black, fuzzy around the lights of the marina. Few cars were in the lot. One set of tail lights took the sharp curve in the road that headed back up into the village. A truck pulled out of the lot across the street and headed the other way, toward Great Island. Rid ran ten yards, squinting, trying to focus on the license plate. He thought he had it. Was that a M or an N, MI 1 B, was that it? Or MIL 8? Massachusetts plates, for sure. But he didn't even know if that was the right vehicle, though the truck wasn't immediately familiar, as the fishermen's were. Decals in the back windows, but he couldn't read them, and didn't even know for sure what color the body was. It could have been dark anything. Not too new, not too old, a Ford. Across the road, the shellfish warden's shack was scarcely outlined. Behind it, the sea was one shade one more black, unfathomable, deceptively quiet tonight.

He hadn't even gone back inside to settle his tab. Billy would be pissed off, but he'd also know that Rid would make it right tomorrow and he'd get over it. In dank December cold, Rid stood staring after the truck, repeating aloud— twice—what he'd thought he'd seen on the license plate, hurrying to his truck to write it down on a paper coffee cup he scrounged off the floor. He'd never even gone back to pick up his jacket, just left it in bar, a couple of hooks down from where the stranger had been.

He'd gunned his truck engine to life; he had to *do* something, but then couldn't think what. He got to second gear following the truck that had gone toward Great Island, but stopped before he got up the hill. Was it a pistol? Maybe just a cell phone. How'd the guy know his name? Rid's mind raced to every dead-end of a maze.

Finally, he'd driven to Tomas' house, a small Cape Cod, similar to his own, except that Tomas' was smothered in Christmas lights and wreaths. Marie must have hit a K-Mart going-out-of-business sale.

The pavement was getting slick, and so were the stones from Tomas' driveway to the front door. The fog was turning crystalline, like so much spilled skim milk. Rid stood on the front step, shoulders hunched up around his neck, pocketed hands drawn up tight against his body, a good minute before knocking trying to compose himself. He hadn't decided whether to tell them.

Marie swung the door open just as his knuckles were moving for the second knock. She stepped back to avoid being hit in the face.

"Hey, Rid. I see you've already had a few and you're even early! It's okay, though, we're just finishing up. Mario's here." Tomas' wife had put on weight since they were married, but she clung to her high-school style, which had been considered pretty. Rid found her intimidating. Now she wore a bright red sweater with a reindeer emblazoned on the front, and her earrings were little blinking Christmas lights hooded by long brunette hair.

"I know," Rid said after a moment, disoriented by the earrings.

"You look like a deer caught in the headlights," she said merrily. "If you drink any more, I'm taking your keys. The guys're down in the basement."

"I better not." Then, needing it, "well, yeah, a beer, thanks." He put his truck keys into her outstretched hand.

"Hold up, you can carry it down yourself. I'm not wearing my little white apron just now." She went into the kitchen while Rid stood at the top of the basement stairs. He heard the refrigerator door open and close, the sound of a church key on a beer, and Marie reappeared with a brown bottle.

"Thanks," he muttered, brushing the wall with his hip as he walked.

"You okay?" she asked. This was more solicitude from Marie that he'd had in the past five years. She didn't appreciate it when Tomas went out for a beer, not that he ever stayed all that long. Rid wished her eyes weren't so narrow, close together. She always looked like she was accusing him of something, no matter what her tone.

"Yeah."

Marie reached around him and flicked on the light illuminating the basement stairs. "Watch your step."

"That you, Rid?" It was Tomas calling from downstairs, in the rec room Tomas had finished himself in knotty pine. It made Rid dizzy.

"Coming."

At first he hadn't said anything, mainly because Mario was there and he couldn't sort out if it would be a mistake. Then, because the two of them kept asking him what was wrong and because he had another beer after the first one Marie had given him, he tried to describe what had happened, taking pains to be exact.

"No shit," Mario said. "I say we go blow up Pissario's fuckin' house once and for all."

"Knock it off," Tomas said, his parental voice. "Settle down. Think about it. You don't carry a pistol in your hip pocket unless you want to blow your own nuts off. What's this thing about monthly payments? What's this about? Where's the paper he put in your pocket? What's it say?"

"Dunno." Rid said.

"Is this about that chick at your grant?" Mario said. "You got her in trouble? She Pissario's daughter or something?" His voice was an accusation.

"What?" Tomas demanded. "Who?" He slid forward, moving his beer aside, as if it were blocking his view of Rid. As always, Tomas was stone sober. Rid knew he himself was sheets to the wind, speaking too deliberately if anything, trying to hide it.

"What's Mario talking about?" Tomas demanded again. His curly hair and beard—gray starting to mix in—needed cutting; he looked like some sort of wild mountain man, especially backlit as he was by an old floor lamp Marie had stuck by the kids' foosball game.

Rid put his face in his hands, leaning forward and resting his elbows on his knees. He'd only meant to take a moment to put some words in coherent order, but his partners leapt to another conclusion.

"Man, you sold us out!" Mario shouted. On his feet, of course. The bozo hadn't an ounce of patience. History counted for nothing with him.

Annoyed, defensive, apologetic. His mind was a mixed drink. "No way. No way. I didn't know she had anything to do with Pissario. I slept with her once, way before the lawsuit, back in September. Never saw her after that. She just told me she's pregnant. That's the whole story. That's the chick that was waiting for me on the grant the other day, Mario. She's from over on the horseshoe beach, not up on the bluffs, but she owns property. That's all I know."

Tomas' voice was a blade. "Let me see the paper in your shirt pocket."

Rid pulled it out and handed it to Tomas still folded.

Tomas read it. "Is Terry DiPaulo the one you've knocked up? On Bradford Street in P-town?"

Rid's face probably answered before his word did. "Huh?" Even Mario dropped back down into his chair, but Rid was too far gone to take much satisfaction in it.

"Terry DiPaulo. Is that her?"

"Never heard of her."

"Well, that's the name and address written here. The one he said you're supposed to 'look out for.' Goddammit, Rid, sober up. What did this guy say?" Tomas got up and went to the foot of the stairs, calling up. "Marie! Put on a pot of coffee, will you, honey? Make it strong." He came back and paused at

Rid's chair, a beaten-up wicker piece, before continuing back to his place back on the threadbare tan couch, speaking to him the way he occasionally would to Mario or one of his children. "Rid. What *exactly* did he say?"

Rid tried to look around Tomas to the motley collection of posters, school pictures, and plaques lined up like uneven teeth on the wall behind him. Tomas stepped to the side to block his gaze. "Rid! Pay attention!"

A deep sigh. Oh God! Lizzie! He hadn't fed her, he hadn't gone home to feed her or let her out. He'd meant to go get her, and then been so upset he'd just come straight here. "My dog. I've gotta go. I can't do this now. I forgot. She hasn't been out in—"

"You're not going anywhere."

"No, you don't understand. She's been in too long, I can't." Rid flashed back to the last time he'd done this, the night he'd spent with CiCi when this disaster was set in motion. He was humiliated by the memory and by the tears that came into his eyes.

"Rid, you can't drive. Look...." Tomas' voice eased off. "Give me your keys."

"Marie already took 'em. I gotta get outta...." He started to stand, wobbled, and Tomas put a hand on his shoulder pushing him back down into the chair but not unkindly. Opposite him, on the couch, Mario muttered something under his breath.

"I'll take care of it," Tomas said, already lumbering up the stairs. Rid sat, faintly nauseated, his head developing a pain on the top and back.

The paper with Terry DiPaulo's name lay on the nondescript coffee table, partly retaining its folds, like a white flower just ready to bloom or release its toxin.

Mario, for once, said nothing for a few minutes, then, "Look, man, sorry for what I said."

"S'all right."

Tomas reappeared with two mugs and a pot of coffee. "Marie's gone to your house to get Lizzie."

"Food?"

"She can have some of Copper's." Copper was Tomas' beagle, an obese little barker the family doted on.

"Thanks."

Tomas set a mug in front of Rid and Mario, each with a dull thud. He filled them with coffee and set the pot on a magazine. He picked up their half-consumed beers and set the bottles up on the window ledge, a clear message.

Mario started to object, wanting his, and Tomas silenced him with a raised hand.

"Okay, Rid. Have some coffee. What does this Terry DiPaulo have to do with Pissario?"

"I don't know what anything has to do with anything. I'm telling you, none of it makes any sense to me. I've never heard of that woman. The one who's in trouble is a girl I knew in high school—named CiCi Marcum. Caroline. She didn't even talk to me then, for God's sake. She does have a house on the horseshoe beach like I said. Lorenz said the landowners might get together. Maybe...."

"That doesn't explain the Terry DiPaulo thing." Tomas said.

"Hold up! I got it. This Caroline chick is offering to trade. No support payments if we back off the lawsuit. Drop our opposition! The bitch is with Pissario." Mario weighed in, excited, tangling words in his hurry to show that he'd figured it out.

"That ... might make some sense," Tomas said slowly, eyes half closed as he thought it through, one big hand on each thigh as he leaned back in his chair, "for your part, I guess. That you'd give up and get out." He sat forward again. "Doesn't really put any leverage on *us*."

"Maybe it's divide and conquer," Rid offered weakly.

"Or he's got some other goons with plans for us. Just haven't shown up yet. Bastard," Mario spit the word. He was agitated, his face reddening as it had since grade school when he wanted to fight. His eyes glowed red-black, as if caught by a camera's flash, a combination of the strange lighting in the room and his excitement. Rid's own eyes were burning and irritated, as if the room were dense, although only Mario was smoking. That was why they were downstairs. Marie's rule. Rid wanted to lie down. He laid his head back against the top of the chair, dared to close his eyes.

Upstairs there was a cacophony of barking and a scrabble of feet. The basement door opened and Lizzie took the stairs in a series of implausible leaps. Rid almost couldn't grasp that she was there before she was on top of him, knocking him backward, the comfort and familiarity of her long-tongued kisses, wide, hard tail swings that would have cleared the table of beer bottles had Tomas not already done so. Copper followed in his waddling run, baying.

"Oh man, here's a headache announcement," Mario said irritably, plugging his ears. Rid leaned forward and let Lizzie wash his face, his hands caressing and scratching behind her silky earflaps as she did, their ritual of mutual affection.

"Okay, okay. Copper, shut up. Rid, you've got to focus. Both of you. We have to figure this out, you hear?" More than anything else, the desperation that crimped the edge of Tomas' voice frightened Rid. Tomas, smart, educated Tomas who never lost control. It wasn't what he was saying. It was how he was sounding, just like Rid himself. Like he had no idea what to do.

 *Chapter 17*

The third time she called them in two weeks, the police took thirteen minutes to get to Caroline's house. They called her "ma'am," and the younger one pointed out that she likely was mistaken as the windows were hard to see through just now. They looked like throwbacks to summer, trellised with blowzy white roses of salt and ice. "Maybe even it was a deer. They won't hurt you," he'd patronized, infuriating her. The older one rolled his eyes and adjusted the brim of his cap. "We'll be taking off now," the young one finished, adding, "just call us if you see anything else and we'll swing by." They were starting to act like she was a charity case: pathetic, alone, hormone-driven to lunacy and someone they simply had to humor as a part of their regular rounds.

"I *know* deer won't hurt me," she'd said sharply. "*People* hurt *deer*, though. They track them, and then they put them in the crosshairs of guns and pull triggers." She sounded hysterical, even to her own ears. *Shut up, just shut up* she said to herself. *You're making it worse.* "All right. Thank you for coming by."

The older one, a five o'clock shadow extending to eight o'clock now, and puffy bags under his eyes that made him look hung over, took mercy. "Ma'am, we'll keep an eye out, you know. Patrol. We'll cruise the area."

Was he mocking her? "Thank you." She kept her tone neutral in case he wasn't. The porch and yard lights were on, as was the light over Eleanor's studio door. She knew—or thought she knew—that someone was stalking her, if stalking was the right word, but the police never arrived in time. There were noises on her telephone line as if someone were listening, thumps against the side of her house, footsteps on the porch. Someone ran up her driveway, she was sure of it, but the police asked if it might have been a neighbor, and it could have been, how would she know it wasn't? One morning, someone had scrawled something on the windshield of her car in the frost, but by the time she got out there, the sun had melted enough of it that she couldn't read the words.

The police didn't come for over a half hour. By then, there were only circles of clear glass with long wet droplets running from them like tears down cheeks. "Shoulda moved it into the shade," a cop she'd not seen before said. He looked to be in his late twenties. Were they all babies? Caroline could tell he was disappointed. Maybe he'd hoped to find her dead next to the car, his chance to break a big case and make a name for himself.

"You said you'd be right here," she snapped, "and not to touch anything." She must look like a wild woman, she realized, brushing her hair back off her face, on which she'd put no makeup. She wore a makeshift, mismatched, uneven maternity getup topped by a field coat of her father's, and her mother's boots because the driveway was a mess of mud and slush where the gravel was too sparse. She really needed to have a load delivered in the spring. A lot needed doing. Not that she was doing much herself right now. She had a hard time keeping her thoughts in a straight line these days. She was terrified, dead tired from paranoid wakefulness, and didn't recognize her own body. Just yesterday, a clear liquid had leaked from her breasts and she'd panicked until she remembered she'd read something about that.

I am losing my mind, she told her mother after the detective left and she drank a cup of tea at the kitchen table. The sun that had made a fool of her, erasing evidence while she cowered in the house, streamed benignly through the kitchen window onto the dishes in the sink, hardening egg yolk remains to an impenetrable crust. She was making herself eat well, but cleaning up after it, *not so much* as her mother used to say.

"I know it," she said aloud, answering Eleanor as she often did. Just then her mother had told her, *You can't go on like this, CiCi.* To get through Christmas— where she had to make an appearance at both Noelle's and Sharon's, neither of whom would hear of her being home alone, was going to require a major pull-together effort.

Elsie. She'd call Elsie, even though it was embarrassing to seem so crazy, so out of control. Even the police didn't believe her any more.

Just Elsie's voice seemed to stitch Caroline back together. "Sure, I can meet for dinner," she said. "I'm in Orleans today, though. It would be late before I could get up there."

Caroline hesitated, considering the earliness and totality of nightfall as it would surround her house. The winter solstice was tomorrow. "I'll come down there. I'd just as soon get out of Wellfleet. Would you be done by five if I come down there?"

"Should be. We could go to The Seascape."

"I know where it is. Sounds fine to me. I'll be there at five, and if you're running late, don't think a thing about it, I'll just wait. I know how these things go. I remember how often Mom and I made you late!"

"I'll try to be on time, dear. See you later. I'm glad you called."

Caroline didn't even replace the phone on the wall. She immediately called Noelle. "I was wondering if I could stay in your guest room tonight? I'm … uh … spraying for ants and I don't want to breathe the fumes."

"Goodness, this time of year? Well, I'll send Walter over. You know, the man can take care of anything."

"It's not necessary, really! I promise. It's not a big deal. It's my fault. I left food out."

"You know you always have a place here." Her mother's friends had been reliable as calendars, unswerving in their loyalty. She'd not confided in them, not about the pregnancy, the stalking, or harassment. They'd either think she was in danger or, like the police, that she had an overactive imagination. She couldn't bear to be the object of pity, although when she looked in the mirror she saw that she *was* pitiful, bedraggled as a flower dropping its petals.

Help me, Mom, she whispered. *Help me.*

Ninety minutes later, she'd showered and washed her hair, changed into the best-fitting outfit she could muster—black elastic-waist pants meant for a Yoga class, a kelly green sweater of Eleanor's over a white blouse, both tops loose over her hips. In the neckline, a wide gold chain, also her mother's. *Okay, okay, okay,* she said to her reflection. *Makeup. You can do it.* Foundation, blusher, eyeliner, mascara.

Better. She definitely looked better. Encouraged, she finished blowing her hair dry. Yes.

Good. Keep going. Was it her own voice or her mother's in her head? It didn't matter. She liked to think it was her mother. *Find a decent looking coat. No, not the old goose down jacket, and definitely not your father's barn coat. Yes, try*

that one. Good, that'll work. No. Not those. Put on the low-heeled black dress boots.
They keep the streets and sidewalks clear in Orleans. Much better. You really need to
unpack your own winter things, you know. And buy some maternity clothes.

A last check in the full-length mirror in the downstairs bedroom, once her mother's, now hers, opening the cape-like coat to check the outfit again. She straightened her shoulders, and poked at her hair a bit. She tried on a smile and it looked real. A canvas bag holding pajamas, toothbrush, toothpaste, hairbrush, clean underpants, enough to get by overnight at Noelle's, was on her bed along with her purse. She fished out car keys and draped the straps of both bags over her shoulder.

Ready? Ready. No more of this shit. Time to take hold, you hear? I hear. Caroline smiled for the second time. It must be her mother. She knew her by the swearing.

Elsie wasn't more than ten minutes late, but Caroline had been twenty minutes early to Orleans, so it seemed a long wait. She'd nursed a pot of tea while wishing for a glass of wine, and kept putting off the hovering waitress who obviously thought Caroline had been stood up on a date. "My friend is coming, I'm sure," Caroline said. "But I'll look at the menu. I'm fine, really."

Elsie came in with a sweep of dank night air. Dark had completed itself while Caroline waited. She waved from the corner table, seeing Elsie scan the near-empty restaurant for her in the low light.

"You look a lot better than the last time I saw you," Elsie said, appraising her frankly even as she was settling in the seat opposite Caroline. "How are you feeling?"

Caroline sighed. "I've been going out of my mind to be honest. Insane. That's why I called you. I just thought if I could talk out loud to a normal person about what to do, it would help. Not that I can't go to my mother's friends—I can, but they'd freak out." Caroline smiled. "On my mother's behalf. I've got to sort things out, you know? I need a listener." Why was it so reassuring, Caroline wondered, that Elsie's clothing was utilitarian, a navy blue pants suit today, with fur-trimmed snow boots. Her straight brown bob bore the marks of the hat she'd worn. Caroline had never seen her with make-up.

"I'm glad you felt you could call."

After they both gave their dinner orders, Elsie arched her eyebrows at

Caroline, a silent invitation to talk.

"I've been floundering, and I realize I can't do that anymore," Caroline said.

"Have you made *any* firm decisions?" Elsie unfolded her napkin and opened a package of saltines.

"Yes, I have. I think I've decided." Caroline laughed. "Sort of an oxymoron, isn't it, to say you've made a firm decision and then start the sentence with 'I think I've decided.' Okay. I've decided I'm having the baby and I'm keeping it. Her. Or him. To raise myself. That's as far as I'd gotten for sure. Then I got derailed by this stalking or harassing or whatever is going on. I'm terrified, Elsie, but nothing has actually happened, you know? I don't know if it's some kid, or what. But I do see that I can't go on like this. I called Mom's friend Noelle and asked if I could stay there tonight."

"Did you tell her why?"

"No. I lied. I told her I'd sprayed for ants and didn't want to breathe the fumes."

"But you did tell her you're pregnant?"

Caroline winced. "Not so much."

"How about telling her at all?"

This time she covered her face and spoke from behind her hands. "Not so much at all."

"Hmm. So these people, your mother's friends, are your only local support system and you haven't told them anything."

"That would be about right. Well, I sort of have another friend, at the library. But that's a really complicated situation and I can't really count her."

"Why not?

"It's too much to go into."

Elsie searched Caroline's face and evidently decided not to pursue it. "You need some people around you now," is all she said. "And I think you need to deal proactively with whatever is happening, trust your instincts. If you feel like there's danger, there probably is. What do the police say?"

"They come, I haven't been dead when they've gotten there, they haven't found a crime going on. I think they have me pegged as a crazy lady, and they only come because they have to. But I think someone's been on my phone line for weeks now, and I think someone's been in my yard and I don't know what he—or they—want." As Caroline ate her chowder, she told Elsie the details of the obscured writing on the windshield of her car. "Maybe I've made it worse for myself. You know, looking a wild wreck when the police come. I finally cleaned myself up to come here tonight. Elsie, it was like I could hear Mom talking to me. Do you think that's nuts?" Caroline's titter was small and nervous.

Elsie reached across the table and took her hand. "You are not crazy, Caroline. Can you think of *anyone*, anyone who might have a problem with you, who might want to hurt you? Or want you to leave town?"

Caroline paused. "I hardly know anyone anymore. Everybody loved Mom. I grew up here, but...." Elsie didn't know about the accident, and Caroline hesitated. How could this be connected? She wasn't even using the same name. She didn't look the same. "The baby's father might not want me around, and it seemed like this started the same day I told him. But too fast. I even thought I saw someone in the yard when I was walking back after I told him."

"Could you have been wrong that first time and right about the times since then?"

Another pause. "I don't know. I guess."

Elsie pointed to Caroline's chowder. "Your chowder's getting cold."

Obediently, Caroline took a spoonful. The chowder clams were tender, dense in the soup. "I wonder if Rid supplies this restaurant," she mused. "I think he makes deliveries down here."

"I take it Rid is his name?"

"Maybe he wouldn't like my telling you. His name's actually Ridley. I went to high school with him."

"But you think he might be capable of trying to run you out of town? He reacted that badly?"

"He got pretty upset. He thought I wanted money, I think."

"But you don't."

"No."

"What *do* you want?"

Caroline played with her soup spoon, took another small bite to stall for time. She wiped her mouth and looked around the restaurant. Real fishnets, wooden buoys, lobster traps, wooden plank floors, votives on the tables.

"Rather avoid that one, huh," Elsie persisted quietly.

Caroline rolled her eyes. "I suppose I would. I really don't know what I want. Maybe I thought he'd want to be part of the baby's life. I don't know. I guess I just thought it was the right thing to do, to tell him."

"Could your baby's father be trying to scare you into leaving him alone about the baby?"

"He did say something about the lawsuit, about was I suing him too? You know, he's being sued by those people up on the bluffs. Do you think maybe the sea farmers are doing things like this to all the people with land on the waterfront? You know, to strike back? Maybe it's all about that?"

"But you're not?"

"Good grief, no. My grandfather was a fisherman, my parents worked here. I've been reading about aquaculture, too, just, well, because I'm here. Anyway, I'd never."

Elsie put her spoon down. She leaned forward. "Have you spoken with any of your neighbors? Is it possible that they're being harassed too?"

Caroline turned the idea around. Her shoulders raised, and her brows arched at the same time. "You know, I really have no idea. I haven't talked with them. It's so obvious. But, surely the police have. I mean, the police would have told me if there had been other complaints in the area, wouldn't they? Elsie, they're treating me as if I'm the local crazy lady they have to humor."

Caroline could see Elsie think it over, noticed she had circles under her eyes. Were they darker than usual or was it the lighting? It was the end of Elsie's workday, and she was keeping her. Who else could she turn to, though? *Mom? Mom. I'm so alone, Mom, too alone. I miss you.* Her eyes watered a bit and she used her thumb and forefinger to press down the tingle in the bridge of her nose.

"Perhaps you're right about the police," Elsie said. "But since the baby's father—Rid, you said?—assumed you were in on that lawsuit, and got so angry, and the fact that now you own your mother's house on the water. I don't know. It's certainly the only clue, so far. But you wouldn't want to accuse the wrong person. Is there a way you—"

Caroline put her head down, pressed her fingers against her temples. "Wait a minute." She shook her head and looked back up. "I know why the police might not tell me, or might not do something if the sea farmers are messing with me. The police are *locals*. Think about it. The big houses up on the bluffs—all those wealthy weekend people? They come in and build their fancy mansions so they can spend summer weekends and vacations in them, and they try to throw their weight around—against locals and natives who were working these tides before those people were born. Heck, the police have a lot more in common with the sea farmers than with the upland owners."

"That does make sense," Else said, laying down her spoon.

The waitress appeared and Caroline fell silent while their water glasses were refreshed. "I feel like I'm in a movie," she said, sotto voice, to Elsie, when the waitress moved on. "This whole thing is surreal."

"But you're scared," Elsie said softly, reaching across the table and covering Caroline's free hand with her own.

"I'm really scared."

That night in Noelle's yellow and white guestroom Caroline lay awake with the light on. Cleaning up, seeing color on her face and body again, getting out, hearing herself talk like an adult had helped her to stop thinking some grownup was going to appear to take over and fix this.

For the first time in weeks, Caroline read a novel for a half hour before she reached over to the nightstand and switched off the light. *I can do this, Mom. I know. I need to pull myself together. I hear you.*

She didn't care anymore if talking to her mother meant she was insane. It was comforting.

Caroline woke under goose down, a pale sunup glazing the east window of the room. She'd only been up once in the night, and had gone right back to a sleep that now seemed blank and dreamless. Bacon and coffee scents floated on top of the air. Noelle, or maybe Walt, was up and cooking already. She stretched under the covers and turned onto her back to feel her belly. Now, even flat out like this, the rise was unmistakable, not like putting on weight anymore, but its own separate shape. His or her own *self.* She was going to have to tell mother's friends. It would be too awkward to have them all just pretend they didn't notice, like the elephant in the room no one mentions.

Caroline's bladder wouldn't let her stay in bed. Her feet recoiled against the cold on the hardwood floor. Where were the socks she'd packed? She rummaged for clothing, dreading the moment of temporary nakedness, and took everything into the bathroom to dress where she could heat the room with shower steam first. Downstairs, she heard dishes and a murmur of voices, so they were both up. A throaty laugh, Noelle's. She felt rested and not afraid for the moment, knowing they were going to feed her breakfast, offer to let her stay another night if her own house still smelled from the exterminator's chemicals, hug her warmly and let her go as long as she promised to come back. Such good people. Caroline took heart.

❀

Over breakfast with Noelle and Walt, she checked the tide table in the *Cape Cod Times*. When she left their house at nearly ten, the tide was almost all the way in, so it was a sure thing Rid wouldn't be on his grant. Spotting someone in Wellfleet off-season wasn't all that difficult. She had a full gas tank and plenty of time, neither of which, it turned out, she needed. She only cruised the village once before she spotted his truck at the Cumberland Farm store on Route 6. She'd not memorized his license plate, but detected Rid's dog in the passenger seat fogging the window with her breath. *Good. An adequately public setting. Safe. Nothing he can do to me.* She pulled in and parked alongside.

Rid came out with an oversize Styrofoam cup of coffee. Caroline opened her car door, stood and called to him.

"Hold up, Rid." She shut her door and started toward him.

"Hey." His tone was on the wary side of neutral. "How are you?" He ventured a small smile in her direction.

Caroline was taken back. This wasn't what she'd expected, but, on the other hand, what was he going to do? Hand her a written confession?

She made her voice hard. "Look, I don't know what you people are trying to accomplish, but it has to stop. I *will* press charges."

"*Me?* What am *I* trying to accomplish? I'm trying to earn a living. Legally. On my own grant. The question is what are *you* trying to do?"

"I'm trying to live peacefully in my house. I'm not bothering anybody."

Rid snorted. "No, you get *other* people to do your dirty work. You just said you're going to press charges. Another suit? Goodness. How *do* you manage to keep all your lawsuits straight?"

Caroline felt her face flush and her heart was beating too fast. "What? Are you crazy?" Two cars down, a teenage girl just getting into her car looked over in alarm as Caroline shrieked at Rid. She was too enraged to be embarrassed.

"Sure. Completely." He made a face at her, to go with the sarcasm. Was it a leer? Rid started to open the door of his truck.

Caroline grabbed his sleeve. "Oh no. You're *not* doing this to me any more. Don't you have any feelings? For God's sake, there's a baby involved."

Rid spun around, coffee sloshing out of his cup onto his bare hand. "Shit!"

He put the cup on the top of the truck and waved his fingers in the air, wiped them on his jeans. Lizzie came to the driver's side and whined.

"I'm sorry," Caroline said. "I didn't mean to do that."

"I'm not the one throwing away the baby's future. Look, why can't you just go back where you came from? You and your washashore friends with your goddamn precious bay views."

"Dammit Rid. I was born here. This is *my* home, too. You're not going to drive me away. Stay off my property, stop stalking me, stop trying to scare me into leaving. I know who you are, I know what you're doing, and I'm warning you."

The day was dank, heavy clouds having moved in from the west to completely blanket the early sun. "Oh, you're warning me are you? Well, I'm warning *you*." His eyes were navy, stones under water, his whole face ruddy as if from weather, different from when he'd smiled at her. He wore a heavy hooded sweatshirt, gray, over a red flannel shirt. She could see the collar of it, and another white T shirt beneath that. The tips of his ears were flaming. He picked his coffee off the roof of the truck, sloshing more there, the ground and himself as he opened the door and got in.

Caroline saw the dog hustle back into the passenger side but quickly reverse position and lick Rid's cheek and neck. Rid turned his face to the Lab, somehow rotating his body to bring his left hand up and over to caress her ears. Then he straightened and the motor roared to life while Caroline stood on the asphalt outside the convenience store as if she'd taken root there, trying to fathom how a man could be so tender to his dog and go out of his way to hurt the woman carrying his baby.

 *Chapter 18*

Rid was so worked up he'd actually turned the wrong way on Route 6, forgetting that he'd been headed to the marine supply in Orleans. Now he found himself with his shorts in a twist and aimed toward P-town for no reason at all except that he'd wanted to head the truck away without having to pass CiCi and her car. Every single damn time he saw that woman he ended up with his heart pounding mad and his truck bed filled with guilt. He'd left her standing there, her mouth half-open like a bitten apple. Like she was talking but nothing was coming out. Just as well. It wouldn't have been good, he knew that much.

He dried his coffee-covered hand on the ratty towel he kept on the floorboard for Lizzie when she'd been swimming in the bay, finishing it off with a couple of swipes back and forth against his jeans which were way cleaner than the towel. Traffic was non-existent. He took a breath, then another, trying to calm down. He'd had the impulse to call Tomas, but squelched it. Sometimes he got tired of Tomas telling him what to do, for one. There were times Tomas acted as if he was the only one with a working brain.

When Rid got to the Truro town line without having turned around, he decided to just go to the marine supply up in P-town. He was halfway there now anyway. What the hell had Caroline been talking about? Stalking her? Like he'd consider it. Jesus. Trying to drive her out? Rid shook his head in disgust. Obviously, the woman knew nothing about him. That was more lunatic Mario's style.

Oh Christ. *Mario.*

His mind did a yoyo reel. Mario had threatened Pissario. Maybe Mario thought Caroline was an easier target. It would be just like him. Was it even possible that CiCi was telling the truth? But she'd pretty much admitted that she was in on the lawsuit, hadn't she? All that stuff about how this was her home. She sounded like Pissario, talking about his stinking rights. A lot that asshole knew anyway. When had all this started? Rid tried to lay out a mental time line but the line wouldn't go straight, wouldn't even stay just one line, but forked and turned all wavy, doubled back and looped into knots. Like his stomach right now.

He crossed over onto 6A where the roads ran close together near Beach Point. All the cottages lined like soldiers along the beach were deserted; you could fly down this road as fast as Route 6 if you felt like it now, but he'd wanted the change of scenery and thinking time, so he slowed a good deal from highway pace. He'd not had the thought consciously until the *Provincetown* sign was smack in front of him and then the road split, Bradford Street to the right and Commercial Street to the left. The marine supply was on Commercial Street but there he was, veering to the right.

He leaned to flip open the glove compartment, pulled out the paper Moonface had given him. Terry DiPaulo 290 Bradford Street. *Just check on things at this address,* Moonface said. *She needs anything, you help her.*

Tomas said, "Don't go near the place. It's a set-up."

He drove past the house deliberately, turned around in a driveway, passed it again, turned around again a quarter of a mile back the way he'd come from, and this time pulled over to park fifty feet east of the house and on the opposite side of the street.

What was he supposed to see? It was a house. An old Cape house with cedar shakes. Fenced, a bit ramshackle, but not falling down. The yard should have been mowed again in late fall, but it was too late now. The shrubbery could use pruning. So what? So could his own. In the small yard, a child's swing set had an unused look, as all children's play equipment does in winter. This set seemed to be for a toddler; the seats were the kind that harness a small body like a parent's arms. The house didn't appear particularly lived in, but didn't look abandoned either. Most of the windows were covered, but not so much as to make it look as if the world had been refused entirely. Curled on the passenger seat next to him, Lizzie stretched, shifted position and sighed as she resettled in her sleep. The tags on her collar jangled softly one against the other. Rid stroked her head without taking his eyes from the DiPaulo house. "Atta girl, good girl," he murmured. "I have no idea what the hell is going on."

His lukewarm coffee tasted of earth and age. The truck windshield was dirty, big streaky fans left by the wipers, which annoyed him, and it annoyed him that he had let Moonface control him this much. It was easier to be annoyed than to be afraid.

His thoughts shifted back to the confrontation with Caroline. Now that he was mad at Moonface again, it was easier to study her in his mind's eye and see she was truly frightened. What the hell was Mario thinking? They'd all agreed not to do anything illegal, especially with Lorenz working behind the scenes. His impulse was to go have it out with him, but he didn't want to hear Mario run his mouth. It's not like it was going to be the truth coming out if it didn't serve Mario's purpose at the moment, partners or not. He and Tomas had already proven that much the night Mario sank his truck.

Pieces of an idea began to occur to him, shifting into different patterns as he turned them like a kaleidoscope and studied various ways the pieces could dovetail. But there were too many. He'd just have to leave the pieces in disarray. He started his truck and drove back to Wellfleet in the bleak of December without remembering to go to the marine supply in P-town and get the rope he needed. He hadn't eaten yet that day, either.

❀

That afternoon he hung out at the Oyster bar, not that he didn't have plenty to do at home with cages to repair, fourth quarter taxes in a mess, and the giant tangle of HAASAP paperwork for which he had no talent or patience. He needed to get more firewood cut, too. He hardly had enough for himself yet, let alone enough to sell. (And he'd promised his sister to bring a load "for Mom," although surely his lily-livered brother-in-law could dirty his hands enough to take care of keeping his own house warm if it came down to it.) But he was here because Billy would have the police scanner on, for one, and for two, the local cops hung out there themselves when they were off duty and hiding out from their wives. This was going to take some time to finesse. He didn't want anyone knowing what he was after.

"Hey, Billy. Gimme a draft, will ya?" He'd hung his jacket up and settled at the bar. "And a Reuben, huh? With fries and a couple extra pickles." Then, in a casual tone, he cast his first line. "Saw an accident up on 6A. Who was it?"

Billy's face registered surprise, then he narrowed his eyes. He was the one who took the town's pulse. "Squad cars there? Nothing on the scanner...."

"Maybe someone was trying to keep it off his insurance record. Only one of the cars looked messed up. But maybe you just missed it."

"Nah. It's a graveyard in here." *Graveyahd*, it came out. South Boston never wears off. The local accent wasn't nearly as broad. "I've had the scanner on all morning," he said, skeptical.

"Huh. Dunno, then. Anything interesting for the flatfoots lately?"

"Some peeping Tom calls, not last night, though. But you'll love this one. That Pissario guy up on the bluffs reported vandalism." Billy gave Rid a sidelong flirtatious look and flipped his wrist, the other hand on his waist in a caricature pose. "Honey, I know that'll just break your heart, you being best friends and all. I'm sure you just have no idea who might want to do any damage up there now, right?"

He'd gotten more than he bargained for. "Shit," he muttered. "Shit. Do they know who did it? I mean did they catch anyone?"

"No arrest *yet*." Again, that infuriating grin from Billy. And his dangling right earring shone and winked in the window light, which made it worse.

"Hey, wipe it off, will ya? If you're thinking I had something to do with that, think again."

Billy feigned innocent surprise. "Oh no. Certainly not *you*. *Your* name wasn't mentioned on the scanner as someone to pick up for questioning. But you'd know the person who was."

That had to mean Mario. Goddammit, why couldn't he just stick to their plan?

"I'm pretty sure Mario was with Tomas last night anyway." A lie, but he needed to get to what he really wanted to know. "Still, I suppose an alibi won't count against Pissario's money."

"Hey, our cops are locals. They'll be looking for a way not to hang it on him. But they've got to make it look right."

"What's the peeping Tom stuff about?"

"Dunno. It's a chick over on the horseshoe beach at Indian neck. She's called in a bunch of times is all I know. They've never found anybody on her property when they get there. I think they're getting sick of her. Maybe she's cuckoo." Billy twirled his forefinger around the side of his head along with a cross-eyed lolling tongue grin. He was wearing a Hawaiian shirt today, with darts. It looked like a woman's XXL.

"They think Mario's in on that, too?"

"I dunno. Didn't hear one way or the other. Ask your partner. Hey, I bet your sandwich is sitting under the heat lamp waiting on me to pick it up. You'd think Chuck could give a holler, wouldn't you? Lemme check." Billy disappeared through the swinging doors into the kitchen.

Rid took a deep breath and tried to quiet his mind enough to sort through what he'd learned, but there wasn't enough time. The doors swung again, and Billy appeared with his food, setting it down hard and then sliding some silverware in Rid's direction. "He actually bitched at me for letting it sit there after it was done, can you believe it? So what? He's got two broken legs and couldn't have brought it out here himself? Like the grand master chef has anything else on the grill. Thinks he's special...." Billy kept muttering, wandering down the bar, wiping the wood as he went.

Rid leaned way over to pick up a Provincetown Banner someone had left on a table behind him. He opened it and tried to look engrossed. He needn't have. Billy had wandered over to the restaurant side where he was sharing his outrage with Jannie Stonegood, who served as both hostess and cashier during the off-season. Rid was free to try to put together something that resembled a plan.

He'd frittered away the afternoon as if minutes were just so much sand blowing around, unable to concentrate on all that needed to be done while he waited for darkness. It was absolutely unlike him, and added another layer to the frustration he was working on, to say nothing of how it was filled with anxiety.

This close to the winter solstice, moonrise was around four, and before five, the afternoon light gathered its skirt over to one side to reveal the blaze of sunset. Evening stars had taken over by five forty-five. Rid waited until six, then headed out to his truck with a full thermos of coffee, two shrink-wrapped sandwiches and a Hershey Bar he'd picked up at Cumberland Farms. "No, girl, you stay home," he said first, as Lizzie automatically scurried to her feet and tried to get out the door ahead of him, but even as she reluctantly backed up, he said, "Oh, what the hell. You can come. You'll just have to stay in the truck, but you're used to that, aren't ya?" The dog's tail swung in furious pleasure, thumping against the door jamb as she scampered out. Right behind her, Rid suddenly thought of something else, went to the storage closet beneath the stairs and pulled out a small beach blanket and a backpack.

"Okay girl. Let's roll," he said, catching up with Lizzie who was waiting for him at the passenger door. "I'll drive, you take shotgun," he said as she made her leap onto the seat the instant he opened the door.

It was only a five-minute trip. He turned down King Philip Lane as if he were headed to his grant, but instead of making the right turn that would have taken him to the access road, he went straight, and where the little road turned off, at Blackfish Creek, to Hiawatha, which in turn would become the access road, he pulled over and parked. "Nap time, girl. I gotta work now."

Lizzie jumped through the cleft in the two front seats to the back. She knew these words and this drill. Rid poured some water into the bowl on the floor of the back seat from the two-liter bottle he kept there, and pulled a biscuit out of his pocket. "I'll be back," he said, caressing her ears. "You be a good girl." Opening his glove compartment, he pulled out the small high-intensity flashlight there, and stuck it in his back pocket. He took a blanket, his thermos and the sandwiches—one tuna salad, one roast beef—stuffed them in the backpack, cracked the driver's side window and locked the truck. Then he started to walk back up toward the access road, pulling the backpack into position as he went.

Once headlights cut through the blackness ahead and he melted into someone's yard, taking refuge behind a hedge. He crossed the access road, and then started to work his way into the woods, staying on property lines as best he could. There wasn't a lot of underbrush; it was all tall pines, sandy yards, but still, oaks, especially, growing where there was more light. The closer he got to the water, the more beach plums and wild roses there were, and the harder it was to make his way.

He kept a wide berth of CiCi's yard. Down close to the horseshoe beach, a lot of people let much of their land go wild. If they bothered with grass, they only mowed the smallest spot around their house, maybe clearing areas for vegetables and flowers, a private area for sitting outside with garden furniture and a patio table with a bright umbrella, that sort of thing. Most of the older houses also had wraparound porches, often screened. But they'd let the larger parts of their yards go wild over the years as the crowds of summer people swelled and were ever more intrusive. There's not much vegetation that's less hospitable when you're uninvited than the daunting impenetrability of beach plums and rose hips.

"Shit," Rid muttered. "Ow," and then a moment later, "Goddammit. Whoever is trying to freak her out—if anyone is really trying to freak her out—she could, of course, be a goddamn liar trying to freak *me* out. Probably Pissario's the baby's father. But if someone *is* trying to freak her out, he wants her to know it, because he's sure as hell going in from the road or right up off the beach path, not this ass-breaking way. With my luck, she'll spot me, call the police and this will be the one time they'll be on the ball. Then I'll be the one accused of the whole fine mess, and any rusted-out prosecutor could make the case stick."

During his diatribe, it occurred to him that the idea that Pissario was the baby's father, did not make him happy. But he pushed that thought away, rolling over it as if it was so much sand beneath his truck's oversized tires.

He had to retreat and detour several times, finally sneaking up CiCi's neighbor's path to the beach, keeping his body as close to the ground as possible. "I'd have been great in special forces. Too bad about those felony convictions," he said, still talking to himself as he did out on the flats. He'd wanted to set up a watch point in the woods above CiCi's house but now realized he wasn't going to be able to get there from here. He'd way underestimated the amount of ground pine, for one. He was climbing on the bushy stuff and it was killing him. If he stuck to his plan, he would have had to approach from her road, which was a couple lanes closer to the water than King Philip, paralleling it, and less than a half-mile long before it dead ended. He didn't want to go in from there; most of the yards were filled with tall pines, their needles silencing the ground, but there was nothing to give him any cover. And it would risk a ruckus of dogs. He ended up walking all the way down the rutted, axle-breaking Hiawatha Lane to where it became the sandy access road to the grants, listening intently for any oncoming vehicles so he could duck into the vegetation on the left where there were no houses, only a marshy inlet. Finally, he was at the Y, where he would normally turn to the left to reach his grant. He went to the right, to the horseshoe beach itself and cut back up toward CiCi's house, which did not put him at a secure, let alone high, observation point.

He reached the ragged hem of her property from the water side, brambled with ground and stunted pitch pine, and impossible to lay low on. There'd be nothing to see except the ankles and knees of the rose hips and beach plums if he tried to sit down here and keep watch. Closer to and sheltering the house was a stand of tall pitch pines, further obscuring the view. She had all kinds of outdoor security lights around the place. The porch light was on, and there were lights on over the driveway and her mother's studio, plus a yard light between the studio and the house.

Still on his feet and well back in the darkness, Rid hunched down, completely frustrated. He'd have to come back and try to figure this out in the daylight by walking Lizzie down the horseshoe beach and scout the place in advance. Maybe he'd just have to risk coming in from above, carry a pocketful of dog treats to pacify any barkers he stirred up. The approach he'd tried tonight wasn't going to work.

Just like that, it happened while he was standing there making alternate plans. At first he didn't see anything. He heard a crack, or a crash, and the sound of glass shattering. Rid jerked his head toward CiC's house, a reflex. Nothing. But then, yes. A shadow, literally a shadow, running up her driveway. Ten seconds later a sedate motor—it sounded like a truck, though from this distance Rid couldn't be sure—drove off at a speed suggesting nothing amiss here.

Rid's first instinct was to barrel toward Cici's house, to see if she was all right. At the very least she must be terrified. She'd told him the truth. If she was in with the lawsuit, it didn't make sense that Pissario or somebody with him would target her. *Oh God. Mario.* Rid stopped short as he circled back to a fear he'd had before. Could it be? Some perverse sense of loyalty to Rid, plus Mario's own conclusion that Caroline was involved in the suit? Hell, until thirty seconds ago, he'd thought the same thing. They were paranoid about all the waterfront landowners.

What was he going to do? Obviously, she'd called the police. How would he explain his presence in her yard? *Oh yeah, Officer, I was here watching to see who is trying to harass or hurt her. No really, it's not me. I was here with my sandwiches and my thermos and my nifty blanket to sit on for an entirely different reason. Yeah I saw the guy. No I can't identify him. No, not his vehicle either. Might be one of my partners, though. I'll talk to him for you and get it stopped if you want. How's that for a deal? Yeah, the cops would sure eat that line up from an ex-con. Holy shit. I've got to get out of here. If they cruise the area, and see me, what am I going to say I'm doing here? Oh, God. What if they spot my truck? Lizzie's in it big as life, not that they'd have to run my plates to know it's mine. What if they ask CiCi about me? She already thinks it's me. She accused me herself. Do not pass go, go directly to jail.*

Rid did an exact reverse course. This had to be one of the most purely stupid things he'd ever done in his life, and he'd done plenty of things that rang the bell at the top of the stupid meter. How was he going to retrieve his truck and get the hell out of here? Not the way he came in, that was for sure. He had to stay off the roads.

Panting, Rid made it back to the horseshoe beach by sneaking onto one of CiCi's neighbor's beach paths, and hunching as low to the ground as he could, doing an awkward run. "Oh, this is peachy, just peachy," he muttered to himself as he jogged, trying to keep his head down. "In Caroline Marcum's neighborhood at the exact same time one of her windows gets busted. What kind of moron are you, Ridley Neal? You've done made Mario look like a frigging genius tonight." Then breath was too hard to suck in to waste any on words, and he just kept moving on the shoulder where the beach grass and low dunes started, figuring he'd blend into the darkness best there. When he reached the access road, he got over the shoulder and, even though it was clumsy, blind-going, slow and miserable, Rid got down and went through wet-footed mucky beach grass, intending to approach the front of his truck by coming up from the wetland. He had a much better chance of avoiding detection.

Cold and wet, he half-crept, half-crawled toward the front of his truck from the marsh side, praying that Lizzie wouldn't put up a major stink. Usually she knew when it was Rid, and didn't make a sound unless he'd left her too long. Then the barking was a warm up for her joy dance or her reproach because she'd been holding her pee. Once the truck was in his sight line, he stopped and lay on his stomach in the dark, to get a fix on whether anyone was around the truck or a squad car might be parked behind it. Nothing he could see.

Trying to be noiseless, he centered the weight of his backpack again and, staying low, made it to the road. There, he straightened up and tried to look unhurried. He opened the truck bed and shifted some crates in it, pulling a sandy rake and a crate half-full of clams forward, so that if caught he could say he had been picking in the wild. Kind of far-fetched when he was this close to his own grant, but maybe not to the police. He opened one of the extra two liter bottles of water he kept in the back for Lizzie and wet the clams down, so they'd look just picked. He pulled off the backpack, got out the tuna sandwich and started eating it, to back up his own story. The tide was too far in, there was the darkness problem, and this wasn't a designated area for picking. "More holes'n Swiss cheese," he said aloud. He put on his miner's hat, so it would look like he could have been using a headlight. He tried to look casual, all the while his hands were hurrying, and the sound of his heart pounding was like surf in his ears. Keeping the thermos with him, he unlocked the driver's side where Lizzie was already at attention in the passenger seat.

Clamping his jaw to keep his teeth from chattering, Rid quickly climbed into the truck, and even while Lizzie was licking his right ear, he was starting it, no motor gun, and then as quietly as he could doing a three point turn and driving back out to Indian Neck Road, and on out on Cove toward Route 6 at a calm speed that denied his every instinct. As he reached the junction of Indian Neck and Cove Road, he saw flashing blue and red lights approaching. He signaled and veered off onto Pilgrim Spring Road well before the police car passed.

It wasn't until much later when he was at home in his recliner with a beer, and the police still hadn't shown up at his door with a warrant (but who knows how long it took to get a judge to sign one of those?) that he started to look at what had happened through a different lens. The television was on, but only to have things look normal—whatever that meant—if they showed up. He couldn't have named the program. What he saw was that CiCi hadn't lied. Someone was terrorizing her. She thought it was Rid, but so far hadn't pointed him out to the police. Why not? Second, it had taken the cops at least twenty minutes to respond to her call. Maybe more like thirty. He couldn't really tell how long it had taken him to get from her yard to his truck, but it was a fair distance and he hadn't taken a quick or easy route. They weren't taking her calls seriously. Or they were protecting someone else.

 *Chapter 19*

December 23. The morning after he'd tried to stake out CiCi's house, Lizzie woke Rid at six-thirty. "Tide's not till ten-forty. Go back to sleep," he tried, knowing full well she wouldn't until he'd let her out and fed her. She leaked out a little whine and nuzzled him softly. "All right, girl. I know," he said. "I'm coming."

By the time Rid himself had peed and was back in bed, Lizzie three minutes behind him with her morning gratitude kisses, the whole mess of CiCi and Pissario barged back into his consciousness and immediately got tangled up in his mind like the wreck of a grant after a terrible blow. He lay sleepless in the dark, aware of how alone he was. Then this unwelcome thought—if I feel alone, how must CiCi feel? Afraid, pregnant, her mother newly dead.

He'd call and offer to help, but that would tip his hand, that he'd been there last night. He stewed in the bed another fifteen minutes, overthinking every angle. Finally, he sighed, and extracted his thigh from beneath the sleeping Lab who'd been using it as a pillow. His feet touched the cold hardwood for the second time that morning. He really needed to get himself a pair of those fur-lined slippers. But he'd been saying that for at least three years, maybe five.

An hour later, he was at The Oyster, happy he'd bothered to wear his rubber shoes because the sandy parking lot was full of frozen-top puddles from the overnight rain. A skin of ice silvered all the beach grass and branches. Likely it would be gone by the time he came out.

"Hey Billy," he forced the greeting out nicely with something near a smile, even though Billy was wearing a dangle earring that looked like a barber pole, and some weird shirt with a cutout around his arm tattoo—Rid never had been able to read more than the first two letters, EL. The outfit was topped with a doo rag covered with tiny Santas.

"Hey yourself. What'll it be?" Billy said leaning over the counter.

"Look, man, your earring is nice, but could you give me some air space? Just—"

"No problem," Billy interrupted, straightening. "It's a candy cane," he said, flipping his earring. For Christmas. You know, with my last name being Cane—sort of a joke?"

"I thought something was going on, sorta over the top."

Billy's face fell a bit. "Anyway, what would you like for breakfast? If I can get The Lord of the Grill to cook something and actually ring the little bell when it's ready." As he spoke, he unnecessarily re-wiped the bar in front of Rid before sliding silverware and a napkin in place. Normally Rid would have taken a table, but again, today, he wanted Billy's chatter so he was enduring the preliminaries, masking his impatience.

"Two eggs over easy, a side of extra crisp bacon, got any blueberry muffins today? And, yeah, hash browns." He slid the menu back toward Billy, not having looked at it.

"Somebody's got an appetite today," Billy said suggestively.

"Listen, Candy, lay off. Go put my order in and then come back and catch me up on local gossip. I've been down on the grant all the time, trying to button it down, hardly seen anyone at all." He'd known the invitation would light Billy up, but he needed to get what he needed to get, and then he could stop playing this game. Not that he didn't like Billy.

"You got it." Billy flourished through the swinging kitchen doors. All the locals let their guard down in the off-season. But this was way more than Rid remembered from last year, or maybe Billy had been warming up to it for years, like a snake shedding skins.

The doors swung back momentarily, Billy carrying two mugs of coffee. He plunked one in front of Rid and took a sip of the other himself. "Slow morning," he said, swiveling his head around the bar as if to show Rid there were no other customers for him to attend to. Rid had counted on it. There were a smattering in the restaurant side, but those weren't Billy's problem. The pretty brunette married to Clint, whose grant was next to Barb's—was handling the restaurant side along with Jannie who was doing double duty, as usual.

"So gossip central is now open," Billy said. "Who is it you wish to dish?" Playing it to the hilt.

"Nobody in particular, everybody in general. What's the latest around town?" Ease into it, he cautioned himself. Don't act too interested in any one thing.

"Well, let's see. You heard about Barb's daughter, didn't you? Oh, she's such a doll, the prettiest girl too, don't you know? Couldn't have happened to anyone nicer. Seems she won the prize for …." Billy went on and on, jumping from person to person, while Rid pretended to listen, drinking his coffee, trying to keep his eyes somewhere close to Billy's face.

"Oh, you wouldn't wanna know anything about Mr. Pissario now, would you?"

"Is there something to know?"

"Might be." Teasing.

Be patient. Keep your hands off his throat. Rid grinned at Billy. "Okay, Candy, spill it."

Just then, Chuck's baritone from the kitchen. "Billy-Boy, you have an order. Would you care to pick it up, or shall I call a courier service?"

Billy's face turned dark. "This is what I put up with." Then, calling to the kitchen, in another tone entirely, this one light and fake-cheery, "I'm coming, Chuck. Thank you."

When the kitchen doors slapped behind him on his return back into the bar, Billy put Rid's breakfast down—already a bit cooled off, Rid noted, without mentioning it—and continued where he'd left off on the subject of Pissario. "Maybe he reported that his car, a Lexus don't you know, was keyed in the Stop & Shop parking lot. I heard it on the scanner. I know this breaks your heart, you and him being so close."

"Oh yeah. I'm weeping. Any idea who did it?"

"Nobody's been mentioned, or more importantly, picked up for questioning."

"Far as I'm concerned, that's a good thing."

"You know anything about it? Not that I'd tell."

Rid made a point of looking Billy square in the eye and holding the contact while he answered. "I'm not about to mess up a court case by doing one illegal thing, and that's the truth." The last thing he needed was gossip getting started that he was behind this and just too clever to get caught.

"So anything else interesting on the scanner? Any good breaking and entering? How about grand theft? Any murders in town? Gotta be some decent auto theft, at least." He forked some bacon and eggs into his mouth, took a swig of coffee, raised his eyebrows expectantly as he chewed and waited for Billy to come up with an answer.

Billy put on a show of trying to remember. "Damn. There was a bunch of that stuff, but a lot of it just escapes my memory. I'm just so busy here all the time, you know, slaving to wait on the hordes of winter customers. Sorry."

"You are at risk of being a boring guy in a boring town," Rid said. "Don't tell me the peeping Tom retired, too." Now, finally, what he was after.

"Nope, but if he's a pervert, he froze his little dick off last night, because he also threw a rock through that lady's window. That was on the scanner, too."

"You're kidding. Man, that's bad. Do you know who she is?"

"I think they said Caroline somebody. Over off Indian Neck Road, one of the lanes that look like ladder rungs down to the beach."

"Caroline Marcum? Geez. I know her. An old friend from high school." Might as well get a witness established as to how and when he heard about what happened and that he told somebody he was going to call and see if he could help. Might help if she accused him later. "She told me this was happening, and it sounded kinda far-fetched. So it's true. I wish I'd asked you about it before." Another bite of bacon and eggs.

"Didn't sound like anybody much did believe her."

"Her mother just died a bit ago. I went to the service. Our dads used to play poker way back when."

"Ya don't say."

"I went out with her back in September once." Rid kept eating, which gave him a reason not to look at Billy directly.

Billy's eyebrows went up. "She a nut job?"

"No more'n you."

Billy rolled his eyes. "Possibly she wouldn't find that description complimentary."

Rid took a long drink of coffee, then elaborately set his mug down. In a long deadpan, he slowly wiped his mouth with his napkin, then looked up at Billy, back at his plate, picked up his muffin, buttered it, and just before opening his mouth, paused to look at him again to say, "Possibly not," before he grinned and took a big bite.

Billy chuckled.

"Anyway," Rid continued, "I feel bad for her. I'll give her a call and see if she needs some help." He thought of telling Billy that she was pregnant, and then thought better of it. The only thing Billy liked better than gossip was sexual innuendo.

"Yeah," Billy said. The morning sun was on his face, side lit by window light from the restaurant side, and he looked older than his years. "Somebody oughta."

"You got my check? I gotta run to my grant. Almost time for the tide."

"Sure." Billy tore it off his pad and slid it face down across the bar. Rid pulled his wallet from his back pocket and turned it over, it was blank. He looked up at Billy, a question on his face.

"It's on me. I like talking to you."

"Hey, man, that's not necessary." He stopped short of saying I like talking to you, too, although sometimes he did. "Thanks a lot."

"My pleasure." Billy grinned and picked up the dirty plate, silverware and mug. "See you soon."

"Hey, Billy—I'm still leaving you a tip," Rid called as Billy backed through the swinging kitchen doors.

"Not necessary."

"Better pick it up," Rid called into the empty space between the doors as they still made their small slapping noises, and put a ten dollar bill under the salt shaker.

When he left The Oyster, he checked the shellfish shack where the warden's office was, across the street. No yellow flag flying over it. Good enough. Harbor open. Still legal to pick today.

He did run out to his grant. He had a standing quahog order, and he could still dig. He'd left some legal size oysters in, too, hadn't pulled them out yet to put in the pit in his yard. The more he could sell while the temperature was above freezing, the more cash he could raise for the lawsuit defense. He couldn't harvest a frozen animal out of the water; that wasn't legal because when it thawed it would be dead and have no shelf life. This was a bit of a risky game he was playing. The safest thing now was to pull all the rest of his oysters and get them buried for the winter. That way he wasn't chancing ice damage if a sudden hard freeze came. December was early for it, but you never knew. *Tomorrow.* He promised himself that every day.

Probably as much as anything, though, he'd come to the grant to think. The bay was home, even in this unforgiving season when his toil and loyalty were what earned his truest claim. Pissario might be still coming out an occasional weekend now, but once Christmas was over, he'd disappear entirely until about May fifteenth. All the weekenders did.

But that wasn't what he'd come to think about as he picked oysters from the big rack in the front of his grant. He'd come to think about how to approach CiCi. Every time he said a word to her, it ended up stuck all over his face, like bubblegum gone wrong. He had to go down to his sister's for Christmas. Laura could live without him for sure, but he wasn't into hearing about how he'd broken his mother's heart again. Did CiCi have someplace to go for Christmas, though? He couldn't see her left alone, scared, waiting for the next stealth rock through a window, or worse. But surely one of her mother's friends. Or maybe she'd made some friends of her own by now. What was she telling people? Or had she had an abortion after all? Rid sighed and shook his head as he carried a crate to the open gate of his truck. "Goddamn," he said out loud.

⚅

His delivery completed, Rid went home and played Frisbee hard with Lizzie under a sky that looked entirely scribbled over in heavy lead pencil. He'd picked up some groceries in Orleans, and, delaying, came in and fried a steak with some onions, peppers and mushrooms while the microwave nuked a potato. He'd killed a beer before he ate, and knocked off another with dinner. Watched the TV news. Rummaged for dessert, cursed himself for forgetting to buy ice cream. Found some Rocky Road in the basement freezer and scooped a big bowl. Watched Jeopardy, challenging Lizzie for the house championship. Was pleased he was able to beat her and retain his title from the night before last. Washed the dishes. Considered whether he could proceed to do laundry. Called himself a goddamn wussy boy. Picked up the phone. Put it back. Picked it up again. Walked a circle around his living room. Lizzie perked an eye and ear at him. "All right, already. Goddamn, I know, I know. I'm doing it." Dialed Caroline's number.

"Caroline? Please don't hang up. This is Rid Neal. Listen, the barkeep at The Oyster, you know, Billy Cane? He always has the police scanner on, and I was there for breakfast this morning. Anyway, he told me that somebody threw a rock through your window last night. I'm … I'm calling to see if you're all right. I mean, I thought you might need some help."

At first there was just silence from the other end. "Caroline?" he said, thinking she'd hung up and he'd just not heard it, although the line sounded open. "CiCi, are you there?"

Finally, "I'm here."

"Well, are you all right?"

Silence again. "I wasn't in the path of the rock, if that's what you mean."

Crap, here we go again. "Look. Please. I'm sorry for our last conversation. Can we just cut through all that? I don't have anything to do with what's happening to you, if that's what you think. I swear it."

"If not you, then who?"

"CiCi, I'm telling you, I *don't* know."

"One of your friends, maybe?"

"I'll be honest with you. It's not impossible."

"And you're telling me, you don't know about it."

"I'm telling you I don't know."

"And I'm supposed to believe you."

"Dammit, CiCi, I'm telling you like it is."

"And I'm wondering why you couldn't tell it to your friend."

"I don't even know for sure. *If* it is him, he's a hothead who's out of control. I will talk to him. My other partner has warned him about a hundred times not to do crazy stuff. So have I. I don't know for sure that he *is*. Only that he *could* be going behind our backs."

"Will you talk to him?" Was that a slight softening in her voice?

"I told you I would. Yes. Is somebody staying with you?"

A hesitation. Rid guessed she was afraid to give him any information. He couldn't sit anymore so got out of the kitchen chair where he'd perched, and walked the length of the kitchen to check Lizzie's water bowl. Outside the window, another starless, moonless night, damp enough to blur every edge illuminated by his house lights.

"Okay. Don't trust me. I'm just your baby's father calling to offer help. I'm presuming there still *is* a baby?"

"Yes."

"And it's still mine?"

"What's that supposed to mean?" Her voice was a just-ignited rocket.

"Are you in on the lawsuit against me?"

"*NO.* Why would you think that?" Gathering energy, flames at the base.

"Doesn't feel good, does it? Sooner or later we're going to have to trust each other. Or not, I guess. Good night, Caroline."

Imagining the blastoff, Rid pushed the button that hung the phone up, and carried the phone in to the living room to replace it on its cradle, feeling a momentary sense of victory. By the time he'd gotten another beer from the refrigerator, dropped in his recliner, given Lizzie a biscuit, and picked up the remote, the feeling was already dissipating, something a bit like shame starting to corrode the edges, and that pissed him off. He had nothing to be ashamed of this time, dammit.

Chapter 20

The day after Christmas, Caroline opened her eyes in Noelle and Walt's yellow guest room again. The air held the cold knife of a New England upstairs bedroom in winter, but her body was suspended in a cloud of warm goose down. Noelle had insisted she spend Christmas night with them; after all, she'd spent Christmas Eve night with Sharon and Charles, when Karen had come for dinner as had redheaded Carol, a widow with her regular companion, an oysterman, and, of course, Noelle and Walt. When she'd refused wine with dinner, Noelle had given CiCi her dreaded single eyebrow arch accompanied by The Look. She was tired of pretending to be fooled.

CiCi had given Noelle a small nod. A few moments later, still not knowing what she was going to say, she began. "I hope you know how much I appreciate all this. I mean you all." Oh, she had no energy, but she couldn't put this off. "I know what you meant to Mom through the years, and to have you take me in the way you have, well, I just thank you so much."

There'd been murmurs of "Oh honey, we love you," and "We miss your mama right along with you, you know that," running together like currents in a river.

"There's something else," Caroline looked down at her hands bunched in her lap, wondering if the rest of them could have missed it and supposed it was possible. She'd worn a long loose black velvet jumper she'd bought at a Provincetown thrift shop for twelve dollars, although there was no reason she had to be so parsimonious. High-heeled black leather boots; the added height hid some bulk. Eleanor's thick gold chain in the neckline of the filmy white blouse, too, called attention away from her middle. *But get it over with.* She looked back up. "I'm pregnant."

A flurry of feminine voices and movement. Sharon and Carol got up to hug her from opposite sides and thumped their heads together. Carol tripped back over herself and ended up on the floor. When Caroline started to help her up, four people yelled, "No, don't hurt yourself!" including Carol, and then everyone was laughing. Noelle hugged Caroline while Carol's companion got her up. Sharon and Karen were behind Noelle with embraces, and it was clear from their excited chorus of "Do you know if it's a boy or girl?" and "When are you due?" and "You better be prepared for a lot of grandmothers spoiling this little one," that she needn't have braced herself for judgment. "Your mother would be so happy," Carol whispered, the last to get her hug in.

"In late May or early June," and "No, I have no idea of the sex," and "We'll take all the grandparents we can get," Caroline had answered variously, then realized that the last response had opened the question of paternal grandparents. At that moment, she had longed for a glass of wine. Or three.

"I think you're all just too goodhearted to ask, but sooner or later I'm going to need to tell you and probably now is best. I don't have the best relationship with the baby's father, and I don't know how much he will or won't be involved. He's one of the aquaculturists with a grant on Indian Neck. That's honestly all there is to know right now." She paused, and looked around the dining table, at which everyone had reseated themselves. They were waiting for her to go on. "He is very upset and distracted, to be fair, because he is one of the ones being sued by that upland owner—you know, trying to shut the oystermen down, saying that their apparatus spoils the view and all. Somehow he got the idea that I was in on that lawsuit, you know, because I own waterfront property, I guess."

"Are you?" That was Charles, Sharon's husband, a chiseled-featured, sandy-haired man whose recalcitrant Southern drawl had rubbed off on Sharon after so many years.

Ben Demos, Carol's date, whose grant was off Mayo's Beach, hadn't said a word but had stiffened and was watching CiCi's face. She felt him study her through the candles.

Carol turned to Charles. "You're not from here. Locals don't think that way. This is a fishing town, always was." Adamant.

There was a murmur of assent. "I'd have something to say about it if she was," Walter said to Ben.

"Hey, I was born and raised here. This is my home," Caroline said.

"Of course, honey." Noelle shot The Look at Walt. "He knows better. Men just like to hear themselves talk."

"Didn't think she would," Walt said, having taken the heat off the other male.

The evening settled with coffee and pecan pie.

On Christmas Day, she cried twice. When she went home, there was a grocery bag at her kitchen door. She'd have called the police, frightened to risk looking in it except that the top had been left wide open. In it was a teddy bear, with embroidered-on eyes and smile, a red satin bow. Its tag said, "For Baby's first Christmas." There was no note. One of her mother's friends, she guessed, had managed to find an open store, and wanted Santa to visit the baby on Eleanor's behalf. Caroline put her face against the yielding plush and cried.

She'd showered and changed, and wrapped the gift she'd reserved to take to Noelle, a basket of things that had belonged to Eleanor that Noelle could use: a beaded necklace that served as a holder for glasses. One of Eleanor's favorite pins. A sachet out of one of Eleanor's drawers. And a piece of Eleanor's pottery, in a color Noelle had collected. Caroline had found it tucked away in the studio, with Noelle's name on it, and surmised that Eleanor had been saving it as a Christmas gift. She wrapped each, using Eleanor's handwritten "Noelle" as the tag. Using her nail, she picked the price off a bottle of good cabernet.

Walter, a retired chef from Duck Creek Inn, was making Beef Wellington, a process he'd begun a couple of days previously when he started cooking an ox tail. When he started explaining the numerous steps in excruciating detail, Noelle asked CiCi to check if the fire in the living room needed wood.

"No wood needed yet," Caroline said to the couple when she returned to the kitchen. "Maybe in fifteen minutes, though. The tree is still gorgeous,"

"I'm so glad you're here," Noelle said. "Think how lonely we'd be without Tina and Alex if you weren't here. And it gives Walter a chance to really show off." Noelle's hair was short and wavy, liberally salt and dark pepper. *People pay a fortune to have that done to their hair, and here Noelle gets it for nothing.* Caroline remembered her mother's mock frustration as Noelle spoke.

"I'm very grateful," Caroline said, hugging Noelle spontaneously.

"So you'll be staying on Cape, keeping the house? I hope—I mean, we'd like to be here for you. Help with everything. And we love babies." Noelle laughed. "Listen to me. I'm stammering."

"No, dear, you're begging," Walt interjected.

"I am not. Okay, I'm begging."

Caroline hesitated. "I'd like to stay."

"Well, then STAY."

"That's my plan for now."

"Excellent." Noelle said, and the word was a period.

After dinner, they moved to the living room with tea and a chocolate torte Noelle had made. Caroline was taken aback when Noelle brought out four gifts for her.

"Wait a minute. What's all this?" CiCi protested.

"Well, I already had this extra gift for you that I was going to give you today *anyway*. But you know Sharon. And it seems like Karen and Carol just had nothing else to do after dinner last night but to run down to Orleans to see if there wasn't any place still open for last minute lunatic shoppers. Musta been. Because on their way to Tara's this morning, Sharon and Charles were here dropping this stuff off. Can you tell the wrappings are courtesy of Sharon? Except for mine, of course, which looks like a normal person wrapped it." Noelle grinned.

"You first," Caroline said.

Noelle lifted the basket Caroline had so carefully filled onto her lap and started. Each item she opened brought a startle of recognition and teary smiles. Caroline went over to Noelle's chair and sat on the arm to hug her.

"I wish you would have let me be there more when she was dying," Noelle said. "I wanted to. I wanted to help more, for you and for her."

"I don't think I was trying to shut you out. I just felt like it was my job."

"Try not to do it again with the baby," Noelle said.

"I'm sorry I hurt you."

"Maybe you just had to be alone with her." Noelle's face was wet. "Hey, poor Walter, he must think all we do is cry. Go, unwrap your presents, honey." Indeed, across the room on the couch, Walter looked as if a taxidermist had got hold of him.

Noelle handed Caroline a tissue as she returned to her chair and pulled it closer to Noelle. Caroline gesturing to Walt, "Okay, it's safe now. I think we're finished crying."

"Ya sure?"

"Can't promise, but come closer and we'll try to behave."

Caroline picked up Noelle's gift and worked the wrapping open. Inside was a crib blanket, hand quilted, one side pastel blue with a bit of pink and white, the other side pale pink with tiny touches of white and pale blue, the blanket edged in white eyelet. Of course, Caroline cried, and Walt said, "Oh sheesh, here come the waterworks again, I thought you said you were done. Noelle's been working on that for the past six months."

Noelle threw a pillow at her husband. "You stop that, Walter. It's not even been three weeks, and you know it."

CiCi blushed. "I *was* going to tell you. I feel like an idiot."

Walt snorted.

"No matter, honey. No matter. I just didn't want the others to be asking me, which I knew would start happening soon. It needed to come from you. But don't worry, they hadn't realized. And pay no attention to *him*. It's not like *he* had a clue."

Caught, Walt chuckled. "Hey, look," he diverted, pointing out the picture window into the thick woods where their deck overlooked Gull Pond. The low-slung graphite sky was releasing snowflakes, which had been predicted for yesterday but never happened.

Meanwhile, CiCi had the blanket against her cheek. "This is so beautiful, Noelle. Perfect handwork. It's exactly what my mother would have done."

"I know," Noelle said, a whisper.

"Thank you, thank you so much."

"Okay, now I guess you can open the rest."

The rest, it turned out, were three unisex sleepers for a newborn, baby toys, a small collection of first books, and a musical crib mobile of bright, dancing animals. The other three women had, indeed, hit the Walmart in Orleans. "What, no bicycle?" Caroline joked.

"Pretty poor," Walt agreed. "The minute I get back from Toronto, I'd best see to that one."

"Well, maybe learning to walk, first."

"I just knew you were going to be a stick in the mud about this stuff," Walt said, trying to duck the second pillow Noelle shot at him.

Later, because of the millimeter of snow on the road, they wouldn't let her leave. Her black toiletries bag with nightgown stuffed in the top was still in the car from Christmas Eve, had napped there all day like a fat cat. Caroline was glad for an excuse to stay away from her own house another night. *Tomorrow,* she mocked herself as she got ready for bed. *I'll think about that tomorrow.*

The next morning Caroline drove home, the back seat loaded with the baby gifts the women had brought to Noelle's. *Wait,* she thought as the replayed the previous day—if their gifts had been brought to Noelle's, where had the teddy bear she'd found on her back step come from?

From that thought, she traveled directly to panic without a rest stop. Was there a bomb, like a secret black heart inside it? She'd left the bear on the kitchen counter. She'd set down her guard as casually as a teacup. And now Noelle and Walt—all the others, too—had left to visit married children. She hadn't even thought to ask Noelle and Walt for a key to their house and make up some reason she might have to stay there. She could have said more ants. Whatever. She felt sweaty in the layers of sweatshirt and down jacket, wool scarf, gloves. Impatiently, she swiped her hood off her head and cracked the car window. Immediately she was chilled and nauseated. The scrub pines along Route 6 looked bent-shouldered and heads-down against the cold, in need of simple mercy. Patches of black ice showed here and there where last night's new snow had blown from the road. The salt trucks hadn't gotten here yet

How strange to be so equally desperate and terrified to get home, her mind perfectly divided against itself. No one to call now.

She drove toward her house because there was nowhere else to go. As she stopped at the top of the driveway, Caroline studied the outside of the house, looking for any broken windows, signs of forced entry or vandalism. Her heart thudded, too loud, too fast. *Shh. Shh.* Still in the car, doors locked, motor running, she talked to herself. *That can't be good for the baby. Calm down. I don't see anything. Help us, Mom. Keep us safe.*

And she didn't see anything amiss. The window she'd had replaced was still intact. The outdoor lights, left on, were still glowing as were the indoor lights, anemic in the daytime and like neon signage that she was away. The east windows were opaqued by the dull light of the barren sky. Caroline started to breathe easier and, at walking speed, pulled the car farther into the driveway where there were no tire marks in the snow. No footprints.

She scoured the house and yard with her eyes again, all still well until, squinting, she made out two little squares, paper maybe, on the steps up the small back stoop off the kitchen door, and a larger, thicker square on the little porch itself. The steps were largely protected by a roof built out over the porch, and there was very little snow on them.

Her heart started up its wild stomping. Why didn't she have a cell phone? She promised herself she'd get one today. She thought of going to get a policeman to come back with her. But maybe what was on the paper were benign notes—even sweet little notes about the baby from her mother's friends, left on their ways off Cape. If she brought the police back with her, they'd decide once and for all that she was plain paranoid, and they'd write her off completely. She'd lose whatever sanity ground she'd gained in their eyes after the rock was thrown through her window.

She pulled the car as close to the porch as she could, ignoring the snow-obscured boundary between gravel drive and grass, and the stone walkway to her mother's studio. Leaving the motor running, she opened the car door and took four steps to where she could bend over to look at what was on her steps.

Confused because she'd started at the top where there was a piece of burned toast lying at her kitchen door, she had to go back and start reading the sticky notes from the bottom up. In that order, the notes read first, *You,* and then *ARe.*

Chapter 21

Rid had the heat on in the truck, but still an involuntary shiver ran down his spine. The late sky, which had been the color of a file cabinet, was darkening toward gunmetal. Dreary. The penetrating cold of humid air, that dankness. He'd finished buttoning the grant today, a relief because the real cold had hit earlier than usual this year. His remaining oysters were in the truck bed, ready to go into the pit. Now his winter work would start in earnest: repairing old cages and trays, building new ones, casting new Chinese hats. He'd check all his mesh envelopes and bags, looking for holes, taking inventory of how many new ones he needed to buy. And, of course, troll for the best deal he could get on quality matchhead quahogs and seed oysters for the nursery. He'd gone as far north as Maine to buy them last year. And he had to straighten out the mess of his paperwork or the state would be after him. Cut firewood. He'd try to pick up work on a scallop boat or a shrimper out of New Bedford, too. A couple of weeks and the cash would front him money for seed. The hatchery down in Dennis let him take seed on credit, and they were a guaranteed market for his mature stock, but he didn't want to be overly dependent on any one place, any more than his father had.

Rid and his stomach were both ruminating on the subject of dinner when he turned down his road. He'd defrosted a precooked pot roast concoction he'd discovered at the Stop & Shop and was ruminating about throwing canned potatoes, carrots and onions on top with a jar of beef gravy and putting the whole thing in the oven. Ought to work. Wouldn't take long to heat up at all.

He swallowed saliva. "Yeah, you can have some, girl," he said, patting Lizzie on the seat next to him. She licked his hand.

"Shit," he muttered. A Honda was in his driveway, somebody in the driver's seat. Not only that, it was blocking his access to his garage. He tapped lightly on the horn and swiped with his hand to show he wanted to get in his garage. He or she didn't seem to get it. The car started up and pulled forward, not what he wanted.

Impatient, Rid got out of the truck and strode to the driver's side. *Jesus.* He should have recognized the car. It was CiCi. Her face was all swollen and bleary-pink, like one of those oversize begonias his mother raised. Crying. Rid tried to open her door but it was locked. He tapped and pointed, saying, "Unlock it." When she did, he reached across her and turned the engine off. "You all right?"

No response. Taking her elbow, he said, "Come on in." She was still crying. And, he realized, shaking with cold. "How long have you been here?"

"A while," she said. Her teeth started to chatter as soon as she spoke.

"You all right?"

"Yes."

He hadn't locked the house. Nobody around but locals in winter. Inside, he led Caroline to the couch, sat her down, and put the afghan his mother had made over her. He turned up the thermostat. "Let me go turn off the truck and get Lizzie—watch out, remember she'll try her French kiss on you—and then I'll get you something hot to drink and make a fire. Or do you want a beer? Hey—CiCi—it's okay. Don't be scared. Are you sure you're all right?" He'd seen she was shaking and didn't know if it was cold or fear.

"I'm okay. Just freezing now. No beer," she shivered. "Can't drink. Pregnant. Have you got tea bags?"

When he came back in with the dog, he saw it was a good thing. Lizzie went to Caroline with wagging tail, jumped up on the couch to lick her face, and then circled her tail twice and lay with her head on Caroline's lap. Caroline stretched her arm over the dog's back.

"She's good as a heating pad," Rid said, tossing his scarf over the back of the recliner. He clomped into the kitchen to get out of his outer jacket and waders, and put them with his hat, gloves and another flannel layer in the utility area. "Want the TV on while I do some stuff?" he called in as he filled the kettle.

"Only if you do. But aren't you going to ask why I was in your driveway?"

Rid padded to the doorway in his wool socks to look across the living room at her. "You told me you're all right. That's all that's important. I figured to let you warm up first. And I'm so hungry my stomach thinks my throat's been cut. So I'm puttin' some dinner on for us. Gotta heat up and all. And I need to make a fire."

"That's very nice of you."

He started to tease her, to say something like *hey, be careful, better remember I'm the enemy* and for once in his life he thought better in time. He just approximated a smile and went back to the kitchen. The truth was he was afraid to start asking what she was doing there. He'd never once talked to her without it ending badly. Or very badly.

A quick succession of opening cans, the refrigerator opening and closing a few times, rummaging for a casserole dish, the can opener click and grind, a clatter of glass on glass and dinner was assembled in the oven. He went back into the living room where he already had paper, kindling and the first small pieces of wood on the hearth. Once those were in small, heartening flames, he went out his kitchen door and brought in three split pieces of seasoned hickory. "These'll keep the cold back a while. Nice slow burners, too."

"Such a beautiful big fireplace," Caroline said. "I really like the hearth."

"Yeah, you can sit on it if you're still got chills. Dad and Mom had this house built and they wanted an extra big fireplace. As you can see." He laughed as he straightened up, wiping his hands on his jeans, and did a grand gesture as if presenting the fireplace. "Ta-da. Lets in a wicked lotta cold when there's no fire in it, though. Wood stove's best for heat. Got one of those in the kitchen."

"I know what you mean. Ours is practically its twin. You've been in our house, right?"

"Is that a trick question? How many crimes you trying to get me to cop to?"

Startled. "No. No! I didn't mean it that way. I forgot. I mean, I didn't mean it that way. I'm sorry."

Rid was affected more by Caroline not throwing a dart at him then as much as he'd ever been hit by the ones she aimed square at him. She looked small on the couch, under his mother's multicolored afghan, her hair all mussed up, no make-up left, and her face showing that she'd recently cried. One of her arms was latched around Lizzie for dear life, too. "It's okay. I'm sorry. I shouldn't have said that," he said.

Caroline started to say something. The kettle whistled.

"I'll get you tea," Rid said, "and myself a beer. Hang tight." A moment later he was back. "Here's your tea. I left the bag in. Starting to smell good in there." He thumbed over his shoulder. "I put the oven up to 450 to hurry it up. Is that going to ruin it?"

Caroline smiled. "That would depend on what's in the oven, and the temperature at which it's supposed to be baked."

"Listen to you—*teacher*." But he was grinning back. "It's a frozen pot roast thing that was precooked. I already defrosted it. I added—oh, why don't you come look at it? I added a bunch of stuff and gravy. I've got the package."

In the kitchen, Caroline lowered the oven to 375. The directions had said 350. "About twenty more minutes, I'm guessing," Caroline said. "To heat it up thoroughly inside the meat. That extra gravy was a great idea. How about I set the table?"

Rid hadn't set a table in three years. "Uh, sure. He took out silverware, plates and napkins and set them on the counter, let CiCi take over with them. "Is it time to feed Lizzie? She's got a lean and hungry look," she said.

Dammit, does she have to be right about my dog? Lizzie was standing at her food bowl, staring into its yawning emptiness, then sadly up at him before swiveling her head back to the bowl just, he was sure, to make him look bad in front of CiCi. Where was her stinking loyalty?

He scowled at Lizzie, whose tail wagged in great scythe-like swoops, while he fed her, and Caroline set the table in the dining room, a nook between the kitchen and living room. Carrying his beer, he returned to the fire, a full blaze now, and waited for Caroline.

"Thank you for taking me in," she said when she did. "Ooh, that fire feels good. Obviously, I've calmed down and warmed up. I should tell you—"

"Okay."

"Okay what?"

"Okay, tell me."

"Oh. I spent the night last night at one of my mother's friend's houses. I went to my house after breakfast, and there were these notes on the steps, and toast, it was burned, and—"

"Back up a minute. What did the notes say?"

"They were going up the steps. One said, 'You' and the next said 'Are.'" Then on the top step was a piece of burned toast. I was so scared I just drove away. All my mother's friends are gone to visit relatives. Elsie, that's my mother's hospice nurse, we're sort of friends now, she's on vacation this week and I wouldn't bother her even if I *knew* where she was, and I didn't have anywhere to go. I drove around trying to figure out what to do and I just didn't know." As she explained, Caroline's eyes started to tear again. "I'm sorry," she said, wiping her eyes with her sleeve.

"Why were you sitting in the cold? I mean, you could have kept your heater running."

"I was running out of gas," she said simply. "I didn't know if I had enough to make it to a gas station. I thought Cumberland might even be closed—so many places are today. I was scared I'd get stranded. Stupid."

"Upset," Rid said, excusing her with a headshake.

"I didn't have anywhere to go," she said. "I thought of a motel, I thought of the police, but they never do anything. Then I thought of what you said about how we have to decide if we're ever going to trust each other."

"So I was your last hope."

"I guess."

"Did you call the police?"

"No," she whispered. "I don't trust them anymore."

"Okay. Well, let's eat, then I'll go to your house and see if that stuff is there. If it is, I'll call the police. Maybe if I call, it'll make a difference."

"Do you think I'm making it up?"

"Hey, I thought you were going to trust me?"

"I am, but—"

"*I'll* call the police."

Caroline nodded. "I see. Okay." She seemed exhausted, circles under her eyes, which were still reddened. Her lips were chapped, too, he saw. Now that she'd stopped crying, her face looked pale and bruisable as the flesh of a pear, accentuated by a too-big khaki-green sweater. He wondered if it were her father's. It reminded him of one his father had worn.

"Come 'n eat," Rid said. "If it's not hot enough, we can stick our plates in the microwave. Does it bother you for me to have a beer around you?"

"No. But thanks for asking. Is there a candle around I can light for the table?" she asked, unfolding her legs which were underneath her on the couch. As she stood up, Rid snuck a look while CiCi stood and turned three quarters away from him to refold the afghan. He saw for the first time the clear tight rise of pregnancy. Her sweater had crept up and her pants weren't zipped, but strained together by an oversized safety pin that bridged the sides, its metal rails pressed against her bellybutton. The sight affected him, though he hadn't words for how. Reflexively, Caroline pulled her sweater down over the whole arrangement just as he wondered if she'd let him feel her stomach. Rather than ask, he just went and dug around for candles left over from some holiday when his mother and sister had been around. And wouldn't *those* two just go berserk if they knew about this?

"You told anybody about the baby yet?" he asked as they sat down. He started to spoon some of the dinner onto his plate, suddenly thought, and put food on her plate first, then his own.

"Thanks. Ah, yes. On Christmas Eve. My mother's friends." She looked down at her belly with a hand gesture that featured it. "I sort of had to." Her tone was maybe a bit defensive but perhaps more apologetic, Rid couldn't tell. "I didn't say who you were by name, if that's what worries you. And Elsie, Mom's hospice nurse, she knows. But she's known a long time. She'd never say anything."

"I'm not worried. I didn't tell my family yet. I was just thinking about them. Hey, get going. Eat! I am." To prove his point he forked in a mouthful. The candlelight was nice, he realized. "I guess I thought—I guess I haven't thought it through enough to answer any of the questions they'll be throwing at me. No. Shooting at me is more like it. Bullets to be exact." He laughed, covering his full mouth with his hand, trying to remember all the manners stuff his mother always harped about.

"They'll be upset?" Caroline said, brow wrinkled, fork mid-journey.

"Didn't mean it that way. If *you* want 'em to know about it, they'll be shooting bullets of questions about what you're doing, every aspect of everything. What minute of what day the baby is due, when can they babysit—and the baby don't necessarily have to be born for them to start that by the way—what color is the nursery, what astrological sign will the baby be, is it a boy or a girl, can they see the sonogram, and what minute of what day can they see it. You know, that stuff."

"Isn't the issue more if *you* want them to know?"

"I guess we've got a lot to figure out. Probably why I kept quiet."

That was the only moment dinner became an awkward silence. Rid was in a maze, afraid to advance in any direction because he didn't know if he wanted to head out or go deeper in. A kernel of an idea was starting to take shape, but he hardly knew this woman, for one, and for two, he didn't know what *she* wanted. It was nice though, he thought, eating at the table with candles, and the fire going over in the living room where they could see it. He didn't want to mess it up, which he knew was his specialty.

Caroline rescued him. "You're right. We do. Probably this minute isn't the time. This food is really good, by the way. Thank you. I didn't realize how hungry I was. So what did you do for Christmas?"

He told her about his mother and his sister's family over the rest of dinner, and while they stuck the dishes in the dishwasher together. She stacked them the same way he did, front to back, not sideways, though they argued about the most efficient way to load glasses. "Wrong, wrong, wrong, you dork," she insisted.

"Pfft. What does a teacher know about managing space compared to a sea farmer? Listen," he said, turning on the dishwasher. "I was thinking I'd just go over to your place myself and check it out and call the cops. I hate to say this, but I think you better come with me."

Caroline blew out a heavy sigh. "If you could just follow me over there and check the house and call, I'd appreciate it. I have to go home, after all. I was too afraid to go in by myself. Maybe, if you're willing, if you have time, I mean, we could talk about what my options are—I mean the police are a joke—and I need to decide so much. I think we need to talk, too, about you and the baby, what you want to do. Rid, have you talked to that friend of yours you thought *might* be involved with all this—harassment?"

"He went off Cape over the holiday. See, he finally got a new truck—he sank his out off Great Island, long story—and when he got a new one, he went on a road trip. But he was still here when the rock thing happened. Not yesterday or the day before, though. And no, I haven't talked to him yet. I swear I will as soon as he shows up back here. He doesn't have a cell phone, don't ask me why."

As he spoke, Rid was getting out their coats and gloves, laying Caroline's on the table and putting on his own. He blew out the candles. "Come on, let's get it done," he said. He held her coat out for her.

"Did I even bring my keys in the house?" Caroline asked.

"If not we'd better get them, not that anybody bothers anything off season. We'll take my truck."

"I need my car," she turned and protested, pulling on her gloves. "I don't want to be stranded there."

"*No gas.*" Rid reminded her pointedly. "Come on, girl," he said, and then realized CiCi might have thought he was talking to her instead of the dog. "I mean Lizzie—but you, too. Anyway, we'll get your things and you can come back here tonight. It's too dangerous to be there alone. I've got extra bedrooms. I mean, you can sleep wherever you want." He added the last in case she thought he was trying something and realized, too late, he'd gone into double back overkill.

She looked at him hard an extra couple of seconds and he thought he was done for. "I appreciate that a lot. I *am* scared to stay there tonight. I have stuff out in the car, actually, from last night at Noelle's, but okay, let's go check the house, so we can call the police. I could pick up some fresh clothes for tomorrow, too," she said. So he knew he hadn't messed everything up. Not yet, anyway.

In the truck as Rid drove to her house through the dark abandoned roads, CiCi said, "You know, I really don't want to be in your way. I realize you're really busy. I have nothing but time on my hands. Couldn't you teach me some things and let me help out? I know that this time of year you're repairing and building cages, for one. Somebody taught *you* to do that. There's not a reason in the world you can't teach me. You're also looking for good seed. I'm good at research. There's probably other stuff you're running around looking for good prices on, equipment you have to buy or replace. I could help with that." Lizzie poked her nose between them from the back seat, and Caroline laughed softly, caressing the dog as Lizzie nuzzled first Rid and then Caroline's neck and cheek.

Rid had remained quiet while she spoke the whole piece. "Why would you want to do that?" *How does she know what I have to do?*

"Why do you sound so suspicious?"

"Habit, I guess."

"I thought we were changing our habits."

"Good point."

"So?"

"I dunno. I never had anybody around but Dad. I just—well, it just feels strange."

"I helped when that hurricane went past." Her face, though partly illuminated by snow and Christmas lights on a lawn they were passing, was inscrutable when he stole a quick look. Her voice was quiet. Factual.

"True." He had to be fair.

She let it drop then.

They rode in silence for another minute and a half, until he came up to her driveway. "Look first," he said. "Before I turn in. Any tire tracks that aren't yours? Anything different from—when? This morning, you said?"

Caroline leaned forward, peered on the ground illuminated by Rid's headlights. "I don't think so. It looks like two sets, but I came in and out. There was nothing when I came in. I did move my car around up by the house. And I drove over the lawn. I saw stuff on the porch, and I was too scared to get out of the car."

Rid started to say something, then stopped himself. He inched the truck down the driveway, his beams on high. Halfway down, he swung sharply to the right and then to the left, angling the truck to put his beams directly on the back door of the house.

He pulled forward, Caroline perched and hunched so as to get as close to the windshield as she could. He heard her intake of breath then the upset, "*Oh my God, my God.*"

"Rid, they're gone. The stuff is gone. I swear it was there. Please believe me. It was all there. And listen, on Christmas morning, too, I found a teddy bear in a bag on the back step. That's still inside the house. I was stupid and I touched it, but I thought it was from one of my mother's friends, because I'd told them the night before but then they all brought presents to Noelle's, so I know—"

"Calm down," he said, "it's okay. Nothing to be scared of."

"No, it's not nothing, you've got to bel—" she had started to cry again as she interrupted.

He broke in, touching her arm, trying to stop her panic. "I mean the teddy bear. That was from *me*. I'm sorry. I should have left a note."

"From you?" She looked at him intently.

"Yeah, but nothing else, nothing else. You hear me? There was nothing else around then, and what I put here was the teddy bear in a bag. Period. It was Christmas Eve, and I intended to hand it to you, see, and when you weren't here, I thought as long as the bag was wide open and you could see what it was, you'd know it was fine."

"Oh." She paused, trying to take it in and still think about the missing notes and toast on the back steps. "It's a beautiful bear." Still upset, and remembering to be polite.

"You stay in the truck." Rid reached under his seat and brought out a big flashlight. He left the truck running so the heat would be on and tried to keep jumping into Caroline's tire tracks while he looked for footprints. Ahead he saw the marks where she'd driven up over the yard and walk. She really had been too scared to get out. Seeing this manifestation of her fear made him realize it differently as he jumped over some of the unbroken snow crust into CiCi's tire prints where they paralleled the side of the house. The yard security lights were still on, as was the porch light. His truck beams lit the place like a prison yard, too. He played his flashlight along the ground and the steps. Could he make out faint outlines of where the notes had been or the toast? Not enough to call the police.

Rid gestured to Caroline to come. She got out of the truck tentatively. "Nothing here now," he called. "Let's get your stuff."

Anxiety pinching her face, she unlocked the door. "Rid, please believe me, there was…." Then she just didn't go on. She looked freezing again. The coat she was wearing, either it didn't fit her or she was just colder than the weather.

Rid put her hood up, tightened the drawstring under her chin, letting his hand linger on her shoulder as they turned to go inside. "How come you're so cold? I left the heat on," he said as they went inside her kitchen and shut the door.

"I'm just completely freaked out. I should have gone ahead and called the police this morning. I don't have a cell phone, and I was afraid to go inside. But I should have just driven to the police station instead of all over the lower Cape and sitting in your driveway. Now it's all gone, and I just don't do anything right. But I didn't think he'd come back in the daylight. Maybe he didn't. It's dark again now. I just don't know." Tears were breaking out again. "I'm losing my mind is what's happening."

Rid put his arms around her, which had the feel of trying to reassure a board wrapped in a quilt at first, and he almost gave up. But then she gave way and let her weight go against him. He took a step back, bracing himself against a wall, to be steady for her, while he stroked her back and soothed her. "It's okay. I'll help you," he said, just as if his own plate weren't already hopelessly overloaded with the damn lawsuit. "The wind could have taken the notes. Gulls most likely took the toast." It *was* possible. More likely, Rid thought, whoever put it there had come back and removed it to play with her mind or to make her look crazy again with the police. He saw no point in saying that to CiCi, though.

"Go get whatever you need," he said when she seemed to be straightening up. While she went into the downstairs bedroom, he checked around the kitchen and living room (so different without the hospital bed and equipment) and noticed the teddy bear bag on the kitchen counter. When she emerged from the bedroom with a plastic bag, he put the bear in her arms. "An extra friend to bring along," he said.

"He's so soft," she said, bringing the bear to her cheek. "I love him. And I want to show you the things Mom's friends gave the baby for Christmas, too. It's all in my car. They actually went out on Christmas Eve night, after I'd told them at dinner, and brought all this stuff to Noelle's to surprise me on Christmas Day," Caroline said as they went out and locked the door again. She went ahead of him to the truck, still talking, while Rid continued to play his flashlight around the steps. "Noelle had figured it out on her own. She'd already made a crib quilt. By hand."

Along the very edge of the foundation behind the shrubbery, where there was no snow thanks to the overhang of the roof, Rid saw it might be possible to walk without leaving tracks. From there, of course, a determined person could round the corner and get to the side of the house that was mostly wild, a thicket of overgrown beach plums, wild roses, rose hips, and scrub pine. Recent experience had taught him about getting through that stuff, but it had also taught him it *could* be done. Too dark now to investigate if there were signs of disturbance there, but he could come back tomorrow and have a look-see.

 *Chapter 22*

Lizzie roused Rid at five fifty-six in the morning, nuzzling his neck and ear, nudging his shoulder with her insistent muzzle. If he didn't get up, she'd start licking his face, guaranteed to get him moving. Beyond the small incandescent glow of the clock numerals near his face, the darkness and silence were equal, complete, heavy. The house felt freezing, the bed just right. The cost of oil was killing him. He'd need to build a fire in both the wood stove and the fireplace tonight and try not to use the furnace so much.

"You know, you *could* let me sleep in. We can't cut firewood until it's light, or haven't you noticed?" he muttered, caressing the Lab's chest as she stood over him on the bed. Sometimes if he rubbed her chest and stomach, she'd let him put off getting up to feed her another twenty minutes. Lizzie collapsed next to him and rolled onto her back, bought off.

The upstairs toilet flushed, right next to his room, and Lizzie was on the floor barking up a frenzy. Rid was out of bed, his bare feet on the freezing floor, feeling the end of the bed, the chair, for anything he could put on as he stumbled toward the door, confused, Lizzie in his way, even though it was best to let her take the lead. *What kind of intruder flushes a toilet?* Too late. He'd opened his bedroom door and Lizzie was all over Caroline, but it was her joy dance and a French kiss. Caroline staggered, laughing.

"I'm sorry if I woke you," she said.

"No, no, not at all—Lizzie gets up earlier than this. I've been trying to hold off feeding her. I wanted you to sleep," he lied. He'd not found anything to put on, so was self-conscious about the fly of his pajamas and shifted the bottom around so it was off to the side. "The house is colder than I thought. Hope you were warm enough, I'll get some heat up right away, soon's I feed Liz," he said, not waiting for an answer and passing Caroline in the hall, giving her wide berth. Contracting muscles, refusing to let her see him shiver.

Downstairs, the kitchen floor stung the bottoms of his feet like dry ice. He turned up the thermostat. Then he let Lizzie out, got out a coat to serve as a robe, and pulled a pair of twice-worn wool socks out of his yard boots into which he immediately stuffed his feet

Lizzie came back in and wolfed her food while Rid made a fire in the woodstove. "She's got to stay here while we're gone, girl. Gotta get this house warm. Geez, I hope the quilt on her bed is that heavy one. Think so. Maybe not. It's wicked cold. Better check. We gotta remember she's here—can't be runnin' outta the shower naked, now can we?" He talked on to the dog as he always did, noticing after the sentence had come and gone that he was expecting that she'd be there a while and he didn't seem to be objecting to it even though he'd turned up the furnace.

There was just the one bathroom upstairs. A bit awkward, but he took his jeans and flannel shirt in there, showered, and dressed fully before he emerged. He needn't have bothered. He found Caroline downstairs, having evidently used the bathroom down there, already dressed and with coffee brewing. She had eggs and bread out on the counter and was just pulling out the fry pan when he made it into the kitchen.

"How do you like your eggs?" Her hair was wet, combed and tucked behind her ears. She must have taken the world's fastest shower. His sister used to stay in the shower so long their father would go in the other bathroom and start flushing the toilet every twenty seconds until she got out, wet hen flappin' mad.

"Huh?"

"I can fix them however you like," she said. She had on a red sweater, which was too big everywhere except her belly. It looked good, though, maybe because her cheeks were ruddy. Probably from being cold.

"You don't have to do that. I usually just—"

"Eat out or grab coffee."

"Yeah." Had he told her that?

"I can earn my keep," she said with a laugh. "I really appreciate your letting me stay here last night."

Last night? He hadn't said anything about her not staying longer. But should he let it go? "Listen, I'm about to head over to your place. After breakfast, I mean. I'm going to look around in daylight, see if there's—something."

"I should go with you," she said, the skin between her eyebrows bunching together.

"You should stay here." He meant more than this morning. Surely she could figure that out.

⚜

After they ate—she made good eggs, with pepper and something else sprinkled on them—he beat back her protests and left her there. More winter Cape, dank, a wet cold, more snow than usual, and his truck splattered with grimy road salt. The seat next to him was cavernous and abandoned as the ocean side beach. CiCi had asked if Lizzie could stay with her. He'd automatically started to say she *always rides with me*, then even while she was interrupting to say *oh, of course, sorry*, Rid realized maybe she was scared to be alone and being worked up might be bad for the baby.

Caroline's driveway looked as it had the night before. He tried to drive in his own tracks, might have widened them slightly, but came close. His tires bit and crunched the snow like celery when he backed up in the three point turn and ate into unbroken snow behind him. This time it was his own footsteps he stayed in going to the back stoop. Nothing.

He inspected the area under the eaves. It looked to him as if the snow, less in that protected area, might have been disturbed, though it was difficult to tell because of drifting. It wasn't clear enough to track. He walked there himself now, edging along the house toward the back, the side that had been left to the wild.

When he reached the corner, he scanned behind the house. In spite of the lack of sunshine, the snow was hard to read beyond his own boots and a few feet ahead. Still, something about the thicket itself looked wrong. Rid waded away from the cedar shake siding of the house—there was hardly any space—to inspect the overgrown maze of beach plum and wild rose. A broken branch. Two more, deeper in. He backed out, scratching his face as he did. Touching the sting with his glove, he went back to the corner and tried walking into the snow between Eleanor's studio and the wild area, where there was a narrow swath of yard. He went slowly, looking up and down, trying to see into the thicket. Even so, he almost missed it, damp and folded on itself as it was.

A small yellow piece of paper caught on a branch of rose hip like a bedraggled flag. Beach trash is all it seemed. Only the faded lemon color made him look twice. He had a struggle retrieving it. He took it to his truck to open so he could take his gloves off, lay it flat. The thing had been soaked more than once as best he could tell, which made sense given the weather.

aRE.

So she'd been right. Not that he'd doubted her. He'd seen the rock through the window after all, but CiCi was so freaked out now that anything was possible.

Rid started the engine to heat up the cab. His first impulse had been to use his cell to call the police. Maybe he'd messed up any footprints, but he could tell the story, show them the broken branches and this paper and then he could be there when they talked to CiCi. He knew those guys, locals every one. He could back her up. But he studied the sticky note, belatedly remembering there might be fingerprints on it, then handling it like a hot cookie, gingerly, at its very edge.

It could be Mario's writing: this was his style, mixing capital and lower case letters, none of which exactly stood up like soldiers. Rid tried to argue with himself. *You can't tell by three letters*, which he knew was both logical and true. This was also how someone would disguise his writing, or how someone who had done about as well in school as Mario might write.

The longer he sat, the sicker he felt. They had a meeting at one this afternoon at Lorenz's office. If Mario was out of the mix, what would happen to their defense? He couldn't call the police yet. He put the slip of yellow paper in his glove compartment and sat another ten minutes staring at Caroline's house. Took it back out and turned his cell phone on. Sat some more, the paper withered and beaten-appearing as a dried flower on the passenger side now. As it dried, its surface looked curdled, the generic blue ballpoint ink another degree of faded. *Anybody coulda done that*, he told himself. *No proof.*

Finally, he put it back and completed the turn to leave Caroline's driveway. Leaving, he still tried to stay in his own tracks though he didn't know why and shook his head to try to clear his mind.

Back at his house, he avoided Caroline's eyes by heading straight for the closet when he came in. That way, he could say, "Snow under the eaves looked like it might have been disturbed there but it was drifted over, no footprints, nothing that could be tracked, couple broken branches behind the house, but, y'know, police would probably say it's deer," and it was all the truth.

"That's what I was afraid of," she said. Her hair was dry now, but her cheeks were still red.

"You cold?" he asked, picking up her hand as if all he wanted was to check if her skin was warm, but she said she was fine, and he felt silly telling her no she wasn't, that her fingers felt icy and he could rub them. Still, she squeezed his hand before he let go.

He spent the rest of the morning building cages. CiCi made a fresh pot of coffee. "I saw a coffee cake in the freezer. How about I hack off a couple of slices and warm them up for us? I can put the rest back in the freezer," she said when she carried the warm mug to his basement work area.

"You can do that?"

"Sure. It's easier if you cut it ahead and freeze slices, but this works too. I'll rewrap the rest in plastic."

"Yeah. Okay, good. Mom sent that back with me after Christmas."

She stayed when she came back with the cake and a refill, watching him cut a rigid piece of plastic that was laid out on a pattern with a sheet rock knife. Mesh screening and wire ties were already cut and laid out on another table. Caroline was quiet, intent, bending over to watch what he was doing.

"Everything about this has to be perfect, see?" Rid said, filling the silence. "One tiny hole, a crab gets in, and well, you can't believe how one crab can go through a whole nursery tray of your three millimeter babies, wipe out every damn one. So I'm a nutcase about my trays when I build 'em or fix 'em." A few minutes later, he finished with one and said, "I got a meeting this afternoon at one, at the lawyer's, y'know, about the lawsuit. I'll see him, the partner I told you about. I'll talk to him and find out."

"Will he tell you the truth?"

"Not necessarily. But he's a bad liar. I'll know."

"What time do you have to leave?"

"A little after twelve."

At eleven-fifteen, Caroline went upstairs. Ten minutes later, she called down to him that she had lunch ready anytime he wanted it.

Five minutes later his feet were heavy on the wooden stairs. "You don't need to do this," he said gruffly, turning out the basement light behind him. "I mean, it's nice, but I don't expect…."

"I'm glad to do it. I appreciate the help you're giving me," she said simply.

"Anyway, you're working right now. I have nothing else to do." She blew her hair off her forehead by sticking her bottom lip out. His mother and sister both did that, too, and it made CiCi look oddly familiar.

Something on the stove smelled good. "What'd you make?"

"I doctored some canned soup you had—you know, added fresh vegetables and seasonings. It's an old trick. And there's a sandwich on the table. What would you like to drink?"

"I'll get it." She was making it hard. Do the right thing, his mother used to say. She made it sound like it was easy to know what the right thing was. Wasn't it as good as calling the police if he handled Mario himself? So long as the job got done it *was*.

❀

Rid had turned down Tomas's offer of a ride to Barnstable with a lie about collecting on two overdue accounts along the way. He'd hoped to corner Mario before the meeting, but Mario was late. They waited for him for twelve minutes, lawyer expense time ticking and Tomas burning like coal, until Mario came in complaining about the on-Cape traffic returning from his vacation, but not appearing as though he'd run from wherever he'd parked or up the stairs, which was a serious error in judgment. If Tomas had been packing a weapon, Mario would have been dead.

David Lorenz picked up on the tension in the room, which didn't require a sixth sense. "If you men are going to be partners and make it work, well, you know, you gotta at least try to be on speaking terms occasionally, or bring a woman with you as interpreter." He was trying for jocularity, but it fell like an anchor.

"We're all right, thank you," Tomas said quietly. "Let's get on with business. Now that we're all *here*." He looked at his watch.

David Lorenz sighed. "I'm trying to give you advice that will help you, because it seems you will have the opportunity to be in business together if you choose. I've located the person to whom the tidal flats at Indian Neck are still deeded."

Mario jumped in. "And it ain't Pissario? Or the real estate developer? You were right?"

"That's correct. Someone was just very careless and didn't record beach rights out to mean low tide, although they certainly could have. It happens.

People make mistakes. Fortunately." Lorenz ran his hand over his head, smoothing down flyaway hair, then adjusted his heavy glasses back up on his nose. He leaned back in his chair and smiled. "I haven't approached the couple who still owns the rights, although, frankly, just owning tidal flats is pretty useless if you're not a shellfisher, and especially if you don't have a license. There's really not a lot of usable beach there, correct? I'm trying to think like they might. Why not turn something useless into cash?"

"That's right," Rid inserted, covering the same ground with his thoughts. "There's some beach that's good at low tide, when we're there, pretty much none at high tide. And you can't really walk the beach, because it leads around the bend into Blackfish Creek. There's no grant space left open there, so nobody can take up shellfishing there, whether they own it or not. Unless, of course, they kicked us all off and—man, I don't even want to go there."

Lorenz nodded. "That's part of the risk we talked about. Also, that this could somehow get to Pissario and he could outbid you. Or the owner of the rights could go off in search of a higher bidder. Remember, you have the option of just fighting Pissario in court and hoping you win. You definitely have a chance to come out on top."

"But then he appeals, and appeals again. And we get farther away from the local court where a judge knows how we live, and pretty soon we go broke anyway," Tomas said quietly, and it was the quiet that was dangerous. "I say trying to buy the flats is our best chance. I want my life in my own hands. I'd rather be executed now than sit on death row for ten years and then get the bullet."

"An interesting metaphor," Lorenz said. "But you're correct, as I've said, that the court process could drag on for years. Honestly, I don't see any fail-safe alternative, so you should pick the one you think you can tolerate best."

"Or the one in which we have the potential to gain the most," Tomas mused, ruddy-faced, in his good overalls, his face gone to an inscrutable mask as he looked into the future.

"Indeed," Lorenz assented, head bobbing up and down behind his desk. The motion made his glasses slide down his nose and he repositioned them before becoming still.

There was a moment of extreme silence, during which the lawyer hiccupped and Mario's stomach complained. The furnace kicked on, and Rid shifted which leg was crossed over the other.

"Let's do it. Let's buy the damn flats," Tomas said.

"I hate waiting," Mario said. "I'm in."

"We've gotta talk about how much we're going to offer. I don't know how I'm going to raise the money, but I'm in," Rid said, trying to smother automatic panic about where he could come up with yet another pile of cash.

"Good decision. Two things you need to do," David Lorenz said, moving his legal pad in front of him and clicking his ballpoint open. "You need to form and name a realty partnership, and make an offer. So let's get to work."

It was good he'd driven down alone. Not that he'd had the confrontation with Mario that he'd planned. Caroline would kill him for that, and she had a right. Now he'd have to do that later. Right now he was shell-shocked. Too much to take in. They'd decided to offer twenty-five thousand dollars for the flats. Lorenz, Rid could tell, thought it might not be quite enough, but with all the legal bills they'd run up already, this was another eight thousand three hundred something, bango, on top of what else he had to come up with. It was all too much to wrap his mind around.

He'd turned them down when Mario suggested a drink at The Oyster, saying he was way behind on paperwork, and pretty much everything else. That much at least was true. He had to go home and tell Caroline the truth, then figure out what he could sell to come up with the money.

Once inside, though, kicking snow loose from his boots at the door, but still tracking some across the tiles on his way to the big closet under the stairs, his resolve was melting like the ice he'd tracked in. As before, he avoided Caroline by going through the hall by the stairs.

"How'd it go?" she called from the living room. He had a quick glimpse of her red sweater. She was sitting on the floor with the pieces of a nursery tray spread all around her, as he went from front door into the hallway toward the kitchen where the big closet and the stairs to the basement were. He started to ask what the hell she thought she was doing, and then there was too much else that filled the space between them.

"Pretty good," he called back. She got up and came the other way, through the dining nook, to meet him in the kitchen. And then, like an offering, instead of telling her about Mario, like putting a big IOU in an offering plate, he told her something far more dangerous to himself personally. "You have to promise me—I mean on the baby's life, that kind of promise—that you won't tell anyone something."

"All right," she said, sliding into a seat at the table. He noticed her belly then, how she sort of pushed it down to make herself fit underneath rather than pull the chair out while she answered without thinking about either her belly or the answer, it seemed.

"The three of us, we formed a company and we're putting in an offer to buy the tidal flats from the real owner. See Pissario *thinks* he owns them, but his land wasn't registered right, and our lawyer found out about it. Pissario doesn't know." Rid sat across from her at the table and explained what Lorenz had learned, how they were trying to do it all without Pissario getting wind of it, and how he had to figure out what to sell now.

"So what's the name of your realty company?" Caroline said, which Rid found a strange question.

"You promised," he said, suddenly nervous about disclosing it all. "Pissario can't get wind of this.

"I'm on your side, remember?"

Rid sat back in his chair and grinned for a few seconds. "Other Foot Realty. As in *the shoe's on the other foot now, and watch out buster, because we may just use it to drop kick you straight to hell.*"

"Great name," she said with a smile. "You want me to put on some coffee—or you want a beer?" She started to lean forward on her elbows and slide her butt back to get up from the table, obviously intending to get him something to drink, like there was no more to say about the subject.

He never knew quite how to take her. "You really think it's a good name? You think the whole thing'll work?"

She hesitated. "What about the—"

Goddammit. A volcano started rumbling in Rid's head. She thought they were crazy. "What's wrong with it? You think the real owners will go to Pissario? Hell, they don't have any use themselves for the flats," he erupted.

Now she was stopped, half-up, half-down, propped on her forearms, leaning over the table. "I didn't say that. You already said you're in debt, I was just—"

"You don't seem to get it. Even if we win, Pissario will appeal and keep us tied up in court forever. Next time he might be able to get an injunction, too." His voice continued to rise, but he couldn't seem to stop it. He unbuttoned the top of his shirt. The house was too damn warm now. And where was Lizzie?

"Where's Lizzie?"

"On the couch. I hope that's okay. I was working in there, and she jumped up next to me. You didn't make her get down the other day, so I figured she was allowed." Caroline shifted her weight to one arm and gestured over her shoulder, toward the living room where the tray parts were spread out on the floor.

What was she doing with his stuff? Not trying to make a repair, for God's sake! She'd only watched him a little while that morning. "Yeah. Hey, what are you doing with—"

Caroline sat back down the rest of the way. "Rid, I could put some money into the realty company for you. I inherited enough from my mother."

"No way."

"Why not?"

"Look, thanks for the offer, but this is my thing, and I want to keep it that way."

"I'm not trying to take anything away from you." Seated, but leaning toward him just the same, keeping her tone reasonable.

"But it would happen, and that's what scares me."

"No, it wouldn't."

Now she was starting to get mad, he saw, but keeping it in check. Well, so be it. He wasn't going to have worked so hard to keep his grant and then go halfsies with some chick just because he needed money in a pinch. "The discussion is over," he said. "No."

"Look, I can loan it to you, then."

"OVER!"

She let loose. "I get it that you're scared, but *I'm* not the one trying to do anything to you, here. *I'm* scared to death. *I'm* scared something's wrong with the baby, *I'm* scared of your nutcase partner—*and by the way, did you talk to him?*—if he's the one threatening me, I'm scared out of my mind if you haven't noticed, and I get it you're scared about the lawsuit but that's no reason to shout at me. I thought we were going to help each other."

Suddenly sober and wild at once. "What's wrong with the baby?"

"Nothing that I know of. I'm scared, because of the accident, and what I did! Do you believe in karma?"

Then, to make things worse, she started crying. He could never do a single thing right around her for more than a minute and a half. "Did some doctor tell you something?"

"I haven't been to a doctor yet."

"What? *Jesus.* Why the hell not?"

She shook her head helplessly. A shrug. "All the chaos—" she started.

"What are you thinking? You're *supposed* to."

"I'll take care of it. How about *you* talk to your partner like you *said* you would and get off my case."

It was too much, too much. Couldn't he manage anything right except to love the flats and a dog? Rid grabbed his keys, whistled for Lizzie, stumbled back into his boots and jacket even as he headed back for the front door, pulling them on as he went. He undermined the drama of his exit by stepping on a loose bootlace and tripping. Lizzie did not appear enthusiastic about going with him, a cut. Still, with the dignity he could gather, and his reluctant dog, he stomped to his truck, revved it and showed her how fast he could get off her case, since that's what she wanted. With nowhere to go, he spun left out of the driveway toward Route 6 because at least that would get him nowhere a helluva lot faster than 6A, which was to the right.

 *Chapter 23*

He drove aimlessly for a while, first heading for Provincetown, shame arguing with anger, trying hard to let anger win. He'd left Caroline trapped at his house—still no gas in her car, at least he didn't think she'd chance it—and now he'd trapped himself away from the house, just as neatly. "I'd do anybody else's whole shit list if they'd do this one thing for me, girl" he told Lizzie. Then, "Don't look at me like that. Your place is with me." He reached over to the glove compartment and took out a biscuit to sweeten the deal. The Lab snuffled it out of his hand. "Yeah, I know what you like," he said, caressing her ears. Then, "Goddammit, it's *my* grant. They're *my* goddamn trays."

Then, when shame won, he was angry about that, too. "She's right about one thing, Lizzie. I didn't talk to Mario, that fucker."

He'd turned his truck around back toward Wellfleet and The Oyster where Mario's truck was in the parking lot. He'd known it would be. Across the street, the shellfish shack was showing the orange ball. No fishing, obvious given that it was well below twenty-eight. It felt like twenty-eight below, what with the wind.

He parked some distance away, figuring Mario might come out mad. He might come out mad himself. They couldn't afford it, though. The partnership had to survive.

The afternoon was dwindling into graveyard weather, smoky with souls and ghosts as another round of snow created a faux twilight of obscured visibility. Rid motioned Lizzie to the back seat and put out her blanket. He'd brought her with him more to irritate Caroline than anything else. It was later than he'd thought, though, past Lizzie's suppertime. He put some water in the dish on the truck floor. "Not long, girl. I promise." Lizzie sighed and settled on her blanket.

Mario was at the bar, still the dressed-up version of himself he'd been in the lawyer's office. Rid mock slugged him on the shoulder. "Come on, man, let's get a table."

"Thought you had too much to do," Mario said.

"Yeah, well, I got thirsty."

"Slide in here." Mario gestured to the stool next to his. He was sitting on his jacket, the limp arms extending to the plank floor, hat and gloves on the bar, taking the space of two customers in season. The hat was new, looked like a fur-lined baseball cap with ear-flaps, Rid noticed, annoyed. There was a time he'd have made fun of it.

"Hey, Billy, how y'doin'?" Rid said pointedly. "Nah, let's grab a table, want something to eat?" He hoped Mario hadn't had more than a couple beers. "Or did you already?"

"No, I'm okay. Just another brew."

"Come on, let's get a table, there's business." He could tell Mario was a bit gone, not too far yet. "Billy, can you bring us a couple drafts, and how about a double order of wings, single order of fries." Something he knew Mario would eat that might keep him from getting shit-faced.

Billy drew the beer, wearing frustration that he was being excluded from their conversation. He plunked the mugs on the bar with too much force. "The rest'll be up whenever King Chuck sees fit. Can you get these to a table by yourselves?" He had gelled his hair, and wore two silver bracelets and a heavy silver ring that looked new, all on his left hand. On his right wrist, a second watch appeared when his sleeve rode up; Rid almost said something about it, but stopped. The goal was to get away, after all.

"We'll manage somehow," Rid said.

Mario started to protest, but Rid picked up the mugs and headed well away from the bar. Only three people were there, two—Rick and Monty—he knew. They had grants over off Egg Island, and Rid nodded to them while he herded Mario to a table against the back wall.

Maybe more sober than Rid had calculated; once they were seated Mario challenged him. "All right, what's up?" The light was low enough in the bar that Mario's eyes appeared black instead of brown and his skin as dark as it did in August. An old scar was visible on one side of his face in the better light coming from the entryway with its glass doors to the waning daylight. There was no light in Mario's eyes, though, which made Rid uneasy.

And, he had no approach prepared. "Uh ... you, uh ... you know the chick I...."

"Knocked up?"

"Yeah, that's the one. Listen, someone's been messing with her."

Mario snickered, stopping Rid cold. "So I heard from Billy. Billy figured it to be *me*, since she's a waterfront owner, and I figured it to be *you* since you're the handy dandy daddy."

Rid leaned back in his chair. "What? *Me?* How do you figure that? She's, for Christ sake, man, she's pregnant."

Mario smirked. "Didn't know you had such family feeling. So you're saying it's not you?"

"No it's *not* me." The realization that Mario was playing him as he'd played Caroline started to come to him.

"No you don't. No, you don't," Rid said, leaning forward, getting into Mario's face, using the side of his arm to sweep Mario's cap and gloves to the side of the table and nearly knocking over Mario's beer as he did. "*I'm* not what this is about. You're what it's about. *You* and rocks through windows and notes in *your* handwriting and burned toast on doorways."

There was probably no faking the confusion on Mario's face when he threw in the bit about burned toast.

"Burned *what?*" Mario said.

"Toast."

"Like bread?"

"Like bread."

"What's the point of that?" Irritated, loud.

"As if you don't know." Sarcastic.

"I *don't* know." Mario was shouting now.

Billy interrupted them with the food, setting it between them. "Do I have to set up a DMZ here?" he teased, a hand on a hip. "You need me to call in some of my boys, break things up?"

"Beat it, Billy." Gesturing with his thumb back toward the kitchen, Rid tried to soften it with a half smile.

"No fighting."

"It's cool, Billy. Go on back," Rid said again. He waited for Billy to get all the way back behind the bar where he couldn't hear, though he continued to watch, wary of fists. That must mean that Mario had been drinking longer than Rid had guessed. "Calm down, Mario. Last thing we need is Billy getting between us. He might lose an earring, and how would we live with ourselves?"

Mario chuckled.

"Here, let's have us some wings." Rid pulled the plates closer between them, picked up a wing, dipped it into sauce, and gestured to Mario to do the same. Mario salted the fries. "Grab that ketchup, will ya?" he said, pointing to the table behind Rid. Both men ate in silence for a couple of minutes.

"Okay, maybe we can get back to this," Rid said, wiping his hands on a napkin. "How about this? It's your handwriting." He pulled the water-warped yellow sticky note with its ballpoint *aRE* from the pocket of his flannel shirt.

Mario shrugged, hands up. Again, his confusion looked genuine. "I do sorta print like that, but I didn't write that, not that I remember anyway. Doesn't go with anything, for one. I wouldn't have no call to write one word on a page like that."

"So you're saying you had nothing to do with any of it?"

"Nah. Can't say I lost sleep over it, though. Figured she was in with Pissario, and I was givin' you the credit for it myself."

Rid took a long drink of beer while he considered how much to say. "She's not. In with Pissario, I mean."

"You know that for sure?"

"Yeah."

Mario narrowed his eyes. "How?"

"Take my word. If you get any wind—anything—on who might be doing this stuff to her, you tell me, right? For some reason, the cops are passing on it. I'm going to talk to Jerry though, now that I know it's not you. It's not you for sure, right? It's okay to talk to Jerry?" He was giving Mario another chance to stop him, although Mario could probably figure he didn't have anything new to take to the cops right now.

"Go ahead man, talk to Jerry or any other cop. It won't be me you sic 'em on. We're cool."

"Okay. Thanks. So, uh, you got your share lined up for the uh… 'shoe'?"

For once Mario didn't miss a beat. "Pretty much. You?" Mario answered, looking out from underneath his brow because his head was bent over a plate at the moment. Rid felt himself being sized up.

"Working on it. Prob'ly pick up some time on a scallop boat outta

N'Bedford." *I could do it easy as you if I was running drugs, of course.* Rid kept the thought to himself.

The two finished the wings and fries and each had another draft. The bar was a quarter full by the time they were finished, all locals and most pulled chairs around Rid and Mario's table. One grant holder from around Mayo Beach asked them about the progress of the suit—"Nothin' in the paper for a while," he said, but Rid held up a hand and said, "Nope, you'll get nuttin from Fort Mario Knox, and I personally am far too drunk to speak," at which everyone guffawed. The shellfish warden said, "Leave 'em alone boys 'n girls. Best you can do is buy their beer and pray for 'em." Tomas came in and joined them. Rid could tell he was immediately nervous about how much Mario had had to drink. Himself too, probably, and whether they'd let anything slip. He tried to sober up his own demeanor to reassure Tomas.

It was after seven when Rid pushed back from the table, calling Mario aside from the group. "I'm taking off. Listen, Tomas is nervous as a cat. Watch yourself. No mistakes."

"Yeah. I know." Mario's forehead was sweaty, and his eyes showed the beer, though. Tomas should get him out of the bar soon, but Tomas would figure that out.

"Hey, no hard feelings about the other, huh? We gotta trust each other."

"Yeah. S'okay." He stuck out his hand for Rid to shake, and Rid had a good five seconds of peace until Mario went on. "It took me a while to get it back, y'know. For a long time I thought one a you guys had a cell phone the night my truck sank—thought you'd stabbed me in the back. I was just bein' stupid. You're right. We gotta trust each other, partner." He seemed to make an unnecessary point of extending the hand shake and their eye contact.

❀

"So what the hell do we tell Caroline, huh, girl?" Rid had his truck barreling down Route 6. "That Mario's off the hook? That the son-of-a-bitch probably did it all, but he'll likely quit now? Yeah, she'll just go for that one, won't she now?" It was still snowing, and the flakes were the main thing his headlights illuminated, but there was so little traffic that he wasn't concerned. He kept his brights on, which probably didn't help except to alert oncoming vehicles he was there. Everybody else would do the same. He had four wheel drive. Some damn fool pedestrian was walking against traffic, doubtless headed to the Cumberland Farms convenience store he'd just passed.

A mile or so further on he figured it out. A disabled car, hazard lights blinking, was on the opposite shoulder. "Poor bastard. Bad night to be stuck. So, Lizzie, I guess we just go with Mario's off the hook. I made my point, he made his. You think?" Lizzie edged over on the seat and licked his face. "Yeah, me too."

He swung off Route 6 toward his house, rehearsing what he'd say to repair the fight. By the time he pulled into the driveway, he thought he had it about right.

"CiCi?" Calling as he opened the front door, which was locked. Rid flipped on lights as he made his way back to the kitchen. "Hey, Caroline!" The house was colder than he'd have expected. Had she let the wood stove go out? "CiCi? Where are you?" Worry in his voice now. He opened the basement door but there were no lights on down there. He ran up the stairs to check the bedrooms, Lizzie at his heels.

It came to him suddenly. Her car. It wasn't in the driveway. *Goddammit.* He reversed so suddenly that he ran into Lizzie, who let out a rare yip of pain. "Sorry, girl, sorry." Then, talking to himself, "Calm down, it's okay. She probably went to her place. Mario was with me, nothin' gonna happen over there," working through it logically as he bent to check the dog, whose paw he'd tromped and shoulder he'd kneed. "I'm sorry, girl, you okay?" On his haunches, over and over he pushed down panic as he caressed Lizzie and massaged one of her front paws. "Mario's not going to do anything else anyway. We'd had an argument, I took off, I was gone too long. She must've got more and more pissed off. Okay, first thing to do is call over there, make my apology, tell her I went to talk to Mario," Rid explained to the dog.

Back downstairs, on his way to the phone by his recliner, he checked the bathroom she'd been using. "Her stuff's not here. That's not good. Shouldn't have gone out in this weather, for one thing, and no need to go off just because."

At once, he knew. Gas. He knew damn well she'd told him there wasn't gas in the car. He'd known it when he drove off this afternoon. *Stupid, stupid.* Then, the image of the snow walker on Route 6, the disabled car with the hazard lights flashing. No. *No.* In a frantic fluster, his manufactured calm in shards, he stuffed his feet back into boots, fumbled for coat and keys, dropping the keys as he tried to pick them up at the same time he pulled on gloves, and stumbled for the front door. *No.* Eyes stinging. *No.*

❦

Caroline cleaned up Rid's kitchen, wiping the counter with enough pressure to make her shoulder ache and then throwing the sponge in the sink as if it were a grenade. "You asshole," she muttered. She went into the living room and finished repairing the cage she'd been working on when he'd come home, then fixed another one she'd already brought up from the basement, all the while listening for Rid's truck in the driveway. "Like this is so damn hard," she muttered to his ghost in the room. "You were just about to blast me for doing it, weren't you? Couldn't *imagine* I could *possibly* do it right, not leave the tiniest hole for a crab to get in. You think I can't watch and learn? You think nobody can possibly do it right but almighty you?"

As the light in the room began to gray and the chill deepened, Caroline's anger became edged with fear. It was snowing again, and she missed having Lizzie beside her. At first she'd thought he'd taken Lizzie with him for meanness, just to deny her company and comfort, but what if Rid didn't intend to come back tonight? The old house moans started to bother her. The wood stove had gone out—her fault—and she didn't think she should push the thermostat up, but she wasn't sure she wanted to start up the wood stove again. She wouldn't leave a fire burning if she didn't stay. And the longer he was gone, the more she wanted not to be there whenever he did return. Still, she was cold, especially every time she peed, which, it seemed was at twenty minute intervals. She paced in front of the television for distraction, then couldn't bear to be distracted while she was trying to think, still arguing out loud. She could see nothing beyond the windows; the snow was a white drape, as if she'd been snatched from the familiar world and deposited in another. A foreign world where she didn't know the customs or speak the language. *Where was he?*

"I have to take charge of myself. That's what Mom would say." Her hand was on her abdomen, rubbing a circle, taking stock of its swell. She'd felt something yesterday, and again this morning, but it was nothing like a kick. More like a gas bubble, and it was too low to be the baby. She was afraid to go home, but too mad to wait for Rid. No telling when he was going to show up. Besides, they'd probably get into again anyway. Why couldn't they have a decent conversation without it devolving into a shouting match? Why couldn't he trust her? Why couldn't—"This is ridiculous," she said finally.

She went upstairs and started stuffing her things into the two bags she had. In the downstairs bathroom, she dumped her toiletries on top where there was space, not bothering to organize them in their neat kit, which she tossed on top. "I look like a homeless person. This is pathetic. All I'm missing is the shopping cart," she muttered, fanning the coals of her anger, which kept her much warmer and more functional than fear. She already had on her heaviest sweater—or, more accurately, her father's heaviest sweater. It had been Eleanor's favorite, a pure red, and one Eleanor had never been able to part with. She struggled into her mother's goose down jacket and pulled the hood up while she slid her sock-clad feet into boots and hands into the thick gloves crammed in the pockets.

She pushed aside worry which kept drifting in like the snow piling up outside, and when the thought of leaving a note came to her, she said "*Fuck you, Rid.*" She thought of her mother, then, first thinking how she'd disapprove, and then thinking *the hell she would.*

At least her car started right up. A good sign. She made it out of Rid's road, and onto Cove so smoothly she began to relax. She'd overestimated the problem and underestimated the amount of gas she in her tank. "See? It'll be all right. I can do this all by myself," she said out loud.

The visibility was terrible, though. The storm had seemed to be ending when she'd first left the house, but as she turned onto Route 6, it was obvious it had only been a lull. Now it thickened, the flakes like white dimes repaving the highway and landscape into one, blurring the boundaries of land and sky as Caroline's headlights, the snow, and the high streetlights combined in a frothy twilight of white and shadow.

She slowed to a crawl. There was no traffic, which was good, although she wished for a set of taillights to follow. *Presuming someone else can see the road better than I can.* She hadn't gone more than a couple of miles on Route 6 when her engine coughed. "No. No, no, no. NO!" The engine coughed once, twice, and then stalled. Caroline shifted into neutral and tried the ignition. It sputtered, tried to catch, but wouldn't. "Oh God, no. No. *Shit.*" She steered toward the side of the road in neutral, wondering *where* exactly the side of the road was. The cushion of snow obscured the feel of the road, and she couldn't tell what was underneath her tires. She felt a bump, and took it as the road's edge, so when the driver's side tires hit it too, she eased on and off her brakes and put the car in park. She banged her hand on the steering wheel, tears coming to her eyes. "Now what, goddammit." Fumbling, she felt for hazard lights, and had to put on the overhead light to find them. She turned off the headlights. *Don't run down the battery,* and sat in the car for a few minutes, telling herself to stay calm and trying to ignore the voice berating her. *You didn't get gas, and you didn't buy a cell phone, the two things you promised you'd do to take care of yourself and the baby. What kind of mother are you going to be? You don't deserve this baby.* Finally another voice came in to argue as she began to shiver, saying, *You're wasting time with this. You'll freeze if you sit here. There's not enough traffic to think someone's going to stop to help you. Take your wallet and start walking. Try to flag down any car. Leave a note on the driver's seat, in case a cop looks in the car.*

It was that voice—her mother's—that got her moving.

❦

This time, of course, Rid was traveling east on 6, so he came on the disabled car from behind where, thanks to the snow covered hazard lights, it looked like an igloo from outer space. There was no telling the make or model, though by general outline, yes, it could be Caroline's Honda. The license plate was buried, not that he'd bothered to learn hers. He'd do it now if he got the chance.

He pulled up behind the car and put his truck in park, leaving the motor running and the headlights on. Somebody might be in the car; it might not be hers at all, of course. If it were, though, he might be able to tell by what was inside. Maybe some of that baby stuff would be there. The thought clutched at his gut.

He wiped a swath of snow from the driver's side window with the sleeve of his parka and peered in. Empty. He opened the car door, setting off a small avalanche from the roof. The wind was in his face, so when he ducked down to stick his head in the car, he had an immediate eerie sensation of stillness and silence. One glance in the back seat told him it was CiCi's car. Among the packages and bags stacked there, which he'd have recognized anyway, was the teddy bear he'd given the baby. "Goddamn," he said, and again, "Goddamn. " He put his forehead on the seat back for perhaps ten seconds, willing himself to breathe. "God*damn*," he whispered, swiped his face twice with his glove, and stood again.

A note was on the driver's side seat. "Out of gas. Started walking (east) to Chevron Station at 7:45. Would appreciate any help. Caroline Marcum." Some errant part of Rid's mind noticed the handwriting—every letter rounded and perfectly formed—how it looked like a penmanship chart hung over a third-grade blackboard compared to his. Stuffing the note in his pocket, he slammed the door of the Honda, loosening another avalanche, and ran against the wind to his truck.

❦

Caroline had made it perhaps a mile and a half from the car, maybe a little less. When Rid's headlights picked her out of the scene, a small forward-laboring figure, head bent, she swung around and started trying to wave the truck down. He knew she couldn't recognize the truck. She'd be blinded by the lights, and the wind was blowing the snow right into her face. She had a gloved hand up partly shielding her eyes even as the other one was signaling. She must be trying to stop any vehicle on the road to ask for help. The thought made Rid crazy. He pulled to the side of the road behind her and got out. Caroline was half running, backtracking toward him, lumbering, awkward and bear-like in her boots and winter gear. She still didn't know who he was.

To get her off the road—not that anything was coming at the moment, but still, it was treacherous—Rid swung his left arm in a giant arc and ran in front of the truck to the passenger side. He had the door open by the time she was close enough to know who he was. He could see the surprise register on her features, and her hesitation.

Skirting the open door, he went to grab her arm, and pull her to the truck. "Come on," he said, raising his voice over the engine and the wind. "Don't be stupid. Get in." It was relief roughening his voice, but the words came out wrong. Even he knew it.

She did. He closed the door after her, ran around and got in the driver's side.

Once inside, Rid took a deep breath, then another. He didn't look at Caroline, but straight ahead, at the darkness and accumulating, blowing snow through which she'd been walking, still several miles from the Chevron station. "What were you thinking?" he demanded finally, still staring into the white. A blinking wetness that could have been from the snow and wind but wasn't shone on his face. He wanted to touch her, make sure she was all right, and was sitting tight, gathering the nerve.

"About the same thing as you when you stormed off, probably," she said.

"Huh?"

"Which word didn't you understand?" Talking down to him again.

He could give it right back to her. "Try speaking plain English. What are you talking about?"

"You obviously wanted to get away from me—"

"You're the one who wanted to get away from me! So you take off with no gas in the middle of the worst storm we've had all winter? At night? And pregnant? To learn moves like this you went to college?"

"I don't answer to you." At this, Caroline turned her head and looked out the passenger window, refusing to let him see her face any longer.

"And I wasn't trying to get away from you," Rid argued, regardless of how right she was. "You only *think* you know what I'm thinking, but you don't *know* what I'm thinking." His words were filled with righteousness fueled by the panic and guilt he'd felt just moments earlier.

"Whatever," Caroline sighed, still looking intently out the window, where the visibility was zero. A black forest edged the highway here. The berm was a narrow shoulder with an uphill slope and a ground cover of browned needles and old fallen cones. A cottage colony, boarded up for the winter, was perhaps a hundred yards down the road, but tonight you'd have to be on the porch of one of them to know it was there, tucked in the pines as they were.

"See, there you go again. Why'd ya have to say that? I was scared to death when you weren't there."

Caroline kept her jaw set and her face averted.

"Scared to death," he repeated softly after a few moments of silence. He gave up then on the idea she would talk to him, so he took the truck out of Park and gave it some gas. The wipers thudded into pads of snow on each side of their arc. He turned the heater back to the defrost setting. Only then did he feel Caroline's head move until he sensed her eyes on him.

"Where are you going?" she demanded.

He knew his face was wet and hoped she couldn't tell. It made him feel like he was back in high school, that much a loser. "Back to my house. The roads are terrible. I'll get your car for you first thing in the morning. It's the safest thing to do."

"I want my car tonight." She put time between each word, conveying that this was not negotiable. "Either you take me to get the gas or I will walk."

Rid didn't answer. He pulled onto the highway and rather than take the next exit off Route 6, he continued east down to the Chevron station, where he borrowed Sam Preston's five gallon can, arranging his face before he went in. "I'll drop it off tomorrow or the next day," Rid told Sam, with whom he'd regularly cut General Math in tenth grade.

"You're supposed to leave me a deposit. Can't you read the sign?" Sam mock complained from behind the counter. Florescent light made the scars from his acne look like craters. Tormented with zits through adolescence, Sam had been caught shoplifting Clearasil at fourteen. The store manager had taken one look at him, paid for the Clearasil himself, and let Sam go. At least that was the story Rid set loose around school, and it was pretty close to the truth.

"Aren't you worried what I might deposit on the can, though?" Rid leered. "If you ain't, you should be."

"Kiss my ass, you pervert, and get the hell outta here. Bring my goddamn can back tomorrow," Sam laughed.

"Or the next day," Rid called over his shoulder, pushing open the glass door and hunching into the snowstorm. He headed to the gas pump where his truck was parked, Caroline huddled inside. Her face was a pale unmoving moon in the starless sky of the windshield.

Before he was back in the truck, though, Rid's grin died. He got in and headed back west on Route 6, neither of them saying a word. As the wipers thwacked back and forth, the blower of the defroster kept up its white noise and so their silence did not sound as utterly strained and unnatural as it really was. He pulled over, climbed out, and put the gas in Caroline's Honda, then replaced the empty can in his truck bed.

When he climbed back into the driver's seat, Caroline was just putting on her gloves and fastening her hood, keys ready in her lap.

"Look," he said. "It's terrible out. We're not that far from my house. Please."

"Please what?"

At first he thought she wanted him to beg and he bit back a snide refusal. In the silence in which he let her words replay, though, he heard the tone, which was questioning.

"Please come back to my house. I'm sorry I left you alone. I'd messed things up, I hadn't talked to Mario, and that's where I went, to get it done. I'm sorry. I did things all wrong. It's not Mario that's been after you. I found out that much if it's any help." If he'd added anything more, if he'd tried to explain the complex layer of the history of men, competitors and friends—now business partners—a fire and a rising tide that sank a truck on a beach at night, his second thoughts about Mario undermining his own denial, it would have undone what he wanted. And all that was like grabbing air, too smoke-like for language. Especially now.

She was quiet a minute, looking down at her gloves. When she looked back up at him, he couldn't read her face. "I don't want to leave my car here."

It was a sideways opening. At least he took it as one. "How about this: I'll drive your car back to my house—you follow me in the truck." Seeing that she was about to object, he raised the ante hastily. "The truck has four wheel drive. If anything's going to happen, you know, any problem, like going off the road or something, don't you think it's better if it happens to the one of us that isn't pregnant?"

She looked down again. She shook her head once, and one hand balled into a fist that nested inside the other. She must have hesitated a full minute, maybe more. It killed him not to say anything, and he didn't know how much longer he could hold out.

"All right," Caroline said finally, and there really wasn't a clue either in her voice or on her face as to why she'd agreed.

He didn't care why, only that she had.

Then, without warning, her wet glove slid between his jacket and the back of his neck, cold where he'd thrown back his hood. A suggestion of pressure pulled him to her as she moved to him, and her lips—dry, chapped—the edgy skin on them brushing his as she kissed him. "Thank you," she said. Just that, looking him in the eye a moment, and then ducking her head as if ashamed.

Like most everything she did, it caught him completely unprepared. He tried to find his voice and barely managed to stammer, "Are you sure … I mean … are you … are you okay from walking out in it? I was frantic when your car was gone, I … hey...." Rid tried to get her to look at him.

She wouldn't look at him, though. But when he reached his arm over, she let him pull her toward him, and pressed her face against his chest. "I thought you weren't coming back," he scarcely heard it, her voice muffled and murky like something underwater. Then she was crying. *I'm sorry, CiC, I'm so sorry* echoed through him and he rested his cheek on top of her head where his regret felt like melting snow.

 *Chapter 24*

She would almost describe it as hovering, Rid was so careful with her. "I'm not a carton of eggs," Caroline said the evening after the snowstorm, then laughed at her analogy. "Well, one egg, maybe." Rid had jumped up to get a blanket when she'd rubbed her arms and said, "It's getting chilly in here." They were watching TV after dinner, Lizzie between them on the couch. Rid had made the dinner, although Caroline had protested that she felt like cooking.

"What's going on?" she finally said. "I'm fine. I can take care of myself, you know."

"Yeah," Rid said, but it was utterly noncommittal, and he didn't look at her.

"I don't mean to keep pushing about this, but did you call the police today? I didn't hear it if you did, and I was wondering if, I mean when, we're going to talk to them. Sooner or later, I need to be going home, of course. Noelle will be back tomorrow. She said she'd go to get some maternity clothes with me. And I need to get to the doctor."

"I thought I'd do that. The doctor, that part, I mean. That I'd take you. Doesn't the father usually go?"

What popped loud as a fat kernel of corn in Caroline's mind then was her father's old expression: *you could have knocked me over with a feather.*

"I guess that's right," she said.

"All right then," Rid said, as if something were settled. As if she'd made an appointment and asked him not only to drive her, but to come in and be there when the doctor examined her, talk to the doctor, hear what she said, as if they were going to raise this baby together. Or as if it was already decided that he was going to be there for her, for the baby, from now on, till death do us part, or something like that. And she had no idea what to say. Or even what she wanted, and the indefinability of her desire frightened her.

"I don't even have an appointment," she said, thinking to put him off. Rid had gotten up to stir the fire, and Caroline thought she could put closure on the subject for the time being. "I'll have to call. Noelle is, well, really Elsie gave me the name of someone she recommended and then Noelle suggested someone else, so anyway, I'll…"

"Look," Rid interrupted, putting the poker down and turning to face her, "this is important. I know you've been taking care of yourself with the vitamins and all, but still, you need to get going with a doctor. If you can't get an appointment right away, I'll get Tomas to have Marie call her OB."

"No, that's all right. I promise I'll get an appointment. I know I shouldn't have waited so long. First Mom died and then I got so freaked out by what was happening at the house, and I didn't think about anything else. Elsie told me what I needed to do in the first trimester, and I've been doing it, and yes, she did say I needed to see a doctor too, but it got away from me."

The overly-rich stock it boiled down to was that Rid never answered her about their talking to the police—or about her going back home—but had gotten her to agree to letting him go to the doctor with her. So she was *de facto* at his house at least another day, and calling the doctor's office from there in the morning.

Then, when she did call right at nine the next morning, even the nurse midwife who worked with the doctor couldn't see her until Tuesday morning, which was six days away. "I should have realized," she said to Rid. "They're covering a big area out here."

His brow furrowed. "You want to go down to Hyannis?"

Caroline was studying his face, distracted by his broad forehead and how the parallel worry lines looked like those little lap marks a tide sometimes leaves. His hands were wrapped around a coffee mug, and she noticed again how work-roughened they were, even now, in the dead of winter, from seasons of planting, lifting, raking, culling, handling nets, cages, rerod, U hooks, cement, clams, oysters, in and out of every tide of the bay. The next time she went to the store, she'd buy him some of that hand cream her mother used to use, the Norwegian kind that was so good for healing. Eleanor's hands used to get like his when she sat at her potter's wheel, hands slick, moving almost imperceptibly as she shaped the clay, or especially when she did more intricate work and ended up with tiny knife nicks.

"Huh? Do you?"

"Do I what?" she said, jerked out of her reverie.

"Wanna go to Hyannis?" A hint of impatience—or maybe worry—in his voice now.

"Why would I do that?"

"Hey, are you all right?"

"Of course I'm all right."

"Should we go to Hyannis to see a doctor sooner than next Tuesday?" Now he spoke slowly, as if she belonged in Special Ed classes.

"No. I'm not having any problems. I'm just extra tired, and that's normal. I'm taking double vitamins. I mean I'm not spotting or anything. Elsie said really the first trimester is pretty routine—mainly prenatal vitamins and blood pressure checks and watching for problems. I did check my blood pressure at the grocery store, you know that free thing they have, and it was normal. Six more days isn't going to make a difference."

"But you said you're in the second trimester."

"I'm barely in the second trimester. Really, I'm okay. Rid, it's six days." If he hadn't been upset, she would have been. In order to avoid looking at him, she got up from the table, clearing dishes as she did, and took them to the sink. As she made her way, a bird thudded against the window. "I wish you could put something outside, at the window, to warn the birds. That's happening a lot."

"Always does in the winter. Must be the way the light hits it."

"Okay then, could you do something to make it stop?"

"You're trying to make this about me, about the birds, about anything, instead of you."

"No, I didn't mean to. If there's any sign of a problem, we'll go right to Hyannis without waiting, okay?" She carefully kept any hint of sarcasm out of her voice, ran water into the sink then, and let the plash and clink of dishwashing make natural, conversation-ending noise.

"How about you just stay here?" The words came five minutes later, through a natural lull, as she finished putting dishes away, and was pouring another cup of coffee. She'd just offered Rid one, he'd said *yes, thanks,* and she brought the pot over to the kitchen table where he had an account book and piles of receipts spread out like the contents of an upturned wastebasket.

"Stay here? You mean today?"

"I mean, for the time being. I don't know. Just stay. I mean, it's safer here. We'll go give a statement to the police, but you stay here while this thing is going on until they catch someone."

❦

"So I guess we'll see. I know he really cares about the baby." Caroline said two days later to Noelle on their way to Eastham for some maternity clothes. A pale winter sun silvered the deserted landscape as they drove down Route 6 with Noelle at the wheel as Caroline summarized the whole story, downplaying it to teenage vandalism. Still Noelle fretted, impatiently fingering peppery waves that had fallen too far over her forehead back into place.

"I don't understand why you didn't tell us sooner. Whatever the police are doing, Walter will want to station armed guards around the house, you know."

"Yeah, that's why I'm staying with Rid. So Walt doesn't have to call up the militia."

"Would you be more comfortable staying with us? Because you know, we're the baby's grandparents, and Eleanor would want that."

"I know I can do that. Maybe this gives Rid and me a chance to work things out about the baby." Caroline felt as if she were calming her mother. It wasn't a bad feeling. Noelle was wearing a black coat with a scarlet scarf and Caroline was fairly sure her mother had given Noelle the scarf.

"Do you think there might be something between you?" Noelle asked, an *ah ha* blooming in her voice.

"He's—very attentive right now. But maybe that's just about the baby. If so, that's a good thing for the baby anyway, right?"

"Right." And Noelle reached over to squeeze her shoulder through Eleanor's jacket. "But I'd like there to be something in it for you, too. Do you think we should look for another coat for you?"

"I suppose. But I like wearing Mom's. Does it look really dumb? Anyway, the police were no help. Even with Rid there. There's no evidence, which is a problem, and no suspect. But nothing's happened since I've been at Rid's."

Noelle tented her brows.

Caroline had to study her face to extract what she was thinking. A whole unspoken conversation went on until Caroline made it explicit. "Oh no, Noelle, no way. I'm sure of it."

"Okay," Noelle said. "As long as you're sure. It's a powerful lot of coincidence, though, that it all stopped when you moved in with him." She inhaled and exhaled audibly, slowly, like a yoga exercise, her chest rising and falling as she did. "So, let's figure out what we're after, shall we?"

Caroline tried to pay attention as Noelle created a list poem of what would carry her through her pregnancy. She laid her head back against the head rest and let the sun warm her face. The tire hum blended with Noelle's voice, and fear melted with the salt slush on the road.

❧

"Tomas is picking me up. We're gonna run to the hatchery down in Dennis. They've got a line on this QXP virus that's been found in Barnstable and we both want to talk to John ourselves, just make sure we get the lowdown. It kills clams, and we've got to make sure it doesn't get to Wellfleet harbor. Has to do with who we buy seed from, see."

Caroline pulled her hands out of the sink water and dried them. She had been distracted all through breakfast rehearsing what to say. Rid had been reading the paper.

"Listen, I can see that you're working on your receipts and your account book. Is that for taxes?" she said.

"Yeah. And the state shellfishing regs." A bit wary, Rid stopped rummaging through pages to look at her.

"I'm good at paperwork. If you show me where you are, I can do that for you. You want me staying here, which is okay if you'll let me pitch in and work with you. Otherwise I need to go home."

"I got it handled."

She shrugged and turned back to the dishes. "Okay, I'll just pack up then."

"Whoa. What's this?"

"You want me to stay here. I'll do that if I can work. Those are my terms. Take it or leave it."

❧

He did need his expenses tallied in order to take his books to the accountant. "If you'll give me a copy of last year's taxes, I can do this year's," Caroline insisted. "I'm *good* at this stuff. I just need to see which forms you need."

"Well, for now, just add up the expenses month by month," Rid hedged.

The dining nook table was covered with receipts in various piles. "I did get behind."

"Just a bit," Caroline observed sarcastically, sticking her pencil behind her ear so she could use her right hand to pick up her mug of tea. "When did you quit writing things down? Last February?"

"Probably about April. When the weather broke, likely. But I'm real good about saving the receipts. Look, CiCi, it's a simple cash in, cash out system. You got enough light? If so, I'm gonna get to work downstairs. When the oysters come out of the pit, I gotta have all the cages ready, y'know. Some of the stock that was in mesh bags is big enough to go into cages, so I gotta build some more, too. And before spring, I need to—ah jeez, too much."

They settled into a routine within a week. He wouldn't let her work on any cages by herself, even though she called him a *diehard egomaniac control freak*, and he said, *I'm not in this to raise crabs, thank you very much*. They were laughing at the time, though on Caroline's side only because he did let her help with tasks like readying pieces for him to cut or fastening wire ties. There was a charge in the air. Occasionally they would touch by accident, smile. Once when she was at the kitchen table, having started on the book work, Rid leaned down and kissed her on the lips. Before either of them could think about it or react, he disappeared downstairs.

They'd gone to her first doctor's appointment. Dr. Silva had examined Caroline and afterward Rid had been called to join them in her office. "Your age alone makes this a high-risk pregnancy," she'd said, herself all of about thirty-two, dark Portuguese eyes darting from Caroline to Rid and back with a question as to why there'd been no medical care in the first trimester. But the year-rounders on the outer Cape are their own people, and Rebecca Silva had been raised in Provincetown, so holding both judgment and her tongue came naturally. "You're doing wonderfully, though," she said, when no answer was offered. "The heartbeat's strong and—" Rid's head had whipped from the doctor to Caroline at that. "Did you get to hear the heartbeat?" he'd said, and it had been almost an accusation, but too filled with some other emotion for the word to fit. She'd nodded. Later, on the way back to his house, Caroline decided to ask Rid if he'd like to go to the ultrasound appointment with her next week, even though she was still resolved this was *her* baby if shove came to push.

Rid was in the basement when Caroline finally got up to December's gasoline receipts and realized that, according to what he'd given her, Rid had spent only twelve dollars and ninety two cents that month. "I don't *think* so," she said in a singsong to herself. From the top of the stairs she called down to him, over his ringing hammer. "Probably still in the glove compartment—I must 'a just forgot to bring them in at the end of the month," he yelled back. "Y'want me to go out and look?"

"I'll get 'em," she called back. "Lizzie wants out anyway."

She ran out without zipping her jacket or bothering with gloves, Lizzie bounding ahead as soon as she'd squatted, circling the truck several times for the exultation of running in the snow. "Glad *you're* so happy," Caroline muttered, since snow was getting into her shoes. She climbed into the passenger side of the truck, leaving the door ajar, and got into the glove box. Rid appeared to have guessed right. There were multiple receipts in there. Caroline pulled them out and started checking them. December gas. December gas. December coffee but no gas—she crumpled that one and stuck it in the litter bag Rid had hanging from the lighter. December gas. A receipt-sized piece of paper with *what?* Terry DiPaulo, 290 Bradford Street, Provincetown. Caroline hadn't even known that much.

Her body didn't feel right. She'd forgotten to breathe. Her head was either too full of blood, or it had all drained. She felt as if she'd been punched. What was Rid doing with Terry's name and address? Were they colluding? Noelle's questioning look when Caroline mentioned that nothing had happened to her since she'd moved to Rid's came back to her suddenly.

Caroline felt the baby move, and this time she knew it was the baby moving, and she also knew she was going to be sick. She put her head between her legs to try to fight off the nausea. *Calm down*, she told herself. *Calm down. Breathe. Think.*

She put everything but the December gas slips back in the glove box. Fear, fear and the earth shifting from beneath her feet. She wouldn't let Rid know what she'd discovered. She'd been safer here than she'd been at home.

"Come on, Lizzie," she called when she'd formulated the first step of a plan. "Let's get on in."

Caroline waited until the next day when Rid left the house to make the call to the library. She'd stayed away since before Christmas, when Terry had fortuitously not been there, and now that she was at Rid's, she'd been plain busier, which helped. She was fairly sure she'd recognize Terry's voice, but it was library practice for personnel to identify themselves when answering the phone, so she wouldn't have to rely on her discernment ability. It was a volunteer who answered anyway, which made things much easier.

"Is Terry DiPaulo working today?" she inquired. She was perched on the arm of Rid's recliner, using the phone in the living room so she could keep watch out the window in case Rid's truck unexpectedly pulled back in the driveway. She'd given him a fifteen minute head start, though, and usually when he'd forgotten something he was back within two or three minutes.

"No, she won't be in until tomorrow at ten," the volunteer answered. "Can someone else help you?"

"Oh, no, thank you. Terry has been helping me with some research, so I'll just come in tomorrow. Thanks so much."

"May I tell her who called?"

"No thanks, it's not necessary. I'll come by tomorrow to see her. Thanks again." And then Caroline quickly hung up, before the library volunteer could persist in her efficiency. Frustrated, she went back to work on the books. She hadn't wanted to wait another day. It would wear her out later to make small talk and dinner, do dishes and the all other chores *with* Rid, and then to plan who would do what the rest of the evening and tomorrow, all as if she trusted him.

"I'll be takin' a couple hours off this mornin', Mr. Slave Driver," Caroline said at breakfast. "And I don't expect my paycheck to be no different, y'hear?"

Rid put down the *Cape Cod Times*, took a long draw of coffee and answered in a manufactured drawl. A pale winter sun buttered a swath of the kitchen table and they'd sat an extra fifteen minutes over breakfast enjoying this light that ended a tunnel of gray days. "Why I reckon I shore do, Miss CiCi. I'll be deductin' nuttin from nuttin and you'll continue to draw nuttin. I trust that'll be acceptable."

"Perfectly."

"So where ya be goin'?"

"The Truro library, then to finally get myself a cell phone and get it activated—a revolutionary idea, I realize. I thought I'd look in the thrift shop for some extra maternity clothes—junkier than what Noelle and I got—just for getting dirty, I guess. And lastly, I thought I'd see if I could get a haircut. Or at least find out when I can, if she can't do it today." What she really intended to do was go to the library and to get a cell phone. But she wanted time she didn't have to account for. Just in case. Not that she thought Terry would tell her outright, but she might say *something*, or it would show on her face: a blush, averted eyes, guilt. Something to give it away that she and Rid were conspiring.

When she was leaving, Rid followed her down the hall to embrace her from behind, saying, "Hey, drive safe, OK?" Rather than turning around, she responded by nuzzling her cheek into the nook of his shoulder and arm and caressing the arm that crossed beneath her breasts. "Hurry back," he said.

"I'll be awhile," she said, "Don't worry, everything will be fine." She tilted her head up to answer him, an oblique angle that avoided his eyes.

 *Chapter 25*

Terry was three times warned. Once by the library volunteer (dying to be hired on) who mentioned that a woman had called for her yesterday "about the research you've been helping her with. I told her you'd be in today." It had been a couple of weeks since CiCi had been flying her "journalist" kite around the library, just long enough that Terry actually had to take a couple of seconds to figure out what Miss Efficient Volunteer was talking about.

"That's fine," she said, covering smoothly. "I'm aware of exactly what she wants," she said, although she wasn't at all. She'd hoped it would be as easy as Cousin Whacko bragged. She'd taken two days off after she discovered Caroline's identity, called Boo, gathered her composure and gone back to work, steeled. The steel turned out to be unnecessary. It seemed Boo *had* taken care of it already when Terry didn't see Caroline again. But Boo said no, CiCi was just laying low, still Terry shouldn't worry at all; he had a good bead on the woman who'd killed her son, and he didn't aim to let her out of his sight.

She'd been informed that CiCi was pregnant. Boo had learned that from the phone tap, and then he'd found a stuffed animal on CiCi's porch with a tag that said "For Baby's First Christmas." He'd gone to fetch material to disfigure it, which he thought poetically perfect. A knife and matches were in his truck, hidden a fair hike away. When he crept back up on the house, CiCi—or someone—had left enough evidence to tell Boo the house had been entered, the bag taken, and the house abandoned again. He'd had to content himself with the notes and toast thing he'd planned all along. Still, knowledge of the ongoing pregnancy allowed Terry to plan a greeting that would give her the edge.

Her third warning was easy. Terry literally watched for her. It was simple to manipulate Rhonda into letting her work the front desk, and from there she had a clear view of the parking lot from the windows behind it. She wasn't going to be caught in any heart-pounding unpreparedness. She touched the gold angel on the collar of her blouse. By chance, she'd worn a severe outfit that day, a starched white blouse tucked into a belted charcoal black skirt, off-black stockings, black heels. A black boiled wool jacket. When she looked in the full-length mirror before she left the house, she'd considered adding a colorful scarf, but shrugged and let the clothes match her mood.

Now, as she saw Caroline's profile emerge from a salt-grayed Honda, her own crisp all-business attire pleased her. Caroline was wearing jeans, oversize boots, and a puffy jacket that was managing to look too big and too small at once. Not exactly a powerful look. Rather a pathetic one, in fact, and faintly ridiculous. If you knew she was pregnant, you could tell now, too. Otherwise she might have passed herself off as big-boobed, thick-waisted, out-of shape, that awkward stage of pregnancy when no one dares ask if you are. CiCi crossed the heavily treated parking lot. The ice beneath the plowed-off snow had turned to slush, and she, like everyone, picked her way. The day was bone-cold, dank, silted-over.

Terry gave the angel pin a furtive caress, straightened her shoulders, and neatened her hair with her hands. She asked Miss Efficient Volunteer to cover the check-out counter for her "long enough for me to get this order finished," moistened her lips with her tongue, and pretended to busy herself at a corner desk with some *Library Journal* and *Booklist* reviews she'd been checking against *Publisher's Weekly* to help her decide on the month's acquisitions, yet another task Rhonda had delegated to her. She didn't allow herself to look up when Caroline entered the building, looked around and failed to notice her (as Terry had hoped) and been forced to ask for her at the front desk.

Miss E. V. was even better than Terry expected. Like a little sergeant, she'd even refused to point Terry out to Caroline, but had taken her name and asked her to wait. She herself had come over to Terry, something Rhonda would never have respected Terry enough to do, stood there in her denim jumper, white Oxford cloth button down shirt—the woman absolutely must have gone to Mount Holyoke—clog shoes and ponytail, and said, "There's someone here to see you named CiCi Marcum. She says she's a journalist and you've been helping her with research, but she doesn't have an appointment. I told her you were working on an acquisitions order and were busy right now. Would you like to see her, or would you like her to make an appointment for another time?" It occurred to Terry right then to hope that Susan's degree in *something* wasn't in Library Science. Rhonda could be waiting for Terry herself (who hadn't yet started on the degree!) to slip up so she had an excuse to give Susan the staff job. On the other hand, if Miss E. V. had a degree in Library Science and was on the payroll, how long would it be until she was escorting Rhonda herself out the door? *Never mind, no danger of Susan collecting any paychecks here unless she tore it out of Rhonda's cold dead hand.* Rhonda only encouraged Terry because she knew Terry was without ambition or design on Rhonda's job. Anyone paying the smallest attention could smell both on Miss E.V., like cologne applied with a heavy hand.

"Susan, I really appreciate how you handled that. It was perfect. In this case, I'll go ahead and talk to her briefly now. You can bring her over."

A moment later, Susan reappeared with a sheepish-looking CiCi two steps behind. Terry kept her head down, writing a title into the distributor's order form (something she'd have to redo on the computer). She kept them both standing there waiting, then looked up as if slightly startled. She gave Susan a professional nod. "Thanks, Susan," she said warmly, so she could cool her tone down a noticeable notch when she spoke to CiCi.

"I'll keep the front covered," Susan said, and left. Terry sat, surrounded by papers, letting CiCi continue to stand a couple of feet back from the table.

Terry had scripted her part. She looked at CiCi quizzically with a small hint of ambiguous smile on her face, and said nothing.

CiCi broke easily. "Hi Terry, how have you been? I hope you don't mind my coming by—I didn't realize I should have an appointment now. Things—or you—must have gotten a lot busier." Terry thought CiCi had a flush starting on her neck. She needed a haircut, and her highlights were grown out a good two inches, which finished the disheveled look started by the coat and boots.

Here Terry inserted a noncommittal noise that would have sounded like "hmmm," only she altered it toward "mmmm" making it suggest an affirmative.

"I'm, ah, I'm still working on that piece for *Cape Cod Life* on aquaculture. The reason I haven't been in here is so long is that I've been working with one particular aquaculturist who's involved in the law suit brought by the upland owner on Indian Neck. You know, Pissario?"

Terry gave her another "mmmm." Now she literally saw CiCi break a sweat. At least there was sheen on her face. She deliberately warmed her tone a bit more. "How about taking off your coat—it's warm in here—sit down, and tell me what you're interested in."

Hook, line, sinker. CiCi unzipped the jacked and slipped it off almost simultaneously with sliding into the chair catty-corner to Terry's.

"I see those books were for you after all." She kept her tone absolutely neutral, giving no clue.

It was a sucker punch, no doubt. CiCi either had no idea or pretended not to know what she was talking about. "I'm sorry, I'm not sure…?" she stammered.

"The books on pregnancy that you said were for a friend." Five long seconds of silence left to purposely give the lie to what she'll say next: "Congratulations."

"Terry, I wasn't sure what I was going to do, that's why I—"

"Oh, I'm sure it's none of my business. Now, what was your research question?"

"I just feel badly that I misled…."

Terry was glad that CiCi was wading in deeper now. It was as good as holy water washing away any guilt she might have felt.

CiCi swallowed and, Terry saw her struggle to meet her eyes. "I'm sorry, Terry," she said. *For what you've done, or for what you're trying to do?* Terry wondered if her thoughts could wave across the table, like laps of incoming tide in an onshore wind.

"So, you were saying, you've been working with…?"

"Uh, yes, an aquaculturist from Indian Neck. I've interviewed him, observed, you know, actually gotten to see him work his grant, even gotten a bit of hands-on experience rather than all library research. You know, primary research of a different sort?"

She was stammering, over-explaining, and Terry knew the blank Caroline left was for her to insert some words of agreement or at least interest, but she left the blank empty, forcing her to plunge on awkwardly.

"So, ah, now I'm wondering if you can help me get some background on him from other sources. For one, do you know him personally? I mean you know most everyone, I've found. His name is Ridley Neal. Rid, people call him."

"I don't believe I know anyone from the Indian Neck area. The name's not familiar to me. But if you say he's befriended you, does it seem a bit ungrateful to go behind his back like this?"

CiCi blinked and put up her hand to signal *stop.* "Oh no, I didn't mean it that way."

"Why can't you just ask him what you want to know?" Putting it to her hard, staring her down.

"I thought you might know him, and give me a, you know, different perspective. Journalists always try to get multiple perspectives."

"I guess you're right. I really have no idea what you *journalists* do to get a story." The faintest emphasis on 'journalists,' tossing back CiCi's flaming lie. "I'm sorry I can't help you. I guess you could try one of the search engines. I presume you already tried the local paper archives and such. All the obvious places, I mean."

"I'll do that." Caroline stood, picked up her jacket, settled her purse over her arm and was backing away from the table. "Thanks, Terry. I can see you're busy today. I hope I didn't distract you too much." She brushed her hair off her forehead. She still looked overheated and uncomfortable.

"No problem. Oh, and good luck with your pregnancy!" Her parting salvo, shot after an extra five second pause during which Terry faked renewed involvement with her paperwork, making a show that her raised head and response were an afterthought.

Surreptitiously, she watched Caroline use a computer for all of four or five minutes, take a few notes, and leave the building. Later, she checked the history and found she'd been looking up hatcheries in Maine on the Internet. Terry had accomplished exactly what she'd wanted—she'd made CiCi feel terribly uncomfortable, even guilty without having any notion as to how or why it was happening or any way to guess that Terry was on to her, so it made no sense that after CiCi left, she went to the staff bathroom, locked the door, and cried.

 *Chapter 26*

It wasn't as if she believed Terry, but there was nothing to do except leave the library. On the way out through the salt-slushed parking lot, Caroline tried to reason with herself. The whole "appointment" business couldn't be aimed at her personally. She hadn't given her name when she'd called, for heaven's sake. But the veil over Terry's eyes had been unmistakable, and the connection she'd felt to Terry had vanished, as if an invisible force field had gone up between them.

Here was the strange part: she'd gone in expecting to fight her inclination to behave differently. After all, she'd found Terry's name and address in Rid's truck. Her home had been vandalized, and she'd been threatened. How could she not be suspicious? So she'd prepared herself to earn an Emmy. Instead, she'd done no acting, not really. The superficial lies had been easy. She'd been so busy reacting to the charged atmosphere around Terry that she hadn't had to make up emotions. There was only one explanation: Terry must have figured out who Caroline was. Or she'd been tipped off.

Still, if that were so, why hadn't Terry confronted her? Caroline would have expected as much, and Terry had every right. At the thought, a pale rose guilt began its hot bloom on Caroline's chest and opened along her neck, throat and cheeks. As soon as the sun shone on her identity, she realized she was a stalker, no way around it. But if Terry was colluding with Rid in all that had happened to her, then Terry bore the same guilt. Caroline's mind spun ruts trying to figure it out.

She sat in her car trying to make sense of it, then reminded herself that Terry, if she chose to look, could be watching. The temperature had warmed a bit, and the day was overcast—again. The western sky looked like it was carrying a payload of snow. Or sleet, the worst of the Cape's winter offerings. *What now?* She turned the key, let the engine cough into an idle. *What now?* Shifting into reverse, she backed out of the parking space, swung around until she was facing the road. *What now?* The baby moved, a little series of hummingbird wings inside her, and she shifted into drive, heading for Route 6 with no plan for the day, no plan for the rest of her life.

✹

She ended up in Eastham where she got her hair cut and finally bought the cell phone she told Rid she was going for.

Eventually everything fell into place, like tricks in a well-bid bridge game. She laid out what she knew as if she were cataloging a wardrobe, checking to see which articles of clothing she still needed.

She picked up the makings for dinner on the way home. Already the afternoon was sliding toward twilight, and it was only 3:45. Rid was home when she arrived.

"CiCi? Where you been? I was getting worried," he called from the kitchen as soon as she opened the door. She heard the chair scrape and Lizzie's paws scrabbling on the hardwood as both got up to greet her.

"Remember, I *told* you this morning? Cell phone?" She held it up as she came down the hall toward him. "Had to go to Eastham for it. You *could* have warned me that Land's End isn't carrying them anymore. While I was there I went ahead and got my hair done. And I went to the library first, this morning. I told you all this at breakfast. *Men.*" But her tone was light, a froth of tease on top. He helped her take her coat off and kissed her cheek as he did.

"Wonk, wonk, wonk," He made a hand motion like an opening and closing mouth. "You know, *some* people buy cell phones so they can call their families when they're going to be gone a long time so their families don't worry."

Family? Okay, why don't you just use a stun gun on me? "I didn't mean to worry you," she said. "I'm sorry."

"Can I see your phone?" Rid said, reaching for it. When it was in his hand, he sat at the table and fiddled with it for perhaps a minute. "There," he said, handing it back. "I programmed the house number and my cell number in it. If you want me to put anyone else's, like the doctor or Noelle, I can. I mean, you probably can figure it out fine, I didn't mean you couldn't."

"No, that's good, thanks."

Rid sat, and busied himself with further programming the phone, using the list of numbers Caroline had tacked up under a magnet on the refrigerator. "I'm putting your number in my cell phone now, too—okay?"

"Sure. Don't forget to put Elsie on mine," she said, trying to keep her suspicion at bay. *Why this, why now?* "I bought stuff for a casserole and salad. I'll get it going now, so we can eat early." Caroline stifled a sigh. She was tired of trying to understand things that didn't make sense, tired of trying to act like she was okay. She went in to the bathroom to pee, splashed some cold water on her face and washed her hands. In the mirror, the woman who returned her gaze looked black-eyed and disheveled. At least her hair looked better. She returned to the kitchen and began cleaning vegetables. In a clatter, Rid pulled plates from the cabinet and piled silverware on top. The baby did a tiny brief dance as she stood at the sink, as if wanting to join in on the "family" activities.

❧

The next day, Rid went up Cape to look at some used oyster cages he thought he could buy cheaply and repair. When his truck had crunched off the gravel drive and been gone for fifteen minutes, Caroline called Tomas.

"This is Caroline Marcum, Rid's friend. I'd like to keep this just between us. Are you comfortable with that?"

"Meaning you don't want Rid to know?"

"I mean not Rid, not Mario, not anyone. It has to do with helping, about the flats, not harming anyone, I promise you."

A hesitation on the other end. "I guess that would be all right."

"You'll understand why when I go into details, and I'm sure you'll be fine with it. Could you and I meet sometime today? It won't take long."

"That'd be all right. I'm tied up until late afternoon, but I can stop at The Oyster on my way home."

"I'm afraid that might be too—public. Is there another place?"

"Billy'll let us use the private room. I'll stop for a coffee this afternoon and check. He can keep his mouth shut when he needs to. You could come to my house, but my wife is about as quiet as a full-page ad in the newspaper."

"All right. Thank you. What time?"

"Five?"

"I can do that. Thank you, Tomas."

The rest of the day she fidgeted or busied herself, Lizzie always at her heels. There was the one necessary bank errand that consumed an hour. She caught up all the laundry, organized and packed her own things. She started to cry when she hugged Lizzie. The Lab fussed at her face with her long tongue. The baby's things—starting to be an accumulation now—she left in the room in which she and Rid had them stored. Once, Rid had actually called it *the baby's room*, but she'd taken it to mean the baby's storage room. She trusted Rid to keep them, and she didn't have it in her to make that many extra trips up and down stairs to try to cram it all in her car. This was only a matter of going to Noelle's until she knew the connection between Rid and the mother of the boy she'd killed, how that fit with a threat on her door step and a rock through her window. Maybe she *would* have to leave for good. Not yet, though. Not yet.

Caroline left for Noelle's before two in the afternoon to make sure she wasn't there when Rid got home. The note she left on the kitchen table, which she knew could be either little surprise if he was guilty or a blade in the heart if he wasn't, read, *Rid, I think it's best if I let Noelle and Walt help me get back into my own home. I need to find out if and how the threats and vandalism are connected to my past or my present, get honest answers, and resolve it before the baby comes. I can't keep hiding here and pretending nothing is wrong. When I know what's really going on, you and I will work things out. All the baby's things are upstairs. CiCi.*

Later, having stashed her things in the yellow and white guest bedroom, tired from the trips up and down the stairs at both houses, Caroline made herself a cup of tea in Noelle's kitchen. Walt was at a doctor's appointment, and it was the first time she'd been alone in their home. The room was cheery— red paint, rubbed wood, gleaming copper and brass artfully hung along with live plants in the large breakfast area windows—but she felt displaced all over again, as she first had at Rid's. Strange how she'd begun to feel at home there, how close she'd gotten to him, or thought she had. Maybe it was Lizzie, who loved her and she loved back without complication, or maybe it was the house, which had become a refuge from danger, and she'd confused the feeling of safety with feelings for Rid.

She sat at the table with her tea, looking out the window in the direction of

the water where Rid and the others tended their grants in a handed-down way
of life based on the tides, her own family home alongside. For a few moments
she cried while inside, her baby moved in primal water, as if tethered to the ebb
and flow of the sea. And then it was time to go meet Tomas.

☙

She needn't have worried about it being too public. There were eight cars
in the parking lot at The Oyster, nine with hers. That had to include the staff.
She recognized Tomas's truck. She parked her own off to the back, where sand
and shrubbery crept onto the asphalt, and twilight had long since overtaken
the area of the closed bookstore.

She'd worn the black sweater that hid her pregnancy best, jeans, and her
boots with the two-inch heels. Even makeup, a necklace and earrings. She
didn't want to look pathetic. She wanted to look like she had choice, dignity,
and knew exactly what she was doing.

"I'm meeting Tomas," she said to the bartender. There wasn't a hostess on
duty. Both the bar and restaurant sides looked cavernous, abandoned, but it
was early.

"I'm Billy. We've met before. You've been here with Rid, aye?" He flounced
a bit, purposefully, as if to say *how could you forget me?* then chuckled. White-
hair partly covered with the kind of scarf her mother wore when dusting
the rafters, heavy white eyebrows over deep set sky blue eyes, a bristly white
mustache, earrings, and several gold necklaces layered over a black US NAVY
sweatshirt pulled over a pot belly, a rainbow flag insignia on the left breast.
Billy made her blink while her brain searched for a category.

"I remember," Caroline said, meaning it. "I'm Caroline. And once again,
dammit, you're jewelry is better than mine." She gestured to his necklaces, and
then, disdainfully, at her own.

Billy threw back his head this time. "Your first beer's on me just for the
flattery."

"Make that a virgin hot toddy and you're on."

"I knew that, I knew that! You're on the wagon. Tomas is in the back
room with his first beer, though. Make that cheapskate buy you something
to eat." He started to lead Caroline down the hall past the kitchen door and
the hallway to the restrooms, and then turned, hand on hip. "Oh my. There's
not trouble in paradise is there? I mean, will Rid be coming or is this a

clandestine meeting?"

"No on trouble. Yes on private. It's business. I'll really appreciate your not mentioning it to anyone," Caroline said, breathing in Billy's broad Boston accent, so like her father's it might have been his cologne.

"Well, honey, you can absolutely trust me."

"Actually, Tomas vouched for you."

"Really? How sweet of him. Damn. Now I'll have to buy *him* a beer. You know, some nights I end up working for nothing here." As he spoke, Billy pushed open a door to a private dining room where Tomas had his feet up on one chair as he slouched with a beer and the paper in another. A bowl of peanuts rested on the table in front of him on another section of the *Cape Cod Times*.

"Ready for another beer?" Billy said to Tomas.

"Hey, CiCi. Sure, Billy, and bring the lady whatever she'd like."

The use of her old nickname—which Tomas had obviously heard from Rid—was startling.

"How about an appetizer?" Billy said to Tomas, with a wink to Caroline. "Some wings? A mixed platter? You're each getting one drink on me."

Tomas faked a double take at Billy and said to Caroline, "Who is this and what have you done with the real Billy? Should we have him bring us an appetizer?"

"Fine by me. I'll help you eat it—nothing spicy, though."

"Do your thing, Billy. Thanks."

When the bartender had disappeared, Tomas got up and pulled out a chair for Caroline. The man was huge, and Caroline would have instinctively been a bit afraid if his voice hadn't been gentle. He had a wild look with untamed gray hair and beard, broad face. One side, his overalls were fastened, the other dropped over his upper arm and chest. A red-plaid flannel shirt was buttoned to the neck under the denim. Work-worn hands, burly as tree limbs, chapped and nicked like Rid's.

"I'll just put your coat over here," he said, laying it on another table. "What's on your mind?"

"I want to give you Rid's share of the money to buy the flats," she said.

Tomas raised his brows. "Why don't you just give it to Rid?"

"I tried. He refused."

"So—you're doing an end run? What do you want that's making Rid say no?"

"I don't want anything. I guess Rid doesn't believe that."

"Maybe I'm inclined not to either." Tomas tipped his chair onto the back two rungs as Caroline leaned toward him, like a seated dance.

"You're doing exactly what he did. Please, Tomas. I'm asking you to hear me out. That's all. Rid can't separate out the emotional part, the baby. Surely *you* can. I moved out of his house this afternoon. I don't have any idea how things will or won't work out. This money has *nothing* to do with Rid and me and the future. Will you just *listen?*" During the last sentence, Billy came in with her toddy, another beer, and a tray of mixed appetizers.

"Sorry to interrupt," he said, putting it all down. "I'm outta here," and literally backed out of the swinging doors with a wave as Tomas was saying, "It's okay."

The virgin toddy was hot spiced cider and the heat of the mug in Caroline's hand along with the scent was good. She breathed it in and exhaled to slow and calm herself.

"You moved out? Was he there?"

The room was small and undecorated, clearly meant for meetings or for people to bring their own decorations. Either way, Caroline was starting to feel as if she'd climbed on a treadmill in a closet. "That's not the point, Tomas. That's the personal stuff, see? What I'm trying to talk to you about is fighting the lawsuit, the opportunity to buy those flats. Can we separate the issues and talk about that?"

He sighed and brought his chair to flat on the floor. "Okay. Lay it out for me."

"Thank you. I'm a third generation waterside land owner. I care about this town and community. I know what sustains the local economy, and it's not the washashores who weekend here. I support the aquaculturists because it's the right thing to do. I inherited my house. You know about what's been going on—the vandalism and the harassment—why I was staying with Rid?"

Tomas nodded.

"I still don't know who or what's behind it. Frankly, it could be aquaculturists, it could be upland owners, it could have nothing to do with the lawsuit. I want to stay here. I admit I'm scared to death. But my situation and yours aren't related." At the mention of the aquaculturists, Tomas started to interrupt, but Caroline put up her hand to stop him and pressed on. "This is a string-free gift so that you all can purchase those flats now. I don't want my name involved. I don't want any rights to the flats. I have enough money to do this." Caroline reached down and lifted her purse onto her lap. From it she drew a cashier's check for $8,350.00.

Tomas took the check from her hand and looked at it. "Whoa. And you're saying there's nothing personal in this?"

"Yes, he's my baby's father. If nothing else, whatever helps him will always help our child. In that sense, it's an investment. Is that what you're trying to prove?"

"Maybe."

"I mean it about wanting to preserve our way of life here, Tomas. Believe me or don't. Just take the money and buy the flats. Keep it between us. Tell Rid whatever you want—another landowner doesn't agree and donated enough for the three of you to buy the flats—whatever. Just so Rid's share is covered."

"Even though the purchase offer is a state secret…."Tomas muttered. "You sure about this?"

"Tell him it was a donation. You'll just have to make it work. Your future is on the line, too, so I know you'll figure out something."

Tomas sighed again, staring at the check. He looked up then and made eye contact with Caroline, holding it for five seconds. He stuck out his hand and she shook it.

"Thank you, CiCi. Thank you very much. Hey, you hungry? Let's dig into some of this stuff. Can't let it get too cold, especially the mozzarella sticks."

Later, after they'd talked about the snow and Tomas' children, and Labs versus beagles, and what to pay for used oyster cages, after Billy had brought Tomas his third beer and Caroline her second hot spiced cider, Caroline said, "You remember that storm in August, just the tail of the hurricane that hit here? I saw Rid way after the rest of you all had left, out there pulling stock and setting U-hooks and I ran out to help. Raining enough to drown the fish, lightning coming, he was dragging the hats out."

"That's Rid all right," Tomas interrupted, chuckling. "'Course I pulled and buttoned down a lot that day, too." He pushed the appetizer platter toward her. "I'm getting more than my share of these. Grab a couple wings. The sauce is really good." He went back to sucking the meat off the bone he was working on, nodding at her to go on.

Caroline nodded, picking up a chicken wing. "That figures. Mario sure didn't, though. Anyway, since I've been staying with Rid, I've gotten into it more. Repairing nets, pricing seed, all the winter work, you know? And I get it. I get what there is that you can't give up or lose. So maybe there is an in-your-blood-thing for us natives. My mother used to say that."

Tomas wiped his hands on his napkin, leaned forward, reached catty-corner across the table to touch her hand a moment before withdrawing his. "CiCi, I promise you that I have never known of any aquaculturist being involved in anything against you in any way. Most certainly myself. Rid was paranoid about you being involved in the lawsuit at first—well, we were all worried about that—but to my knowledge, he never did one thing."

"Why would *any* of you think that? I just don't get it. Why didn't somebody *ask* me if I even *agreed* with the suit?" Caroline's voice was quiet but the pitch rose and her heart was a fast uncomfortable thudding in her chest.

"Probably because things got crazy between you and Rid with the personal stuff, and then a stranger—a weird guy, not seen him before or since—talks to Rid right here at the bar. Look, I'm talking out of turn here. This is Rid's business."

"I can't ask him. I can't tell him I've been talking to you. *You* tell me."

"CiCi, I'm sorry. I can't go there. If going into Rid's business is the price tag on this check, then—"

"I *told* you there were no strings. But don't I have a right to know who said something to Rid about *me*? If that's what got you all thinking I was involved with the lawsuit? Goddamn, this is so unfair." She could feel her neck and face flushing with anger, and the tail of the last sentence sputtered off.

"It's just not how we do things. I'm sorry."

Fuming, Caroline pushed her chair back from the table as if to demonstrate the distance between them. "In other words, I'm an outsider. No better than a washashore upland owner because I don't have a grant."

Tomas shrugged and answered calmly. "I didn't say that. I'm just saying I only know a little piece about it. I personally apologize for being wrong about you. You'll have to work the rest out with Rid, but you can take my word on one thing. He didn't do anything to harm you. For one thing, CiCi, he knew you were carrying his child, if nothing else."

"What about Mario?"

Tomas closed one eye, raised the other eyebrow, and gave a small, hands up shrug. "I admit Mario's a wild card. I truly don't think he was involved, and I know Rid grilled him pretty good. There was a stretch of time he didn't even have a truck. Rid and I were carting him most everywhere. If you have the dates that things happened, I could at least tell you if he had a vehicle. But Rid musta already done that."

It calmed her enough to hear Tomas be honest about Mario that she was embarrassed by her outburst. "Rid couldn't rule him out, but then he talked to him and said he was okay." Caroline's voice was conciliatory now, and she ate a fried mozzarella stick with the last of her toddy.

Tomas glanced at his watch. "CiCi, I've got to run. My wife is already pacing, and since I can't tell the truth about who I've been with, you know—"

"You go on ahead. I need to get to the bathroom. Baby's dancing on my bladder again," Caroline said with a smile, and pointing at her belly. "Thanks for hearing me, Tomas. Good luck with the purchase."

"We'll be on it tomorrow. You want me to let you know how it goes?"

"I meant what I said. No strings, except that you keep this between us. I'll read it in the paper when the story breaks. It'll be a big one."

"You're a gracious lady, Caroline," he said, taking her hand. "I hope Rid—well, I wish you and the baby well, and if you need a hand with anything, I hope you'll feel free to call me."

"Thank you. That means a lot."

They stood and picked up their coats at the same time, and Caroline started to go into her purse.

"I got the check. Billy'll have it out at the bar." Tomas said.

"I'll get the tip," Caroline answered.

"No you won't. I got it covered," and Tomas laid down a twenty dollar bill. "A little thank you for his discretion and the back room," he said. "He'll know. You sure you're okay? Want me to wait?"

"You go on. I'm fine."

Tomas made eye contact with her. This time he did take her hand, lightly, making a crooked swinging bridge by their thighs. "Thank you. Really, thank you," he said, dropping her hand after a squeeze and leaving through the swinging doors without waiting for an answer. Caroline put another ten dollar bill under her mug, gathered her things together and headed to the ladies' room. Afterwards, her hands still damp, she pulled her coat on, and went out past the bar to the door, slowing down enough to wave and say, "Thank you so much, Billy."

"Anytime, anytime. If you give me twenty-four hours' notice, next time I'll try not to look exceptionally stunning. It's probably not good for you to get upset, y'know."

She was laughing when she went out the door. A full black night had crept in the sea and down from the sky while she'd been inside, so as the door closed behind her and she turned to the right and then right again to round the building and get to her car, she was engulfed in it, and silence.

The Honda was a huddle of black against black. She needn't have worried that Rid might see it there. For a moment she was uneasy and then, internally, laughed at herself. *You're not in Chicago, dodo bird. This is Wellfleet. In the middle of winter. Every damn parking lot looks like this. Next time, park in the front like a normal person, over there, across from the shellfish shack, where it's all lit.* She turned her head toward the shellfish shack just as a bag of rough fabric was dropped over her head and jerked tight, while her right arm was grabbed and yanked up behind her in a grotesque, excruciating hold. Someone, a man she was sure by size and shape, was dragging her now by the head and bent arm, blind face up, her ankles and heels scraping in the ice and slush. She got out a muffled scream and he pressed the arm under her throat and jammed her right wrist deeper and higher into her own shoulder blade.

With her left arm, Caroline tried to punch at her assailant's face, but he just leaned out of reach as he dragged her. She clawed at the arm on her throat, tried to maneuver to bite him. He was choking her with his arm and she felt herself blacking out. *"Baby … don't hurt … please … Mario? No!"* Her voice was a gasp, and through her fog she thought that if she was right, if it was Mario, she'd done the worst thing she could by saying his name.

Then there were heavy running steps, a male voice shouting. Then it was close, upon her, and suddenly she was wrenched loose and falling. Two heavy kicks to her side, a sear of pain as she tried to roll, get her right arm pulled back around her body to meet her left and protect her mid-section, her clothing quickly soaked in the icy slush puddling in the gravel. More kicks. Caroline was on the ground between two grunting, fighting men, huddled, the bag still over her head, but if she raised her arms to pull it off, she'd leave the baby unprotected. Another kick, then no breath, a tangle of stumbling blows as someone fell over her head. She tried to wriggle away, just as one of the men stepped over her, landing on part of the bag over her chin. "Caroline, get away, get away," she heard. "I got this fuckah." South Boston. Billy.

She wasn't right beneath them anymore, but the effort to get to her feet failed. She heard flesh hard on flesh, the terrible noise of fists on bones, the wet, gruff noises of hurt, and Billy shouting. Caroline wrestled the bag off her head. A man in military fatigues was just getting off the ground. He used the momentum to launch a body blow to Billy's sternum, his own skull as the weapon. From where she was, the man's face seemed to have been cut out of wax paper—a perfect round circle, its own source of eerie pale light. Billy staggered back, arms windmilling. The man managed to keep his footing and kept going. The night swallowed him.

Billy tottered, regained his balance, his eyes still on his opponent, then looked to Caroline, on the ground. His hands went to both sides of his head. "Fuck" he spit, and limped to Caroline's side.

"You all right?" he said, kneeling.

"I think so. It hurts. Bad—my side. Hard to breathe."

"He got away, Caroline. I'm real sorry."

"S'okay. Thank you. You're bleeding."

"Can you stay put while I call for help?"

In the other parking lot opposite the shellfish shack, on the other side of the restaurant entrance, a motor started. Billy got up in a hobbled run toward the sound. A truck exited the parking lot and headed toward town. Caroline was seized by a pain that took her breath, and then finally let her go as she fainted into a place as lightless as the Cape night, oblivious to the panicked flurry led by Billy when it spilled from the restaurant to gather around her.

Chapter 27

She was on a train, or no, a plane. Only a dim light somewhere in front of her eyes, but that sound, a dull roar of engines reverberating in her head. Then distant, but again, louder, her name. Not a voice she knew. She thought of opening her eyes but it was as if she didn't remember how. *Concentrate. Open your eyes.* Was the voice saying that or was that her own voice? *Open your eyes.* "Open your eyes. Caroline, can you open your eyes for me?"

She opened her eyes and winced, blinded.

"Good, good. Sorry, I'll swing that light out of your eyes. Try again now. Do you know where you are?"

"No," she croaked, a hoarse whisper, although she could see that the man talking to her wore a stethoscope and she was probably in a hospital. Her breaths were narrow wary slits like her eyes.

"Sir, can you step up here?" he said, stepping aside. Billy appeared, one cheek scraped and swollen. "Hey girl. At least you kept your jewelry." He took her hand in his, which was moist and icy. "Remember what happened? Parking lot of The Oyster, you were—" As he spoke, Billy switched an ice pack from one hand to the other.

As Caroline shifted slightly to look at him, a new pain stabbed her. That, and seeing Billy brought her back to herself. She didn't need to hear what he was saying. "Baby. Is the baby all right?" she gasped.

"Honey, I'm just fine," Billy said, grinning. "But you're not my type." Behind him, the doctor or nurse was came forward. "Here's the guy with the answers.

I'll get out of the way."

"I'm Doctor Rockwell. We have you on a fetal monitor—you can see it right there—and the baby's heartbeat looks fine." He was middle-aged, with a southern accent, strange in this neck of the woods. Groomed formally, atypical for locals, the doctor wore a white shirt and blue print tie. "I think you've got some broken ribs, and a bruised kidney. We need your OB involved, obviously, so if you'll give us a name, we'll give him a call. We're admitting you for tests, and as soon as you're ready, naturally, the police want to know if there's anything additional you might remember, about the assault. How are you feeling?"

"Hurt. OB, Dr. Silva. You sure baby's fine?" Tears were in her eyes, running into her hair. Lifting her arm to wipe them was out of the question. She rotated her head and tried to smear them against the pillowcase. "Rid. Elsie. Noelle." It seemed no one knew what she was talking about or no one heard her. "Billy?"

He didn't hear her. He'd been banished to the nether regions beyond the curtain while they fussed with machines near her. She could hear the swoosh and muffled thump of swinging doors. The overhead light was still too bright, though the examination lamp had, as promised, been pushed aside. Caroline closed her eyes.

"Caroline, were you raped?" It was a nurse asking her, one with an aura of hair so red it was its own source of light, like a sunset.

"No," she whispered, opening her eyes half way. Her head ached.

"You're sure?"

"Yes."

The nurse smiled. Good, big wide-set hazel eyes beneath high cheekbones, crooked teeth. "That's one good thing, at least," she said. "Would you like me to wash your face?"

"Please." Caroline was still crying, it seemed, but maybe her eyes were just watery from the light. She could hear an argument going on somewhere.

Then a voice that rose above the others, then over two other voices saying no to the first voice that she was trying to hear, like trying to catch the words to a distant song. "She's my ... won't go that way, buddy ... going in ... I brought ... a nurse," as the first voice got louder. Rid. And he'd brought Elsie.

In the morning, she opened her eyes as gray light gave shape to objects in the room they'd finally given her. The amorphous lump in the corner stirred and became angular. With effort she raised her head to look. A face. A whisper.

"CiCi? You okay?"

"Who?"

"Don't be scared. It's me. Just Rid." He pushed a blanket off him and struggled out of the chair. His legs wouldn't cooperate and he staggered. "Shit. Got stiff sleeping like that, but you can hear it's me, right?" He'd taken his voice out of the whisper. The room was intended for two people but the other bed was empty.

"They can ... hear you ... down on the flats," Caroline said, gasping as she tried to raise herself.

"Don't do that! Wait, I'll help you," he said, making his way sloppily to her bed and finding the controls for her.

"I have to go to the bathroom. Did Elsie pull strings to get me a room by myself?" It was easier to talk in a more upright position.

"Yeah, told 'em you were dyin', hospice and all," Rid said, straight-faced, taking her hand. When she didn't laugh, but searched his face for more, he immediately said, "CiCi, I know Brenda down in admitting. She's married t' Bogsie, he's got a grant past mine, down toward Blackfish Creek. I told her you're carrying our baby, and hey, no sweat."

"Thank you. And thank you for bringing Elsie last night. You didn't have to stay."

"Why'd you move out? What happened? And what the hell happened in that parking lot? Billy said it was the guy in fatigues."

Caroline's eyes narrowed and she pulled back deeper into the pillows even though it hurt her ribs and back. She coughed, which hurt more. "You *know* him? He's your friend? I thought you said—"

"Hold on, I *don't* know him, *no*," he interrupted, gesturing impatiently. "Weird guy, real squashed-like moonface, y'know?" he said spreading his hand over his face as if to flatten it. "I can't prove it, but I was sure he had a pistol in his pocket. Dressed all military and acting like he was on some top secret mission. He came around when I was at the bar a couple months ago and started saying this crazy stuff about how he was gonna take care of *my* problem and all I had to do was check up on some chick that lives in P-town and make sure *she* was all right. I just thought the guy was a whack job. But now this—if he's the guy that did this to you—"

"A stranger comes up to you? Offers to take care of your problem?" Her voice was suspicious, sarcastic.

"Yeah." Rid's hands and shoulders went up as if he was carrying a tray. "I know it sounds crazy. It *is* crazy. I'd never laid eyes on him before or since."

"What problem?"

"I assumed he meant the lawsuit, that it had to do with Pissario. Then Tomas and Mario thought it might have to do with you, too, because he said something about how I wouldn't have to make any payments. They thought he might mean support payments, like child support. That's what gave them the idea you were in on the lawsuit, see?"

"And you couldn't have asked me?" Her voice was flinty as a drill.

"Not back then. Now I could."

"And what about this 'chick' you were supposed to see was all right?"

"I have no idea what that's about. I went to the address once. It's some Terry DeSomething, lives on Bradford Street in P-town. I didn't know what I was supposed to look at. I left, figured with my record I'd end up arrested for stalking. Guy said I'm supposed to make sure she gets any help she needs, like I owe him a favor."

Caroline blinked several times, remembering the clicks on her telephone line, then lay her head back and kept her eyes closed.

"Hey, you okay? Breathe, will you?"

She released a long exhalation. Rid was right; she had been holding her breath. She turned her face toward the window away from his. Daylight was advancing deeper into the room and colors were beginning to emerge from the shadows, though they still had an overlay of pale charcoal. Still, she could see the door to the room and it made her think of an escape route now, just the way the falling-down dune fence in front of her parents' house had when her mother was dying. It was all her fault. Everything that had happened since her mother died, all the injustice that had flown wild in her world was now folding its wings and lighting on her shoulder, back home where it had fledged.

He might as well have been a barnacle, he stuck that close to her. "I've heard about how you're not supposed to leave someone alone in the hospital," he said. "They make mistakes, you know. Amputate the wrong leg, give the wrong medication. You've got to have somebody watch out for you."

"I'm not having an amputation," Caroline answered, stifling a smile. The early afternoon light was in her eyes and even as she squinted, Rid was adjusting the blinds. He handed her a plastic cup of water, bent the straw toward her. "Drink," he commanded. "Remember what the doctor said."

They'd talked much of the morning, after Caroline picked her way through breakfast. At first, she'd just been silent with her own realization of what must have happened. Her assailant had been sent by Terry. Rid's connection was innocent and unknown to him. Shame had covered and smothered her like a stifling blanket, and all she wanted was for him to leave. He, however, was having none of it.

"Sorry. You can tell me what to do some other time. I ain't sayin' I'll pay attention, but you can try."

"Lizzie will never speak to you again," she whispered, trying for a light touch.

"Nice try. I called Tomas. Last night, when that shirt-and-tie doc who sounds like a Confederate general had me banned to the waiting room."

"Just give me some time."

"Not until you explain why you up and left when everything was going good. What did I do?"

"Nothing. It's my fault, Rid. My fault."

"That's not good enough."

And so it went, round and round, until there was nothing to do but pay what she owed and tell the truth. Who Terry was to her, and how she'd lied her way into the library day after day. How she'd found the paper in Rid's glove compartment and thought they were conspiring against her. The ridiculous irony of that, when she was the guilty one all along.

"You're guilty of not talking to me, that's for sure," he said. "But you're not guilty of mugging yourself. Okay. So now there's pretty good evidence that he came from this Terry person. You've got to file charges against both of them. I'll call Jerry, have him get a detective back here today."

"Maybe she doesn't know, just like you didn't. Maybe she didn't send him. I can't do that to her, Rid. I have to know for sure, first." She paused, shifted, winced. Rid got up to help her move.

"Want this pillow underneath your neck more?"

"Can you lift me a little higher in the bed? Thanks." Her eyes were watering and she held eye contact as she took his hand. "I'm so sorry. All I can tell you is how sorry I am."

"Hey, it's all right. Just so we get the guy that's been doin' all this. Jeez, he goes around like he's some commando. He's gotta pay, CiCi. They both do."

"Rid, it's my fault. I have to do this my way. I can't do the same thing to her I did to you. Please don't call the police back here. They already *took* a report. I can't make any accusations. Not now, not yet. Let me talk to her first."

He stood, pulling his cell phone from his pocket. "This is wrong, CiCi. We can't risk losing him. If the guy was a local, one of us would recognize him. Jesus, how can you not get it, the longer you wait, the farther away he gets?"

"The doctor said I'm probably being released this afternoon. As long as the baby's all right. Hey, Dr. Silva says I'm going to be a terrific mother because I did such a great job of protecting the baby." She allowed herself a self-satisfied smile. "My kidneys are working all right, one is bruised the ER doc said, and you know they don't really do anything for broken ribs. Noelle and Elsie will be here soon to get me to Noelle's."

"That guy already has too much of a start. We have to get the police on him. What he did could have been attempted murder. We don't know. And I don't like it, you going to Noelle's. Walt can't keep you as safe as I can."

"Walt may be old but he's fierce when he needs to be. He's a Vietnam vet, y'know. Navy. Listen, please respect this. I *have* to give Terry a chance. I *owe* her."

Rid waited to answer. His eyes were unreadable. He'd placed himself so as to help block the light from her eyes, but he was backlit and it made his features less distinguishable. What stood out was the heart shape of his face, and his hair, more dusky than in summer. "All right," he said, putting the cell phone in his pocket, and she had to take him at his word.

"Come home with me, and we'll do it the minute the library opens tomorrow."

"Noelle is taking care of me for my mother. Rid, I'm trying to right wrongs. I shut her out when my mother was dying. Let me make amends. It's just one night."

"But we can go tomorrow?"

"Tomorrow."

"Together?"

"Yes, together."

※

But Dr. Silva didn't get back until twilight to check the baby again and okay Caroline's release. Rid waited down the hall in a little sitting area with

Noelle and Walt, wondering what they must think of him. He rehearsed a good ten different starts in his mind, wanting to explain something to them, but reticence took over. He only said hello again, having met them the night before, calling Walt *sir* and Noelle *ma'am*, as his mother had taught him, and updated them on what the doctor had said about CiCi in the morning, noting that they, too, called her by that nickname. Of course they would.

Walt had been flipping through a fishing magazine. "You fish?" he asked Rid, looking up after an awkward silence.

"Uh, sure. I'm a sea farmer, actually. You mean deep sea?"

Walt chuckled and blushed, shaking his head. "Stupid question. Sorry. I knew that. Just makin' conversation. Obviously you fish."

"Actually, sometimes one of my buddies and I go out after tuna."

Walt perked up. "Really? You must make a pretty penny."

"If we get one, we do. Sell it to a Japanese boat, to go back there for sushi, you know? We can pick up five thousand dollars."

"You don't say. Hard to get one?"

"Well, they're not easy to bring in, but we make a good day of it, y'know?"

"Man, I'd love to see that."

Rid was about to answer when he picked up Elsie coming down the hall in his peripheral vision. He excused himself, pointing at Elsie as he got to his feet and headed in her direction. Noelle and Walt were shortly behind him.

"She's going home," Elsie smiled. "And right to bed," she added to Noelle.

"*No* problem," Noelle answered emphatically. She wore a cranberry-colored sweater that brought out the deep brown of her eyes and high color of her cheeks. Rid could tell it wouldn't be wise to mess with her. "No visitors, I presume?" she asked, pinning Rid like a butterfly with her eyes even though she clearly meant for Elsie to respond.

"Neither doctor said that, exactly. Just extra rest. Dr. Rockwell said a day or two. Her ribs are wrapped, for comfort more than anything." Elsie answered.

"Look," Rid said. "Nobody wants what's best for her and the baby more'n me. *She's* got a pretty hot agenda, though. There's somebody she's got to talk to, and she wants *me* to take her. It's not my idea."

"I'll handle that," Noelle said. "Where's she want to go? I mean who's she want to talk to?"

"That's CiCi's to tell," Rid said after hesitating a minute. It was just too complicated. In his mind, Noelle had a purse full of grenades ready to be tossed at him.

❀

In the morning, Caroline didn't call. Rid could have used the time well doing any of ten tasks that had fallen behind in the past few days, things CiCi had been doing, and better than he. The books were in much better shape. The accountant would be shocked and thrilled, especially if CiCi finished them out for the past tax year. Had he thanked her? He must have. He should mention it again, though. She was so good at researching on the Internet, comparing prices for seed and scouting out used equipment. He didn't know squat about computers, though she said he could really develop a Midwest market using the Internet if he'd let her help him. He could have at least cut firewood, but no, he fidgeted, drank coffee, checked out the window, staring to see if he'd lose his eyesight by looking at the glare of the winter sun on the snow as his mother always threatened he would. It kept Lizzie stirred up, making her think something was about to happen so instead of curling up on her red plaid bed by the woodstove in the kitchen, she kept roaming the first floor and checking out the front window.

He picked up the phone to call Noelle's and put it back down for the third time. The thought of Noelle barking a refusal was intimidating. Walt might answer, which would be better. In his mind, Noelle had confiscated CiCi's cell phone. Of course, in his mind, Noelle was also wearing a prison guard's uniform complete with a loaded gun in a hip holster and a jumpy finger.

This is stupid, he told himself, using the words like sticks and rubbing them together emphatically. *She's not a child. It's up to her.* Now a spark and a flame to blow larger. *Noelle doesn't have any right.*

As he stomped and muttered, Lizzie on his heels, he pulled on his boots, parka, scarf and hat. "You can come, girl. In case I can bring you in to see her. She'd really like that." Lifting his keys off the hook by the door into the garage, he reassured the dog, "It's best this way. If I just show up, I mean. Better than calling. Noelle can't hang up if I'm there, can she?" just as glad Lizzie couldn't offer an opinion.

There were slow leaks in his bravado on the way over. He left Lizzie in the truck, thinking it best to ask first, though he'd have rather had her by his side when he rang the bell.

Walt answered the door, in bib overalls a red flannel shirt. Rid let out the breath he'd been holding.

"Good afternoon, sir. I was wondering if I could please see CiCi." Pure high school.

"Of course you can. In fact, she just woke up about a half hour ago. She had a rough night, with the pain, you know, but once she got to sleep with the Tylenol and whatever else she was allowed to take, well, she slept in. Come in, now, just step on the rug there." Walt stepped back, reflexively running his hand over his balding head and then down over his beard, pleased that he'd remembered Noelle's instructions about the rug this time. He'd earn some points for that.

"Sir, before I come in, well, CiCi really loves my dog, Lizzie. I brought her. Might it be possible for me to bring her in, too? I brought a towel and I'll clean her feet before I bring her inside. She's a small, very gentle Lab."

Again, the reflexive scalp rub that slid down to the beard. Walt's hearing wasn't good, but unfortunately he was sure he'd gotten this one right. Noelle wasn't the biggest dog person on the planet, and he could already be in trouble about Rid. On the other hand, he was going to clean the dog's feet for which there would be points added, and if CiCi loved the dog and if the dog made her happy, well then, more points.

"Okay, I'll put the cat out."

"Thank you so much, sir. I'll get her."

He carried Lizzie to the house, talking to her all the way, and still wiped her feet. Put her on a leash, absolutely unnecessary, but it would look good. Gave her a treat and had her sit and give Walt a handshake and a kiss. Watched Walt fall in love, as Lizzie's eager-to-please personality took over and did tricks for him.

"Let's go find the girls," Walt said. "Noelle's gotta love this."

"Heel," Rid said and Lizzie fell into step at his left, her paws scrabbling a bit on the hardwood. "And don't scratch the floor," he whispered, below the range of Walt's hearing aid.

☙

He left almost three hours later, having won Noelle over to Lizzie, raised CiCi's spirits with Lizzie's presence and, he thought, his own, but having had to accept that if CiCi left that house on that day it would be over Noelle's cold dead body. CiCi wouldn't hear of his telling the police about Terry and the moonfaced guy —not yet, she said, not until I talk to her—and the trail was getting colder and colder. He pounded his fist on the steering wheel in frustration. Goddamned felon could be halfway across the country by now. He knew this guy, knew his mind. He'd lived with his kind. *Tomorrow,* CiCi had whispered. "We'll go see Terry tomorrow. I called the library before you got here, and she's working tomorrow from nine to five."

CiCi called him a little before eight-thirty in the morning. "Can you come get me at nine-thirty? I have that appointment with Doctor Silva, just a follow-up baby check, and we can go to the library after that."

He'd hadn't forgotten about the appointment, but he was focused on getting to Terry, which he saw as a means to an end—catching the assailant. For all he knew, Terry was a criminal, too. The doctor's appointment was important, but it was also another delay. He took a breath and calmed himself. "You got this by Noelle? Or do I need to come in body armor?"

"Well, she doesn't know about the library part. She wanted to take me to Doctor Silva's, but I said Doctor Silva prefers that the father come to appointments."

"She does?"

"She does now."

"Thanks. I'll be there at nine-thirty."

The day was sunny and headed toward forty, maybe even a little higher. January thaw. An ideal day to check the grant for damage. This wouldn't last; icy teeth would be back to bite them. Still, no question what came first. It didn't occur to him then to be surprised at that, though nothing but his grant and loving life on it had been the priority for a very long time. Still, when his thought swept like a gull over his tidal flats, he looked at his watch and thought *almost mine,* and wished he could be two places today of all days. Plus, he'd had the news from Tomas—news that made him even more eager to be out there working.

CiCi was ready when he got there, moving gingerly, Noelle circling her like a cross between a flapping mother hen and an antsy Doberman, pulling on her boots, getting her in her jacket and tucking in her scarf so CiCi wouldn't have to reach in a painful direction. She did not like the idea of CiCi going out without her, Rid could tell. More to the point, she didn't think CiCi should be going out at all. "It's an appointment with Dr. Silva," he heard CiCi remind her quietly in response to something Noelle muttered while she fussed over CiCi's jacket. "To check the baby again. It's a good thing. Rid and I will get something to eat afterwards. Please don't worry."

"You'll get her in all this stuff, right?" Noelle said to Rid, gesturing at

CiCi's boots and jacket. "You watched what I did? No pressure on her arms, chest, back. It's very painful."

"I promise. And I'll get her in and out of the truck at the doctor's."

"Oh, no. No truck. You'll take a car. What are you thinking? She can't climb into a truck. Period."

"Great idea," CiCi said, mollifying Noelle. "Elsie and Billy brought my car over. Walt, could you get the keys for Rid?"

"That is a better idea, ma'am. Of course you're right. Thank you very much," Rid said, getting it. He was overdressed, sweating in the front hallway, not even considering a mention of the fact that CiCi was now overdressed, too. The outdoor temperature was irrelevant. Forget high school. This was junior high.

He knew damn well that Noelle was watching—probably with binoculars—and doubtless Walt, too, as he backed out of the driveway. "They've probably got cops tailing me, you know. Ready to do a Breathalyzer, ticket me for failure to wait a full two minutes before proceeding at a stop sign at which there is no traffic coming from any direction, and failing to yield to a car down in Connecticut that wants to merge into my lane of traffic next Tuesday."

"Probably. But it's sweet. She loves me."

He didn't even think about it. "Well, I do too, so I guess I'll just have to put up with it. And you ain't seen nothing yet. My mother can out-hover Noelle hands down."

Although Caroline had shifted her head to look at him sideways when he made his offhand declaration of love, she didn't respond to it. "I take exception to that. Noelle is not hovering. She's taking care of me. That's exactly what I'm going to do with our baby, and don't you forget it."

"That's exactly what I'm going to do, too. I just also plan to let him grow up when he's thirty-five."

She punched his shoulder and winced. "What makes you think it's a boy?" She wasn't going to correct him about her age just now.

"I just do, and don't punch me again 'cause you're hurting yourself."

They teased that way on the drive to the doctor's office, in the waiting room and up until the doctor came in. Neither mentioned Terry. Rid wondered if she felt his tension, if she were hiding her own.

The heartbeat was vigorous, the baby moving normally just as it had during the hospital sonogram, no spotting, and no blood in Caroline's urine. "I'll say it again—you really took care of your baby. She's going to be a great mother." The last was directed to Rid.

"I know that," he'd answered. "It's a boy, isn't it?"

Doctor Silva's whole-face grin crinkled the edges of her dark brown eyes like a pie crust. "A boy," she laughed, nodding, and Rid, dancing in place, whooped to CiCi, *told you.* "Or a girl," the doctor added, she and CiCi laughing at him together. The sonogram hadn't given them a clear view of the baby's sex.

By the time they were back in the car, CiCi was pale, a bit glassy-eyed. He reached across the gearshift and touched her thigh. "You want to stop for a break? Get a bite to eat? Gather yourself a bit and then head to the library?" Fifteen minutes more wouldn't make a lick of difference, and Rid could tell she was in pain.

"I could use some milk and more Tylenol. That would be good," she said. They stopped at The Post Office Café, since they were already in Provincetown, and when she ordered a full breakfast, he sighed and ordered one himself. Clearly, CiCi didn't get the urgency about Moonface. He was crawling out of his skin at the same time he was vigilant about not pushing her too hard, a combination that left him roiling.

"You look good," he said, ignoring the scrape on her cheek and the pallor of her skin. She held herself like an egg in a shallow basket, and he was tender with her as he helped her out of her coat. She'd ditched the scarf and gloves right away, and wasn't even zipping the jacket, the rising temperature was that much a tease. She'd lifted her face to the sun in the parking lot.

CiCi took three more Tylenol with her juice and seemed to feel better as soon as she started on eggs, bacon, wheat toast and milk. "Wow. I was starved," she said. "That seems to happen all the time. I'm much hungrier than I realize."

"Hey, do you feel well enough to get some amazing news?"

"Good news? Absolutely."

"You'll never guess where Tomas is right now. Mario's with him. I was supposed to be, but he's gonna bring me papers to sign in front of a notary. This is much more important right now, and Tomas even said so."

"So where is he? What's going on?" Caroline said. She held her fork aside and stopped eating.

Rid looked around, checking who was in the restaurant and where. He gestured to CiCi to lean in close and he put his head to hers and whispered. "They're at our lawyer's office with the owner's lawyer. We got the money. We're buying the flats today."

"That's fantastic! I'm so, so happy for you. You deserve it. This is it, then, it's over? They're yours forever?"

Glancing at his watch he said, "Yeah, I think they should be finishing up now. See, some waterfront landowner on the bluffs has a stake in aquaculture and made a fat donation for our defense fund. Didn't know anything about how we had an accepted offer to buy the flats, I guess—I mean, how could he?—but Tomas says it's going to pay my part, it's the right thing. Don't even know who it is. He doesn't want to piss his neighbors off by going against them, I suppose. Anyway, Tomas had the paperwork all drawn up before he even told me." He straightened up and said very quietly, "Every bit still confidential, of course. Until it's signed and sealed."

"You should be there with them, not dragging me around..." Sorrow in her voice, shaking her head. "You should be celebrating. I don't want you to be missing that."

"I'll celebrate with you, when they catch that thug. CiCi, I know his type, I was caged up with his type. I don't think you get it. You and the baby aren't safe. He's got to be stopped, and Terry, too. Are you about done? Can we *go*?"

❦

At the library, Caroline was adamant. No, he couldn't come in with her. She had to deal with Terry herself. It wasn't negotiable. What did he think, that Terry was going to beat her up in the library? Still, as she gingerly lumbered in the door after struggling to open it, her heart was thudding the way Lizzie's tail did against the floor when she was on high alert, waiting.

Terry wasn't at the front desk, but Caroline could see her off behind the reception area at her own work station. Miss Efficient Volunteer was covering the desk, Caroline saw, in a courage-deflating moment.

"I'd like to talk to Terry DiPaulo," she said to the volunteer. "It's personal," she added, to try to head her off. "My name is Caroline Marcum."

"I'll see if she has time," Ms. E.V. said. She had on her preppy denim jumper and the same black velvet headband Caroline had seen before. Caroline watched her bend and whisper to Terry and then the two of them looked at her, Miss E.V.'s face neutral but perhaps a tad professionally suspicious, and Terry's tightening into a mask. Terry nodded, touched the angel pinned to her kelly green sweater, adjusted her hair, and walked toward Caroline.

 *Chapter 28*

"What is it you need, Caroline?" Terry said.

Either the unflattering green of her sweater made her skin look sallow and the bubblegum pink she'd applied to her cheeks and lips created that terrible Kewpie doll look, or Terry was sick and trying to hide it, Caroline thought. Dark roots emerged from her scalp, too, which accentuated the artificial color of her long blonde curls.

"To talk with you. I'd like to talk with you privately." Terry started to shake her head no, but Caroline intervened before she could speak the refusal. "Please, Terry. I want to be honest with you, and I hope you'll be honest with me."

"Go ahead," Terry said.

"Could we please speak in private?" Caroline used the reception desk to brace herself. It was some kind of fake surface, less shiny than Formica, but dark and cool underneath the hands she spread there as if casually. She was clammy in her coat, glad she'd at least left scarf and gloves in the car.

Terry made a show of looking around. Miss E. V. was a short distance away. Caroline guessed at what Terry was going to say and countered it. "I don't think either one of us wants anyone overhearing any part of what's gone on, in the past or now." She pointed to the scrapes and cut on her own cheek, an artificial bravado to the gesture.

Terry yielded. She went to the hinged section of the counter, raised it, and signaled Caroline to follow her. Her two inch heels clicked in a crisp counterpoint to the mushy sound of Caroline's boots as they crossed an uncarpeted section of slate flooring near the library entry.

It had to be deliberate, although Terry revealed nothing right away. She led Caroline to the children's room which, as was common on a weekday in the middle of winter at lunchtime, had no patrons in it. Young children were home being fed and put down for naps. Older children were in school. Once inside, she closed the door, walked to the end of the room where there were some adult sized chairs and a table, which she moved until she was satisfied. Pointing to the chair she wanted Caroline to take, she sat herself and, finally, fire-eyed, looked at Caroline whose eyes were streaming tears.

"I know who you are. I assume this is what you wanted," Terry said bitterly. "You wanted to watch me suffer. Well, have at it. You could have just said so from the beginning and saved yourself all those ridiculous lies. But I guess that would have required human decency. Even Rhonda doesn't make me come in here, but maybe this will satisfy your craving and you'll finally go away forever."

"You thought that's why I came? To watch you suffer?"

Terry turned up the volume. "People with good intentions don't pack their suitcases full of neatly ironed lies. Look, I want you out of here for good. I'll get a restraining order." She nearly shouted the last sentence.

Caroline fought to keep her voice level, quiet and steady. "I think I'm the one with the grounds for a restraining order. You've had me stalked, you've had my house vandalized, you've had me threatened, and now you've had me beaten up in a way that could have killed my baby. Or were we *both* supposed to be killed? I have to wonder if that was your intent. But at least a child for a child, right?"

Terry's right hand fluttered up in the direction of her pin. "I have no idea what you're talking about." Her eyes slid over the bruising on Caroline's face, then darted away. "Whatever happened to you, I had nothing to do with it," her tone as defensive as angry for that moment. Then she went back on the offensive. "*You're* the one that took my life. Don't you think once was enough? Just get *out!*"

Miss E.V. appeared at the glass door that Terry had closed, a confused look on her face. Terry got up and went to the door. Miss E.V. whispered something, and Caroline heard Terry reply very quietly, "No, it's fine. Really. Thanks. You just cover the front desk. Thanks," and she surmised that Miss E.V. had heard Terry shouting, or perhaps even been lurking about to check on things. Ironic, she thought. I'm the one who was beaten up, but Terry's the one being guarded. She reminded herself that it was she who'd forced Rid to remain in the car, blurring the lines between independence, loneliness, and stupidity.

Terry returned but didn't sit. "Are you finished?" Bitter, spittle-filled.

"No. Because now it's you who isn't telling the truth. Terry, I freely admit that I was here under false pretenses. Not to watch you suffer, though. I discovered you completely by accident when I came to the library. What brought me back—after I knew you were here, I mean—I'm not so sure about. I think it was that I'd also discovered I was pregnant and I was scared to death." Terry sank into the chair, but her face showed no sign of capitulation. Caroline continued as if Terry hadn't moved. "I felt like I needed to know if you were all right. I thought I should have an abortion—that I certainly didn't deserve to have a child since I was responsible for you losing yours. Then I thought that wasn't right either, that maybe my baby would have defects like yours, and that was what was supposed to happen. I'm almost forty-one. But I didn't think I could handle that, either." Caroline was scrutinizing Terry's face, which was unreadable to her, except that now her eyes were small overflowing ponds. "I admit I lied about who I am. But I didn't have a hurtful intent toward you any more than I did with the accident. Terry, I am so, so sorry. For everything," Caroline finished, fishing in her pocket for a tissue. Overheating badly now, she struggled to get out of her coat and then realized she couldn't do it alone. She stood up and tried to let the coat just slide off her shoulders and down her arms, which she put as far behind her as she could, onto the floor. Still, it stuck about halfway down, hung up on the taping around her back, trapping her. She backed up to Terry, "Would you just push the coat onto the floor? Thanks."

"What's wrong with you?"

"I think you know," Caroline answered, kicking the coat toward her chair and sitting back down. "It's why I'm here today, before I tell the police."

"I hardly know what to take on first," Terry said, the pools spilling, and she angrily wiping her eyes with the back of her hand. "How dare you think that having a child like Alex is a punishment? He was a *blessing*, a grace! He was everything to me. You are not worthy of such a child."

"I didn't mean it that—"

"No, you never *mean* to hurt anybody do you, that's just what you *do*."

Caroline tried to take a deep breath, but her ribs wouldn't let her. A cough seared her. She was tiring and her head was throbbing. She wished Rid would appear and take her out.

"Terry, please. I came for two things today. First, to tell you I'm sorry. I'm so sorry. I understand you'll never forgive me, and I don't expect that. Second,

I came to see you about the man you sent to harass me and beat me up. He's done it, and it's going to have to be enough for you now. It has to stop. I've decided to have this baby and do the best I can. I can understand if that makes you hate me even more, but I felt like I owe you this—to at least warn you—I'll name you to the police if you don't put a stop to it now."

Terry's resistance didn't flag. "I've done nothing. Don't try to shift your guilt to me. You've no proof."

"But I do. We have a partial license plate, a description of the man who attacked me—which is pretty distinctive—and the fact that back when all this was just starting, he told Rid to look out for you and he'd do him the unsolicited favor of making sure he wouldn't have to make any payments. We've figured out that he meant child support payments. Unfortunately for you, he gave Rid your name and address in his own handwriting. I don't think that's a connection the police will ignore."

A physical change came over Terry. She leaned back, shoulders sagging, exhaled, and said, "Do the police already know all this?"

Caroline paused. "No. I haven't told them. They just have the man's description and the partial license plate. The bartender who saved me from him gave them that."

"And why haven't you told them?" Maintaining the distance, head turned a little sideways while Terry's chin went up and her eyes got almost imperceptibly smaller.

"Because I wanted to talk to you first. To give you a chance to explain or, I don't know, just to put a stop to it yourself. Because I don't want to bring more trouble and pain into your life."

"You want me to owe you? Like then I'll have to forgive you or something?" Terry was clutching her pin now, leaning forward again, her voice raspy.

"The mercy I can show you is in not asking for your forgiveness. Here's what I'm asking: if you stop that man, I won't send the police to you."

"He's my cousin, Boo," Terry whispered, shrinking, face crumpling. Then, she pulled herself up and the whisper took on the sound of a hiss. "Taking care of me because of *you*."

"Can you stop him now? And stop him for good?"

"I don't know. Maybe. I can try." A whisper this time.

"If you stop him first, and the police find him, I won't press charges. I don't know if the police can override me, but I'll do my best. I won't help them, and I won't say anything that connects any of this to you. *But you have to stop him.*"

The heat in the room was oppressive and the bright red, green, yellow, blue bears on the border below the ceiling seemed to be moving. Caroline felt light-headed and steadied herself by gripping the table. "I have to go now."

Terry's face was covered by her hands, and she was sobbing now. She did not look up to see Caroline struggle out of her chair and struggle again to pick up the coat on the floor. It wasn't her pregnancy size, not yet; it was the stiffness of her injuries and the pain in her ribs that made her so awkward. Caroline, too, had tears running down her face, but they were silent. She pulled two more tissues from her coat pocket and released them onto Terry's lap. She wanted to touch the other woman, comfort her and tell her that she understood, and she started to but then drew back. In the end, Caroline put the lightest, briefest touch she could manage, a feather, milkweed seeds released from their pod, a butterfly, a baby's kiss on Terry's shoulder and left the room.

※

When he saw Caroline coming, Rid scrambled out of the Honda and hurried to meet her. She was carrying her coat bunched up in front of her and using a sweater sleeve to swipe at her eyes. "Goddammit, I *knew* I shouldn't let you go in there alone. What did she *do* to you?" He put his arm around her as if she were an invalid, trying to avoid hurting the broken ribs but hurting them anyway as he steered her toward the car. Caroline flinched but didn't pull away from him.

"Shit, I'm sorry," he said, immediately moving his hand down to her hip. "Or here, just give me your coat and purse. Are you cold? Let me put this over your shoulders."

"Who are you? My mother, my grandmother, Noelle and Elsie all rolled into one?" Caroline said, touching her head down on his chest briefly. She raised her head to face him. "Honest, I'm okay. Let's get away from here. I don't want her to see us in the parking lot. I'll tell you everything, just not here. Let me get myself together."

They stopped at the Village Café, where CiCi went to the bathroom and Rid bought her tea in a paper cup. Then he drove out to the access road in front of his grant, CiCi's house right there, intact across the horseshoe beach. One aquaculturist was out, antlike in the distance, down toward the Blackfish Creek. "Here's home for both of us," Rid said as he set the brake. "Look at that sun scattering itself on the water. Diamonds. Hmm. And who's that son of a bitch out, getting a jump on the rest of us. Looks like—Clint? What the hell is he doin'? Okay, never mind, forget that stuff," he said, shaking his head like a dog. He shifted in his seat so he was three-quarters facing her and extended his hand asking for hers. "I'm not good at this patience thing. Let's hear it now."

Caroline took a deep breath. "You were right. The guy who did it—the guy who grabbed me—is her cousin. I don't know exactly what she told him to do, but I guess it was to run me off."

"You're shitting me! She confessed?" Rid tightened his grip on her hand and then in his excitement, let go of it, needing both hands to gesture. "You've got her cold? And you've got him? I can't believe it. Good job, CiCi. Oh baby, I'm so proud of you. It's really over! Wow. Good job. Okay, we go right to the police and make the report. And then, hey, you ever thought about getting married?" He leaned over, grabbed her shoulders and contorted himself over the gearshift so as not to pull her forward but to make all the movement come from himself, and smacked her with a full wet kiss on the lips. "Nice," he said. "Umm." A grin, and then he did it again before he started the engine of the car.

Caroline reached over and covered his hand. "No." she said. "Turn it off. Please."

Rid switched off the ignition. "What's the matter?" he said.

"I'm not going to the police."

"The hell you're not. That moonface psycho dickhead attacked you and he could have killed you, coulda killed *our* baby. What the hell are you thinking?" Incredulity laced with anger.

"I'm thinking that whether on purpose or not, Rid, I hurt her once the worst anyone can hurt someone else."

"That was a fucking *accident*. Completely different. She might be too dense to see that, but the rest of the world isn't. And besides, you paid for that. You did your time."

"So she hurts me on purpose," Caroline continued. "Maybe has her cousin try to kill my baby. Let's say she does."

"Or try to kill you *and* our baby. On *purpose*."

"Okay. I'll give you that. So I, in retaliation, press charges and she goes to jail."

"Her and moonface psycho dickhead. Right on."

"And then she gets out. Then what?"

"She's eighty-two and on a walker, I hope. You can get a lot of time for attempted murder."

Caroline put her hand on Rid's thigh. "Rid, someone has to stop the pain, and

I choose it to be me. This all started with something I did, and I have some small power now to be—to be decent or kind. I'm not sure what the right word is."

"CiCi, no. It leaves you wide open. She can come after you again. Psychodick can come after you again, nothing to stop them. Do you think they want you to have this baby? You can't live like that. Worrying about them being right around the next corner."

Caroline saw the frustrated anger in the red flush rising from his lower neck steadily toward his face, a thermometer of emotion. She'd seen it before when he'd had it in his head that she was involved in Pissario's lawsuit.

She tried to take his hand, but he withdrew it. "I don't want to make you mad, and I don't want you to have to worry, but Terry said she thought she could get him to stop. I'm trying to make things right, so I can live with myself. It's a matter of *mercy*, Rid.

"You believe her? After what she's done to you?"

"I'm going to give her a chance."

"And risk yourself and our baby?"

"There's some risk, yes. I want to give her a chance is all." Caroline looked out the windshield toward the water, but had to squint because of the intensity of the light. She wished she had some sunglasses with her. Rid was right, though. It was home. The sand and the water were soothing. The back of the tide was creeping up toward the wrack line, high and thick as always in winter. The worst of the weather was ahead. The harbor would likely freeze by the end of the month and she was worried about the potential damage to the buried clams. Big blocks of ice would shift with tides, scraping the sand and netting off them.

"Well, I don't. An accident is one thing, CiCi, but what she did was on purpose. Don't you get that?"

"Please, Rid—"

"I don't think I can live with this."

"But—"

"Are you going to be rational and protect yourself and our baby, or are you gonna put yourself out there with a target on your stomach? Because I'm not gonna watch that. I'm not going to sit around and just wait for that."

"I wouldn't expect you to. If I thought that's what I was doing, I couldn't either. Hold up, just please listen," she said as Rid started to break in. She picked up his hand, half to restrain him, half to soothe. "I thought about this a lot when I was in the hospital and in bed at Noelle's. You know, the whole idea of why this happened, if it was retaliation. I felt like it was at least spiritual punishment, that I somehow deserved it. Now I know it was real, direct human retaliation, which at least makes more sense."

"No way, CiCi. The baby could have been killed. The baby is *innocent*. That's not how things work. You have *no right* to put the baby's life in danger for one unnecessary minute. It's *my* baby too." Rid's face was flushed right into the half-moons where his hairline had receded, the ones that made his face heart-shaped. He was furious, yanking back his hand, but Caroline wouldn't let it go and he wasn't going to jerk on her because of her injuries. "Please let go," he said.

"Just hear me out. Please. It's all I'm asking. Okay?" She waited for him to take a couple of breaths and meet her eyes again. His were so blue, now, against the flush on his skin, maybe because they were newly wet like beach stones when the rising tide first covers them and recedes. With beach stones, their color intensifies and they glisten like joy; she was always sad when it faded.

It was a good fifteen seconds before he nodded.

"Thank you. Listen, I know you're right. There's some risk. But I have to take that chance if I'm going to live at all. I've been afraid to, because so much goes wrong all the time. But not living hurts, too. That's the problem. You love, you hurt. You don't love, you hurt. You trust, you forgive, you get hurt. You don't trust, you don't forgive, guess what?" Caroline was like sand and rockweed flying down the beach in a blow, that speed, that intensity, trying to sweep Rid along with her. "Which choices let you live the best, most decent life? Which gives you more chance at goodness? I don't want to live in a wasteland anymore and I don't want our baby to, either. Tell me something: who am I quoting now? 'I throw my life savings into the bay, and hope?' Do you recognize your own words? The way we live here is all about risk and love, isn't it? That's what sea farmers do. You don't give up. This is my chance to not give up, to have a little hope that Terry and I can somehow move on to something better in our lives."

Rid shook his head. "You don't get it. What you're asking is the same as…," he cast for an analogy and hooked one, "asking me not to button down the grant before winter, just take my chance that nature, which I already know can turn lunatic-destructive, will make nice and do me no harm. Yes, I *hope*. But I act responsibly, too. I can't just rely on hope."

"What are you saying?"

"I'm saying I'd go to the cops myself, but that's not going to do any goddamn good if you won't press charges." Rid looked away from her, out the window toward his grant. A wet sheen was around his eyes, gathering in the bottom lids. "I'm saying you're tying my hands, and I can't stand that. You might as well put me back in that cage."

She still didn't get it. "Rid, please try to understand. I love you." She reached for his hand where it was in a fist on his thigh, and wrapped hers over it like paper takes rock in *rock, scissors, paper.*

"Do you realize that's the first time you've said the words outright to me? And you're saying them to get me to do what you want."

"But I *do* love you. So much I'm scared of it. I'm sorry I haven't said it upfront before. Neither one of us has been exactly a fountain of words about our feelings, have we? Maybe we should have been. Sooner."

"But I've at least given you a clue, haven't I? I've said it, not just when I wanted something." Both of them now unsheathing a blade. Rid took his hand out from underneath Caroline's and shoved it under his own leg. It was junior high again, but he couldn't help it.

It was the back side of the tide, coming in fast now. Clint's truck bumped over the sand. Upon the most subtle signal from Rid he'd have pulled up and rolled down his window for a chat, but failing one, he gave a slightly quizzical look—they were in a car rather than a truck, for one—checking to make sure they didn't need help, and when Rid waved, Clint waved back, accelerated and drove on by.

When he'd passed, Caroline said, "Wait. This isn't about love, it's about going to the police or not, and I can't do that yet. I have to wait to see if she can make it stop. I owe her that."

"You *owe* her that? Jesus, CiCi, If you don't go to the police—don't you understand? I can't be helpless again. You're putting me back behind bars, locking me up and telling me I can't do what I need to do to protect what I love. I can't sit back and wait for Moonface to come along and destroy everything. I can't love you and the baby and go through this just waiting for him to attack you in the dark again. I did it your way, to give you time to talk to Terry. I showed my respect. But now you won't do the same."

"What do you mean?" Now Caroline's eyes were full, disbelief mixing with a frantic effort to come up with something, *anything.* Anything except altering the decision by which she was earning her redemption.

"I can't sit by and watch while you give those two license to hurt you and our baby again. I can't do it. I won't."

"So that's it? What about loving each other? What about loving our baby?"

Rid turned to face her, angry. "I do love you. I thought I'd made that clear. You're the one who just said this wasn't about love. You're making unilateral decisions about your safety and about the baby's safety that I can't abide."

CiCi stared at him, unbelieving.

"I can't do it," he whispered, his voice ragged. "I'll take you back to Noelle's now."

Both sat as if made of stone. Caroline looked out the passenger window, positioned so her tears would slide silently into her scarf so she wouldn't have to wipe them. Rid put on the radio so she would not hear him sniffling. He swiped at his eyes with his sleeve, glanced over and saw she was sitting at an angle and worried that her ribs must be hurting, then told himself she'd made it clear she didn't want him taking care of her. Noelle and Walt could worry about her now.

 *Chapter 29*

Frigid Canadian air had chased behind the worst weather of the season, freezing the harbor. Not only that, the last winter storm had come hard from the west, which meant Rid had to worry whether Mario's stuff had come loose in the blow before the ice hit. If it had, it would have gone to the east and would be all over Rid's raceways, putting holes in his nets or even scraping them off his quahogs. Typical Mario. He hadn't pulled out his cages for the winter, playing fast and loose with his own and other people's livelihoods.

Rid hadn't let himself call Caroline, hadn't let himself go to his grant since he'd taken her back to Noelle's. Going to his grant would mean seeing her house, and how would he be able to keep himself from checking it? From checking on her? It was taking all the self-control he could gather. And it didn't help that he'd slept better in prison than he'd slept in his own bed lately. He was fitful, a wing beat of a bad dream he couldn't remember troubling him again and again. Still, he was determined to ride it out. He hadn't finally learned to do things by the book—after so many wasted years and impulsive mistakes— to deliberately unlearn it now.

On Thursday, he couldn't stand it anymore. There was enough dark gray wind that he put on his parka rather than waterproof sleeves; he wasn't going to work, just to look, after all, but still, he added a wool cap under the hood, it was that bone-piercing cold. Two Christmases ago his mother had given him insulated jeans that had turned out useful for cutting wood in bad weather, and he wore those, too, with long underwear.

"Come on, girl. Wake up. Let's go." The Lab roused from the couch and climbed down joylessly. "Oh for God's sake, Liz. Cut me some slack, will you? I'll give you a treat in the truck."

He didn't drive across the beach as he normally would, but left the truck at the end of the access road. Too much snow. He knew where the biggest rocks were, of course, and they were visible snow-mounds, more like small igloos, anyway. But he saw no point in risking his muffler by pretending he was certain where every rock huddled in the deep snow. He opened the driver's side door and gestured for Lizzie to follow him, sneaking a glance at Caroline's house while the Lab scrambled out and bounded into valleys between drifts. He could barely see the top of the dune fence between her house and the beach, the storm had blown that much snow against it. There appeared to be a light on in the kitchen window, but it could have been a reflection. It wasn't his business, he told himself for the umpteenth time. He turned toward his grant. The wind picked up snow and flung it at his back. Twice he tripped on completely covered obstacles. There were patterns on the unbroken snow like those left by retreating waves on sand. Several sets of footprints had already traveled to and from the grants.

Mario was down on the beach, between his own and Rid's grant. The wind obscured the sound of his feet in the snow until Rid was almost on top of him, but as he approached, Rid saw what Mario was looking at: the detritus of cages frozen into the front of Rid's grant, which would certainly be over raceways. Who knew what kind of disaster the back would be in?

"Jesus, man, I'm sorry. Caroline's already been down here. I'll make it right—I'll clean it all up. Whatever stock is lost, I'll replace it."

Rid looked at the grant and then looked at Mario, trying to process Caroline's name at the same time he took in the probable devastation to his quahogs. "You don't know that your cages didn't take out all *your* clams along with mine," he said, trying to keep his voice steady. He couldn't ask about Caroline, about what she'd been doing down here in this weather. It was too much. It was all too much. "How're you gonna fix this? How you gonna replace mine if your nets and stock are gone, too? Goddammit, Mario. This is all I've got, and I did *everything* by the book. Everything by the goddamn book." His voice was raw, sad, spilling anger.

"Look, next year I'll button the grant. This summer I'll dig a pit and next winter I'll button the grant, my word on it. I promised Caroline this wouldn't happen again. She made me see I'm not being fair. I promise I'll clean this all up, and I'll make it right. You know, man, we've got to wait to see—maybe it's not so bad. There's no telling right now, not till it thaws. Okay?"

Rid swallowed and breathed hard a couple of times. His mouth grim, moving only his eyes, he took the measure of his grant, the seasons of work that lay beneath the ice, where seed had been planted and nurtured like something sacred. Where he'd done all he could to not mess up again like he had in the past. Where he'd done his damnedest to carry on his father's legacy and build something that would last.

"Man, I'm sorry, I'm sorry. Give me another chance, will you?" Mario's voice was hoarse. Like Rid, he was in a heavy parka , but he wore high waterproof boots, too. Footprints onto the frozen bay revealed that he'd tried to dislodge the closest displaced oyster cage a corner of which was jutting out of the ice. It had been an exercise of equal parts desperation and futility.

"The damage is done, Mario." Rid's tone said he wasn't necessarily referring to the grant.

Rid turned to meet Mario's eyes and saw tears.

"I swear I'll make it right," Mario said, a naked plea. "You gotta give me a chance. We're partners, right? I keep thinking how you helped me when I sank my truck, and I probably never said thanks. And now I let this happen. I know I fucked up. Just give me a chance. We're in this together. I swear I *will* make it all right."

Mario's words washed over him like a rip tide, and Rid looked back toward his grant, not seeing it this time. *Oh God*, he thought, *is there only one story in the world?* He put his head down on his chest a long quiet moment while his eyes filled and he closed them. Finally he lifted his head and met Mario's anguished gaze. He nodded and put out his gloved right hand for Mario to shake.

"It's okay, man. I know you'll work it out."

Rid left Mario behind him and headed back toward his truck. A light snow had started up again, magnified by the wind so it swirled around him like a cloud. He didn't stop at the truck, but lumbered on, Lizzie bounding ahead, then coming back and circling behind as if to gather him in. The land and water were indistinguishable now, and because of the frozen harbor and sky, they too merged until the world seemed all of one substance and he and Lizzie alone in it. He crossed the horseshoe beach and turned to face Caroline's house where now he saw smoke mounting from the chimney. A fire had been lit. She was there. Thank God, she was there.

 *Chapter 30*

The day's warmth was a bonus for late April. Spring was often late, then chilly and damp on the outer Cape. Usually the sea farmers fought rain clouds for breathing space, but this year, they were all coatless thanks to days of robust sun. The lilacs were budding early beneath Caroline and Rid's window, their fragrance faint but present enough that she and Rid lifted the sash at night for the scent as well as the sound of the bay.

Caroline sat on an overturned milk crate on the beach with a slotted box, culling oysters. Rid, sweaty in waders, bent from the waist in shallows picking stock to fill what order they could. He filled a crate and hauled it up to her. Lizzie thumped her tail where she lay next to Caroline but didn't get up.

"Yeah girl, I know who you love best now," Rid said, leaning over to scrub behind her ears. He pulled a treat from his shirt pocket and fed her at the same time he leaned over and gave CiCi a kiss on the mouth. She had sunscreen on her lips which made them slippery as she returned it. "How was that last bunch? Any of 'em need to go back?"

"Those," she said, pointing. "Not legal size, but all healthy."

"I can't figure how those got in that rack. Mario probably," Rid mused, rubbing his face, tired-sounding.

"I guess we can't complain about his trying to replace some of the stock you lost, even if he gets it in the wrong cage."

"There's no way he can...." He shook his head to cut himself off. "Okay. You all right?"

She pointed at her belly this time, sunk between her spread knees. She wore denim shorts and a green top that revealed advanced pregnancy, swollen breasts. "I can't sit like this. We need to bring a real chair out here, and find a way to lower the box. Maybe you could dig a hole in the sand?" She stretched, pulling her elbows and shoulders back.

"Why didn't you tell me? Geez, I should've realized."

He'd told her to stay home and rest for this tide, the second of the day, but she brushed him off, teasing, "You think you're the only one with the blood?"

Now, with mounting frustration, he said, "Look, there it is again, you're putting your hand on the same exact spot that asshole broke your ribs. You do it all the time, and I know damn well it means you're still hurting, no matter what you say. We should've pressed charges. We still can. Jerry said so." He made a visor of one hand to shield his eyes while using the other to stroke her neck and back.

"Haven't we had enough of the law? Terry seems to have stopped him, and—"

"Except for the air outta the truck tire in February," Rid interrupted. "The mailbox busted in March. And the skiff loose last week. If Mario hadn't spotted it on his way in, we'd be doing without." As he recited this litany, he ticked off the fingers of his right hand.

She inhaled then spoke on the exhale, to calm him. "Sweetheart, you and I both know stuff like that happens all the time. We can't assume."

"You're naïve. You don't want to believe there's crazy or evil that can't be fixed your way. I wish you were right, but look at how things spiral out of control." This was a practiced conversation he'd not found a way to advance against Caroline's conviction. He hated it when he begged. "I want to be done with that asshole. What if it's something bigger and more dangerous next? *Then* will it be time to call up the posse?"

Caroline winked at him. "Hey, I know one asshole we're done with. Pissario's whole outhouse of cards—make that glass cards—collapses around him while he sits on the toilet pants down. And here *you* stand, on the flats you three guys *own*. Now how fine is that?"

He let her deflect him for the moment. "Yes ma'am, very fine." He gave her a quiet, satisfied grin, his eyes joining hers. "That guy who donated the money saved our lives," he said, and pressed his lips together, nodding slowly for several seconds while he raised his head and scanned the shallows. But then he remembered his point and swiveled back to Caroline. "However owning the flats is not relevant to pressing charges against Terry and her psycho-agent-orange-sniffing cousin."

He knew she'd won again by the smile she tried to hide. "It's relevant because things *do* spiral out of control. And how's this for relevance: you and Tomas and *your* agent-orange-sniffing-psycho Mario could be renting or selling your friends' grants to them, but are you? Ha! Gotcha. The Indian Neck sea farmers work their grants without paying you a cent. Why? "Never mind—" she said, holding up a hand as Rid started to interrupt. "I'll tell you the real reason, whatever garbage you're about to spew. It's because you three know what it's like to be down, just like your friends did when they pitched in to help you fight Pissario. So don't talk to me about what I'm doing, because we're exactly the same."

Rid closed his eyes. When he opened them he said, "Look, about the flats. That's the way it is now, the 'no charge' business. That's the way I hope we can keep it. I'll really try on my end, but I'm one of three partners, remember. People are people. Hell, nature is nature. Things happen, life gets in the way."

Caroline ran her hand—a working hand now, calloused, and her nails short and a bit dirty—through hair that needed a cut again, but they'd been so busy out on the grant she'd not gotten to it. *Don't worry about it. It's okay if your hair gets long again. You don't have to keep trying to look like a different person,* Rid said yesterday; Caroline claimed he'd been eavesdropping on her mind.

"And anyway, you gotta stop talking like you're not part of us on the flats. Don't say 'me,'" Rid said, pointing to himself. His face was reddening in the sun, his nose, forehead and neck, and she tossed him the sunscreen, something he'd disdained for years. "Say 'us,'" he continued, catching the tube.

She smiled at him and pointed at his face, meaning *put that damn sunscreen on.*

"I put it on this morning."

"You need to reapply, my love," she said lightly. "Always reapply. There's enough here to fill the orders I think—you need to get raking. Look, it's the back of the tide already, and we've got to get the babies planted. We really got lucky. Have you seen what beautiful seed came in?"

Rid saw how Caroline looked at the sunset over the shallows when the tide was late, how rain didn't keep her away, the satisfaction she took in planting, how she could pull an oyster and judge it by its heft in her hand. Used to laboring alone, he hadn't expected this, that she would go to the tides with him. Weeks ago, he'd gone to the town clerk's office and signed to have her name legally added to his grant without telling her, to seal them in the way that meant most to him. Soon Rid would add another name, as his father had added his, knowing the child's blood was his and Caroline's, and the tide always returns.

~ ✿ ~

Acknowledgements

Special thanks for support and invaluable help along the way to Nancy Pinard. I'm especially grateful to Kristina Blank Makansi, Amira Makansi, Janice Rockwell, Ciera deCourcy, Alan deCourcy, Audra Shields, Brad Cook, and to Barbara Austin and other aquaculturists of Wellfleet, MA, who so generously shared their lives and work.

About the Author

Lynne Hugo is a National Endowment for the Arts Fellowship recipient who has also received grants from the Ohio Arts Council and the Kentucky Foundation for Women. She has published five previous novels, one of which became a Lifetime Original Movie of the Month, two books of poetry, and a children's book. Her memoir, Where The Trail Grows Faint, won the Riverteeth Literary Nonfiction Book Prize. Born and educated in New England, she and her husband currently live in Ohio with a yellow Lab feared by squirrels in a three state area.

Connect online with Lynne or find resources for readers and book clubs at www.lynnehugo.com.

CPSIA information can be obtained at www.ICGtesting.com
Printed in the USA
LVOW10s1153160914

404244LV00007B/8/P